PRAISE FOR M. I

A fabulous soaring thriller.

— *TAKE OVER AT MIDNIGHT,* MIDWEST BOOK
REVIEW

Meticulously researched, hard-hitting, and suspenseful.

— *PURE HEAT,* PUBLISHERS WEEKLY,
STARRED REVIEW

Expert technical details abound, as do realistic military missions with superb imagery that will have readers feeling as if they are right there in the midst and on the edges of their seats.

— *LIGHT UP THE NIGHT,* RT REVIEWS, 4 1/2
STARS

Buchman has catapulted his way to the top tier of my favorite authors.

— FRESH FICTION

Nonstop action that will keep readers on the edge of their seats.

— *TAKE OVER AT MIDNIGHT,* LIBRARY
JOURNAL

M L. Buchman's ability to keep the reader right in the middle of the action is amazing.

— LONG AND SHORT REVIEWS

The only thing you'll ask yourself is, "When does the next one come out?"

— *WAIT UNTIL MIDNIGHT,* RT REVIEWS, 4 STARS

The first...of (a) stellar, long-running (military) romantic suspense series.

— *THE NIGHT IS MINE,* BOOKLIST, "THE 20 BEST ROMANTIC SUSPENSE NOVELS: MODERN MASTERPIECES"

I knew the books would be good, but I didn't realize how good.

— NIGHT STALKERS SERIES, KIRKUS REVIEWS

Buchman mixes adrenalin-spiking battles and brusque military jargon with a sensitive approach.

— PUBLISHERS WEEKLY

13 times "Top Pick of the Month"

— NIGHT OWL REVIEWS

GRYPHON

A MIRANDA CHASE ACTION-ADVENTURE
TECHNOTHRILLER

M. L. BUCHMAN

Other works by M. L. Buchman: *(* - also in audio)*

Action-Adventure Thrillers

Dead Chef
One Chef!
Two Chef!

Miranda Chase
Drone*
Thunderbolt*
Condor*
Ghostrider*
Raider*
Chinook*
Havoc*
White Top*
Start the Chase*
Lightning*
Skibird*
Nightwatch*
Osprey*
Gryphon*

Science Fiction / Fantasy

Deities Anonymous
Cookbook from Hell: Reheated
Saviors 101

Contemporary Romance

Eagle Cove
Return to Eagle Cove
Recipe for Eagle Cove
Longing for Eagle Cove
Keepsake for Eagle Cove

Love Abroad
Heart of the Cotswolds: England
Path of Love: Cinque Terre, Italy

Where Dreams
Where Dreams are Born
Where Dreams Reside
Where Dreams Are of Christmas*
Where Dreams Unfold
Where Dreams Are Written
Where Dreams Continue

Non-Fiction

Strategies for Success
Managing Your Inner Artist/Writer
Estate Planning for Authors*
Character Voice
Narrate and Record Your Own
Audiobook*
Beyond Prince Charming: One Guy's
Guide to Writing Men in Romance

Short Story Series by M. L. Buchman:

Action-Adventure Thrillers

Dead Chef

Miranda Chase Stories

Romantic Suspense

Antarctic Ice Fliers

US Coast Guard

Contemporary Romance

Eagle Cove

Other

Deities Anonymous (fantasy)

Single Titles

The Emily Beale Universe
(military romantic suspense)

The Night Stalkers
MAIN FLIGHT
The Night Is Mine
I Own the Dawn
Wait Until Dark
Take Over at Midnight
Light Up the Night
Bring On the Dusk
By Break of Day
Target of the Heart
Target Lock on Love
Target of Mine
Target of One's Own
NIGHT STALKERS HOLIDAYS
*Daniel's Christmas**
*Frank's Independence Day**
*Peter's Christmas**
Christmas at Steel Beach
*Zachary's Christmas**
*Roy's Independence Day**
*Damien's Christmas**
Christmas at Peleliu Cove

Henderson's Ranch
*Nathan's Big Sky**
*Big Sky, Loyal Heart**
*Big Sky Dog Whisperer**
*Tales of Henderson's Ranch**

Shadow Force: Psi
*At the Slightest Sound**
*At the Quietest Word**
*At the Merest Glance**
*At the Clearest Sensation**

White House Protection Force
*Off the Leash**
*On Your Mark**
*In the Weeds**

Firehawks
Pure Heat
Full Blaze
*Hot Point**
*Flash of Fire**
Wild Fire
SMOKEJUMPERS
*Wildfire at Dawn**
*Wildfire at Larch Creek**
*Wildfire on the Skagit**

Delta Force
*Target Engaged**
*Heart Strike**
*Wild Justice**
*Midnight Trust**

Emily Beale Universe Short Story Series
The Night Stalkers
The Night Stalkers Stories
The Night Stalkers CSAR
The Night Stalkers Wedding Stories
The Future Night Stalkers

Delta Force
Th Delta Force Shooters
The Delta Force Warriors

Firehawks
The Firehawks Lookouts
The Firehawks Hotshots
The Firebirds

White House Protection Force
Stories

Future Night Stalkers
Stories (Science Fiction)

ABOUT THIS BOOK

WITH THE RISING THREAT OF RUSSIA, SWEDEN JOINS NATO FOR ITS own protection. But someone wants to make them pay—in blood.

Sweden's home-built, world-class jet fighters, the Saab JAS 39E Gripen—named for the mythological half-eagle / half-lion Gryphon—are falling out of the skies. The stability, the very existence of NATO could be shredded, as if torn by the Gryphon's mighty eagle claws.

Can Miranda's team of air-crash investigators solve the crisis before the lion's deadly power tears them asunder?

————

A list of characters and aircraft may be found at:
https://mlbuchman.com/fan-club-freebies
Scroll down to: People, Places, & Planes
And return afterward for a free bonus story
and a recipe from the book.

1

DECEMBER 13TH

ROLM LINDGREN HUNG UP THE PHONE WITHOUT QUITE SLAMMING it down, though he wanted to drive it straight through the top of his desk.

He'd spent the last two hours on the phone while dictating press releases, checking in with key personnel, and trying to control the disaster. Every time he hung up, there'd been two more calls waiting. Finally, it had quieted for three whole minutes—before it gut-shot him again. He'd managed it all smoothly until now, but this had been one phone call too many.

In the echoing silence, without any more calls to make, he could finally start to think.

He glared at the calendar. He remained old-fashioned enough to keep a paper one by his desk for quick reference. Right now, it irritated him almost past reason.

With only eight days until its final retirement, the last Boeing 737-700 in Rolm's fleet had gone down—hard.

He'd purposely planned his own retirement to follow the day after that of the 737's. The way he felt, he might well be dead by tomorrow—from sorrow, if nothing else.

A hundred and thirty-seven passengers (only four empty seats), two flight crew, and four cabin crew had boarded the LuftSvenska flight under their own power. They would all be departing the flight, or at least the rolling hillside of the Fjällberget ski area, very differently. He'd been told that DNA testing would be required to straighten out who some of the parts belonged to. There was also the matter of eleven skiers still unaccounted for on the ground.

Rolm shifted his glare from the calendar to the cold sky outside his window and did his best not to read anything into today's date. Easier said than done.

December 13th.

He considered himself to be no more superstitious than the next Swede, but it was the precise seventieth anniversary of the airline's first disaster.

Not that he could do a damn thing about it from here, not until he knew what had happened. As if. President of the airline never did a damn thing anyway except PR—and suffer a thousand headaches.

His desk offered a sweeping view from the top floor of the headquarters building. Stories below, the waterfront of northern Stockholm inspired guests in his office to exclamations of pleasure. But all he'd ever really cared about was looking up. There, he caught glimpses of their LuftSvenska planes headed in and out of Arlanda Airport thirty kilometers to the north. As the country's flagship airline, the King had granted permission to paint the planes flag blue with wide yellow stripes down the window line and diagonally up the tail. Distinctively Swedish from miles away.

Rolm's service boss had been one of the many calls, assuring him that the bird had passed all safety checks and the maintenance was fully current. There'd been no slacking off as the aircraft approached end-of-service.

Then *why* had the 737 gone down?

Had it looked at a calendar? His wife, Gertrude, had suggested that when he'd called to let her know. Unlike him but like so many of his fellow countryman, she was deeply superstitious about the number thirteen.

The press was sure to make a heyday of that and the seventieth anniversary of that first disaster combined. LuftSvenska's first crash, a midair collision over London that had killed all the crew and passengers, thirty-four in all, had almost killed the airline. Always remembered as the second-worst disaster in the airline's history. Would it now be remembered as the third or finally relegated to the chronicles of the past? No, the newsies would make sure it was prominently remembered for a good while yet.

Yet another call: the PR department asking goddamn questions about the rework of the diamond jubilee of the airline's founding campaign. Intended to kick off in two weeks —the *Seventy-five Years of Happy Customers* campaign would require a complete and horridly expensive rebuild.

The one other great tragedy in the airline's history, the newly demoted to second-worst disaster, had been the nine days *after* he'd taken over the airline twenty-five years ago. This one nine days *before* he left it.

That wasn't a coincidence, that was some cosmic joke on his career. The media would probably label him as the President of Crashes. Like that headline could possibly be more important than all the people who'd died.

The first crash of his presidency—and the only one until today—had been a collision in fog between a departing LuftSvenska passenger jet and a bizjet crossing the runway it shouldn't have been anywhere near. The Italian airport management and ground traffic controllers had been found guilty of that one, served jail time (when they should have been run through with a sword), which hadn't mitigated the disaster.

And now...

Rolm stared at the garment bag hanging on the back of his office door. Tonight was supposed to be the first of a series of retirement dinners. How the hell to put a good face on that? Besides, he hated wearing suits. He'd told Gertrude that in ten days, the day after he left the airline, they were going to have a suit-burning celebration. Her look said that wouldn't be occurring, she had a penchant for fancy restaurants he didn't much share. He hadn't conceded the win on that one yet.

That damned Boeing plane.

In the early decades, until Boeing bought McDonnell Douglas, LuftSvenska flew the MD aircraft. After Boeing purchased MD, everything began slipping sideways. MD aircraft were being phased out, but not fast enough. Boeing jets were brought onboard, but MD parts and Boeing parts didn't match. Machinery, engines, pilots, service people, service *methodologies,* none of it. Then the former management had picked up a couple of Airbus jets. And yet other makes for short-haul connectors: Fokkers, Bombardiers, a couple of BAEs, even a lone, home-grown Saab fifty-seater.

And the idiots wondered why it had all spun out of control.

Holding the fractured mess together made for hard years, compounded with each bad decision. Rolm thanked the gods that he hadn't been around to see them, at least not on the front lines. Not until he'd been elevated from the rank and file to clean up the mess. For his entire first year he'd raced from fire to fire, plugging holes as fast as possible. Including the ripples of the worst crash in the airline's history—up until two hours ago.

Had he even *seen* his Gertrude in those first months? Probably not. Blessedly more tolerant than he deserved, which meant he would be keeping a dinner-out suit.

Knew that battle was lost before you even started it, Rolm. Acknowledging it didn't make him any happier.

Despite the appearances his presidency required, he sat far

more comfortably around a half-rebuilt engine with his team, sharing falu sausage sliced with a greasy mechanic's knife and eaten on black bread with mustard.

Why had he left the line?

Because it hurt him to see what others were doing to the airline. Even as a kid fresh out of airframe and powerplant school, he could see it. He'd joined, led, then left behind the mechanics.

But he hadn't forgotten his roots. Not long after he'd solved the worst of the messes from the prior administration, Airbus had come around with an offer of quality planes and massive EU-subsidized discounts. Locally-sourced parts, a single primary platform, and a focus down to only two brands for the short-haul connectors. It was heaven. The bottom line cleaned up as parts and training had harmonized around fewer and fewer variables.

It had taken twenty-five years.

And in nine days it would have been done. He'd planned to retire the day after the Boeing 737 and hand off the reins to a clean-running thoroughbred. He'd led LuftSvenska through the great pandemic intact—not furloughing a single crewmember or team lead. They'd come out healthier than they'd gone in.

LuftSvenska had picked up routes that others couldn't service. In addition to all of Scandinavia and much of Europe, they now flew nine prime US routes connecting Oslo, Copenhagen, and Stockholm to New York, Chicago, and Denver.

Perhaps the old 737 hated him on principle.

He *had* been the one to make sure it was the last of its kind at the airline. A poor service job on the last rare bird?

No, the line guys wouldn't have let him down. The first thing he'd done on taking over was a salary bump and double the training budget for the line staff. Every minute a plane wasn't aloft cost a small fortune. Investing in keeping the aircraft aloft, and simplifying the workload to make it happen, had paid bigger dividends than any other single action he'd taken in twenty-five years.

And *this* was his reward.

It wasn't enough that the 737 had gone down in the largest single loss-of-life event in LuftSvenska's history. That had been the first awful call.

This wasn't only the first moment he'd had a chance to sit and think in the last two hours. It was the moment he could finally feel! All those dead, by his airline's hands. All he'd really achieved in his hours on the phone was to delay imaging the dead.

And this final call had been one too many in a day of horrid news.

He'd hoped for a rapid, unbiased investigation. Maybe even one that could be done before he left office so that he wouldn't be dumping this on the next president.

But rather than wrapping it up nicely and putting a neat bow on it in proper Swedish fashion, the SHK—Swedish Accident Investigation Authority in English, the "Breakdown Commission" *Haverikommission* in Swedish—had already declared the crash as *problematic.* They'd at least had the courtesy to inform him before they called in the US National Transportation Safety Board.

The bloody Americans.

The only good news was that they had a team attending the International Society of Air Safety Investigators conference in Reykjavik. Only two hours away once they were on a plane.

He'd been a keynote speaker for the ISASI a couple years back, on a panel with United, Delta, Quantas, and Lufthansa. The other airline presidents had warned him not to stick around for the rest of the conference, but he'd ignored the advice.

It was the scariest four days of his life.

These people listened to lectures on every topic from atypical structural failures to improper software behavior to patterns of CFITs, controlled flights into terrain (known among his old mechanic's crowd as PFUs, pilot fuck-ups). Each conference session had been about ten times as horrific as it sounded. And now LuftSvenska Flight 1308 would become another presentation at a future ISASI conference.

For ages after attending that conference, he'd had waking nightmares every time a flight took to the air. He could picture fifty new and horrifyingly spectacular ways a plane might come back down: wet runways, bird strikes, FOD (foreign object debris) ingestion by an engine at takeoff... The list had been unending.

But calling in the Americans? They were so brash. They certainly didn't need paparazzi over there; Yanks were their own most vocal selves. Still, he understood SHK's reasons. With LuftSvenska phasing out Boeing aircraft over the last twenty-five years, very few of the Swedish investigators had deep experience with them. Hardly anyone in Scandinavia did anymore. And even less experience with them crashing.

Maybe it was a sign he hadn't retired soon enough.

He should have stepped away when Gertrude had wanted to do that knitting cruise last spring. He'd have kicked back and read a book or drunk himself blind in the ship's bar.

No, instead he'd decided to stay on until the last step of standardizing the fleet and operations was complete.

The old 737 was already sold to the Democratic Republic of the Congo, where they'd fly it until it either lost the ability to take off or dropped out of the sky. Which wouldn't take long to happen down there. They didn't believe in maintenance; just use it until it broke, then move on. It was an ignominious ending for such a fine plane—it had performed flawlessly throughout his entire career as airline president—but a typical end in today's market.

Not anymore. Today the 737 once again counted as *his* problem, not the DRC's.

Nine days until his retirement.

There existed no chance that this mess be done in time for Hanna Berg's takeover.

He could dump the whole thing in her lap and go get drunk now. Or at least hide out in his country place in Västerås. The cross-country skiing in the woods out his back door was supposed to be very good, not that he visited there much.

Gertrude had chosen it, the former biathlete Olympian who had swept him off his feet forty years ago, and still skied with a grace like she'd been born for no other purpose.

It was very un-Swedish of him but, other than the joy of watching Gertrude, he hated cross-country skiing.

The winter sky shimmered outside his office window. It looked as if it had been carved from blue sapphire. His last time to look out this window? See his planes soaring aloft?

Only one plane was in sight as a tiny black speck climbing aloft out of Arlanda. He grabbed the big binoculars, the finish worn smooth with that precise gesture repeated thousands of times over the years, to check the paint job.

It wasn't one of his.

Stockholm to Fjällberget. Fourteen minutes in the air. Driving time of three hours. Anything would be an improvement over sitting in his office, achieving nothing for the next three hours except feeling heartsick. And if he went, there would be no possibility of being back in time for tonight's retirement dinner; the first good news of the day.

Ten minutes later, he was in his car and driving northwest along the E4.

Why *had* the damn thing gone down?

2

"Ms. Chase?"

Mike looked up at the man who'd approached their table at the conference luncheon. And kept looking up. Not that he stood particularly tall. But it *felt* as if he did.

Not even on Mike's best days, when he was skiing every weekend and hitting the gym most weekdays to keep himself in a steady supply of Denver ski bunnies, had he looked like this guy. Not quite six feet but a chest you could land a 747 on. Well, maybe only a Gulfstream 550 bizjet, but it was still ready for prime time.

Bald, black, and built. He didn't know that guys looked like that outside of the movies.

He'd addressed the question to Holly, who pointed at Miranda.

Miranda had retreated in many ways over the last few months. She wore top-of-the-line Bose noise-canceling headphones and gold-mirrored Randolph Engineering sunglasses that she probably wished were mirrored on the inside too—so that she didn't have to look at people at all.

Meg, the autism therapy dog she'd been given after Andi

Wu's abrupt departure, lay on the floor between her feet, snoozing off the small plate of raw ground meat that the conference chef had thoughtfully provided.

It was his first ISASI conference and it felt like being battered in a wind tunnel test. The International Society of Air Safety Investigators conference in Reykjavik made international the key word.

Jeremy was chattering away with the three delegates from the Japan Transport Safety Board in a rapid patter that wholly eluded Mike's own *konnichiwa* and *arigatou* command of the language.

The thick Indian-accented English from the AAIB guys at the table behind him sounded almost as foreign as the group at the next table the other direction from the French BEA laconically discussing the first morning's lectures in their native tongue.

Miranda's attention remained riveted on her plate of grilled langoustine and lemon fettuccini. She'd been staring at it without touching her fork; Miranda wasn't a big fan of foods touching each other, especially unfamiliar foods. Mike separated the two on his own plate and dumped all the mushrooms onto a side plate; she didn't like their squidgy texture.

Holly tapped Miranda's arm, then pointed at the newcomer.

While her attention was diverted, Mike switched their plates, giving her the prepared one.

Holly, who always noticed everything, typically nodded her approval when he did something like that. But she hadn't noticed while too busy admiring Mr. Chest.

He tried to ignore the letdown. Since when did he need her approval? Or anyone else's? For his entire life before joining this team he'd never needed anyone. Never *trusted* anyone. And now he felt *hurt* because Holly hadn't acknowledged him taking care of Miranda? Since when had pathetic become a line in his team job description?

Miranda tapped the button on her left earmuff, turning down the noise-cancellation on her headset without removing it.

"Ms. Chase?" Mr. Chest had a bass voice low enough to make Vin Diesel sound like a tenor.

"I'm Miranda Chase," her sunglasses focused on the man's left elbow.

"I'm Tad Jobson. That's short for Tad Jobson. Pop wasn't big on fancy names. He claims it comes from me being just a *small tad of a thing* when I was born. Mama has more than a few things to say on that any time he brings it up—most of 'em along the you-try-passing-a-watermelon-out-of-your-body-and-see-how-you-feel lines. Either way, I'm your new rotorcraft specialist." He flashed a big smile.

Miranda turned into an absolute statue long enough for Tad Jobson to look up and around at him and Holly.

When she snapped back to life, Tad didn't jump, but he sure twitched.

"I...have a..." Miranda stopped again, stuttering like a robot with a short in its power supply. No, her team *didn't* have a rotorcraft specialist—anymore. Even after months, Mike knew that Miranda hadn't integrated Andi Wu's abrupt departure from the team and her life.

"Mr. Jobson—" Mike started.

"Tad."

"I'm Mike Munroe." His handshake didn't crush down on Mike's as he'd expected. "Why don't you have a seat for a moment? Eat some lunch." He had to get Tad away from looming into Miranda's personal space. He was back far enough for a normal person, but that wasn't Miranda.

Mike noticed something else. It was still a new factor, but he was getting to know it better and better.

Meg the dog had come up out of a deep sleep the second her mistress had frozen. Short enough to do so, she stood before stepping out from under Miranda's chair. Mike snagged the handle on the back of Meg's therapy-dog harness and lifted the gray Glen of Imaal Terrier. Not as easy as it looked as she was a solid little scamp. As soon as she was high enough in the air, she stepped forward and Mike released her onto Miranda's lap.

After a long few seconds, one of Miranda's arms came around the little dog. And then, as if nothing had happened, she picked up her fork and inspected her plate. Carefully avoiding the grilled langoustines that Mike had placed neatly around the edge of the plate, she twirled up a forkful of the olive oil-and-lemon pasta—without mushrooms—and began eating.

"What the...?" Tad had sat in the only open seat at their table. The seat next to Holly.

Mike hadn't thought that through very well, had he?

Miranda set down her fork and turned the noise-canceling function back to high. He knew she'd now be able to ignore anything below a shout. As usual, Jeremy remained utterly oblivious to everything except the three Japanese engineers beside him.

Mike turned to Tad. "We recently lost our rotorcraft specialist. Miranda was very close to her."

"Well, that had to suck the big one." He glanced at the oblivious Miranda, then raised his eyebrows like a shrug. At least he'd taken her preference for another woman in stride. Andi had made an amazing couple with Miranda, until Andi's betrayal six months earlier that had shattered everything and nearly destroyed the team.

"It did and it does. For all of us."

Tad raised his hands just in time for a waiter to place a luncheon plate before him. "Hands off on the topic. Reading you five-by-five, buddy." Another glance at Miranda to which she didn't react. "And the rest of it?" He had the decency to lower his voice despite the headphones.

"You ever work with an autistic, Jobson?" Mike kept his voice steady to avoid attracting Miranda's attention. He had better luck at that than at keeping the testiness out of his voice.

Holly's raised eyebrow said he did even worse than he thought.

Meg looked up to drive the point home, but Miranda didn't and that was all he cared about at the moment. She cut off a tiny piece of the grilled prawn, then held it out to Meg. After sniffing it carefully, Meg ate it, confirming its acceptability with a rapid wag of her stub tail and perking of her ears.

Miranda cut off an even smaller piece and tried it herself.

The rest of the prawn disappeared quickly enough between the two of them, and it never touched the pasta.

"With an autistic? Nope." If Tad took offence, he did a good job of hiding it. "My kid brother's a raging ADHD, does that count? Taught me a passel o' serious patience early on. Oh, and my gunner was way on the OCD side of things. Didn't bother me any 'cause it meant he triple-checked everything, and I do mean everything, probably even wiping his ass. But when it be *my* ass depending on his missiles flying true, I'd have let him do it fifty times to keep him happy."

"What did you fly?" Holly spoke for the first time since his arrival. Her Australian accent wasn't too broad, but it wasn't her normal accentless tone either. She'd pulled out her playful accent without tipping over into mocking or dangerous.

It was a rare balance, one she typically reserved for him. His own prawns weren't sitting nearly as comfortably in his gut as they were in Meg's and Miranda's.

"Zulus," Tad answered as he bit off an entire langoustine and chewed on it. "Tight fit for a dude like me," he flexed his massive shoulder muscles, "but I managed." Also, like Holly, he managed to talk around his food without garbling his words. Perhaps it was a military trait.

Mike had to think for a moment. Zulu for Z? That rang a bell. Oh, Zulu Cobra, the AH-1Z Viper attack helo—the thin one with the pilot seated above and behind the gunner. Only one outfit flew those, but which one? Army? Navy? Marine Corps. Bingo!

The conversation had flowed on without him. Tad and Holly were trading place names, half of which he didn't recognize, the other half that he knew were the horror spots of the globe.

Ex-Marine, except there was no such thing according to a Marine. Which meant Mike had to be careful how he asked the next question.

"Why did you stop flying?" Without meaning to, Mike cut them off in mid-laugh over what crap passed for food at yet another African place with far too many vowels for the number of consonants involved.

Tad tapped his left ear as he twirled a load of pasta and secured it to his fork with another massive chunk of prawn. "Blew it out. Wasn't even in my bird. Riding a cougar that was supposed to be getting me out of theater when it caught an IED. Big one, lost three, jostled me pretty good. Damn loud, I'll say that much."

"A cougar?" Mike clamped his jaw shut. Too late.

"MRAP," Holly answered for him. "Mine Resistant Ambush Protected vehicle," as if he were a simpleton. "An IED is—"

"I know what the hell an MRAP and an IED are, Hol." She was buying into the whole Tad-the-underplayed-hero thing. *Three dead. But jostled him. Damn loud.* "Crap!" He was *not* jealous. It wasn't in him. Jealousy meant attachment and he'd sworn off that the day he'd turned nine and watched his parents die from the back seat of that car wreck.

Holly looked at him askance. He never swore—once a

Catholic orphanage inmate, always a Catholic orphanage inmate—and she knew it.

"What other types of rotorcraft have you piloted?" He ignored her and kept his focus on Tad.

"More than a pilot, I'm a jumper. Old man was an Army helo mechanic down to Mother Rucker."

"Fort Rucker, Alabama," Holly injected helpfully. "That's where Army ACE is—the Aviation Center of Excellence for training their helo pilots." She was lucky Miranda was seated between them or her shins would be hurting. Holly knew what it was from the same source he did. As a former Army Night Stalker pilot, the world's best, Andi had told them all plenty of stories about ACE.

"I followed in Pop's mechanic footsteps but went Marines. Sometimes feels that if it's got a rotor, I've spun a wrench on it. Then some up-and-up spotted me doing the shakedown flight test when I might've been fooling around a bit; slammed me straight into Warrant Officer School and combat pilot training. Next thing I know I'd jumped from working the line into seats —hell of a shock for a wrench like me. Pop near enough burst his buttons though, so all to the good."

He took a moment to wash down his latest mouthful with iced tea, then kept right on talking like he'd be glad to talk about himself until Armageddon struck and the four horsemen trampled him underfoot. Maybe even then.

"I spent most of ten years in the Zulu Cobras before that IED knocked me sideways. Got shuffled off into air safety for the rest of my tour, but neither of us were real hot on me re-upping. Watchin' my buddies go aloft while my ass stayed parked on the ground was worse'n a roll of cheap toilet paper and a case of the runs. So, with the old ear gone and me outta the Corps, NTSB made some sense. Anything else you wanna know?" Tad said it easy, casual. No hint of threat or annoyance.

Mike wanted to see the man's ID, but Holly looked at him like he was the one being a total shit.

Had she missed what he'd said, the single most important thing? *I'm your new rotorcraft specialist.* That meant he'd been assigned to Miranda's team.

And no one hated change more than an autistic.

Holly and Tad turned back to their war stories.

At the moment? He'd give Miranda a run for her money on disliking change.

3

"WHO'S HE?" JEREMY ASKED AS THEY WERE MOVING FROM LUNCH back to the lecture hall.

"She. Her name is Meg." Miranda nodded toward the dog trotting close by her side in her bright red Therapy Dog vest.

The delegates from Germany and Australia were nearby, moving from the ballroom back toward the main session room, speaking in their foreign tongues. Years of working with Holly hadn't prepared her for the curiosity of male delegates from the Australian Transportation Safety Bureau speaking in a soft Strine. The logic that men as well as women would, didn't decrease her surprise each time one spoke.

None of them were close enough for her to worry about them tripping on Meg. That was good.

Jeremy laughed. "I know *that,* Miranda. The big guy who joined our table at lunch? I was talking to the team from JAXA, the Japanese Aerospace guys, when he came in, I guess. Remember the Epsilon S engine that blew up and the H3 that had to do a programmed self-destruct in flight a couple months before that? The engines are really giving them trouble. I made a few suggestions on what to look at and they wrote them down. It feels so cool when I can help out like that. Don't you think so?"

She made an agreeing sound, and that seemed to pacify him for the moment. She'd found that simulated concurrence often bought her a moment to consider conversational content. *It feels* implied emotional content, something Jeremy would know that she never understood. But in his excitement, and he was always excited by something, he rarely remembered such details.

JAXA's recent engine issues *were* intriguing. Should she leave the NTSB? After all, her original reason for making air-crash investigations her Special Interest when she was thirteen had proven to be utterly false. Her parents hadn't died the way she'd been told. Or even, she now understood, particularly cared about their only child except in some unconstructive intellectual way. Did that make her angry? Sad? Frustrated? Why did there have to be so many different emotions?

She wished she could ask Andi, but Andi was gone.

Maybe...

Miranda veered to the side of the foyer, out of the smooth stream of the delegates changing conference center rooms. There were predictable flow eddies near the two restrooms, primarily the men's as they predominated in air-safety investigation roles—though there were enough women, typically members of various airlines' air-safety programs, at the conference to create a typical holding pattern outside the women's facilities as well.

She checked the primary corridor's pattern when she arrived at the side of the foyer, seeing that her departure had created only minor turbulence in the overall hallway flow.

Meg had followed her effortlessly as usual. Jeremy joined her after nearly walking square into the lead safety manager for JetBlue.

"Why are there so many emotions, Jeremy? Why can't there

just be the basic five I learned as a child?" They'd come to rest in the unlikely shadow of a potted palm tree placed along one side of the hall. The pictures on the walls were mostly of Iceland's geothermal and volcanic features, making a curious contrast.

What if she pretended it was Hawaii?

No. Hawaii had a very different type of volcanology, shield volcanism rather than Iceland's steeper and more violent stratovolcanoes. Images of erupting stratovolcanoes amid potted palm trees didn't make any more sense in Hawaii than it did here in Iceland. Perhaps in Indonesia?

"Five emotions?" Jeremy squinted at her.

"My parents had a chart for me to point at how I was feeling, or I'd look in the mirror to try to figure it out: happy, okay, sad, worried, and upset—big smile, small smile, no smile, frown, and tears. A neat continuum that made emotions much easier to comprehend."

"Well, the five are useful for general categorization, but there's more."

She opened her personal notebook to the four pages of pasted-in charts of emojis and identifying words. "This is out of control."

"But," he waved a hand to the southwest. "Taz is at home with our Amy. I miss them both so much, which makes me sad. Having a child, Miranda, is so beyond awesome that I can't wait for her to talk so I can ask what she's thinking. She's only four months old, but I can see her learning every second of the day. Every time I hold her, I'm so happy that it's a wonder I don't self-destruct like Japan's H3 rocket engine. It was so hard to leave her, to miss a single day, but Taz said I had to come to the conference to see you and *get out from underfoot,*" he imitated Taz's Latinate tones. "Which made me happy to see you and laugh at Taz's joke."

"But those are all covered by my five."

"Well, you didn't mention excited. Aren't you *excited* about being here? Aren't you *pleased* with Meg the superdog?"

Meg looked up at them and wagged her tail at the mention of her name.

"And *saddened* or even *annoyed* by some of the safety methodology failures that we've been hearing about?"

"I guess." Would she be down-frown sad if she left the NTSB? In September of last year, the NTSB had signed an agreement with the FAA stating that the NTSB would lead aerospace accident investigations only if someone was hurt or property unrelated to the launch was damaged. In other words, hands off if anything technologically interesting occurred.

She'd been with the NTSB for twenty years, half her life. Would she have to leave its familiarity to join the FAA to work on the newer problems? She didn't like the sound of that.

"Anyway," Jeremy looked around, then leaned closer. "Who was the guy at the table?"

"Rotorcraft," there was a sharp tightness in her throat and her stomach roiled. Was it the langoustines she'd eaten? Miranda looked down at Meg, who had taken the opportunity to lie down and fall asleep at the base of the potted palm's pot in her usual position (on her back, legs in the air). Her prominently displayed belly didn't appear to be bothering her. Was the discomfort an emotion? None of the faces on her reference chart showed choking and she didn't have a mirror handy to check her own face even if it did. Did she need a Heimlich Maneuver? No, her breathing was overly rapid but functional.

"Rotorcraft? Like replacing-Andi kind of rotorcraft? Took them long enough."

Miranda looked up from Meg, almost to Jeremy's eyes.

"I mean it. None of us was ever a tenth as good at those as she was. If this guy's at all decent, you need him."

There was a look on Jeremy's face. His eyes aimed upward,

but not as if he was looking at something and there was an odd twist to his mouth. Wistfulness? She studied the pages of her still open personal notebook. Yes, it was the only one that fit his facial pattern.

"What are you feeling wistful about, Jeremy?" she asked to test her hypothesis.

"Oh," he looked down at her and she looked aside quickly.

Knowing that her eyes were hidden from others by the reflective sunglasses helped less than she'd hoped. They might be looking at their reflections, but that still lined up their eyes with hers. In fact, they watched their reflections *more* intently than they'd ever looked at her eyes. And *she* saw *their* eyes. She sighed and took off the sunglasses, tucking them carefully into the pocket of her vest that she'd dedicated to their use.

"I just miss being on your team, Miranda. I mean, Taz is happier in Washington, DC. And I love the problem-solving needed at the NTSB Headquarters lab. But I miss...you."

Did she miss him? "Yes. Not as much as Andi, but I miss you too."

He laughed again. "Good to know. So, he's rotorcraft, but who is he?" Jeremy hooked a thumb back towards the banquet room.

"He's the Big Bad Wolf," a deep voice said so close behind her that she leapt away. After tripping on Meg, who gave a sharp yelp of surprise at the rude awakening, Miranda would have landed on the floor if she hadn't run into Jeremy first. She managed to remain upright, but he tumbled backward into the palm tree, landing sprawled across the big pot with his butt planted in the plastic ivy covering the dirt.

"Whups! Sorry, buddy." Tad lifted Jeremy back to his feet as if he weighed less than Meg, who was up on all fours and snarling at Tad.

"What the hell?" Holly grabbed Tad's shoulder and yanked

him away. He almost dragged Jeremy over Meg before letting go of Jeremy's arms.

"Ow! Shit, woman." Instead of collapsing in pain as most people did when Holly did one of her vice-grip things, Tad reached up and peeled her hand off his shoulder. "Got a good grip on you."

"I'll grip your damn face off!"

"About time," Mike whispered from close behind Miranda, almost making her leap again.

"Just chill, woman. You on that hair-trigger all the time?" Tad rubbed at his shoulder.

Mike answered for her. "Count on it. Now, what did you just do?"

"Surprised them is all. Heard Jeremy asking about me, chimed in with my Big Bad callsign. My squad tagged me as the Big Bad Wolf when I told them about being typecast in a high school play. They were doing *Into the Woods*. Let's just say I tried out cause Little Red Riding Hood was one hot chick—dark as midnight with hair bleached to match the summer sun. Turned out well for me, I can tell you that."

Miranda supposed that his grin could be described as wolf-like, not that she'd ever seen an actual wolf grin. She pulled out her phone and searched on *wolf grin image*. Photos showed big fangs, bared teeth, and expressions like Meg when she was angry, only much worse. Miranda blanked the screen quickly. Then she cleared the app to make sure the images didn't stay on her phone. Then she deleted it entirely and told it to reinstall a fresh copy.

Tad Jobson's grin possessed no discernable relation to a wolf's except they both had teeth.

He started in on some other story about skits he'd done with the other Marines on long ship-board cruises to pass the time.

Why hadn't she thought to do this before?

She opened a different browser app to make sure she didn't see the wolves again, just in case the first one had somehow bookmarked them despite the reinstall. She searched and located a number of charts of dog emotions. Then she sat cross-legged on the foyer carpet with her back against the confusing terracotta palm pot. Meg sat in front of her and Miranda began trying to identify the dog's emotions.

The first several charts on her phone were very confusing, mostly because there were too many options. The next set didn't match anything about Meg. That's when she understood that they'd all portrayed human emotions on a dog's face; she'd have liked that when she was younger but it didn't help her with Meg. Miranda discarded those as well. The simplest one turned out to be the best.

Eight basic dog emotions, more than the five she'd been raised with but still manageable. Meg's eyes were wide open, her tongue lolling out, and she did indeed appear to be smiling as she looked up at Miranda's face. *Happy or excited.*

It was good to know.

She waited for Meg to change her expression, but she didn't. Then she pulled in her tongue and tilted her head to the side without looking away. Miranda found a match. "Oh, look. That's a *curious* face."

Tad squatted down beside her. "Yep, that's a curious face you got there, buddy."

"*Her* name is Meg."

"Yep, that's a curious face you got there, Meg."

Jeremy laughed.

Miranda didn't understand why a nonconstructive repetition of information was funny.

4

THEY WERE HALFWAY THROUGH A LECTURE ABOUT BEST AIR-safety practices for designing nighttime helicopter landing platforms on offshore drilling rigs.

Miranda, Jeremy, and Tad were riveted. Though only Tad was taking notes, pages of them as if he was trying to copy down the whole lecture.

Holly looked as if she'd rather be at a beauty salon, something she'd once described as a special hell perpetrated on women by insecure men. Her sole concession to society's pressure was hacking off the bottom of her ponytail with a knife whenever she deemed it too long. Mike's offers to use actual scissors were always brushed aside as too much trouble.

Thank God they kept these sessions short, twenty-five minutes apiece with a five-minute break between. Images of destruction due to landings on oil platforms under tow and...

Mike closed his eyes. The conference certainly drove home the stupidity of amateurs, the deadly complacency of pros, and the flat-out bizarre ways people managed to die. It was very hard to open them again.

He wanted to stay awake until the next session on Human

Factor Failure Methodologies Analysis presented by NASA. The conference chair appeared on the stage as if by magic between one slow eyeblink and the next.

At lunch, he shouldn't have had the second chocolate mousse cake on top of the big meal but it had just been sitting there. To his left had sat Jeremy and the JAXA team. They'd shifted to English and were discussing metal fatigue and fracture analysis with an enthusiasm usually reserved for overtime play at the Super Bowl.

To his right, the silent Miranda. When he'd stopped her from giving chocolate to Meg because it wasn't good for dogs, Miranda had refused to eat it herself. It was very good mousse, lighter yet richer than his recipe, which he had no idea how to reproduce despite eating two of them.

And the eyeblink after that, the chairwoman was the one at the microphone, "I'm so sorry for interrupting. Where is Miranda Chase in the audience?"

Mike shook himself alert as Miranda rose slowly to her feet.

"Oh, excellent. Could you please proceed to the back of the room? Sorry for the interruption." And she was gone.

Miranda was most of the way to sitting back down when Mike caught her arm. "I think she meant now, Miranda."

"Oh." She looked once more to the stage where the speaker was trying to recall where he'd left off squeezing every possible word into the twenty-five-minute time frame. "But I've only heard half the talk." Miranda hated incomplete things.

"Would you like me to go for you?"

Miranda nodded and sat down again. Then her attention re-riveted on the speaker's slide of the shortcomings of navigation electronics when landing a heavy helo on a moving object like a towed oil drilling platform.

He left her sitting beside Holly with Tad on the far side. Jeremy had ended up beyond Tad, as good as a mile away. Meg lay on her back across Miranda's toes with her paws in the air and her head thrown back, fast asleep as usual. What did the little beast know that he didn't? She hadn't bothered to wake up when Miranda stood, already knowing she wasn't going anywhere.

"I was expecting Ms. Chase," the elegant woman waiting by the conference room's back door looked anxiously over his shoulder. Tall, slender, her hair Nordic blonde (a true one, based on her roots and eyebrows), and the softest blue eyes versus Holly's golden hair and gem-blue gaze. She had a slight Swedish accent, placing Chase closer to Shase. She'd been built to tick every box on the master entice-Mike list. Including, she could be a twin of ABBA's Agnetha Fältskog at her peak.

The band had broken up before he was born, but as a kid, he'd shoplifted every cassette of their music. He hated disco, but Agnetha had been his first major crush and this woman awoke every one of those dreamy memories.

"I'm Mike Munroe, the Human Factors specialist on Miranda's team. She's fascinated by the current lecture." He didn't bother explaining that, courtesy of her autism, Miranda was fascinated by anything she chose to focus upon—to the exclusion of all else.

Klara, by her attendee badge, used those big blues on him. "By your tone, you are not so intrigued." Her handshake was firm and warm despite her slender fingers.

"Human factors," he tapped his chest and tried not to think of Tad Jobson's massive pecs. "Oil platform electronics," Mike waved at the screen, then offered a friendly shrug.

"Klara Dahlberg, Swedish SHK. Very technical, I'm afraid, airframe design engineer before I move into Swedish *Haverikommission*." She said it with a bit of humor and a dazzling smile, as if teasing that *Two such as us, so different, there would be no future.*

He returned the smile that said it might have been fun to find out, but it didn't feel right on his face.

As if she sensed the internal miscue, she continued, "I am to be requesting Ms. Chase's—"

That soft Shase sound was going to kill him.

"—attendance to a crash site in Sweden. A Boeing 737 has gone down, the airline's first accident in two decades. The next flight from here to Stockholm is in two hours, but I've arranged to reserve the last two available seats and a late check-in if we can escort her to the airport in time. A helicopter will be awaiting her at the other end."

"Why us? Why not your own people?"

Her lovely face turned grim for a long moment, but such a face couldn't sustain it for long. "Our Minister of Defense and her husband were on the flight. Your government offered any support. I'm supposed to mention that a General Drake Nason recommended we contact Ms. Chase." Shase.

"Oh, that certainly explains it." The Chairman of the Joint Chiefs of Staff had become a great champion of Miranda's team, with reason for the number of times Miranda had bailed him out. Over the years, Miranda's success rate had made her in high demand for politically urgent investigations.

Mike glanced back at his team.

Tad was leaning in close to Holly whispering something. Mike wanted them apart...in different directions. Not a chance would he send Miranda without himself along, but leaving Holly and Tad here together looked like a crap idea as well.

Mike turned once more to face Klara. "Miranda has a talk scheduled tomorrow morning."

"I will speak to the organizers about moving it to the end of the last day in case she can make it back in time." Her tone filled with sorrowful doubt, but she didn't know Miranda. She had a habit of tracking down the cause of crashes faster than most.

Mike gave himself a seventy-thirty odds bet Miranda would return within the three-and-a-half remaining days of the conference. "You can let the plane go. We can do you one better than that. Are you coming with us or remaining here? Plenty of room."

"I will be remaining here."

Mike paused for a heartbeat, then two.

Klara Dahlberg was everything a man might ask for. Tall, breathtakingly lovely, smart, a sense of humor, and no ring. And a young Agnetha's twin.

And Mike felt not a single thing about her not joining them.

Now was not the time to wonder why he wasn't doing everything to sweep her off her feet and onto her back, but it was like an itch he knew he'd have to come back to unless he remained very careful to avoid it. He vowed to hide from it as long as humanly possible.

It wasn't as if he and Holly were in a monogamous relationship, at least not a declared one. Holy Christ! How long *had* it been since the last time he'd looked seriously at another woman? Way too long! And here stood one to look at and he felt nothing that could be construed as a proper attraction to—

A round of applause marked the end of the talk. There would be a brief window in which to break Miranda free as the session leader did the obligatory gift presentation of a boxed pen and posed for a handshake photograph.

"Wait a moment, please." He went to fetch the team. Time to break up the dance going on there.

He wasn't going to pay any attention to Holly's quiet laugh shared with Tad.

Mike leaned in to block Miranda's sightlines to the stage. Some part of him had noted that the poor presenter had never rediscovered his true stride, flashing through the last eight slides in the final fifteen seconds. It was unlikely that anyone, other than perhaps Miranda, absorbed their content.

Ten minutes later, they and their luggage were out front.

Miranda hadn't said a word, but Meg was trotting along happily enough for Mike not to worry.

"Going with us?" Mike pulled Jeremy aside.

"Wouldn't miss it!"

"Did you call Taz?"

Jeremy held up the phone clutched in his hand as if the blank screen was proof.

"Good boy." Since when had he decided that tending a marriage was important enough to make sure Jeremy did so?

Mike had been a serial monogamist his whole life, but his relationships never extended more than a few months—before Holly. He'd been with her since two years *before* Taz returned from the dead. Now Taz and Jeremy were a year married and had a newborn. He and Holly were still dating, or sleeping together, or whatever they were calling it. Thank God they were both terminal bachelors. That's all they were. Two single people fine with sleeping together every night. Marriage would never be—

Klara arrived at the same moment as an airport shuttle, the flow of her fine blonde hair arriving well behind her. She went through the expected apologies for pulling them from the conference and thanking them for coming to the SHK's aid.

As they were loading up, she held out her card. "If there's anything I can do to help, anything at all, please don't hesitate to call." Except she didn't present it facing him. Instead, she presented the back, which had a handwritten phone number and a word that looked misspelled. Then he guessed that the Swedish word was only one letter different from the English one.

He made a show of tucking it carefully into his wallet before thanking her and joining the others in the van.

Beside the handwritten phone number was the word: *Privat.*

In the past, he'd have definitely made use of the card at the first opportunity. Where had the charge gone? He was glad to admire but felt none of the normal need to pursue.

He climbed into the front seat and glanced back at the others. Jeremy and Miranda discussing the latest session. And Holly, sitting in the back row of the van beside Tad Jobson's shoulders, made his gut wrench. He faced forward.

Jealousy was ridiculous. It wasn't like he'd *ever* wanted a committed relationship.

5

THE FLIGHT FROM REYKJAVIK TO SWEDEN WAS A CRAZY juxtaposition of variable speeds. Miranda's Citation M2 bizjet covered the thousand-plus miles in two and a half hours. Just that quickly they crossed from Iceland to Scandinavia.

But the trip *felt* as if it took forever. Mike always flew copilot to Miranda. With Meg lying behind Miranda's seat, that left Jeremy, Holly, and Tad in the main cabin's four facing seats. Despite the headset tuned to cockpit-only, he heard the three of them yakking it up like old times—like when the team had first come together.

He missed the early days. Miranda's planes often made it more efficient for the rest of the team to fly themselves to an incident site. Before acquiring the M2, Miranda always flew a step ahead, leading the way at the edge of Mach 1 in her Korean War-era single-seater Sabrejet. Then he, Jeremy, and Holly would follow along, rubbing shoulders in the close confines of the slower Mooney M20V. But, along with the easy camaraderie, the little plane was gone now, burned up along with Miranda's home. Instead, the luxury bizjet whisked them all together to crash investigations with effortless ease.

Effortless.

He was not going to think about whatever the hell was going on back in the cabin. Instead he'd think about what lay ahead.

That constantly renewed determination didn't last him a single tick past ten seconds.

After Tad and Miranda had left the lunch table, he'd texted Jill at NTSB headquarters. If ever there was anyone wired into everything happening there, it was her. Every launch to an incident crossed her desk first: air, sea, rail, pipeline, and highway.

She'd confirmed that Tad Jobson was for real and had been sent to their team. Only knowing that Jill could as easily hand them the mundane launches as the highly technical ones that were Miranda's specialty had kept him from lambasting her for not giving them a heads-up. Not that she was the vindictive type at all, but certain risks weren't worth taking.

Once they were up to cruise altitude, he hunted down a tiny airstrip less than twenty kilometers from the crash site. He'd never have attempted to put Miranda's jet down on such a short runway, but she eased it in as if it was the most normal thing in the world. Of course, the runway on the island she used to live on had been two hundred meters shorter.

At least the little strip had runway lights. They'd flown out of day into night. The winter sun had set two hours earlier, the leisurely passage of a winter's evening at three in the afternoon drastically accelerated by their eight-mile descent from the lofty and still evening-lit heights. Welcome to winter in central Sweden.

They still had five hundred miles of fuel in the tanks. It was a good thing because Ludvika Airport boasted no services, only three small hangars, and a house with a very startled owner standing on the porch. He'd probably never seen a jet land on his airstrip before. His eyebrows had only gone higher when a pair of white, blue, and yellow police cars had raced up his driveway to load them aboard.

A call to Klara's number—with no greater purpose Mike could identify in himself—had arranged for special customs clearance and the police escort. The cops whisked them away, directly to the crash.

En route, Mike contemplated the thick woods cut neatly back to either side of the two-lane. They were in a channel sliced through a dense, sixty-foot-tall conifer forest, lined on both sides with three-meter deer fencing, lit in the blue stroboscopic flashes of the police cars' emergency lights. The verge bore only a few inches of snow, blades of brown grass still poking through the white sheen. Occasionally, the road would curve around the shore of a frozen lake, revealed by the abrupt break in the forest. A glimpse of stars above a sky gone jet black.

He twisted from the front seat to look behind him. Jeremy and Miranda sat in the back seat of the police car discussing the ISASI lectures. Holly and Tad had ended up together in the other car without his noticing.

Stop being paranoid, Munroe.

Though for every single woman since Sister Mary Pat at the orphanage until joining Miranda's team, being paranoid about women had served him very well.

The one time he'd let his guard down, he'd almost eaten the wrong end of a shotgun. There'd been a little family spat that had wiped out half of the Denver Giovanni mafia family—including the incredibly lustful Violetta who he'd unwittingly been helping to defraud her older brothers. Then Mike's FBI controller's bosses had stepped in to wipe out the other half, again almost taking him down as a not entirely innocent bystander.

Violetta had almost out-conned his best con, until it cost her life.

The next day Mike had been dragged into the NTSB and met Holly. And, against his usual nature, had flown straight ever since.

Dealing with Holly and Tad flirting was his payback for toeing the line?

Well, he sure didn't need that garbage.

6

"LOOKS LIKE A WAR ZONE," TAD WHISPERED.

"I've never been to a war zone," Miranda looked around. "It looks like an airplane crash to me."

"Man, don't know if I'm cut out for this shit."

Fjällberget ski resort was a small area cleared among the thick trees. The hill's prominence stood only a hundred and thirty meters above the surrounding topography. There was a single lift climbing a half kilometer through the dark conifers and three trails winding down. Typical for the rolling landscape of central Sweden. It was Norway that claimed all the high mountains and rugged slopes. The most notable things about Fjällberget were that it lay beneath no regular flight path and that there was a Boeing 737 that had planted nose-first in the middle of the primary ski run then flopped down onto its belly.

A line of wide-spaced high-pressure sodium lights mounted on the ski lift support poles cast a yellowish glow across the snowfield. A snowcat had been driven up near the wreck and its high-intensity white lights chopped the wreckage into sharply delineated areas of sun-bright and deepest shadow.

Miranda turned away before she saw more.

Not yet ready to study the crash, she kept her back to it—and Tad. Seeing Tad where Andi was supposed to be...hurt. Right in the center of her chest.

First, she checked her vest to make sure it wasn't pinching her there. It wasn't. Then she verified that every tool resided in its proper pocket. Then she pulled out a headlamp and turned it on.

As soon as she'd chosen a fresh notebook and labeled it with *LuftSvenska Boeing 737-700* and the date, Jeremy began reading out the weather data from his handheld meter.

"Three degrees Celsius below freezing. No wind. Winter-low humidity of twenty-seven percent." Just as she'd trained him, he kept the white clouds of his breath directed to the side as he took the measurements to not skew the readings.

"Dark," she looked around and recorded it dutifully along with his data.

"Local sunset at 1450 hours today," Jeremy announced after accessing his phone.

She'd forgotten they used to work this way. None of the others had adapted as neatly to her methods as Jeremy had. Or hadn't she let them? Had she kept Andi at a distance? Is that what had happened between them?

Before she had considered that question, Jeremy began describing the sloping terrain and the low altitude of the crash site. The jet should have been at thirty thousand feet, not three hundred meters. Yet it wasn't.

The next sphere of her investigation method after weather and terrain was the extent of the debris field. It had—

"Ms. Chase? I'm Kurt Anderson, the lead investigator for the SHK." Like most older Swedes, his English sounded slightly stilted. The younger ones could have been American-born by their accents.

She looked at his extended hand. He wore heavy gloves and she wore light ones. She still didn't want to shake hands.

Meg was looking up at her expectantly.

Miranda sighed and shook Kurt's gloved hand as briefly as possible, hoping that satisfied Meg. "My name is Miranda Chase. I'm the Investigator-in-Charge for the NTSB."

"Thank you for coming so quickly. We have focused so far on body recovery," he waved toward long lines of body bags laid out on the snow along the track of the ski lift. The black bags absorbed the yellow night lights until they looked like rectangular black holes in the hillside. It seemed that should be a metaphor for something, but she wasn't sure what.

"Did you photograph the bodies in position?"

"Each one. To all appearances, they were killed by blunt force trauma from the impact of—"

"No, I don't want to know."

"But—"

"Kurt," Mike stopped him. "It isn't that she's squeamish. It's that she likes to approach a crash in a logical fashion."

"And that doesn't include the victims?"

"Not yet."

At least Mike understood. She was never happy when another team was involved. They always had their own Safety Management System methodologies, even other NTSB teams. One of the conference talks had quantified the usage by sixteen different agencies of eight distinct SMS's—many agencies using multiple methods.

She knew that no one else used her own Miranda's Nested Sphere New Methodology, MNSNM. She'd added the *New* so that it would form a palindrome but the S and N blocked her attempts to make the entire title symmetrical about its center. Rotating it one-eighty created WNSNW, but her attempts to change the words to match had yet to prove noteworthy.

Her NTSB mentor had developed MNSNM specifically for

how her autism needed to approach an investigation. She adhered to it whenever possible: environment, debris perimeter, debris field, airframe, electronic records, and finally human factors. She'd ultimately added an outermost Conjectural Sphere of Causality, CSC (also an asymmetric palindrome), to temporarily store various hypotheses that emerged from the other spheres of the investigation.

Despite concerted effort, she'd never managed to create an acceptable acronym for the spheres themselves. She'd come close, but then the addition of the CSC had thrown out earlier efforts. CEPFARF served no identifiable purpose and sounded silly even to her.

She'd never worked with the Swedes on an investigation before and had no experience of their process at all. Did they use Reason's Swiss Cheese method, SHEL(L), or one of so many others? Removing the bodies first, she knew people liked to do that. The team from SHK had photographed them, which many failed to realize offered crucial analysis information. But were they the right type of photographs?

"Mike, find their photographer, then inspect and copy what they have. Make sure they're what I need. Jeremy, you can begin photographing the wreck." He knew what she liked, even better than Mike did.

He began conferring with Kurt of the SHK.

"Tad and Holly, you can start reviewing the debris field itself."

"Really?" Holly's voice had a tone that had Meg looking up at her.

"What's the deal?" Tad asked.

Holly didn't answer him directly. "Are you sure, Miranda? Isn't that out of order for you?"

"No, I can see they've already staked the debris field." There was a line of orange tape spread on the snow, with occasional ski poles jabbed into it. "I'll go see if I have any adjustments to the perimeter marking. Only one person should be needed for that."

As she turned to go, a Volvo XC90 painted in the same style as LuftSvenska's airplanes skidded into the parking lot and nearly sideswiped one of the police cars. A tall man clambered out, shrugged a parka on over an expensive suit without zipping it, and didn't bother with gloves or a hat over his silvered hair. He ducked under the tape line the police had erected to keep people out.

"Who's in charge here?" he demanded.

Kurt of the SHK looked in her direction. No, that wasn't correct. Hadn't he heard? She'd been very careful.

"I'm the Investigator-in-charge for the *NTSB*." No one laughed as if her repeating the phrase was funny—perhaps neurodiverse people didn't have the knack for doing that. But her point was that the NTSB always remained subordinate when called to assist in a foreign country. She decided to try a clarification to reinforce the correct status. "*Only* for the NTSB. Not for the SHK."

It must have worked as Kurt nodded, then turned to the new arrival. "Hello, Rolm, haven't seen you in a while." Kurt pushed back his parka's hood as he greeted the man, which earned him a smile in return. They shook hands in a way very different from the one Miranda had managed.

Why didn't her greetings ever earn her a smile? Was it the handshake? A secret handshake among neurotypicals? She'd never heard of one but that didn't mean that one, or perhaps several, didn't exist.

She pulled out her personal notebook and turned to a fresh page. It only took a few moments to develop a ranking and coding system for categorizing handshakes. She then charted the two she'd witnessed, her own and Rolm's with Kurt.

Kurt made introductions, interrupting her before she completed her notes. "Rolm Lindgren, this is Miranda Chase from the American NTSB. Ms. Chase, Rolm is the president of the airline."

"Oh. Well, at least your pilots were neat."

He glared at her. She'd learned that meant she'd said something wrong. Clarifying often repaired such conversational issues.

"Rather than skimming in, as if they were fighting for recovery or a long sliding crash, they impacted almost directly perpendicular to the slope. It saves us from looking for the rest of the plane."

A glance revealed no identifiable change in his overall expression.

She'd done what she could and now walked away to start circling the perimeter of the debris field. Was the orange tape pinned to the snow with ski poles a standard Swedish methodology or did they avail themselves of multiple practices, which in turn implied possible inconsistences in other areas of the investigation?

As she followed the perimeter, she observed that whatever the markup method, it was highly accurate. The impact of the plane at a steep angle to the slope had severely limited debris dispersal. And while the impact and short slide had churned up the snow, where it hadn't, the ski slope was well packed and scattered debris lay on the surface with only the larger pieces penetrating deeper.

The only disruptions were where teams were digging along the edges of the fuselage and wings. They were not being very careful about where they were tossing the snow.

Before she could complain, she saw them drag a body out from under the starboard wing. The corpse still wore parka, ski goggles, and parts of a ski clipped to her boot. They took a photograph, the flash more blinding than the floodlights, removed the ski, then shifted the woman into a body bag.

Miranda made a note in her crash notebook to personally

inspect the areas of the debris field covered by this disturbed snow.

The orange tape created a very efficient perimeter: like a chalk outline around a dead body, a tape outline around a dead plane. She considered it compared to the small flags that the NTSB used. For a larger wreckage area, miles of tape might be required. Perhaps she'd stick with her reusable perimeter flags.

Meg was light enough to trot over the packed snow surface that she herself kept sinking into. If she'd known she was headed here, she'd have brought her snowshoes. Her first-ever crash investigation had been in deep snow in the high Idaho wilderness. She had sorely missed having snowshoes. She now kept a pair in every plane. But in the whirlwind of the afternoon, she'd left them strapped into her jet's rear luggage compartment.

I'm your new rotorcraft specialist. It was a horrible phrase. She missed the old one. She'd *loved* the old one. Andi hadn't called, written, or simply dropped in since her abrupt departure.

Miranda's chest hurt even more than before. It felt as if her heart cried and the tears burned her insides.

7

"WHAT THE HELL, KURT?" ROLM TURNED ON HIM. THE TWO OF them had been mechanics together a lifetime ago. As Kurt had risen to lead the SHK, they often ran into each other at industry dinners. "Sorry. Long day. Thanks for coming out yourself. But what the hell?"

"Biggest accident ever on Swedish soil, of course I'd be here." Then Kurt glanced toward the departing woman and shook his head. "I'm not sure what's up there. Didn't even offer me a hello. Or want to look at the plane. Brought quite the team with her though." He pointed out the other four who had come with her—already in and out among the shadows—each marked with a bright headlamp.

Rolm couldn't tell anything about them from here. "They any good?"

"Haven't seen enough to tell. NTSB's dispatcher said they were sending their best. My people are still working with fire and rescue, pulling out the bodies. She comes in with her little dog and dispatches her team to tasks without so much as a by your leave. Never seen anything quite like it."

"Damned Yankee arrogance." Exactly what he didn't want.

They'd find a way to hang this on his maintenance or flight crews—he had no idea which was the worse scenario. But he knew an American team would never hang the fault on an American aircraft.

"No, Rolm," Kurt beat his hands together to keep up circulation.

Rolm's own hands and head were getting cold despite it only being a few degrees below freezing. They'd become office jockeys, losing...*lost* the edge that had them working on cold planes in frigid hangars with only normal amounts of griping.

"Whatever it is, it isn't arrogance."

"Just do me a personal favor, Kurt. For old time's sake."

"Will if I can, Rolm, but I'm not going to mess with the report if it's your guys who screwed the pooch on this."

"No, nothing like that. Just keep a damn close eye on them."

"*That* I can do for you. You know that a determination, if we can make one out of this mess at all, might take months? Or longer?"

Rolm felt sick to his stomach. He definitely shouldn't have stopped at Günter's Korvar for a double Polish sausage on baguette on his way north. But they'd always been one of his weaknesses whenever he was passing through that part of North Stockholm.

"If that's the case, then it becomes Hanna's problem."

And he hated himself hoping for that. If it *did* turn out to be his guys' fault, he didn't want to have to see it and report it firsthand. And definitely not be the one to hand down any form of blame or justice. *Yeah, you just killed an entire planeload of folks with your negligence. Live with that, why don't you? Oh, and I have to fire you, which means you'll never be employable in the industry again.*

Kurt headed off.

With nothing else to do, just as useless as an airline president always seemed to be, Rolm stood at the base of the ski run and stared upslope at the shattered pile of steel, aluminum, and people that had been the last Boeing in his fleet. He spotted the first of the news vans pulling into the lot behind him. He zipped his parka and pulled up his hood to delay the inevitable. Once he'd been recognized, there'd be a thousand questions, all blasted out nationwide.

He hadn't visited the wreck in Italy twenty-five years ago; there hadn't been time. The incident had been in the middle of an active airport. The authorities cleared the bodies and wreckage before even the Italian investigators arrived because it had closed the main runway and crashed into the luggage-handling building. In fact, the cleanup happened so fast that the flight recorder wasn't found for a week, mixed in with the wreckage taken offsite for disposal. There'd certainly been nothing left to salvage—everyone forward of the wings dead from blunt trauma of the plane shredding, and everyone aft by a fire that had raged through that portion of the plane.

This crash was different. It spread over only a very small area of the ski slope.

Lying on the snow, it looked too improbable to be real. The black sky above, the bright lights and the hum of activity all around it; almost as busy as if it sat parked at an airport gate and teams were preparing it for a departure that would never happen.

The pilots had been the first to die.

The nose was crushed inward until it was mostly within the forward part of the passenger fuselage. The entire passenger compartment had concertinaed behind it—the plane a third shorter in death than it had been in life. The entire empennage, along with the rest of the tail, had folded over forward—the vertical stabilizer punched like the can piercer on a church key can opener into the middle of the fuselage.

The wings and engines lay to either side, the inboard sections knifed into the snow by their leading edges. Angled as if still trying to fly straight down into hell. The wings had broken and crumpled badly outboard of the engines.

And along the left side of the slope, tracing the lines of the Poma lift—not running at the hour, its long poles hanging like hooks to fish for the souls of the dead—lay lines of body bags. Black on the white snow, each bag so dark it looked like a line of graves waiting to be filled.

He knew the scene would haunt him the rest of his days. He looked down at what he was wearing. When he was done, he *would* destroy all of his suits. He'd have Gertrude buy him a new one for nights out and entertaining. One suit in which he could pretend at least on the outside, at least for her, that he'd never seen any of this.

8

"YOU REMEMBER I'M ROTORCRAFT, RIGHT? I DON'T RECOGNIZE half this shit." Tad nudged a crumpled piece of metal with his boot. "Especially not in the dark."

"Wing slat. Outboard by the look of it," Holly twisted about to shine her headlamp on nearby wreckage. The port side engine was jammed into the snow close to her right. The broken-off end of the wing well to her left. "Mid-wing slat. It's the bit that extends out from the front edge of the wing to give it more curvature, more lift for departure and landings."

"So is it telling us anything? Or is it just a piece of broken crap?"

Holly used to leave this part of it to Miranda and Jeremy. Once he'd transferred from the West Coast office to DC, she'd picked up what slack she could. But *why* wasn't one of her strengths.

"Well, it's still tucked against the wing, rather than in the extended position. Means the pilots weren't trying to take off or land. Not even an emergency landing. If they were, they'd have the slats well out to set maximum lift and achieve the lowest possible airspeed on touchdown. That's unless there was a total failure of all systems and they couldn't, which would be unlikely."

"Meaning they dove into the hill while hustling."

"Something like that." Holly looked around but didn't see any of the other team members. "Might be they were already dead."

Miranda had started walking on the starboard-side perimeter, so why had Holly started them on the port side? She used to keep a close eye on Miranda. Something was off with Miranda, so was Holly avoiding the problem? That certainly sounded like the Holly she knew.

If he'd stayed true to form, Jeremy would be somewhere deep inside the wreck itself, oblivious to the danger. Sure enough, she spotted the bright wash of a photo flash strobe through the cockpit windows, or all that remained of them. He'd be going after the Quick Access Recorder and then be headed aft for the cockpit and flight recorders mounted in the tail section.

Mike was...over by the ski lift talking to a ski patroller in a blue-and-yellow parka. A patroller with long blonde hair spilling out from under her yellow safety helmet. Why wasn't she surprised? Pretty women always went mush-brained around Mike. As if she hadn't noticed that Klara Dahlberg woman at the conference giving him her card and the *Call me soon, Baby* look.

How did he do that?

And two in one fucking day. Blatantly.

She'd never caught him doing anything overt. Never overheard him flirting more than was normal to do. Hadn't ever caught him having an affair.

An *affair*? Like being with another woman when he was supposed to be with her? They'd have to be a couple for him to have an affair just by definition.

Which they were. Which she'd sworn she'd never do.

Bloody hell! The man was messing with her head.

Like cutting up so stiff about Tad Jobson joining the team.

Except Mike *never* made mistakes about people. And Tad had clearly leaned on one of Mike's buttons—hard.

"'ang on a sec." She wasn't sure if she was speaking to herself or Tad.

Mike was turning from the pert ski patrol girl and headed toward the nose of the wreck where Miranda must be on the other side. She'd have bet he'd be another half hour chatting up the ski patroller.

What if that's wasn't what he was doing? It meant...she had no idea what.

"Hang on?" Tad laughed. "To what? I still don't know what any of this shit is."

Holly jabbed a finger. "That's an engine." And again. "That's a wing. Add two and two, Sherlock."

"I'm just a big bad wolf," he called after her. "Not some damn plane detective."

She managed to catch up with Mike by what was left of the nose of the plane. "Hey."

"Hey what?" Mike didn't stop.

Holly grabbed his arm and spun him around.

He shrugged off her grip with a hard shake but at least he stopped.

"Why you chuckin' a wobbly?"

His glare said whatever had pissed him off had done it but good.

Mike hunched in the shadow that the snowcat's searchlights cast from the wreck. They had both turned off their headlamps so as not to blind each other, but he now stood in deep shadow with his fists jammed in his pockets. With all the glass blown out of the cockpit's forward windows, the plane's crushed nose had taken on a darkly sinister glower as if it only needed the smallest excuse to leap forward and crush them all.

Holly considered waiting him out. She never had much patience with angry men, one of the things she liked about Mike: not much riled him. Then she remembered his look when Miranda had been kidnapped by Russia. He kept his anger off his face, usually, but below the surface there was a whole other story happening.

One deep breath.

Two.

By three she'd lose her patience so she spoke instead.

"What don't you like about Tad Jobson?"

"Want a list, Hol?" It was that same rare slice of him that she'd only glimpsed a few times but made her suspect he'd have been a top soldier in a different life. Or a ruthless assassin by the look of him at the moment.

"I guess I'm gonna need one, because I have no idea." Not something she liked admitting. Mike would know that about her. Weak wasn't her.

"Okay. Number One. Did you think for a single second to check his story?"

"I didn't need to. No one can fake the kind of operational knowledge he has. He is what he says."

"Sure," Mike nodded but he wasn't smiling to match his tone. "He knows his rotorcraft. Even my *idiot brain,* that you think doesn't know what an MRAP or an IED is, heard that. But, Number Two, he *says* he was sent by the NTSB. To, Number Three, join *Miranda's team* without any notification to us. And, of course Number Four, you verified that he has the security clearance to be on the team for the type of ugly that Miranda keeps getting us snarled up in."

Holly opened her mouth, then snapped it closed. Mike was absolutely right. She was supposed to be the suspicious one on the team. She hadn't had Miranda's back last spring in the UK and it had almost cost both their lives to fix it. And now she'd—

She loosened the vicious Fairbairn-Sykes dagger she wore in a thigh sheath. She'd go and get a few answers for herself, even if she had to carve them out of Tad Jobson. A twitch of her hip and she felt the second blade she kept at the small of her back was in place. One of the advantages to not passing through airport customs.

"Holly, give it a rest, will you? He checks out. All the way down the list. They kicked him to us for field training rather than sending him through the Academy because we're the only NTSB team that stays permanently staffed. And we do need a rotorcraft member." Mike's face looked serious. Not messing with her. "First thing I did during lunch while you were distracting him with all your eyelash batting."

"I don't bat my eyelashes at any man."

"Whatever you say, Harper."

But it was harder to let go than she expected. Not once had she thought to check Tad Jobson on any of those factors. It didn't matter that he checked out, *she* should have been the first one to the line on that. Her adrenaline had latched open, and it didn't want to stop pumping into her system. Even a conscious effort to breathe didn't ease her system back down.

"Okay. Okay. Sorry. I should have been on it." Contrite had a bitter taste. Who knew? One more deep breath. "What else am I not seeing?"

Mike simply stared at her. Didn't even blink. Staring like he'd never speak to her again.

"What?"

He turned on his heel, flicked on his headlamp, indicating the conversation was done when it totally wasn't, and walked off toward Miranda. She'd come around from the far side, following the orange tape on the snow with broad zigzags aside to make sure no debris lay outside that perimeter.

"What?" But she didn't raise her voice enough to carry to him.

As she turned, she saw Jeremy watching her from inside the windowless cockpit.

"What the hell's up with you?"

"I didn't say a thing." He raised his hands in surrender as if she was about to shoot him. In one hand he held his tablet computer, in the other, a hard drive that must have come from the Quick Access Recorder. His gaze flickered downward for a second.

She followed the line and saw that her dagger was no longer in its sheath, but instead clenched in her fist. Very slowly and carefully, she slipped it into its sheath, pushing down to make sure it was fully seated.

"You know..." Jeremy glanced after Mike's retreating back, then apparently thought better of it. Instead, he waggled his computer at her. "Wanna hear something weird? According to this, the pilots didn't say a single word once they flew clear of local air traffic control in Stockholm. From climb out to crash, fourteen minutes, not a word."

9

"I NEED THE PILOTS' BODIES," HOLLY SPRINTED OVER TO SKI Patrol Girl with Tad lumbering along close behind. She'd show Mike who was paying attention to the details.

In fact...

She pulled off a glove to put a thumb and finger into her mouth and unleashed a shrill whistle. Mike's headlamp turned in her direction. She waved for him to come along. When he didn't respond, she noticed that she was standing in yet another of the heavy shadows cast across the bright snow. She aimed her headlamp at her own arm so that he'd see it and waved again—following it with the military double fist-pump of *hurry* that she'd taught him.

Mike bent to scoop up Meg, then he and Miranda headed in her direction.

Jeremy had crawled out through the broken cockpit window and arrived on their heels.

"The pilots are—" Ski Patrol Girl looked at the long lines of body bags. Obviously not a clue. Her face pale, even by blonde Swedish standards. Probably trying not to toss her cookies. Another airhead conquest for Mike, an easy target because she'd obviously need consoling after this. Except, knowing Mike, what he'd probably been doing was giving her a chance to vent followed by a pep talk. Damn man was inscrutable.

"Do the bags' tags have seat numbers?" Jeremy leaned in to inspect one where he stood downslope of them. "Nope."

"They're laid out by seat number," the girl said. "Each row of bags is a row of seats."

Holly looked down and saw that they were indeed laid out in a neat pattern: three bags, a gap for an aisle, and three more bags.

"And you're going in the wrong direction. The flight crew's bodies would be in the two body bags at the upslope end of the line. We've been putting the cabin crew where we located them. Those off to the side include severed limbs that could not be identified to a particular seat and are grouped by general area in the cabin."

Holly felt sick. She hadn't had to gather up unknown body parts since her team's deaths. But the girl didn't even blanch; her skin must be normally that pale.

Not so airheaded.

She headed upslope, trying not to count the rows or acknowledge that the body in each one had been alive and breathing this morning. It wasn't very often that they reached a crash site while the corpses were still there. So, maybe she wouldn't blame the ski patroller for her blanched complexion. A bag lay in the center aisle area, probably one of the cabin crew.

There were a few gaps. Unrecovered bodies? No, they were Swedes, they would have worked methodically through the plane. Were the empty seats actually empty, or some numb-nuts out of his seat during a pending crash?

No scattered bags. The cabin crew had gotten the passengers seated and strapped in, for what little good it had done them.

They had to know they were going down; it had still been daylight at the time of the crash and someone must have looked out the window.

At the head of the line, she saw true proof of idiocy; a body bag lay all by itself on the forward right side ahead of the front row—some fool had chosen the lavatory as his final place of refuge. Not even a seatbelt in there.

Past the last forward cabin crew member, where the fold-down seat would have been, lay the two flight crew members.

"What are you thinking, Holly?" Jeremy knelt beside her.

She didn't answer, instead pulled down the long zippers, then folded the sides back. As she'd expected, one was covered in blood, the other one not.

Mike had arrived. "I know that look."

Holly glanced up at him.

"DOA." He was studying the one who hadn't bled much.

Holly knew he was right. The copilot, so bloody she'd first thought that he'd been the one murdered, wasn't the issue. It was the pilot, with barely a drop on him. There were plenty of lacerations from the crash, but they hadn't bled much.

Why?

Because the pilot's heart had *already* stopped beating. No pumping blood. DOA—dead on arrival.

The two pilots had been in a locked cockpit together. Which meant that the copilot had to be the one who killed the pilot. By...

Holly pulled on Nitrile gloves and gingerly tested the pilot's neck.

Mike put on gloves and shifted the man's head for her.

She felt the bones grating together. Snapped.

She'd bet it wasn't with the forward wrench of the crash, but instead from a sharp twist. He'd probably been dead from the moment the cockpit door closed and locked—with no one the wiser.

They were less than fifteen minutes by air from Stockholm.

"Copilot as a terrorist?" Tad asked. "Like some kinda 9/11 scenario?"

"Why would he try to kill a ski slope?" Miranda, of course, asked the key question.

"They weren't," Mike answered. "Klara said the crash killed the Swedish Minister of Defense who was a passenger."

Klara! He said the name of that woman from the conference like he'd been practicing it in his head. *Oh, Klara! Ooo, Klara!* Holly was going to murder both of them.

Holly looked around. She'd wait to kill Mike Munroe until she wasn't surrounded by dead people.

10

Rolm Lindgren didn't know whether to feel better or worse when Kurt came to get him. At least he was taking him across the security line before the first of the newsies had identified him. It was a long trudge up the slope toward the American team squatting around a pair of opened body bags. His leather office shoes were full of snow by the third step.

He did *not* want to see this.

"Sorry, Rolm," Kurt's kind voice did little to steady him. "I don't know your flight crews. I'm hoping you can offer positive IDs."

The gallows. That's where he was headed. The Poma lift's poles dangled from the high tow wire, held aloft by the built-in spring to keep the empty ones out of harm's way. High enough to hang him by, but it wouldn't work because the integral spring would let his feet reach the ground. A pity.

He understood the layout of the body bags immediately. How many hours had he studied cabin configurations against profit-and-loss statements? He'd opted for quality and comfort, the famed LuftSvenska experience that had been the final keystone of his leadership: top crew on the line and in the air, unified aircraft platform, and high care for the passengers. The 737-700 had the hundred-and-forty-one-seat layout at the more generous thirty-two-inch spacing, rather than the far more typical one-forty-eight at thirty.

Rather than the three cabin crew required by law, one for every fifty passengers, he'd mandated one-to-forty, which put four aboard this flight. Now it meant one more of his people lay dead on this frozen slope.

Two body bags lay all the way at the rear where only the cabin crew would be found. He'd studied the flight manifest for an hour before he decided he had to come here: Chanda, the utterly charming woman who'd left Air India to come to Sweden, and Erik, the rather vivacious local boy from Uppsala —at least he was relatively certain that *boy* would still be the politically correct term.

Row upon row he climbed the slope. Looking aside didn't help, the lines of corpses to his left and the shattered aircraft to his right.

He spotted the bag in the aisle a third of the way from the nose. Rolm had no doubt who he'd find there if he dared look. The lovely Alva wouldn't be strapped into her seat, not if there was a chance to save even one more passenger. After eight years, their affair had ended two months ago; she'd met the Right Man, but he'd never forget her generous body and her bountiful laugh.

He walked up to the group of Americans standing around a pair of partially unzipped body bags.

Rolm looked down, and there was the Right Man, Kapten Olaf Olsson—known as Double O, like a secret agent who stole Alva's heart. Of course Rolm had granted Alva's request to fly with her fiancé. Little knowing he'd be condemning her to an untimely death on their first flight together.

"That's Olaf," he managed a steady voice by pretending he was his suit, not himself. "You'll find his future bride in the aisle by Row Seven." He waved a hand behind him, careful not to turn and look.

"And this one?" The blonde American asked softly but with a hint of an Australian accent.

Rolm looked over... Only their faces showed. Olaf had looked like he was simply asleep in a black plastic cocoon. Marco looked like he'd been through the wrong end of a prize fight, battered and bloody. "Marco Marino. New hire six months ago, immigrant, from Italy. Exceptional credentials."

The woman zipped up the two body bags before standing. "We're thinking that one," she pointed at Marco's bag, "snapped that one's neck." Like the Grim Reaper, she aimed a blue-clad finger at Olaf. "Probably before they were off the ground."

Rolm didn't recall sitting down until he'd been there long enough for his body heat to melt the snow and soak him through the seat of his thin suit pants.

Kurt squatted beside him, not saying a word. His hand rested on Rolm's shoulder.

Rolm shook his head to clear it. Then stood to avoid freezing himself to the ski slope and having to wait for the spring thaw to escape this nightmare. He closed his eyes for a long moment, but when he opened them, no one had gone away. No path to freedom.

The lead woman, Miranda, began speaking to the dog sitting at her feet. "Excluding hijackers, there have been twelve confirmed suicide-by-aircraft in the twenty-first century, totaling a hundred and ninety-four fatalities. The worst of those totaled a hundred and fifty passengers in a single flight—the Germanwings crash in 2015. Considering that against an average of twenty-nine-point-eight-million flights per year—that's over the last decade and inclusive of the statistically anomalous Pandemic, approximately thirty-one-point-three without it—it makes it a very rare but not unheard of event."

Rolm knew the general statistics of flights, but crashes by

suicide? The cold of his wet shoes and wet butt seeped into his bones.

"We'll continue the investigation," she continued talking to the dog, "until we can prove that the downing of your aircraft was a deliberate action."

Her manner left Rolm wondering if she thought the aircraft belonged to her dog.

"Jeremy, was the autopilot engaged?" She still didn't look up.

A man young enough to be one of his grandkids swiped at his tablet computer through several photos before answering, "No, it was switched off. Along with the system that would have attempted to auto-recover from a catastrophic dive. You can see in this photo that both were manually disabled." He turned the tablet toward Miranda and her dog and then toward Rolm himself.

A closeup shot of the top-center section of the cockpit console that contained the autopilot controls.

Rolm saw that the relevant switches were indeed set to the Off position. Just because he'd flown a desk these last twenty-five years didn't mean he'd forgotten his roots. He wasn't current on anything bigger than a Beech twin-prop, but he'd been through the full sim course and several training flights on each aircraft type before he'd certified it to be part of the fleet. He felt seriously old that he remembered the 737 from those long-ago days. It had been added to the fleet when he was still a junior mechanic.

Miranda continued speaking to her dog. "It is a reasonable addition to the hypothetical Conjectural Sphere of Causality that the aircraft was deliberately crashed. An intentional CFIT, controlled flight into terrain."

"But..." Rolm ignored the sphere thing but understood the message, "...why would someone do that?"

"That," she primly addressed her four-legged audience of

one, "is outside the scope of our investigation. We're only interested in why the aircraft physically came down." She turned away and set the dog on its feet. "Jeremy, next we'll recover the data recorders. We need to map the control inputs from the cockpit to verify the conjecture that it was an *intentional* controlled flight into terrain."

"Take Tad for muscle instead," the Australian waved at the big black man who'd been last to arrive. "I need Jeremy for a moment."

"Least I'm good for something," the black man muttered. "None of this makes any damn sense."

Rolm wouldn't have heard him if they hadn't stood side-by-side.

Rolm wanted to strike out at the Miranda woman. Strike out for the dead plane, for the lovely Alva, for...himself. So that he wouldn't have to face the pain.

All other releases denied, Rolm fell to his knees in the snow and screamed at the dark night. Then puked up the entire sausage sandwich he'd eaten on the drive up. Sick until any meals behind that one lay on the snow before him as well.

Rolm pitied his wife, Gertrude. Not for the affair. She was the one who'd announced herself *done with sex.*

But he pitied her nonetheless. Perhaps it was very Swedish of him; he didn't know or care. After all her years of patience and support, from this moment on she would only have a hollow shell pretending to be a husband—all that remained of him.

His airline, his life's work, instead of reaching its culmination in eight days, had been shredded by a suicide.

"By the way, mate," the blonde Australian spoke softly.

The strange woman and her dog had moved on.

"He may have an Italian name, but look at his face. Looks more like a Russian prizefighter to me." For some reason she knelt and unzipped the bag again to his waist. She slid up

Marco's sleeves, but he saw no markings on either of his forearms.

The young Asian man snapped several photos of Marco's face. He also pulled out a small device that imaged Marco's thumb and fingerprints. The blonde held out a blood-stained wallet. He photographed the contents.

Rolm stared at Marco's bloody uniform and broken body. Too numb and sick at heart to look away.

"I'll send these to a friend of mine and see what she thinks." Then the Asian walked away while tapping on his phone.

The Australian tossed the wallet on Marco's bloody chest and zipped up both bags, shed her blue gloves, and followed the others toward the plane.

She'd been right, he didn't look very Italian. But Russian? LuftSvenska might have been attacked by Russia?

11

HEIDI GELLER RETURNED FROM HER AFTERNOON RUN READY to die. The Imagine Dragons track "Enemy" pounded over her earbuds, as if she needed a reminder that everyone was the enemy. Today the London weather definitely ranked as Enemy Number One.

She ran in DC all the time; why was London so freaking cold by comparison? Two degrees above freezing, but wrapped in a thick, chill mist that soaked everything it came in contact with. Her Outdoor Research jacket's Pertex waterproof had utterly failed. Not because the water went through it, but because the chill London fog slid in via every tiny opening worse than a desert dust storm.

And she'd thought she'd been so smart by skipping a run in this morning's freezing sleet so she didn't actually pitch under a London bus—coming from some drastically un-American direction. Sleet, at least, might have frozen on her like a shell, offering its own layer of insulation.

She went straight into her hotel room's shower fully clothed. Of course, the jacket worked great against a mere inundation, sluicing the water off her body before it warmed her in the slightest.

Heidi forced her frozen fingers—frozen right through her sixty-dollar winter running gloves, *thank you so very much*—to peel off layer by layer. Though the temperature looked to be set to lukewarm, her nervous system rang fiery-intruder alerts as loudly as possible about the comparatively scalding water blasting her skin.

Twenty minutes. That's all she had.

In twenty minutes, warm or not, she had to be downstairs ready to present her keynote address. Her hair could stay wet, it always curled enough to avoid a drowned rat look. Besides, she was a woman at a hacker conference. She could mesmerize most of the guys by reading the terms and conditions for an iPhone's operating system.

Her job took care of the rest of the doubters. As head of the CIA's cyberattack division (which of course didn't technically exist), her keynote, *New Cyberdefense Tactics and Methodologies,* would rivet them to their seats. If she said even a serious percentage of what she knew? Their brains would melt down— and she'd spend the rest of her life in solitary confinement in Leavenworth prison.

Damn Harry for tearing out that tendon in his ankle and sticking her with this on her own. He's the one who headed up Cyberdefense, though he wasn't as good at dancing along the edges of the secrecy directives surrounding their jobs, even without the injury. Now, he'd had the tear repaired but was on his back for the next two weeks—*foot must remain elevated to "toes above nose" for eighty percent of the time.* No plane flights from DC to London. No long days at the Black Hat Europe conference.

At least he could crutch around and feed himself during the other twenty percent. And he'd appeared clearheaded enough already for her to go on her own, as she was one of the keynote speakers.

They had rigged a lie-down console setup for him, both at home and the office, but she hadn't thought to make him video-in for the talk. It might have been fun as he was still loopy on the opioid painkillers. Probably not the best choice for a public presentation—who knew what would slip out. Be fun to watch though.

Heidi, finally naked, kicked her clothes to the corner of the shower and began edging up the hot water, trying to raise her core temperature. Or at least stop the shivers shaking her like a failing hard drive.

Black Hat Europe was always fun. Whatever idiot scheduled Black Hat USA during August in Las Vegas was clearly a punk hacker, probably never left Mom's air-conditioned basement except for the conference. Certainly never considered how deeply stupid it was to travel to a city at a time of year ideal for frying eggs on the sidewalk.

USA also took themselves far too seriously. All the heavy security geeks were there, from the NSA and DIA on down. Mixed in with all the beginner wannabes who'd read too many William Gibson novels, it was a mess. Here, her far-more-rational NATO-member counterparts predominated.

A loud buzz cut off the follow-on to "Enemy", Lady Gaga belting out "Hold My Hand." Heidi had left in her earbuds. Her hands were still shaking when she reached up to squeeze the earbud's stem to accept the call.

"This is me."

"You in a rainstorm?"

"Shower." Then she recognized the voice. She'd been expecting Harry, not Jeremy.

"Uh..."

She imagined the bright blush racing up his face.

"...should I call back?"

"Why?" Heidi couldn't resist the tease. Jeremy had been Harry's best man at their wedding. She'd discovered that he was embarrassed by the strangest things. Harry was sweet, for a vicious hacker, but Jeremy was simply too cute.

"Because you're..."

She wondered if he'd manage to say the word *naked.*

"Is Harry around?" Nope, no *naked* with Jeremy.

"He's still in DC with his foot up in the air. I'm at Black Hat."

"Oh. Uh, that's great. Good program this year, but I didn't sign up. You know, with Taz giving birth just a few months ago I didn't want to leave her alone, except I did go to the Air Safety Investigators conference at the last minute with Miranda—Taz accused me of hovering too much and getting on her nerves. Wait until you and Harry have a kid; it does crazy things to how you think about stuff. When is that anyway?"

"When is what?" She played stupid to buy a second, at least long enough to *not* swallow her tongue. How had he started discussing Black Hat and finished by scaring the shit out of her?

"Having a baby. You two. You'll love it."

She laid a hand on her belly. Her belly was warm, the only part of her that was, but her fingers felt as if they were far colder than the run had made them. The chill claw of doom threatening to invade her womb. She *really* wasn't ready to think about going down that path. "Sure, why don't *you* carry a growing alien lifeform inside your body for nine months and see how you like it?"

Jeremy laughed. "That's what Taz kept saying."

Which, Heidi realized, was where she'd heard the phrase. In the birth room no less, as if witnessing the event had been insufficient verifiable proof. The shivers were back. She nudged the temperature up another notch.

Jeremy and Taz had reproduced almost right away, and fatherhood looked good on him. Herself and Harry? "We haven't really talked about it yet. There's plenty of time." The two of them *were* older than Jeremy, but they were younger than Taz.

"Well, you should talk about it. I'll text Harry. Hang on..."

"No, wait, Jeremy." He would too—she needed to run interference. "Why did you call?" She turned her back to the spray and the burning sensation shot to life again.

"Oh right. We've got a corpse that probably isn't who he said he was. I've sent you photos, fingerprints, and a copy of his pilot's and driver's license."

"Pilot's?" Of course, with Jeremy being part of the NTSB that made sense.

"Copilot for LuftSvenska. Or he was until he snapped his captain's neck and then crashed the plane."

"Any other fatalities?"

"A hundred and forty-three with cabin crew and both pilots." And there was the weird contrast of Jeremy. He could stare at a battered corpse and start modeling the necessary kinetic forces and external trauma to do to them whatever had been done to them. But he wouldn't be able to speak to her hundreds of kilometers away if she reminded him that she was naked in a shower except for a pair of earbuds.

"Um, I'm on as a keynote speaker in a couple minutes. Send it all to Harry but remember, if it's a truly deep cover, it can take a while to run. And Jeremy?"

"Yeah."

"Please don't bug him about having a baby. I'd rather have that conversation myself."

"Oh, right. Enjoy your, uh..."

"Naked shower?"

"Yeah. That." And Jeremy was gone. She clearly heard his blush long distance.

Sometimes all it took was a good friend to make you feel warm—at least on the inside.

12

"Is it down?"

"It is." He sat in his cubical and wished he was sitting ten thousand miles away, like the middle of the Pacific Ocean.

"Good. Cleared to Phase Two."

"Yes, Chief." He hung up the phone carefully. He'd created the plan—or at least the idea—ten months ago.

That had been his first mistake.

It was a drunken night in the Bunker Bar and he'd been slamming back Lebowskis like the White Russians were straight cream. The Bunker, an ideal place to feel miserable after a breakup. They'd remodeled a World War II brick bomb shelter into a long series of arched chambers: the dance room with a tiny stage jammed at the far end, next the bar room for serious fuel mixed with close-body mingling, and a tiny kitchen at the other end for pumping out a steady stream of Western-style appetizers, burgers, and quesadillas. The Bunker's website was hosted on the high-security Telegram app and the menu bore the stamp *Classified*.

A lot of intelligence service folks came here, drank hard, and rarely met each other's eyes. Talking to each other outside the walls of headquarters wasn't safe—on even the most innocuous topic. Even here. Despite the roar of the band. Yet, here they gathered together with enough general populous that they could avoid each other.

That night's country-western cover band, mangling surprisingly few of the lyrics, had kicked out rhythmic blasts worthy of being in an underground bunker. The dance floor was jammed to the limits with plenty of likely young ladies in the mix and overflowing into the bar as usual. But the scars from Elene Burduli had still smarted. He'd gone down there with his ears drooped like a sad dog to bury his sorrows in the old shelter, not create new ones.

He'd had vague notions, which had become foggier as the night dragged on, that it had been his bar before she'd come along, and it would damn well be his afterward.

He'd turned to tell her so—

And for the hundredth time that night, she hadn't been at her usual spot on the next stool over.

He'd sat at the bar, barely bothering Max, the bearded owner/bartender. And not quite watching the hockey game on the big screen above the lines of bottles. They slapped the puck back and forth like they were slapping him upside the head, like the band beating the time with a sledgehammer, like Elene Burduli—

Yep, his thoughts had plunged once more down the same snake hole they'd been traveling all that night.

Wouldn't it be nice, he'd thought at the time, if they were all beating on someone else other than him?

Which gave him the idea. What if they were?

His second mistake had been making his way up out of The Bunker and not going home to sleep off the idea in a drunken stupor that guaranteed a hangover able to eradicate all memories—except Elene dumping him, of course.

She hadn't merely thrown the ring back at him, she'd

laughed in his face on top of it. Marry *you?* She'd laughed harder, until he tossed her out of the apartment wearing only her sheer suggestion of a nightgown. He'd ducked out the back door through the chill February rain—nothing worse than a cold night's rain in February—to avoid the new tone of the howls. Not a court in the land would convict him on that one.

Nope, he didn't want to be anywhere around his apartment that night. The only surprise when he finally did return home was that she hadn't fire-bombed the place.

Instead, after he'd crawled out of The Bunker—since her memory hadn't left him alone there either—he'd gone to the office and typed up his idea. Dumping it in an Eyes Only envelope and shoving it into his boss' secure drop constituted his last functional, if not coherent, act. Then he'd passed out face down on his desk, effectively erasing the memo from his memory.

For two months, it had stayed that way.

Then he'd been called into the service chief's office, without his boss or either of the managers two tiers above him. He'd been utterly mystified about what the hell he'd done so wrong to be pulled up on the top carpet in the entire operation. Pavle was an analyst. He'd never had a private meeting with the chief since his six-minute welcome aboard five years ago.

We've vetted your plan at the highest levels. You're no longer in the Analytical Directorate; you now report directly to me. I have a few suggestions on how we can get the assets in place.

He'd had no idea what the chief was going on about until he spotted his original memo in the open folder on the desk. His only coherent thought at the time was being impressed that he'd been sober enough to write it in the first place.

Even now, eight months after that first meeting and cleared to launch Phase Two, he wished he knew if he'd fallen into good fate or obliviously buried his head in the sand—like when he'd thrown Elene out into the February rain...or like when he'd taken her back a week later.

13

Major Ingrid Eklund of the Swedish Air Force waggled her wings in greeting as she pulled alongside the Finnish F/A-18C Hornet jet.

Kapten Liisa Salo waggled back. In the early morning and this close to the Artic Circle, they saw each other only by their nav lights and the shine of the half-moon scraping the horizon.

They'd never met in the flesh, but Liisa had been damn cute in the pre-mission video briefing. The Finn possessed more prominent cheekbones than a typical Swedish woman, the amber eyes accented by the extra-dark-chocolate hair so different from her own true blonde. They both wore it long and had shared the easy smile of fighter pilots knowing exactly who ruled the skies. Unless Ingrid had misread the subtext, the more personal interest was also mutual.

After today's patrol she had two days off. If all went well, maybe she'd take a Grisslehamn ferry across the Gulf of Bothnia and see what happened.

For now, they had a mission to fly.

She felt a little sorry for Liisa. The American-built F/A-18C Hornet was a nice enough jet, but dated.

And it couldn't touch her Saab JAS 39E Gripen.

The Saab Gripen—Gryphon in English, named for the mythical beast of a lion's hindquarters and an eagle's head, wings, and talons—was sometimes called the first sixth-generation fighter. She wasn't stealth. She didn't have massive payload capabilities. The pilot wasn't wired into her plane with a half-million-dollar helmet like the American's fifth-generation F-35 Lightning II.

However, her Gripen had been designed elegantly with one sole purpose in mind—killing Russians. And if the time ever came to test that, Ingrid had every confidence in her mythical creature's speed and firepower.

Her baby boasted the lowest operating cost of any fighter jet aloft by almost a factor of two. The Gripen's entire system was based on a single suite of software so that she was easily maintained at the very leading edge of technology. Most nations' fighter jets required years of lag-and-leap between system upgrades due to conflicting software systems from multiple manufacturers unwilling to share proprietary architecture.

There were also extreme maneuvers that had been first achieved in Saabs. Supermaneuverability was the Gripen's home turf, all the agility of an eagle in flight. Only a handful of fighter aircraft designs could make that claim...and Liisa's Hornet wasn't one of them.

For the kick-ass lion's behind? Her Gripen could drive ahead at Mach 1.2 supercruise—one of the few jets able to fly past the sound barrier without firing off the fuel-guzzling afterburners. Or seriously hustle along at Mach 2.2 when she did light them up.

Someday, Ingrid might grab a two-seat Gripen JAS-39D and

show Liisa what a jet fighter could really do. All part of a friendly forces exchange program, of course.

Today's flight had a simple profile. They'd met up at the Swedish-Finnish land border in the snow-covered north. Fly south into the light, over the Bay and then the Gulf of Bothnia. The seven-hundred-kilometer subsonic run would give them fifty minutes of flight time to get used to each other. Once over the Baltic, they'd fly east to the Finnish-Russia border. South across the narrow opening near St. Petersburg to Estonia, and then home.

Their countries had flown any number of forces coordination flights, but this was the first one since Sweden joined NATO—about freaking time. Now Article 5 ruled: an attack on any NATO-member nation would be treated as an attack on all, including Sweden.

Today was a reminder to Russia not to mess with Finland—or Estonia for that matter. The Gripen could cover the four hundred kilometers from Stockholm to Helsinki in twelve minutes or, if need be, start bombing St. Petersburg's port out of existence in twenty. Today's flight would be far more sedate, staying firmly in international waters.

After a few minutes of straight-and-level, Ingrid considered her first move. But before she had decided, Liisa nosed down. When she followed, Liisa nosed up until they were roller-coastering back and forth, one descending while the other climbed. A neat way to offer two constantly changing angles of fire while still staying tight on each other's wing.

The next time she was high and Liisa was low, Ingrid did a wing-over-wing passing from Liisa's starboard side over to port as she flipped once upside down. In moments, they were twisting one around the other like they were fired from a gatling gun.

All down the long stretch over the water between their two

countries, they tried each other on for size until they were flowing like a single plane in two separate airframes.

They barely had to speak. A glance across the narrow air gap between them (once there was enough light to see each other by), a nod, a tip of the wing, a flirty kick of the tail: faultless communication to know to figure what the other would do next.

Reaching the Baltic proper, they carved to the east around the Hanko Peninsula, keeping well over Finnish territorial waters.

Twelve minutes later they reached Kotka—the last major Finnish town, thirty kilometers from Russia. In such perfect sync that Ingrid's breath caught in her lungs, they turned southwest to avoid Gogland Island before cutting back southeast toward Estonia.

Women who flew jets. There was nothing sexier. It wasn't an opinion; Ingrid knew it was purest fact. And they were two hot women in two very hot jets.

14

AFTER THE ARRIVAL OF THE PRIOR DAY'S LAST FREIGHTER, THE *Koidutäht* harbor tug hadn't stayed in the Sillamäe, Estonia, port. Instead, hired at five times its normal hourly rate, the tug had struck north into the chill December darkness.

By dawn, it floated among the scattered winter ice halfway between Estonia and Finland, close off the north shore of Bolshoi Tyuters Island.

15

"For four hundred years before the Russian's renamed it, we Finns called it Tytärsaari or Daughter's Island. During the Winter War of 1939, when Russia attempted a takeover of Finland, we had to evacuate. In President Ryti's godforsaken peace agreement, a tenth of the country, including Daughter's Island, was ceded to Russia." As Liisa told this in snippets over the radio, her tone of voice stated she was still warrior-pissed about it eighty years later.

Ingrid liked that about her. "Ouch!" She knew about Ryti, of course.

The Russians' inability to quickly overrun the far smaller Finnish force had led Hitler to decide that Russia itself would be easily conquered and to launch his own attack, creating the Eastern Front of World War II.

Then President Ryti commanded Finland's troops to side with Hitler's Germany to take the war to their historical enemy, Russia. It hadn't worked out well for the Finns.

"The Germans took the island next," Liisa continued. "But even after their hasty overnight retreat in 1944, the West decided to cede it to the Soviets without asking Finland.

Instead the West honored the 1940 peace treaty that had ended the Winter War, though they'd still insisted that war itself was an illegal act by the Russians."

And then the Soviets had whupped on the Finns horribly in post-war reparations and land grabs as payback for Ryti siding with Germany against them. All Ryti's own fault. He hadn't merely sought to reclaim the prior land lost while sided with Germany in the Continuation War; for that he might have been forgiven. No, he'd then tried to invade the Soviet Union and grab a wider territory. The whole effort, and Ryti's reign, collapsed in 1944 with the German retreat.

"My grandparents were born on Daughter's Island. They and over four hundred former residents, who had carved a living for centuries from the exceptional fishing grounds around there, were never allowed to return."

Which had to suck.

Then Liisa had laughed. Not a friendly laugh, but a warrior's.

"For all that, the Russians won crap. Their lone lighthouse keeper knows better than to explore the two-mile-wide island beyond a few carefully cleared paths. In addition to massive amounts of abandoned equipment, the Germans left an untold number of mines. To this day its nickname is Mined Island."

16

Aboard the tug *Koidutäht*, by prearrangement, the captain and crew were locked in the windowless hold for the duration of the operation. *What you don't know won't kill you.*

Whether that was true or not, the next few hours would tell.

The agent unfolded the half-meter-wide, two-point-five-gigahertz dish antenna that he'd picked up for a hundred euros online. When this was over, he'd tip it over the side into the depths of the Baltic without a trace. Attaching a transmitter, he readied himself to wait.

Two hours later—with nothing to keep him company but the occasional bumping of the ice against the hull—the sun broke fully clear of the horizon. Soon after, he spotted the two flecks of light approaching from the north. Two jets, exactly as this month's joint-exercise roster had listed.

He turned on the transmitter and raised the handheld dish to aim it toward the passing jets.

17

Ingrid hated flying border patrols near Russia.

She'd never been comfortable with it. Sweden shared no border with Russia—Norway to the north and west and Finland to the east wrapped their arms around Sweden like mothers protecting a child.

Oh, she'd flown joint missions through both the Nordic Battlegroup and NORDEFCO, the five-country Nordic Defense Cooperation. Each time it took her along the Russian border it felt like the worst flight imaginable. A lone Swede ghosting along the edge of the brute, half afraid he'd wake up and half wishing he would so that he could be put down hard once and for all.

But one didn't anger the bear in his den, especially not a bear armed with nuclear weapons.

NATO had slowly wrapped around Russia, but it was far from the cage everyone hoped for. The Russian bear kept swiping out with its claws: Georgia in 2008, Crimea in 2014, and now the Ukraine. Who would the Russians war on next?

By joining NATO, Finland and now Sweden were yet

another part of the cage, but many of the bars were weak and the bear kept testing them.

She shook her head, trying to clear away the miasma of gray hopelessness that threatened to swamp her.

Did Liisa feel it flying beside her? She flew with such joy, such a reaching that Ingrid felt better for simply flying beside her.

And it *was* a beautiful morning. The sky shone with a crisp winter blue. The dark Baltic waters speckled with snow-dusted islands.

A scan of her instruments showed no threat warnings coming up out of Russia. And because of the flight restrictions since the Ukraine War, there was little commercial air traffic so close to the border.

And she flew in.

She performed a pair of four-point snap rolls—knife edge-hold, inverted-hold, other knife edge-hold, return to straight-and-level flight, then the same in reverse—to remind herself that of all miracles, she'd earned the right to fly her Gripen.

A motion caught her eye.

A motion where there shouldn't be one.

18

THE SIGNAL BROADCAST UPWARD FROM THE TUGBOAT *KOIDUTÄHT*
washed over the two jets flying side-by-side. The signal was too
weak to cause an alert from any of the onboard threat-warning
mechanisms. Especially not at the frequency transmitted—
close below air traffic control frequencies. Battlefield and
missile targeting radar were typically five times higher in
frequency.

The signal strength wavered several times as the agent
aboard the tug attempted to keep the small dish centered on
the passing aircraft. Not an easy task against their motion
across the sky and the tug's rolling in the winter waves.

Due to the cold, the transmitter's battery strength was less
than calculated and it wasn't strong enough to penetrate
through the lower section of the fuselage.

But then the Gripen JAS 39E performed a sharp four-point
snap roll.

During the first roll, the agent's aim drifted wide because of
a wave that threw him against a bulwark hard enough to bruise.
He almost lost the antenna overboard sooner than planned.

But then the plane rolled back.

When it entered the inverted position, the signal passed easily through the canopy, the inside of Ingrid's right thigh, and was picked up by a small antenna embedded under her seat cushion.

The signal triggered the receiver hidden there.

The receiver in turn closed a relay connecting a pair of batteries to a high-force linear actuator that had cost the agent another forty euros at everyone's favorite online package provider. He'd installed it himself last week when this mission was first listed, during a routine seat maintenance check. The device wouldn't be seen until the next seat inspection not scheduled for another five months. Of course, now this bird would never see that maintenance check.

He'd liked Ingrid—always polite to her bird's mechanics. A pity she didn't like men, what a waste of a pretty woman. But not having slept with her saved him from feeling the least bit bad when it was her name that came up on the duty roster. Could have been anyone. Wouldn't matter to him, they paid him for the result, not who did the flying.

The actuator's lower end was anchored to the structure of the seat and the upper end to the back of the ejection handle.

The mechanism began extending its central thrust arm.

19

HAD HER SEAT EJECTION HANDLES ACTUALLY MOVED?

The yellow-and-black-striped loop lay close between Ingrid's thighs—an easy grab no matter what g-forces slammed the jet during an emergency.

She knew there'd been a crash early in the Gripen's deployment when a series of hard maneuvers had caused the pilot's lower-body pressure suit to inflate and deflate repeatedly. It drove blood out of the lower body and back toward the heart during high-g actions. The section of the suit along the inner thighs had also repeatedly squeezed and raised the ejection handle until the pilot abruptly left his aircraft without intending to.

But they'd fixed that fifteen years ago by altering the circular handle into a reverse teardrop shape, narrow between her thighs with an easy to grab loop above.

Right now, her thighs were loose to either side of the handle.

Her g-suit hadn't inflated for a simple snap roll, a null-g maneuver.

Yet the handle kept rising like a guy's pants when they

thought they had a chance with her after too many beers at some flyer's bar—as if.

She tapped the autopilot to life, then took her hand off the throttle and pressed down on the handle. It fought her. Pushing harder didn't force it any lower. It continued to move upward inexorably at several millimeters per second.

Ingrid leaned forward to look down at the mechanism at the moment the actuator had raised the handle to its trigger point.

The ejection seat's computer initiated the launch sequence —the whole of which required a mere one-point-two seconds.

First, the haul-back yanked Ingrid's body and shoulders tight against the seat itself. Her attention remained on the self-rising ejection handle loop between her thighs, tipping her head forward. She saw the top of the raising mechanism emerge from below the seat cushion, a shiny aluminum shaft anchored to the back of the ejection loop handle.

Next, the MDC—Miniature Detonating Cord—embedded in the canopy fired. The thin explosive strip ran from front to back along the center of the main canopy, the only blemish in the sweeping view aloft from the cockpit. When it blew, it split the acrylic in two. With a hard bang, the secondary MDC placed all around the lower edge where the canopy locked onto the upper lip of the cockpit cut the canopy aloft. The two halves tumbled aside in the six-hundred-knot slipstream.

Next, the seat cannon fired to drive Ingrid and the ejection seat clear of the jet.

The barometric pressure informed the ship's computer that they were at twenty-thousand feet. It fired with only fourteen g's, rather than the twenty-five that would be necessary if it had triggered at or near the ground. In a low-altitude ejection, it would have to throw her far enough aloft to have a chance for the parachute to open and slow her return to Earth. Here all she had to do was clear the jet's tail.

Ingrid had been trained to lean back in her seat, fold her arms over her chest, and brace for launch as soon as she'd pulled the handles.

However, Ingrid's position, head tipped forward and down as she'd continued her efforts to fight the rising handle, meant she was out of position when her head's weight jumped upward from five kilos, five-point-six with her Saab Cobra helmet. For a brief moment of hard acceleration, it weighed eighty kilos— more than her entire body, including her flight suit, boots, helmet, and sidearm.

She was tall and fit, an inch taller than Liisa Salo, but light with slenderness. Had the ejection proceeded normally, with Ingrid sitting upright, she'd have become an inch shorter than Liisa due to permanent spinal compression.

Instead it fractured her neck.

With care, trained placement on a back board, and immediate surgery, she could have eventually recovered. Not enough to ever again risk flying a military jet that she might have to eject from, but enough to have had a very enjoyable life with Kapten Liisa Salo of the Finnish Air Force. She had not misread Liisa's signals of personal interest.

But that wasn't what happened.

Because she'd ejected straight up, the seat assessed that *no* additional corrections were needed to right the seat or fire it higher. Any of which would have severed her spinal cord and made her a quadriplegic at best, or left her with no functioning heart or lungs but giving her brain enough time to understand the true terror of imminent death.

No guidance rockets fired.

Instead the computer released the seat harness. The seat dropped away and freed the drogue chute. That in turn pulled out Ingrid's main chute.

During the sudden deceleration of the booster rocket ceasing fire, her instincts had shifted her head squarely over her neck, though not in perfect alignment. The hard snap of the opening chute pinched her spinal nerves sufficiently to debilitate her arms. Her training tried but her arms wouldn't lift to the chute's control toggles. Ingrid's fall remained at the whim of the winds over the frigid Baltic Sea.

Without control of her hands or arms, the emergency survival kit stowed below the seat pad and dangling from her harness by a short tether would never be of any use.

The chute restricted her descent to thirty kilometers per hour. From six kilometers, twenty-thousand feet, she had plenty of time to observe the world around her.

She heard Liisa's emergency call, "Pilot down. Pilot down. Under a parachute. No sign of attack. Launch CSAR." Then their coordinates.

As the chute spun her one way, then the other, wholly out of her control, she saw her beloved half-bird / half-lion winging its way south.

Undamaged except for the loss of the canopy and pilot, the Saab JAS 39E Gripen's automated flight attitude recovery software compensated for the shift in the center-of-gravity loading caused by the abrupt departure of seventy kilos of ejection seat, eighty-three of pilot and her gear, and ninety more of the canopy blown aside.

Once restabilized, the autopilot Ingrid had engaged to wrestle with the ejection seat handle would guide it safely for over seven hundred kilometers. Eventually, a Polish F-16C Fighting Falcon would shoot down the pilotless Gryphon, the mythical guardian of gold and kings, rather than risk it crashing into downtown Warsaw.

Even when the remaining pieces were returned to Sweden, there would be no useful information. Nothing aboard had detected the odd frequency of the signal and the entire sabotage mechanism had been ejected along with Major Ingrid

Eklund's seat, which was even now falling independently into the sea.

Liisa dove down to fly by her.

Ingrid attempted to turn her head to follow but the pain in her neck stopped her instantly.

"What happened?"

It took Ingrid a thousand meters of descent to realize they were words sounding over her helmet's emergency radio. And then five hundred more and another full spin to understand they were directed at her.

"Hi, Liisa."

"Hi, Ingrid. What happened?"

It was a good question. But one of many she had. She had questions for Liisa too, but couldn't recall what they were at the moment.

Then she recalled the feel of something pushing up against her palm. It was...

"The ejection handle! It pushed up on its own."

"That can not happen."

Ingrid didn't feel like giving a history lesson about the early days of the Saab Gripen. "I felt it. Pushing up against my palm. I managed to slow it down, but couldn't stop it. There was—" What had she seen? "I saw...an aluminum arm. Attached to the handle. Square shaft. Pushing it up..."

She tried to look down, to remember.

But again her neck pain stopped her. What she did see wiped away any attempts to understand what had happened.

By squinting through the lower edge of her visor but over the facemask feeding her emergency air from the small bottle integrated into her harness, she saw a lot of blue—nothing but blue with scattered sheet ice dotting the surface. Individual waves rippled forever below her. None of the ice would be big enough to land on, but plenty big to crush her after she'd fallen into the water between them. She spun

right to left, then left to right as a gust swung her abruptly
about.

Frigid, winter Baltic, blue so dark it was almost black except
for the whitecaps being ripped from the tops of the waves and
the sunlight blinding off the white ice.

Very bad.

"I'm sorry, Liisa. I wish..." But that all seemed very far
away now.

"Me, too, Ingrid. You hang on. Steer the chute."

"My arms..." she wanted to shrug, but if it worked, she
didn't feel it.

On the next spin, she saw an island. Two more times of
slowly twirling about before she understood she'd hit the
island rather than the sea. A strong westerly wind drove her
along.

It would be a good thing, right?

Her feet. She tried flexing her feet and felt those. Maybe
she'd be okay despite the battering she'd taken.

"Hey, Liisa. If I get through this..."

"Don't talk like that, it's a date. *Mysa, Sisu.*" The Finnish F/A-
18C Hornet shot by close enough for her to see Liisa looking at
her though Ingrid couldn't turn her head to track the flight.

Two words. Two languages. No easy translation to English
for either but they meant the world. Swedish *Mysa,* to lie
comfortably together snuggled up. *Sisu,* Finnish, to face with
great bravery, as an endearment by Liisa's tone.

"A date," Ingrid confirmed.

"Absolutely!" Liisa offered a choked laugh of
encouragement.

But the island was approaching fast.

Unable to brake the chute, Ingrid bent her knees to absorb
as much of the impact as possible. It looked as if she'd clear the
thick trees that covered much of the island and would land in
the sandy patch along the east side.

She made ready to kick down hard against the sand to ease the impact on the rest of her body.

It wasn't her fractured neck or paralyzed arms that killed Major Ingrid Eklund of the Swedish Air Force.

Time hadn't yet destroyed the fuze on the World War II German Teller landmine lying beneath the soil. Designed for blowing up tanks, it required ninety kilos of pressure to trigger the five and a half kilos of TNT.

Ingrid in her full gear weighed under eighty and could safely walk over it. Time had buried it deeply enough that she and Kapten Liisa Salo—both lean and fit, totaling a hundred and fifty-three kilos—could have made reasonably energetic love atop it in equal safety as long as they left the extra weight of their gear and clothes off to the side.

However, unable to brake the parachute, Major Ingrid Eklund punched the sand hard with both feet to ease the impact on what she'd correctly assessed as a broken neck. A step to either side wouldn't have triggered the old Teller mine —but she struck dead center above it.

The last thing she ever did was land on Daughter's Island. Nothing readily identifiable as human remained in the three-point-one meter blast crater.

It was the first Swedish Air Force pilot death since 1996.

Kapten Liisa Salo received no medal for the hardest thing she'd ever done. She hadn't, after watching Major Ingrid Eklund be blown to pieces, destroyed the Russian lighthouse and its lone keeper with a Hellfire missile.

She didn't know, but her restraint changed nothing. The Russian lighthouse keeper had stepped out onto the back deck of his house to watch the jets pass over, not a common occurrence over his remote border island.

He held a cup of morning tea heavily laced with vodka in one hand. The tea for the December chill. The vodka to grease the wheels of murder he'd been pouring into his first-ever novel. Half the pages on the pad of paper in his other hand were already covered in a first-rate murder mystery. The victims? His treacherous wife and the supply boat captain she'd run off with last week without telling him to his face.

Though he stood two hundred and fifty-two meters—the length of four ice hockey rinks—from the center of the explosion, the signal mirror from Ingrid's emergency kit spun into his neck and severed the left carotid artery. Unable to finish pouring out his ire upon the page, nonetheless the writing pad he carried was well soaked in blood before he died.

20

"MISSED YOUR BEAUTY SLEEP?" TAD DROPPED INTO THE CHAIR beside Jeremy, facing her. Only an empty chair kept her company on this side of the restaurant's table.

Holly considered drowning Tad in his bowl of muesli, but the *filmjölk* yogurty stuff the Swedes used instead of milk was probably too thick to kill him.

Tad laughed. "Yep, that's about how Ma looked anytime Pop said it. Like he didn't have the sense God gave a chicken some mornings. Course he also always told her she was the most beautiful woman on the planet, so it musta balanced out enough to keep him alive."

If he was asking to be murdered, she'd definitely consider it...after having her coffee.

Instead she glared at Mike's back two tables farther into the restaurant.

Last night Mike had locked the hotel room door on her and refused to answer. She'd fetched a second key from the desk and been almost angry enough to kick the door down—and far too angry to speak—when she discovered he'd thrown the deadbolt as well. Angry enough that she'd left a single boot print beside the lock, but her heart hadn't been in it. Which was probably a good thing because, if she'd gotten in, there would have been bloodshed.

Mike never presented a clear target; his most annoying trait. Instead he slipped past her guard in ways she could never quite pin down. Thinking to check out Tad's story, when her role was team guardian. Giving her shit about Tad and at the same time not chatting up Klara Dahlberg. She *knew* what sort of man she was sleeping with—except he wasn't. And it was starting to seriously piss her off.

She'd ended up on the crap couch in Miranda's room as the hotel was full with all the investigation folks from the crash site —only place for twenty kilometers in any direction. Fjällberget was a locals' ski slope, not some fancy resort.

It was the first time they'd slept apart since...

Holly really didn't want to think about this. Because if Mike wasn't the sort of man she knew he was, what the hell kind of a chap was he? And what did that make her?

She focused on her coffee, which didn't help. If she drank it instead of staring at it, would it make any difference?

The last time they intentionally slept apart, other than when one or the other was out on a different part of an investigation, she'd been the one to lock Mike out of their room. That would've been the US Air Force dorm at Groom Lake back when Andi Wu had first joined the team two years ago. All the evidence had said he was hitting on the cute new Chinese girl while sleeping with Holly herself.

But he wasn't.

Turned out Andi's interests didn't include men at all. And Mike had only been trying to help her get through a bout of PTSD Andi hadn't wanted to admit to. Bastard had honored her request, leaving Holly to draw all the wrong conclusions.

Which didn't explain last night.

Or did it?

Not wanting to learn anything new, Holly risked another look at him anyway.

Mike sat, not with the cute ski patroller who'd done yeoman service until the last body bag was off the mountain and the last investigator off her slopes. Mike sat with Miranda (both of their backs to her). Opposite them sat the head Swedish SHK investigator and the president of the airline. Rolm Lindgren looked as rough as she felt, which meant she ranked right down there with a dingo's bum.

Still, Tad would at least choke a bit if she shoved his head into his muesli for pointing it out.

Miranda's couch had been comfortable enough, not that Holly had managed a second of sleep on it. She had *not* been batting her eyelashes at Tad Jobson. They'd just been...trading war stories. It was a relief to talk to someone who she could share with at that level. Didn't know she'd missed it until she did.

Like why it was so funny that a drunken Marine Corps major had driven an up-armored Lexus into an obstacle course mudhole. He didn't have to explain that the heavy up-armor meant the windows only rolled down inches—enough to let mud in but not people out. And that the little window-breaker hammer he'd been beating the inside of the window with didn't touch bullet-resistant glass rated NIJ III against multiple 7.62 mm rounds. He'd have gone down with his car if the Marines hadn't been quick about hauling his ass back out.

The punchline wasn't the Marines and all the explanation. It was that in his drunken state he'd accidentally taken the Navy base commander's personal vehicle after a lusty fling with the guy's wife. His career had, literally, turned to mud in that instant.

Tad had kept his face intent while making frantic-beating-a-tiny-hammer-against-a-window gestures.

She laughed until her gut hurt.

She hadn't done that in a long time. Taz might be a colonel in the Pentagon—and had grown up on a barrio street rougher than anything Holly could imagine—but she'd never served in the field. And, while Tad hadn't been in Special Operations Forces like she herself had, he'd flown into plenty enough ugly to share a language.

The last person she'd had that with had been...

Oh shit roasted on a stick! Andi Wu. The pip-sized Night Stalkers pilot, who'd flown missions Tad never could. Andi's brain had been seriously cutting edge. Which only made what she'd done ten times worse.

Holly refused to miss her.

But Mike had a point. Holly should apologize to him... somehow. Didn't have a whole lot of practice doing that. She certainly wasn't going to try it in front of the Holy Trinity he was having breakfast with.

Probably help if she knew exactly what she was apologizing for.

She rubbed her fingertips together hoping for a little magic, like rubbing a genie's lantern. Instead she felt the memory of the neck bones of the dead 737 pilot grating against each other.

Who the hell was she supposed to talk to about that?

Mike was squeamish at the strangest of times. Miranda could be interested in a technical way that would have her visiting morgues to calibrate different vertebrae fracture patterns. Tad? Not a chance. He was a whirly-boy, not about to get his hands dirty.

But that left only Jeremy, who would start telling her the anatomical variations of different types of breaks until she was ready to shoot herself rather than listen to another detail about—

"Incoming on your six," Tad said in that perfectly even tone designed not to draw anyone else's attention. It was the sound of her past, mission deep and ingrained by years of training.

Affirm: The restaurant door had a conspicuous squeak she hadn't consciously noted earlier, but it had sounded less than two seconds before Tad's warning.

Assess: Her position? Between Miranda's table and whatever threat Tad had identified as inbound. She wouldn't fail Miranda again.

Assets: Sole line of defense.

Action: Best defense—give no warning before going on offense.

Holly kicked her chair back with a crash to create a distraction as she rolled into the aisle between tables. With her left hand, she reached along her back waistband and yanked out her horizontal-carry SOG Altair fixed blade. Ready to slash a femoral artery or punch it into the groin for the iliac artery. Landing in a squat, she had her other hand on the long Fairbairn-Sykes dagger on her thigh, ready to drive for the heart or lunge up and slice from under the chin directly into the brain.

Her target—

Frozen.

Stock-still.

He was a tall man in a sharp-pressed Swedish military uniform. Sporting an Air Force major's bars and wings. His hands were empty except for a slim portfolio.

An abrupt silence permeated the restaurant.

"Shit, woman!" Tad's whisper was the first sound in the utter void.

Her knee joints creaked with adrenal-forced tension. Again her heart was racing like a triple-espresso hit, not the three sips of coffee she'd managed.

Without a word, well aware of everyone watching her, she

tucked her knives away, righted her chair, and sat on it as if it might explode—which would be a relief at the moment.

Instead, with a soft crack, the right front leg gave way.

She braced her feet to keep the chair level as if nothing had happened.

Her coffee spread across half the table—Jeremy fought the tide bravely with their napkins.

Out of the corner of her eye, she saw the major scoot by, giving their table a wide berth.

"So not messing with you," Tad whispered once he was gone.

"Fuck off."

"Guess Mike wasn't kidding about you being hair-trigger all the time." He ignored her warning.

When she didn't speak, Jeremy answered for her. "She's former Australian Special Air Service Regiment. Like our Delta Force only with a funny accent." He mopped up more of the coffee after grabbing a few napkins from the next table over.

Didn't matter that it wasn't in her cup anymore, not a chance she'd keep anything down until the adrenal punch to her system chilled out a bit.

"SASR?" Tad whistled softly. "No shit?"

She gave him the finger without looking up from her lost caffeine supply.

"Sorry."

She kept the finger up high and dry, which finally shut him up, leaving her the peace to feel truly idiotic.

The major stood by the head table. He was addressing Miranda; though occasionally casting a wary glance in her direction.

Holly should be there. She knew it. But she didn't trust her legs at the moment. Didn't trust herself to not find yet another way to screw up. And definitely didn't want to face Mike after overreacting to Tad's miscue.

Instead she stared down at the puddle of coffee that had survived in her saucer and did her best to be invisible.

In the field, she often became invisible with the right camo and SASR trained stillness. Too bad she couldn't turn invisible to herself. Because whatever she was feeling and didn't understand, she—times ten—didn't *want* to see it.

21

A WAITRESS HAD CLEARED THE WORST OF THE MESS HOLLY HAD made and departed to fetch her a fresh coffee.

As only Mike could ever do to her, without her situational awareness triggering at his approach, he arrived at the end of the table—she'd know his boots anywhere. No longer the Rockport walkers he'd had on the first day. Nor the high leather he'd worn for the next two years in case of snake attacks, even on snow and ice.

Now? Who else purchased designer work boots other than Mike Munroe? *Six hundred bucks buys utility* and *luxury,* he'd claimed. Hard to believe she was sleeping with a guy like that. For four years now, he was always the best dressed member of the team, of any team they met in the field. Personally? She'd rather invest in pizza.

For all that she scoffed at him, he was damn good at his job, in ways she didn't begin to understand. Easily half of the incidents they investigated eventually boiled down to his territory—human factors and operations.

Christ, even last night, the copilot snapping the pilot's neck fell under human factors. Everything the other four of them had done in the long hours after that discovery—make that three of them plus Tad fumbling gamely along in their wake—had found nothing wrong with the aircraft.

"Jeremy, Tad. We're on the move."

Holly looked from Mike's boots to his face in shock. Stone-faced. No way would she be the one left behind for a single—

"You too." Then he twisted on his heel and headed for the door.

The major, Miranda, and Kurt from the SHK followed close behind.

Rolm, the LuftSvenska president, sat alone, studying his coffee as she'd been doing. Except in proper Swedish noir fashion, he looked like he wished to drown himself in his. Rather than drowning someone, *anyone* else.

As he rose to his feet, Tad started telling some story about going fishing with his Pop. But with neither coffee nor breakfast, she didn't bother engaging the part of her brain used for talking, listening, or telling him to shut the fuck up.

When she shifted her right foot out into the aisle to stand up, the broken chair almost pitched her headfirst into Tad's arms. Would have if he hadn't caught her arm. Mike scowled back at her from where he was holding open the restaurant's door for Miranda.

She shook off Tad, but Mike was already gone by the time she found her equilibrium.

At Miranda's little bizjet, and it was obvious that the SHK investigator and the Air Force major were sticking with them, she let them take the cluster of four facing cabin seats along with Jeremy and Tad. She took the side-facing seat opposite the door. The cabin only had five seats, if you didn't count the cushion on the lavatory at the very back.

That was the seat they'd always stuck Jon Swift in, back when the major occasionally flew with them. Back when he'd been dating Miranda despite the rest of the team's distrust. The outcast / loser seat; one he'd ultimately proven that he deserved before Holly had tasered him and thrown him off the team.

Much the same way she'd thrown Andi off the team.

The two of them shared no traits, yet—

As the engines spun to life, Meg wiggled her way out from behind Miranda's pilot seat and climbed up into Holly's lap. At least someone was still talking to her. She tickled the dog's nose until she got a sneeze, then gave the terrier a good scritch to apologize for the teasing. Soon the dog was asleep. She rested her palm against Meg's curly gray fur and felt her heartbeat and slow breathing.

"You just like my lap because it's warm."

Meg snored in response.

Holly avoided looking aft when Tad's laugh rang out.

And looking forward? The main thing she saw was the back of Miranda's head. Mike in the copilot's seat was invisible behind the partition by her right shoulder.

Doing her best to follow Meg's example, she leaned her head back on the curve of the hull and prayed for sleep as the takeoff dragged at her sideways.

22

Mike decided it was an awkward distance. Uppsala Air Base lay only a fifteen-minute flight from Ludvika. Definitely not long enough for him to go back and find out what the hell Holly was thinking. Yet long enough for him to think about the plusses and minuses of doing so. Did he even want to know? Now, that was an ugly question.

Normally he always wanted to know what a person was thinking so that he could second guess their next action. At the moment, not so much. Besides, that had never worked on Holly anyway.

A glance over his shoulder revealed Holly's well-scuffed Australian Army Redback boots stretched out across the narrow aisle. Woman had the longest legs on the planet, a feature he'd had plenty of opportunity to appreciate over these last years.

And a sure bet, Tad Jobson had noticed them as well. Every time he'd turned around, they were glued together. Even last night by the corpses, Jobson hovered at her side. Though Tad tried to hide it, it looked to be a close thing that he hadn't puked on the corpse.

There'd been a dark rage that had flashed over Holly's face when Mike told her that Sweden's Minister of Defence had died aboard. It had made no sense. Was it that he'd spoken at all?

He hadn't heard Holly's arrival at breakfast. Hadn't even been aware of her until the loud crash of her chair being kicked aside. He'd twisted around in time to hear the Air Force major's yelp of surprise as he stared bug-eyed at the lethal apparition crouched by his feet on the restaurant's worn carpet.

When Mike had glanced back to see if she was okay after she returned to her seat, she'd given him the finger.

For locking her out last night? She'd sure as hell deserved it. Not just for how she was so buying what Tad Jobson was selling, but for treating him as if he was a preschool idiot in front of Tad. He'd worked just as hard as she had since joining Miranda's team and for that his reward was being called stupid? It royally pissed him off.

He supposed that the morning's only surprise was that she wasn't in Jobson's bed. Still might have ended up there with the way they were both leaning toward each other over the table this morning. And practically embracing her as she rose from the table.

She'd shown no interest in Mike last night, on the snowy slopes of the aircraft investigation—other than trying to kick in the hotel door afterward. Thank God that the Swedes built to last. It had only been one kick, but it had resounded in the small hotel room. This morning he'd also discovered that it had bent the lock enough to have him consider making his exit through the window before he managed to free the bolt.

He'd never had this kind of trouble with a woman before.

Though, if not for his FBI handler pulling him out against orders, Violetta Celeste Giovanni would have gotten him killed —twice. And there'd been that lovely lay sister at the orphanage. She'd done so many things right but Father Stevens hadn't taken well to Mike, beating Mike unconscious with a Bible. Apparently God had marked the sister exclusively for the Father's dalliance. Or there was—

Okay, his past track record with women couldn't be viewed as wholly hazard free. Time for Holly to be added to that list of unmitigated disasters?

He half wished that the lovely Klara Dahlberg had joined them rather than staying at the ISASI conference. That would show Holly that he still knew how to treat a woman—at least a normal woman—right.

Except somehow Klara *wasn't* the right woman. Had Holly psychologically neutered him using some top-secret SASR voodoo? He wouldn't put it past her.

He glanced once more down the plane's aisle, beyond Holly's boots to Tad's shoulder sticking out into the aisle.

Whatever Mike himself was, apparently that wasn't enough.

He turned his attention back to the flight, they were fast approaching Uppsala Air Base. From now on, that's what he'd do: focus on the job and the female companionship. He didn't need to be The Guy for any one woman.

23

JEREMY HAD SPENT THE SHORT FLIGHT TEXTING BACK AND FORTH with Taz. Tad chatted with the Swedish Air Force major who'd come to fetch Kurt, the head of the SHK investigation team, about a lost Gripen fighter jet. In turn, Kurt had asked Miranda's team to accompany him.

We cracked the first one, he texted Taz. *Sleeper-agent-copilot crashed a full 737—probably to kill Swedish Minister of Defence. Heidi and Harry are trying to trace his real identity. But now their Air Force lost a plane and they want us to look into it. Okay?*

Taz answered. *Yes, definitely stay with Miranda for a couple days if you want. I'm fine. Other than losing my mind.*

??

No one warns you how your world goes completely sideways when you become Mom. I have no brain for anything beyond Child. I'll be dead or a certified nutcase before maternity leave ends.

Jeremy had sent back a laughing face.

He had to puzzle over the emoji she sent back: gritted teeth, red cheeks, and steam shooting out its ears.

Thought you were making a joke. I was laughing WITH you. Wasn't!

He decided that his best tactic was a thoughtful silence for a response.

How are the others? Taz finally answered.

The plan had worked. Then he sent a short version of Holly nearly stabbing a Swedish Air Force major in a hotel restaurant along with a line of laughing smiley faces. Yet as he'd described things, he realized that something weird was going on between Mike and Holly though he couldn't be sure what. *Neither one is talking much.*

Not even to each other???!?!

She was right. Mike chatted easily with anyone, but Holly rarely did more than tease anyone other than Mike. He was the only one she usually spoke to in any consistent fashion. And sometimes Miranda. But Miranda emerged from her noise-canceling headphones so rarely of late that there wasn't much talking around her. *Nope. Weird, huh?*

Not weird, just totally them. Tell Holly I'll kick her ass if she doesn't just come to a stop and talk to Mike.

But there's a crash.

Don't care. Jeremy, seriously, don't let the two of them off the plane until they've spoken. Oh crap! She sent a crying-baby emoji and didn't respond again.

Make them talk? How was he supposed to do that?

24

"You all, uh, go ahead. There's something that, you know, I need to kinda ask Mike and Holly." Jeremy waved the others off the plane.

Mike would rather be dipped in boiling oil.

Holly didn't look ready to be a-waltzing Matilda anytime soon either.

But since it was *not* a typical Jeremy-style request, he was usually more likely to just blurt out whatever entered his brain, this had to be important.

"Just a sec," Jeremy held up a hand when it was only the three of them aboard: Holly in her sideways seat, Mike twisted around in the copilot's seat, and Jeremy in the doorway. A chill wind sliced in through the jet's open door. He hustled down the steps, then folded the door up to close it in their faces. The latch thunked home, sealing them in the plane together.

"What's he doing now?" Holly asked.

Through the windscreens, Mike watch Jeremy circle around the nose and race toward the main building without looking back. "He's hurrying after the others like his tail's on fire."

Holly slouched in the seat, once again stretching her legs sideways across the aisle. "What's he doing that for?"

Mike rose, then felt like a mountain troll standing at the gap between the pilots' seats. The ceiling of the Citation M2 was under five feet. "He's... Aw, hell."

Holly looked at him askance for swearing.

"A buck gets you twenty that this is his way of saying we need to talk."

"You and me?" Holly looked up at him in utter disgust.

"No, Tad Jobson and a freaking lamppost. Yes, us."

There was a long silence before she repeated his curse. "See any way out of it?"

Mike considered, then shook his head. "He'd never have come up with this on his own. Taz is behind it. And I'm sure not going to take her on."

"I can handle her."

"No, Hol, you can't. US Air Force Colonel Vicki the Taser Cortez, the four-foot-eleven Latina powerhouse? Even money on that bet. But Taz is a mom now. It confers some kind of a superpower on women. I've seen it before."

"I'm sure you have."

"I never once went after a married one."

"Sure hit on single moms plenty, I bet."

"Give me a break." The crick in Mike's neck was starting to hurt.

"Go whine to your girlfriend Klara."

"What are you— Never mind." Sitting back into the copilot's seat, he wouldn't be able to see Holly. Sitting sideways on Miranda's seat would have two issues. One, experience had taught him that these seats were absolutely not designed to do that and, two, it was a bit like sitting somewhere holy that he didn't belong. Knowing that it was his Catholic orphanage upbringing didn't make it any less true. The left-side cockpit seat of this plane belonged to Miranda and Miranda alone.

He slouched his way aft like the *grumpy* mountain troll he felt inside, knocking Holly's legs aside when she refused to move them. In the main part of the cabin he dropped into one of the four facing seats ready to wait her out. *He* sure as hell wasn't going to take on Taz in Mom-mode.

It took less than a minute before Holly must have reached the same conclusion. She groaned as she climbed to her feet— and cursed as she banged her head hard on the low ceiling. Moving into the cabin, she sat kitty-corner across the aisle and propped her boots on the opposite seat. "So talk."

"Me? You're the one slobbering all over the Marine Corps flyer."

"Well," she studied the ceiling. "He is awfully pretty."

If it wasn't for the threat of Taz, and the hopeful puppy-dog look that Jeremy would be sure to have stored up when they got out of this mess, Mike would leave now.

"Not as pretty as Klara," Mike couldn't resist the shot.

Holly looked about as pissed as Mike had ever seen her. "Damned woman should be on a runway. The fashion kind, not the accident investigation kind."

"I know what you meant. And you're right. She's not pretty, she's gorgeous," Mike rubbed it in.

Holly's scowl soared hot enough to make this worthwhile.

"She's funny, too. Smart besides." And what in Christ was he doing? Not a chance in the world of Holly ever being the first one to back down. And if he kept pushing, she'd be gone. And the thought of that twisted his gut up in such a knot... "And she doesn't do a thing for me."

"You just can't wait to get your hands on all that pale Swedish perfection until she whimpers like *Oh, Mikey! Ooo, Mikey!* All to the tune of some old ABBA song about—"

He never should have told her about his childhood crush on Agnetha.

But Holly didn't continue.

Mike waited while her face went through a whole series of contortions that were almost fun to watch as her brain tried assimilate his words.

"Say what?" She wiggled a finger in her ear as if to make sure it was working.

"I know." He sank lower in the seat.

"You never slouch."

Out of ideas, he gave her the same finger she'd shot at him over breakfast.

"And you *certainly* never do that. What the hell's going on with you, Mike?"

"Says the woman panting around after Chief Warrant Tad Jobson."

"You don't get it, do you?"

"Explain it to me."

25

AND FOR JUST A MOMENT HOLLY WISHED SHE COULD BUT, "I can't."

"Why not?"

She looked at Mike. Really looked at him. Even slouched and pissed off, he was about the handsomest man she'd ever been with. Not just his features, which made for very easy viewing, but his kindness. "That's what I have no experience with."

"What?"

"Kindness."

Mike squinted at her.

"You. Kindness. I don't even know how to deal with that. With Tad I don't have to think. He's easy."

"I bet."

"Not that way. We share a warrior's background and vocabulary. That's what makes him easy. We're just talking."

"Oh, sure. That must be why he laughs at even your lamest jokes like you're the entire cast of *Saturday Night Live*. He also hasn't left your side for one second in two days."

She opened her mouth, then closed it again. He hadn't?

Mike, being Mike, read the question on her face. "Never more than a foot away. He'd take you down in a heartbeat if you gave him the go ahead. Assuming you haven't already."

"Well, I haven't and I won't. I don't want him. He's just..." Holly covered her face and kept it covered as she spoke. "You know what Andi did to me the day before everything went sideways?"

Mike kept his silence.

"She called me on my shit. Not woman to woman. Not even soldier to soldier. She did it Spec Ops warrior to Spec Ops warrior. She was always so chill and mellow. Didn't even know she had it in her."

"Former Night Stalkers pilot, Hol. Even I guessed that one, though I admit she didn't pull it out very often."

"I suppose. Anyway, she crawled right up in my face the way no one ever does." She needed to shut up—right now. Because Andi had been all over her case about—

"About what?"

"You." Why couldn't she keep her mouth shut? She waited. Then some more before asking, "What? No answer to that one?"

"Depends on what she said," he kept his voice soft. Goddamn kindness. What guy ever listened? It was unnatural.

Holly shook her head, she wasn't ready to go there. So? "Then there you are, going after Klara like there's no tomorrow and—"

"Will you drop the Klara shit!" Mike's shout echoed loud enough in the small cabin to make her ears hurt. "You want to know what happened with her? Fine. This gorgeous, smart, funny woman—who is *not* a daily royal pain in the ass— makes me the offer. The come-on smile, the dropping shoulder with the slight turn that accentuates a woman's breasts to perfection especially ones as nice as hers, the artfully unthinking but oh-so-practiced hair swish, the personal number," he yanked out his wallet and flung the card at her.

It smacked her in the nose and tumbled into her lap. She glanced down long enough to see the handwritten *Privat*. Then looked up again in shock as Mike continued to rage. That was *very* new.

"The whole bit! And you know what happened? *Do you?* No, you don't. So I'll tell you...nothing. Absolutely nothing! My pulse didn't jump. My nerves didn't tingle or whatever it was they do when the hunt is on. I didn't think about how nice it would be to get naked with her in front of a stone fireplace after a day schushing along some Nordic ski track filled with evergreens and silence. None of it happened. There should have been heaven-sent lightning bolts with the way that woman looks. Instead I shook her hand and said *thanks*. That's just wrong in so many ways. *Especially,* while you were getting all cozy with Tad bloody Jobson."

"I wasn't..." But Holly couldn't finish the sentence. Did Mike know what he was saying? The same thing that Andi had chewed her out for months ago. How close had she just come to pissing away the longest relationship in her life?

The *best* in her life. Period.

There wasn't a question mark there, and there bloody well should be. A big one! Size of a big red Roo—two meters and ninety kilos of kicking, biting kangaroo-question mark! One as tall and broad as Tad Job—she winced. She'd come up with worse analogies, though she couldn't think of one at the moment.

"This is scaring the hell out of me," she barely managed a whisper.

Mike closed his eyes and thumped the back of his head against the padded seat. "Well, at least we're finally on the same damn page."

She heard Andi's words about Mike like they'd been burned

into her brain. *Shit, Holly. Did you think he was hanging around for the great sex? Ain't nobody that good, not me and not even you. He puts up with all your mayhem because he loves you. Not that he's any more likely to admit it than you are.*

What if they *were* on the same page? She'd never met a better man. Maybe she never would. Not that he believed in himself.

"I—"

There was a loud thunk as the outer latch of the plane's door was thrown. A blast of cold air drove into the plane sending a chill down Holly's spine. What the hell had she been about to say?

With the door open and the stairs swung out and down, Tad stuck his head in. "Y'all decent?"

No idea of what she'd been about to say and not trusting herself to open her mouth in case it came spilling out, she gave him the finger.

Mike looked from her hand to Tad's face and then her own as if he'd been struck by something very funny. She started to give Mike the same, but it didn't feel right and she didn't finish the gesture.

He raised his eyebrows in a silent question, which she ignored. All he said was, "It wasn't me you were pissed at during breakfast." He sounded surprised.

She had no idea what he was talking about. "Not *only* at you." As far as she recalled she'd been pissed at everyone on the planet this morning. Not a whole lot of people had come off that list in the time since.

His smile said that he could think of several royally embarrassing statements. That finally gave her the motivation to give him the finger he deserved.

All it did was increase the size of his smile.

Tad spoke into the silence with only his head sticking in the door. "Miranda needs you, I think. Hard to tell with that woman, but she's sounding pretty disjointed, then asked for you, Mike."

Holly waved him ahead.

Waited until they were both gone and the cabin had chilled down to December-near-the-Arctic icebox levels. Mike had left the door open assuming she'd be on his heels.

She wasn't.

She had some serious thinking to do first.

26

"Mike, you need to talk to her. She keeps crying and you know I don't know what to do with that." Then Miranda looked down her dog. "Good dog, Meg. Walkies."

"Who?" Mike asked too late.

Miranda had already slipped on her noise-canceling headphones—set to high he'd wager. She and her dog headed out of the main building's security entrance here at Uppsala Air Base. Out into the cold. Miranda's newest avoidance tool; he hoped Meg's paws held up for how often they went on extended walks.

He made a mental note to get Meg some leather booties for Christmas—even if he'd left the team and returned to Denver. Now there was an interesting idea; the first one he'd had in a while that made any sense.

He stared out the glass doors at the airplane, Holly's head still visible through one of the small round windows. Not watching him, just staring straight ahead.

What *had* Andi said to Holly about him? And why had she assumed he was out to bed every woman he met? Who had she slept with since they'd been together?

She'd sure acted strange about that airline pilot in Australia a couple years back. Pretty clear something had happened there, though he'd never tried to find out what. She didn't want to talk about it, that was her business.

He could corner her. Somewhere that Tad or Miranda or Jeremy or...any of them couldn't intrude and get some straight answers out of her. Or maybe he already had them if he could find five minutes in a row to think?

For now, he had another weeping woman to deal with. Perfect, just perfect. How many weeping eyewitnesses and survivors had he been forced to coddle—his sole worth on the team. *Let's send Mike to talk to her. He's always good with the ladies.* He'd ruined enough shirts with running mascara to outfit a decent men's store.

Other than that? He was less useful than stupid wads of Kleenex.

So he hadn't studied engineering like Jeremy and Miranda, become a pilot like Andi or Tad, or a superwarrior like Holly. No JFK Special Warfare School diploma like Taz kept on her office wall along with her twenty-year Air Force career.

He had a lifetime's training in the art of the con. Not a lot of prestigious diplomas or medals handed out for that particular education. He'd managed to avoid the law the whole way through, which ought to count for a gold star or something. He supposed it had, he'd passed his security check to work with the FBI and now Miranda's classified military projects.

Steps to Denver: one last weeping witness, move there, and never, ever, for any reason on the planet have a need for a security clearance again.

That sounded just fine.

The only thing he'd ever been good at in this world had no place in his present life. How had he landed in a place where he was playing for the *good guys* instead of himself?

Then it slapped him hard in the gut.

He almost laughed, but was afraid he'd be sick if he did. He wasn't running the con, *they* were. He was the dupe, getting all bent out of shape to run their game for them. If it was his game, where were all the cool side benefits and sweet women?

No! He wasn't going to think about women right now.

Mike couldn't get out of here fast enough.

"Down the hall, Interview Room Three," the receptionist waved him through after checking his ID, away from her desk and down the long hall.

Miranda. He owed Miranda this one last-*ever* interview because she'd never done wrong by him. After that, he'd be gone faster than the Road Runner racing past Wile E. Coyote.

When he didn't move, the receptionist eyed him in with a cool professionalism, probably considering whether to smack the button to call out the security team to take him down.

Mike nodded his appreciation; if she'd thrown herself at him, he didn't know how far he'd race over the horizon without stopping. With the way his luck was running, he'd end up in... Wisconsin. No skiing in Wisconsin; their biggest ski area didn't top seven hundred feet. Twice Fjällberget—twice puny was still puny. He missed Snowmass' forty-four-hundred-foot vertical drop.

Four years. He hadn't so much as put on skis in four years. How the hell had that happened?

Okay, fine. One more weeper, but then he was done.

He staggered down the hall, veering about like a drunk. He could feel the receptionist smirking at his back.

Maybe he'd restart his advertising firm. That had started out being legit. Being paid to sell people what they didn't need had to be the perfect con—a hundred percent legal and very profitable.

At least until the FBI came along and insisted on screwing it up because he'd inadvertently signed on a money laundering front. For two years he'd raked in money from both sides, the clients and the FBI's finder's fees. He'd had the hot car, hotter women, and his own plane for flying them up for weekend to the Aspen ski slopes or mountain summer pastures with all *kinds* of splendid views.

Gave it up for what? Not much. He'd never imagined his life turning out this spectacularly lame.

Go interview a bunch of passengers. Get those pilots to tell you what they were really doing. And spend untold hours with thousands of eyewitnesses whose statements contradicted and had nothing to do with what Miranda unraveled from the plane and the flight recorders.

Death like last night's 737 smeared over the snow and now some weeping woman? Not a lifestyle he'd ever signed up for. Well, he had, but it wasn't on purpose. It had been like the universe dropped him on a narrow raceway over shark-infested waters, then loosed a lion behind him. One choice, one single glimmer of a way out, and he'd grabbed on.

Landing on Miranda Chase's NTSB air-crash investigation team definitely counted as an improvement over winding up dead—*missed getting gunned down by the Denver mafia by the hair on your chinny chin chin, didn't you, Mike?* And the FBI's heavy clean-up squad, too, while they were tying up loose ends. With Sister Mary Pat gone, it wasn't as if there was anyone alive to miss him.

Come on Room Three. Show up so I can get out of here. Who made these halls so long? All the charm of an insane asylum.

Working on plane crashes ranked as the weirdest place he'd ever been in his life. His previous record of stability since running away from the orphanage had been his two years operating his own advertising agency in Denver.

Four years with Miranda's team now, three of those with retired SASR Sergeant Holly Harper in his bed. Perhaps the problem was his DNA lacked the genes or chromosomes or whatever for staying legit.

He glanced back up the hall, which he'd moved only a few doors along despite his walking forever along it, at the heavy door Miranda had exited through, leading outside. Would she climb on the plane and fly away, taking Holly with her? He wouldn't put it past either of them.

No. There was a crash, a new one. Miranda would never leave without solving it first.

And the job did offer a few plusses—he'd never been with a warrior before. Soldiers and fliers had abounded in Denver bars—not a lot of sailors in the Mile-High City—but never a true warrior like Holly. And she was...

Well, she was coming through that door at any moment. And no matter how much Jeremy wanted him to, he wasn't ready for whatever came next in his conversation with her. He headed down the hall painted a white as nondescript as any US military base. Fluorescents had given way to LEDs, but they managed to remain coldly institutional.

Yep, resurrecting his ad agency sounded fine. Keep the old Advanced Ads name? Sure. There were probably still rumors around Denver about the agency's colorful demise—mafia gun battles and FBI cleanup squads. Good old PT Barnum knew what he was talking about: *No such thing as bad publicity.* Especially not in the ad business.

Whereas weeping women? Definitely some skills he'd rather not be known for.

The moment he stepped into Room Three, he realized this wasn't his average weeper. She wasn't some civilian *so overwhelmed by events.*

The woman waiting for him wore a green flight suit with the Finnish flag on her left arm in a Swedish military base. He didn't know how to read her rank by the three horizontal stripes on her insignia patch. Jet pilot typically meant officer, he knew that much.

Despite the obvious helmet hair, and the seriously high-end pilot's helmet on the bench that had given it to her, her thick dark-brown hair was lovely. Actually, it was all he saw of her as she leaned forward with her hands clasped and her elbows on her knees.

"Hi there. My name is Mike Munroe. I'm with the crash investigation team. They said you needed to talk to someone." Not his smoothest opening.

"Right here," she pointed between her thighs.

Mike groaned to himself. He didn't need the *come on* right now.

"That's where her ejection handle would be."

He logged *her* as a question for later and reminded himself not to jump to conclusions. Neutral observer, that was the trick. Besides, he didn't know squat. While locked in the plane with Holly, he'd missed any initial briefing that would have explained what was going on. "Uh-huh," he tried to sound encouraging as he sat down on the bench with her helmet between them.

"She said it moved on its own."

"They're not supposed to do that, right?"

She raised her face and shoved aside a handful of hair. "Who are you?"

I'm the idiot they send to calm down distraught witnesses. He pulled out his NTSB ID and his CAC card. "Mike Munroe. Sorry, nobody briefed me on what's happening. They called me in to assist but I, uh, wanted to hear what happened directly from the—" he made a wild guess and hoped it stuck "—*only* witness without the bias of any other, um, interference. So, if you don't mind starting at the top, taking your time, I'd appreciate it. Your English is very good, by the way."

She rolled her eyes. "It's the second language of Finland. Third actually after Swedish. Most of us are at least trilingual."

"That's great. I'm trilingual in English and bad Russian. Of course, I do have trouble with things like counting sometimes."

It didn't even earn a crack of a smile. But, she did hand back his ID and his security clearance after reading both carefully and comparing each to his face. She had a face that wasn't out in Klara Dahlberg territory, but didn't disappoint for a second.

Then she started her account. Most of it sounded pretty routine, so he listened to the second part of the conversation, the part she wasn't saying.

Kapten Liisa Salo may have never met Major Ingrid Eklund in person, but there'd been a deep affinity between the two. The kind of connection that sounded as if it went beyond sisters-in-arms; or would have.

Liisa became more and more precise as she neared the end of her story and he tuned back in to the primary thread.

"The Gripen is an amazing plane. I wish that we flew it in Finland. And I wish I flew half as well Ingrid."

He felt the downward spiral that must be at the end of her story. Rather than letting her reach the end, probably when she had burst into tears in front of Miranda, he circled her back to Ingrid's last few transmissions both before the ejection and during her descent.

Coming at them several ways—he even had her tell him every detail in reverse order—to check for every nuance he could uncover. He circled back to the self-raising ejection handle multiple times, eliciting every nuance she could recall.

Only then did he let her tell the end of Major Ingrid Eklund.

And again, he had a weeping woman on his shoulder.

Thankfully no mascara.

At least this was the last time.

27

HOLLY STOOD CLOSE BEHIND THE ONE-WAY GLASS ON INTERVIEW Room Three. Her chest hurt, no matter how many times she rubbed the side of her hand up her breastbone.

Tad leaned against the back wall with his arms crossed over his chest—almost three feet away this time. But she'd bet he was watching her ass. The SHK crash investigator who'd accompanied them the whole way stood stiffly next to him.

Jeremy stood close to the one-way glass beside her. He kept wanting to talk about each detail the Finnish pilot told to Mike. Wanted to analyze aloud the maneuverability of the JAS 39E Grippen versus the F/A-18C Hornet. To—

She'd had to threaten bodily damage if he didn't shut up.

The fact that he was more hyper than even his norm in her presence told her he was still worried about forcing her to talk to Mike.

Nope. Jeremy counted as one too many things to think about at the moment.

Holly ignored him and Jeremy finally fell silent.

Not once did Mike look toward the window. Not until the major was weeping on his shoulder. Not until he'd finally given her the permission to purge her pain. He'd gone far above and beyond his duty, making sure that the pilot fully understood from her own words that it wasn't her fault in any manner, shape, or form before allowing her the release.

Only then did he look at the mirror. His face was complete...blank.

He'd know she was there, watching. Know that she'd heard and understood every word.

Two women who'd never physically met had cared that much about each other. Their connection ran that deep.

Her and Mike? Three years in each other's arms almost every night. What did they have to show for it?

When Jeremy's phone rang in the observation room, so loudly it might cause deafness at twenty meters, she still couldn't look away.

Why was Mike's blank look causing so much pressure in her chest?

28

HARRY LAY ON HIS BACK WITH HIS LEFT LEG UP ON A STACK OF pillows as high as his thigh was long. The surgery on his ankle had been orthoscopic and required no cast. What it did require was immobilizing his leg between two side braces held in place by enough elastic bandage to hog-tie an elephant.

Doom.

Four days already felt like four weeks and he had ten more days to go. He wanted to be at the CIA, working on the latest cyber defense upgrades he'd designed. Or at Black Hat Europe with Heidi. Not kicking around the apartment going quietly insane.

He'd become pitiful. When had that happened?

Where was the hacker he'd been? Heidi too, once they'd e-met. Together they'd wreaked merry havoc on servers from Beijing to Belarus like there was no tomorrow, flouting everyone's attempts to pin them down—until the CIA.

Caught, they'd been given a choice—entrust their future to the US justice system or take over the CIA's cyber division. Not a bad deal, but he missed the old days where he chose his own targets and what to do to make them suffer for transgressing *his* definition of truth and justice. Now it was the US government's game in the highly questionable form of Director Clarissa Reese.

That had all been back before he'd bunged up his ankle by merely stumbling while carrying a new computer.

He never asked if Heidi missed those days, too, for fear that the answer was yes.

Back then he'd never been pitiful.

What had the CIA done to him?

Well, one good thing, they'd finally met in person. That had turned out to be a *very* good thing. It still startled him that she'd agreed to marry him; not that he'd ever complain on that point.

He missed her even though the woman was only a couple tenths of a microsecond away electronically. Actually with the one-third slowdown in the speed of light over fiber optic cable and various computer switching delays, it was closer to a millisecond—irrelevant on all except the most extreme hacks. Still better than satellites and their heavy handshake latency in most conditions.

Because she wasn't here to clock his opiate usage, Heidi had forbidden his taking any of the oxycodone painkillers without her express instructions. He hadn't told her that he hadn't needed or taken one since the first day. At least that way he had an excuse to talk to her every six hours. It broke up the utter tedium—now his big daily excitement was dinner and sponge-bath break. The drawback of stringing Heidi along about the drugs was the two a.m. wake-up calls to remind him to take his next pill—*you have to stay ahead of the pain, Harry.* There wasn't any pain other than itching, but the extra chance to talk to Heidi was totally worth it.

Twice it had devolved into utterly spectacular phone sex that he eagerly awaited to try in person.

Eighteen hours since Jeremy had asked him about the

mystery copilot. He wasn't much farther along than he'd been eighteen hours before, but he called anyway, mostly to have someone to talk to. Except he'd never admit to that as it sounded even more pathetic.

"Hi, Harry!"

"Hey, Jeremy. Your 737's Swedish copilot is a real black hole. I have him at an Italian flight school."

"Well, that's something."

"Except it doesn't exist."

"That sounds pretty clumsy and a little obvious."

"Sure," Harry pulled up his research on the screen. "But you can call their main line for references and you hit a live operator, with a majorly hot Italian accent. She's breathlessly willing to send you verified coursework, student grades, even the pilot's former mailing address in Italy."

"She's probably a ninety-year-old grandma."

"Yeah probably," Harry wouldn't be surprised. "Then I ran him through all the Russian databases I managed to slip into."

"Meaning all of them," Jeremy laughed.

"That takes time. But the ones I could do fast, gave me nothing. Though Russia definitely runs pilots through the same Italian non-school to get Western pilot credentials. I may have dumped those names into the databases at Interpol, the FBI, Mossad, and a few others. Or maybe not."

Again Jeremy laughed on cue, because they both knew he absolutely had.

"But no joy on your guy. They require that all their enrollees are already fully trained pilots. The school exists for one purpose, to convert unreportable hours into Western-world acceptable hours, but they don't keep the proof afterward. Slick, huh?"

So easy he wished he'd thought of it back in his hacker days. Need a sleeper agent? Train them up on an Airbus, Boeing, or even a Cessna. All hours in Russia, China, or wherever were rewritten into certified experience in the West as part of the service. Nobody claiming that they were more than they actually were, so no incompetence existed—only disloyalty.

He'd cracked their dark-web page and their bank accounts.

A quarter-mil euro for a 737 pilot with five thousand hours. Write a little conversion code, pay the sexy-voiced receptionist, and pocket the rest. Oh, there were a few bribes to obscure airlines in Africa, Southeast Asia, and the like to verify hours that were never served. A flat fee of ten-k per call for the reference source eased verification significantly.

"You'll keep digging?"

"Sure. But no idea if there's more to find. What if there's a name change in there somewhere that I missed? Huh. Name change going into the flight school, coming out a different person with all those hours. I'll check that out. Not like I have anything else to do than to lie here like a lump and stare at my bare toes."

"Wiggle them for me."

Harry did. Then he tapped to switch from a voice call to video. Jeremy did the same. Harry focused the camera on his toes and wiggled them again.

"Good job. Everything's still connected."

"Sure, the doc was slick as can be. Hey, Jeremy?"

"Yeah."

Harry didn't know how to ask the question. Jeremy had been a hacker too, except he'd never finished his first big hack—cold feet an inch from the goal line. He claimed to have played it clean ever since and, because it was Jeremy speaking, Harry believed him.

"What is it, Harry?"

"You ever sorry you didn't go through with it?"

"But I did. I married her and we have a kid. That's what you should do, Harry."

"No, wait. I was talking about... Never mind." Dumb question anyway.

"Oh, not doing that hack?" Jeremy paused longer than was usual for him. Even his listening typically felt breathless. "No. And not just because it was for the wrong side. I don't regret it. But I don't think about it much. That's the past. That's before Miranda, and Taz, and now Amy." And Jeremy kicked into high gear. "You'll never understand the way having a kid changes your world view. I feel like there's so much I never understood. I'm All-powerful Dad and totally freaked out at the same time. There's nothing like— No, wait. Never mind. I didn't say any of that."

"Jeremy? What the—"

"I promised Heidi. No, wait! I didn't say that either. Gottagobye" And he was gone without putting a period on the sentence.

Harry wanted to laugh; to tease Jeremy about an incomplete line of verbal code. But it caught hard in his throat.

Heidi pregnant? With their kid?

A girl with her mom's unruly mop of hair, brilliant mind, and zest for life.

How had he never imagined that before?

29

"FOR SHORT-THROW, COMPACT LINEAR ACTUATORS, THERE EXIST wide variations in power." Miranda pulled up the images of three she'd found on a common shopping website and projected them onto the conference room's main screen. It was good, because it focused everyone's attention forward rather than toward her. She'd been careful to sit at the far end of the table so that all she saw was the back of anyone's head in the dimly lit room.

Except Meg. When Miranda looked down at where her dog lay by her feet, she saw the top of her head, not the back.

"These three devices are all readily available and would fit in the very tight confines allowed by the ejection seat's construction."

Nobody spoke, not the attendant military, no one on her team, nor the Finnish pilot. At least she wasn't crying any more. Mike had done well.

"Heavy-duty devices, in the nine hundred newton category like the one on the right, can extend the central shaft with two hundred and twenty-five pounds of force. These are predominantly round-shaft devices. At the other end of the spectrum, the one on the left, does have a square shaft but offers only sixty-four newtons of pressure. It would be very easy for a pilot to override such a thrust with one hand as Kapten Liisa Salo reported that Major Ingrid Eklund claims she attempted."

"If she said it, she did it." Liisa's voice was very strong, though Miranda couldn't read the emotion. Strident? Had she ever identified strident before?

"We only have her word on that, but we have no reason to doubt it as she stated it *in extremis* moments before she died, meaning she had limited motivation to state inaccuracies. Did I get that right, Mike?"

No one responded.

She looked around the table.

Holly and Jeremy were there. Along with the head of the SHK and several military personnel—two Swedish, one Finnish, and one from NATO in addition to Kapten Liisa Salo. But no sign of Mike.

"That's right, Miranda," Holly spoke up without looking at her. Instead, she searched for Mike in the room far longer than was necessary for someone not in the room.

"The middle actuator," Miranda resumed, "is a likely candidate. It's small enough to fit in the space. A two hundred-newton thrust can be briefly slowed by a harnessed pilot pressing down with one hand or even two overriding the forty-five-pound shaft thrust, but not sustainably. All these units I've selected have a thrust rate between ten and fifteen millimeters per second. Slow enough to be noticed and allow the pilot at least one attempt to respond."

She pulled up displays of the Martin-Baker Mk10 ejection seat.

"This is the seat that would have been installed in the Saab JAS-39E Gripen. I've mocked up the middle unit on the most likely attachment points, which would initially set the shaft of the linear actuator at a thirty-degree angle."

Miranda added a closeup side-on drawing of the configuration that best fit the captain's second-hand description and the seat's mechanics.

"Due to the angle, this would decrease its rate of on-vector effective motion fourteen percent as a first-order approximation—without integrating for the decreasing angle as it extended. This gives it a travel time between two-point-seven and three seconds from initiation until it lifted the handle the twenty-five millimeters necessary to trigger the ejection sequence."

She tapped the next slide, which showed an animation of the linear actuator lifting the ejection handle and the seat launching upward. She'd set this animation to two-point-eight-five seconds as the average of her best estimates.

Liisa's voice sounded rough when she spoke. "Three seconds. Plenty of time for a fighter pilot to perform the OODA Loop." She reached her hands out to the control positions, imitating the necessary motions, a method Miranda thoroughly approved of as it provided more realistic timing.

Miranda launched a stopwatch on the screen next to the stopped animation timer.

"Observe," Liisa kept her hands on the imaginary controls and glanced down. "Orient," she leaned forward to look more closely at her thighs. "Decide, then Act." She pulled her left, throttle hand from the imaginary control and made as if to press down between her mid-thighs. Then moved the flight-control right hand to reinforce the downward pressure.

Miranda stopped the timer. "Two-point-six seconds."

Liisa started to look up.

"No, don't!"

Everyone turned to face her.

"No, Liisa, look back at your hands."

Liisa finally did after making a down-frown.

"Stay there, just like that. You reported that Major Eklund made no effort to steer or slow her parachute?"

"Yes, even after I reminded her." She kept looking down, then popped her head up to stare at the screen showing the ejection seat mechanism in mid-launch. "Oh no! The old fighter-pilot's saying: Before ejecting, place your neck in the position you want it in for the rest of your life."

Miranda had always liked the neatness of that adage. "By leaning forward to focus her attention on the ejection handle's mechanism, she fractured or broke her own neck during the ejection, incapacitating her arms. This entire sequence is an unverifiable hypothesis, but it aligns reliably with the available data."

"Oh, my poor Ingrid," Liisa started crying again. Apparently, she didn't appreciate the neatness of the solution.

Miranda looked around the table, but there was still no sign of Mike to deal with the crying woman.

"What asshole do I get to kill for doing this to her?"

Miranda considered explaining that question lay outside the scope of her investigation. But that hadn't gone well the first time; she'd needed no emoji chart to understand the president of LuftSvenska's scream of despair. It still echoed inside her from when she'd discovered the multiple lies—by her parents —and about their deaths.

Rather than attempting to explain, she did as Mike had done for her earlier, lifting Meg from the floor into her lap. As soon as Meg settled, Miranda slid her noise-canceling headphones into place.

30

"Hey, buddy? Need a hand with anything?"

Mike closed his eyes. He didn't need this. *Especially* not this. He turned to face Tad Jobson.

"No, I'm good." So not. He'd come out to Miranda's plane and found his bag in the nose cargo compartment. The access door in the side of the nose folded upward, placing the luggage at chest height. There he'd ground to a halt deciding about his NTSB site kit. Take it or leave it? He'd built it up over four years. Not some utility vest filled with all the tools of the trade like the other team members. He'd started out that way, but their trade wasn't his. Time had honed it down to the essentials of his role as Operations and Human Factors Analyst.

To interviewees he needed to look more approachable and less like a walking toolkit.

On the job he carried a pair of voice recorders. A notebook with a set of colored pens in several weights, less for notes and more because many witnesses wanted to draw detailed images as they recounted events, though most couldn't form a decent stick figure. Tissues for the weepers—would have been useful an hour ago—and a neatly pressed monogrammed handkerchief for the especially attractive ones.

God his life was pathetic.

That's what had stopped him, stuck him in place by the plane's forward swing-up cargo hatch as surely as if he'd been frozen to the runway.

Women always liked that personal touch, but when had he last used that ploy? Two years? Three? He used to order them in ten-packs and always made sure they were neatly pressed for the occasion. Women liked that.

"Hey, nice bag."

"Thanks." The tobacco-brown-leather Boston Bag from Aspinal of London balanced on the edge of the cargo deck. Worth every penny of the grand it had cost him. The supple leather had that well-traveled look that only time authentically created. It was the very last thing he had left from Advanced Ads. They'd traveled a long way together. *Got some distance to go yet, pal.*

"The way you handled that pilot," Tad leaned one of his big shoulders up against the little jet's closed main door two steps aft of where Mike stood. "Damn, that was smooth, brother."

"Thanks."

"Where did you learn to do that? I mean, I can chat up the ladies as fine as the next flyboy, but that was Next Level."

Wonderful. His life's great achievement was chatting up women so well that a Southern-fried 'Bama hound dog like Jobson wanted lessons. He should charge by the hour like that Will Smith movie, *Hitch*. Which completely backfired on the character, so maybe not. Mike couldn't remember which woman he'd impressed into bed by suggesting that particular rom com for a date. He'd always kept track of such trivia in case he ran into a former lover at a later time.

Nope. Completely gone.

Even his last date before the dangerous Violetta who'd almost gotten him killed? Not a clue.

The tall Latina lawyer he'd planned on meeting the night after Violetta but before he knew he was a fugitive *for* justice and joined the NTSB on no notice? Name started with an A... Yeah, A-shaped like her spread legs when she was doing warm-up stretches in tight Lycra at the gym they'd shared. Alexia... Anna...Alejandra! Okay, not completely braindead.

...he was *fairly* sure it was Alejandra...

Mike tucked one handkerchief into his parka's pocket, then slid the NTSB vest into his daypack, along with the sun hat, heavy gloves, and the few wrenches he needed on rare occasions. He slid the pack deeper into the cargo space, behind Miranda's bag and Meg's dog carrier for the rare times they traveled commercial.

Tad still hadn't moved.

Maybe Mike always had the right words for the ladies, but he had no idea what to say to Jobson.

"Had my eyes on that fine lady," he tipped his head toward the administration building. "Hard not to."

"Pretty damn obvious."

"Yeah, but I hit a brick wall somewhere that I can't get around," Jobson didn't so much as grimace. "You slid in smooth on that pilot. Me? I go with sweeping 'em up so fast they never have time to think twice."

"It's a method." If the guy was fishing for tips on how to woo Holly, let him go to Hell along with Father Stevens back at the orphanage and all the rest of them.

"That's how Pop swept up Mama. Served him just fine going on forty years now."

Forty years? He and Holly in forty years? A cold chill shook him, one that had nothing to do with the midday sun reaching a bare handspan above the southern horizon.

Jobson rolled until his back lay against the closed passenger door as he stared up at the sky. "Seriously heavy shit you folks deal with. I had no clue. I flew plenty, shot my fair share on missions. Saw some buddies there one second and blown out of the sky the next. But that line of body bags last night. That pilot lady in there," he nodded at the building, "dying inside because of her friend going down. Not clean. Not in battle. Going down in the fight is part of the gig and you grow used to the idea that your ticket on the life-ride might be the next one punched. But not this shit. Sabotage? That's just wrong."

"It killed the US Vice President." And some others he wasn't cleared to name but were a part of Miranda's team legacy.

Tad glanced at him, though his body still leaned back and faced the sky.

His posture mimicked the disconcerting memory of the 737 pilot's snapped neck—the way his head had moved so wrong between Mike's hands.

And Ingrid's. He knew her through Liisa; come to admire her by the testimony of another. But he also knew the neck was gone when she'd described how Ingrid never reached for the parachute toggles. She was dead long before she hit that mine; a stay of execution that would only have lasted until she hit the ground—with or without the land mine.

"The VP? That was you guys?"

Mike nodded. "Especially Miranda and our former rotorcraft specialist. But, yes, it was us." Sabotage had downed the VP's helo, too.

"Shit, man. Big shoes to fill, I got that message loud and clear. Don't even know if I can." He turned back to facing the sky. "How do you hack knowing all that shit?"

As if Mike was doing such a sterling job of that at the moment.

31

Holly checked throughout the main building at Uppsala Air Base.

No Mike.

Interview Room Three where Mike had interviewed Liisa? Empty. The other side of the mirror? Nope.

Busted in on a couple officers in the men's bathroom busy dangling it at the urinals and laughing about who-cared-what. One-star Swedish and Two-star NATO stared wide-eyed, dribbling on the walls beside the urinals as they turned to look at her.

"Reconfirm your target lock, boys," she called out as she looked under all the empty stall doors.

No Mike.

He was around. Another of Mike's standards: always there when needed. Not soldier trained, but nobody had your back like Mike Munroe. Miranda's, Jeremy's, Andi's, right down to defending Taz's motherhood as if it was second nature. Hers— even when it pissed her off. The shocker? That he had any attention left over for himself.

No bludger of a layabout our pal Mike.

As she hurried out the front door, she wondered why she kept treating him like one?

Nothing out of place out here.

The blinding sun low enough to shine sideways through the windows of Miranda's plane. No heads in any of the windows.

Half turned back to the admin building, she spotted the shadow of the open lid of the Citation's front cargo hatch sticking out from the shadow of the plane's nose. Squinting against the sun, she spotted two sets of legs. She knew one was Mike's. The other guy's calves were so big, it had to be Tad Jobson.

Was Mike digging around for some weapon she didn't know he kept in his luggage? About to kneecap Jobson?

No, that wasn't Mike's style. He'd be polite if it killed him.

She moved closer, keeping the raised cargo hatch between her and Mike until she was close enough to overhear.

"Look, Tad, this is *the* top NTSB team. It draws the ugly shit: military crashes, launches I can't tell you about even with your clearance because they're code-word classified, attacks that are political rather than military, never mind the merely civilian pilot error. To survive on this team, you need to decide if you're up to the challenge. You, personally."

Holly had never made such a decision in her life. Or was it that it had never been a question?

And after how pissed he'd been at her about Tad Jobson, he was talking as if trying to help the guy. What was up with that? She'd wanted to slash Mike a new smile, from ear-to-ear by way of his throat over Klara—who'd they spent about twenty minutes around, a thousand klicks away in Iceland. How must he feel about the way Jobson came panting after her?

"How did you figure it, when it was your time?"

Holly smiled to herself, waiting to hear which version Mike gave. As far as she knew, she was the only one he'd told any degree of the truth and she wasn't sure about the accuracy of that. Mike might tell you five wholly different pasts and convince you each one was absolutely real in turn.

"Sweet Jesus, Tad, open your eyes. If you can't see the people on this team, you don't deserve to be here."

"Including you?"

Holly heard the humor in Tad's response.

There was a long pause, so long it started to hurt. Whatever Mike whispered to Tad, she missed it.

"Aw shit, bro," Tad's reply didn't bode well.

She had to break this up.

Holly walked around the nose of the plane as if she was just arriving. "Hey. You guys up for a beer run?" Then she nearly choked when she saw Mike's bag pulled most of the way out of the cargo hatch. Not as if he'd been digging through it, more as if he was readying to walk off with it.

"It's..." Tad looked at his watch. "What the hell time zone are we in anyway?"

Mike nudged his bag into the cargo bay and pulled down the door as if he was trying to hide something.

"It's after sunrise," Holly waved at the sun, "isn't that all that matters?"

Tad laughed. He'd been on as many night missions as she had. Morning was often the end of the day and time for a cold one before sacking out.

"I'll pass." Mike nodded to Tad, circled wide around her and kept walking. Not toward the admin building but out along the line of hangars.

Tad was watching her.

"What?"

"Some things are clear as the sky on a summer's day; you don't look stupid to this boy, Holly. Why the hell are you still standing here?"

Holly rested her hand on the closed cargo hatch. She felt

Mike's bag still there, safely behind the door. It did nothing to stop the shivers running through her. She should have grabbed her parka before coming outside to look for Mike.

"You're right. It's cold." She walked around the nose and headed for the admin building.

"Mother Mary and Joseph!" Tad said it like he meant it.

He strode up beside her. Yanking off his parka, he tossed it in her face, then grabbed her shoulders and turned her ninety degrees to face in the direction Mike had gone. He slapped her butt—hard. Hard enough to sting and send her stumbling forward.

"Stop trying to prove that the stories about airhead blondes are true." Then he headed toward the admin building. "Nice butt by the way." His laugh was the last thing she heard before he headed inside leaving her out here. In the wind.

32

THE SLEEPER AGENT'S REPORT ON PHASE TWO MADE PAVLE WANT to kill the man, and then himself.

The agent wasn't quite gleeful about betraying one of his own pilots to death, but certainly convinced that he deserved all the praise in the world. In fact, that had been the service chief's request but there was no way he was passing it on.

If a mechanic had sabotaged one of their own force's planes, he'd be dragged out into a dirt lot and *Ka-pow!* No trial. One and done—straight to the head.

His plan was working; according to the chief he'd been born on a happy star.

What's more, last night Elene had asked for the ring she'd tossed in his face ten months ago. Since her return, she'd been far more contrite and attentive.

Something had happened to her during that week gone. Something that had made her impossibly sad. She'd looked as if she hadn't slept more than minutes since she'd left him.

You never hit me that night, Pavle. I made you so angry, yet you never lashed out at me.

How low a standard was that? He'd never given such things

any thought. The mere idea that a woman like her had been reduced to such a basic criterion filled him with a rage like no foreign aggressor.

He asked who had hit her. She only shook her head, but rested a palm over her heart. Someone had hit right there— from the inside. Who was an easy guess: her father. Never violent, but a man given to dark depression. At heart, Elene was a gentle woman.

Father had never attacked Mother. They'd raged at each other from time to time, occasionally slept apart for a few nights, once for a whole month that had struck terror into his young boy's heart. But afterward? He'd learned to make himself scarce when the make-up sex kicked in. Pavle still blushed at the memory of the sounds coming through the bedroom wall despite his headphones cranking Phil Collins, Foo Fighters, or whoever was hot that week.

He should have been a drummer like Collins. Sexy groupies, road tours, drunken camaraderie of the band. Except he'd never seriously thought about music when he was young. Instead of rhythm he'd had a gift for languages. Instead of his father's path, teaching science at the university, he'd followed in Mother's footsteps—straight into the intelligence service.

That had been one of Elene's other revelations during her week gone.

I followed you to work one morning after you threw me out. I'd never done that before.

She didn't mention why or that it was probably to slash his tires or cause him trouble at the office.

Then I saw what building you went into.

The Service's triangular building stood inside its own, high-walled compound with heavy security at either gate. The only sign was the blue-and-white 51 of the street address screwed into the face of the concrete wall topped with razor wire.

Everyone knew what lay behind that wall and no one talked about it.

She'd waved off his protests that he couldn't explain. She'd always hated that he wouldn't tell her about his work.

I understand that now. I thought you were a lowly office worker or something, ashamed of what you did. So low that you didn't want to talk about having such a pitiful job with all your brains.

At least she hadn't equated him with being an often-out-of-work steelworker like her father.

I thought you'd put away your head. I don't want a man with no ambition who never tries for more. Again her father. *But you aren't, are you, Pavle?*

He'd shaken his head. He'd always liked the way she said his name. And he knew exactly what she'd been referring to.

She wanted to marry up. Almost *anyone* would be a step up from her father on the ambition scale. Her father didn't care about anything other than his dinner being on time and ice hockey or football depending on the season. He wasn't cruel, at least not that Pavle knew about, but he certainly thought no honest work ever came from being educated. Refusing to support his daughter's wish to go to the nursing school she so desired fit him to the bone.

Ever since her return, they'd simply fit together. He didn't think she was shamming. It wasn't some great love, but...they were good together. She liked working with the preschool kids and was finally talking about starting on a nursing degree with a specialty in pediatrics. Plenty easy to read what that meant about his own future after he married her—he'd need to think about a bigger flat.

Last night when she'd asked if he'd propose to her again, he'd seen such hope that he couldn't say no. Her bright squeal of joy as she'd launched at him finally made him appreciate the passionate bursts of noise his parents had always made when they made up after a fight.

Talking about his job remained out of bounds. They didn't have security clearances for girlfriends. Or fiancées for that matter. He wasn't ready to ask about wives.

Besides, even if he did talk about how he'd spent this year, he certainly wouldn't want to. How many lies could one man live? Apparently a lot of them.

Senior analyst on special assignment to the chief's office. With the raise they'd given him, he could send Elene to nursing school without worrying about her bringing in even part-time daycare income.

And reporting directly to the service's chief offered immense cachet at the office. People now came to him with their operations proposals for vetting and advice. The teacher, so recently the underling, now pretending wisdom. And the pretense often proved sufficient to make the ideas roll until a solution was found and fine-tuned.

He wished he had someone to take *his* plan to. Someone to ask for advice without sabotaging his whole future.

A trap of his own devising. Become the acknowledged expert, founder and manager of a key intelligence initiative— with no measuring its true worth.

Or morality.

He'd wanted to ask Elene about that. But he didn't dare, not even late at night whispered under pillows.

The whole operation was out of his control now. For the timing to work, the escalation that was Phase Three had been initiated days ago.

Just like his marriage to Elene, he knew it was too late to stop it. In her case he hoped it would be a good thing. In the operation's...

33

Kapten Arne Sorenson fired the engine on his Saab JAS 39E Gripen fighter jet. Three minutes from alert to departure didn't happen by chance, it took constant practice by the whole team.

Today's hot drill—straight up noon as the December midday sun lay on the horizon here at a hundred and sixty kilometers south of the Arctic Circle—fit right in.

Within five seconds of the single engine firing off, Maja had unplugged the ground-power connection and yanked the wheel chocks. Johan held up a fistful of pins with flapping red tags with one hand and offered a thumbs up with the other—the safeties had been pulled on all of his weapons and his ejection seat. At minus fifteen Celsius, Johan's clouded breath almost masked the red tags from view, but Arne knew he'd have counted them twice to verify none were missed.

Arne gave them both a salute, followed by a wave, and rode the throttle forward. He owed them both a beer; they'd gotten him out of the hangar five seconds ahead of his wingman, Hugo Bodin. Totally worth the price. The harsh payback? Standing them both to a beer would make him the designated driver, sticking with nonalcoholic beer to stay below Sweden's strict legal limit. Still worth it.

Per the alert's instructions, rather than turning west toward the runway at Storuman Air Base, he turned east. Riding the throttle up to a very fast taxi, he raced his jet out of the hangar and along the winding road leading into the trees.

This air strip was one of the first restored to the full Bas 90 standard. The Cold War-era Swedish air bases were unlike any other in the world. They were small and generally had short runways, making them harder to spot. By design, Swedish fighter jets were short-field specialists.

Any attacking force, meaning Russia, could bomb the runway into uselessness with a few hits. During the Cold War, still meaning Russia, Bas 90 strips had been placed all over Sweden. Rarely home to more than a flight of four jets.

In addition to making smaller targets than a big base, the Bas 90 setup also had narrow taxiways that shot through the trees in different directions. These connected to the nearby highways. The old Saab Viggen and now the Gripen were designed to take advantage of these.

Go ahead, Russia, bomb the runways. We won't care. We'll use the roads instead.

After the Cold War with Russia ended, most of these small bases had been retired. But with, yet again, Russia's new aggression, they were being restored as fast as possible.

Arne's dad had been stationed here at Storuman for much of his flight career and the old man loved that his son was the first squad back on the field. He'd started telling many stories of close calls that had never made the news: standoffs with MiG-21 Fishbed fighters and chasing off Tu-22M Backfire bombers that the Soviets constantly sent to test Sweden's air defenses.

The moment Arne had received the drill's alert from the tower, they'd informed him of which road to use. *E12 lights on.*

The E12 was a two-lane motorway that passed close by the

east side of the base. Called the Blue Highway for weaving between some of the best fishing lakes in central Sweden, near Storuman it ran straight as an arrow through the trees for two kilometers. The taxiway from his hangar cut close along the southern end of Bränntjärnen Lake and met the E12 in the middle of that straight stretch.

After this flight, he'd talk Maja into going skating on the lake. She was as magnificent on the ice as she was at maintaining his plane. He managed on the ice, but come the spring thaw was his time. He and his trusty fishing pole supplied all the Arctic char, salmon, and perch for the crew's grill parties. Maja wasn't big on fishing, but still looked lovely lounging in his boat reading a book on lazy weekend afternoons.

"E12 clear," the Tower reported.

The earlier E12 *lights on* call had been reporting that the stoplights placed at either end of the straight stretch were set to red. At the speed most people drove the motorway, it would take under a minute for the traffic to clear the straight stretch. It had now been three.

"Winds from the south at ten."

He slowed only slightly as he turned right at the end of the taxiway. The road surface was well salted and the jet barely skidded as he lined up on the centerline and punched it.

The GE F414 turbofan kicked his ass hard just like it was supposed to. His wingman would be close on his tail, but still behind. He'd make Hugo buy the round for his ground crew. Even talk him into being designated driver while he was at it. He liked that.

Maja always raved about the ease of care on a Gripen; Arne loved the kick-ass. The funny thing was that they were exactly the opposite in bed. There, she was the wild one.

The lion's hind-end strength of the Gripen kicked him aloft

in four hundred meters though he had a thousand of road before him.

Eight cars were waiting at the southern stoplight as he tore aloft above them.

A blue van slid open its side door and someone stepped out to watch Arne race toward them. The man then reached back inside his van—and swung out a long tube.

Red alarms blared across Arne's cockpit.

Threat detection!

No details as even the new, wider-range AESA radar couldn't see the van now directly beneath him.

He was barely aloft, moving at no more than a few hundred knots with his landing gear still dangling out in the wind.

Arne firewalled the throttle. The Gripen had one of the fastest engine spool-up times of any fighter manufactured, but even the GE F414 didn't respond instantly. Two-point-nine seconds to full thrust, and the Gripen was running a full load of fuel and ammo. Fourteen tonnes of aircraft didn't magically jump from V4 initial climb speed to exceeding Mach 2.

He punched the electronic countermeasures to War Mode. But the Gripen wasn't trying to hide from a threat either ahead or behind. The attack wasn't inbound from over the horizon. It was a tracking tone from a bare hundred meters directly below his belly.

The countermeasures offered no help.

The FIM-92E Stinger had been stolen from a NATO warehouse in Hungary and moved across the borderless European Union into Sweden in a worn crate labeled Uppsala University Telescope. This variant boasted multiple upgrades including digital enhancements to distinguish aircraft from countermeasure flares.

The meter-and-a-half-long, three-finger-wide missile drove upward.

Weighing only ten kilos compared to the jet's fourteen

thousand, a Stinger attained two and a half times the speed of sound in the first two seconds of the initial boost phase. However, the Gripen was so close that the missile had barely crossed Mach 1 when it drove the warhead into the belly of Arne's jet a hundred and seventy meters above.

The impact fuse fired the charge and the kilogram of HTA-3 high explosive launched the fragmented shrapnel in a lethal forward-aimed cone.

To either side, the shrapnel riddled the wing tanks with dozens of holes. Extremely volatile Jet A fuel began dumping through the holes. This had no significant relevance to what happened next.

To the rear, the shrapnel impacted the General Electric jet engine's primary intake fan, shattering the blades. Finally answering the peak thrust Kapten Arne Sorenson had hoped would drive him clear, the result was that the fragments of the intake fan's broken blades were sucked that much faster into the core of the engine. They struck the inner titanium blades of the smaller high-pressure compressor fan spinning at twenty-seven thousand rpm deep within the engine.

For the briefest moment before they shattered in turn, the engine jammed on the fragments. The entire force of the stalled turboshaft was transferred to the engine housing. The quick-change guide rails, allowing for an emergency engine change in an unexcelled sixty minutes, were stout enough to transfer the full rotational force into the rear chassis of the Gripen.

Like green carrot tops twisted off a slender carrot, the snap roll of the rear section of the aircraft as it absorbed the jammed engine's momentum tore away from the forward fuselage. The rear fuselage, with its long delta-shaped wings and engine core, impacted the frozen Rusfors Reservoir hard enough to break the ice and disappear below. Other than the Black Box retrieved by a lone diver sent through the ice, it wouldn't be seen again until after the spring thaw still four months ahead.

Arne cared about none of this.

At the last moment, he'd yanked the ejection handles.

The MDC, mild detonation cord, split the cockpit canopy and launched it into the slipstream. The two large curved sections fell to earth like the wings of a wounded snowy owl, fluttering chaotically as they abruptly slowed by several hundred knots and gravity took over.

A section of the shrapnel cone cast by the FIM-92E Stinger's warhead missed the top of his helmet by mere centimeters. But the missile itself had sliced through the ejection seat's controller. Receiving no sequenced signal, the seat's rocket motor didn't fire to launch Arne clear of the wreck.

He rode the arcing flight of the remaining forward fuselage, aerodynamically balanced on its stubby canard wings mounted to either side of the cockpit. The unpowered flight granted him five long seconds to appreciate the airfield his grandfather had flown from, his favorite fishing lake, and the first place he'd made love to Maja.

After a long morning, skating miles on the frozen lake, they'd shaped a snowy bowl that blocked the wind and reflected the sun's warming heat until they lay comfortably naked together on the narrow blanket he'd had the foresight to bring.

At the sixth second, almost clear of the trees, wondering if he'd survive a long skid on the ice—what a story *that* would be to tell, finally outskating Maja—the starboard canard wingtip caught the trunk high on the final tree. The only thing higher was the single branch that decapitated Kapten Sorenson. The cockpit landed belly-first, indeed skating well down the frozen reservoir.

If he'd kept his head, he'd have had a fine chance of survival.

But he hadn't.

His head tumbled down through the tree branches to bury itself in the snow that had gathered in the lee of the trunk. It would greatly puzzle the boy scout troop that literally stumbled upon it four years later.

The Arctic char asleep under the winter ice, briefly startled from their somnambulant winter slumber by the crash, possessed no way of knowing they'd be that much safer when spring arrived but Arne Sorenson didn't.

34

Löjtnant Hugo Bodin saw the streak of the Stinger take out Arne as he rotated aloft from the E12 roadway.

Too late to abort, Hugo hit full thrust, then reached forward to slap the Gear Up lever the moment he rotated. By the time Arne's Gripen was shredding in midair, Hugo was accelerating hard and climbing above it.

The curve of the road and his position behind Arne had initially hidden the missile's launch point behind the towering Norway spruce trees on the inside of the bend. As he climbed aloft, it was hidden directly below.

Tipping over seventy-five degrees, he carved a hard turn to the east. Looking down and back from his steep-angled turn, he spotted a blue van. Beside it, a man tossed aside a Stinger surface-to-air-missile launch tube, separating it from the distinctive front-end targeting block. He reached into the van and pulled out another ten kilos of ugly-in-a-tube to fit onto the block.

Hugo didn't need to see anything more.

"Tower, Gripen Three-three is down hard. SAM attack. Three-seven engaging."

Unlike Arne, Hugo now had maneuvering speed and altitude.

And he had a JAS 39E Gripen, the best plane in any air force.

He'd never done a J-turn Herbst Maneuver at this low an altitude before, but there was always a first time.

Right now, headed away from the attacker, he blasted through Mach 1. How many seconds could he stretch it before he took a Stinger missile up his tailpipe?

Don't think.

Hugo yanked back on the throttle and put the nose up in the air—all the way up.

The Gripen's belly faced flat into the forward airflow and his speed plummeted far faster than he climbed. Like a cyclist using momentum to coast up a steep slope, then turn at the top and come racing back down before falling, he spun a hundred-and-eighty degrees on the proverbial ten-krona coin.

Except he was doing it with an eighty-five-million-dollar fighter jet. At the top of the bank, he kicked the ass over hard and punched the throttle straight into afterburner. He let himself half-fall, half-dive as he returned by the direction he'd departed.

The engine spooled up past its normal thirteen thousand foot-pounds of thrust all the way to twenty-two thousand. It was enough to slam him back in the seat despite his nose-down attitude.

A hundred meters above the ground, he yanked the nose up —hard. Riding the edge of the stall, leveling out five meters over the ice that had swallowed the aft section of Arne Sorenson's Gripen, he raced toward the van.

Any lesser jet would have taken fifteen to twenty seconds to make the turn, which would have required a much wider loop. Hugo's jet achieved the complete change of direction in six seconds and sent him back exactly along the route he'd departed by—the least expected angle of attack.

At the shore he jinked up to thirty meters. The sudden blast of the pressure suit on his lower body squeezed him hard for the brief moment he crossed five g's. It eased off the moment he leveled out, flying mere meters above the tops of snow-shrouded pines.

During that time, the shooter had loaded the second Stinger, but fumbled inserting a fresh BCU. The Battery Coolant Unit powered the sighter and supercooled the missile's target seeker. He finally inserted the round cartridge properly and gave it the quarter turn to activate it.

After aiming it at the sky, he depressed the safety-and-arming switch with his thumb at the back of the handle. The seeker registered the ultraviolet color of the background sky.

Hugo was cracking two thousand kilometers an hour, coming in at a right angle to the road, by the time the slice of the E12 came into view on his targeting screen. The turbulence of his wake ripped a snowstorm off the branches of the trees close below.

The blue van shone clear in his radar's sights despite the intervening treetops masking him visually from the shooter.

It was parked in a line of civilian cars, so using missiles wasn't an option.

Hugo selected the Mauser BK-27 revolver cannon mounted on the left fuselage close by his thigh.

The shooter by the van kept looking for an attack from the north, the direction Hugo had been turning before executing the Herbst turn.

He came in low from the east, his supersonic approach far faster than the sound that might reveal his line.

When the shooter finally spotted Hugo's plane, he swung to correct. With the jet moving at Mach Two, there was no time to center his aim. Despite not having tone on the target lock, the man by the van squeezed the forward Uncage button, which freed the missile's own target-seeking software to track the plane.

The moment Hugo had the van in his radar's sights, still not visible through the treetops, he unleashed a rain of the twenty-seven-millimeter rounds from the Mauser. In the one-point-eight seconds from target acquisition to his passage overhead, he dumped thirty-one rounds toward the van.

At Mach 3.3, half again the speed of the jet, the rounds drove toward the target outstripping even the Gripen on full afterburner. Each round—over an inch in diameter, six inches long, and weighing more than a can of Red Bull energy drink—was tipped with high explosive.

The shooter by the van squeezed the trigger, which then required three seconds to initiate the missile's release.

Eleven of the thirty-one rounds that Hugo fired struck the ground before the van, plowing into the snowbanks alongside the road and impacting the frozen ground beneath. The explosives blasted clouds of snow into the air blocking all visibility, which didn't measurably slow the rest of the rounds already in flight but blocked the Stinger missile's targeting system's view of the inbound Gripen jet.

Five more rounds punched into the road surface itself, forming large potholes that would be patched but never be quite smooth again until the whole stretch of road was repaved three years later.

The road surface, turned into shrapnel, struck the shooter several times in the legs, taking him to his knees, but he kept the Stinger aimed roughly east. Additional frozen chunks of tar made loud noises but did little damage as they sprayed the side of the blue van and took out the headlights on a Tesla Model Y that had stopped next in line at the red light.

A further nine rounds from the Mauser disappeared into the woods beyond the van. Two trees were cut down by the explosive rounds, including a twenty-five-meter Norway spruce. It would land atop the van long after it didn't matter.

Of the remaining six rounds, five hit the van. Four merely struck thin paneling, punching thumb-sized holes in the near side before blowing half-meter sections out of the far side of the van. The fifth struck the engine block, exploding on impact and blasting whole sections of the van's front-end into the trunk and rear window of the VW Passat parked in front of it—killing the driver. Which was a pity as that was supposed to be the shooter's getaway ride after he'd abandoned the van.

The final round struck the attacker in the face—after passing through the sighting mechanism of the FIM-92E Stinger missile's launcher. Because of that, the damage to his getaway car proved to be of little consequence except to its driver.

Like Kapten Sorenson, the shooter lost his head in that moment—it had ceased to exist in any readily recognizable form. Unlike Kapten Sorenson, his finger remained clamped on the trigger as his body fell, swinging the launcher's aim wide.

The sonic boom of the Gripen's passage less than fifty meters above the line of cars shattered every windshield. The safety glass in all the vehicles fragmented into thousands of tiny cubes. All the cars, except the VW Passat of course, remained drivable. However, the nearest town with a car window specialist lay thirty-six kilometers away. Three of the drivers would get frostbite driving there with no windshield despite the heavy clothing and goggles they each had donned.

Despite no verified target lock, after three seconds the Stinger launched from the dead man's hands headed southeast.

Hugo's JAS 39E Gripen raced to the west, then arced wide to return from the north.

The missile's top speed matched the Gripen's but it would never catch it anyway—failing to achieve a positive lock on target through the thick snow blown aloft by the first rounds from the Mauser gun.

A Stinger's targeting system was designed to scan for infrared to locate its quarry by its engine's heat. The purpose of pre-calibrating the weapon toward the empty sky was to register radiant ultraviolet light. By comparing that reading to the amount of UV light blocked by the aircraft's physical size, the onboard computer would attempt to distinguish the actual aircraft from hotter but smaller magnesium heat flares released by the jet's defensive system.

Finding no jet—Hugo's Gripen was returning from the north while the missile was racing to the southeast—the Stinger continued its flight.

Near the limit of its range, seven-point-nine kilometers downrange, the armed FIM-92E Stinger's computer continued to seek a target.

It identified a significant infrared signature, far lower grade than a burning flare, but perhaps a well-masked engine exhaust. It remained the brightest target available.

The UV light that had been initially registered against the sky was brightly reflected off the snow and ice on the ground. The missile's software determined that the targeted object's size blocked sufficient UV light that it wouldn't be mistaken for a mere countermeasure flare.

With a final adjustment in its flightpath, while traveling at seven hundred and forty meters per second, the Stinger missile struck.

It hit Josef—within twenty centimeters of dead center. A true testament to technological innovation.

By the time it penetrated half a meter into its target, the fuse triggered the warhead's high-explosive charge.

Josef the bull—a Rödkulla, Swedish Red Polled breed—stood in his outdoor pen pulling hay from a feeder as the ground was covered with snow and ice.

He'd won first prize at the summer Västerbotten County Fair. His owner anticipated earning a nice income from breeding him during the next season. Not unreasonable, as the locals were working to save the breed from dying out and judges had compared Josef favorably to the four bulls of the Norse Goddess Gefjon, who oversaw foreknowledge, virginity, and ploughing as part of her realm—though *none* of those three attributes were embodied in the massive bull.

Afterward, not enough remained of Josef's scale-topping seven hundred and thirteen kilos to make even one decent steak.

35

"Mike."

The call that he'd both hoped for and feared.

"Mike! Slow down or I'll hog-tie you like a water buffalo."

He kept moving toward the thin warmth of the low sun. "*Can* you hog-tie a water buffalo?" he called over his shoulder.

"You can try if you're having yourself an almighty death wish."

Not having one, or being a water buffalo, he stopped walking.

Holly stumbled up through the calf-deep snow to stand beside him.

He hadn't been aware of moving fast but saw they stood well away from the plane, the admin building, and out past the end of Runway 26. He hoped he hadn't strolled across an active runway. No, if he had, they'd already have come racing out to arrest him.

Then he had to cover his ears as a pair of Gripens punched into the sky along Runway 03. The sound took a long time to fade as if declaring how annoyed the Swedes were at losing a plane. Just wait until they found out it was sabotage.

It was Holly and Jeremy who were always the ones in the big rush, hurrying everywhere. Miranda didn't move particularly fast, but she did it with such absolute determination that it appeared she did, with Andi typically close by her side—until recently. And Taz had always looked like a streak of lightning as she shot by with her long dark hair curling in the wind she left behind.

"Looks like I finally won the hundred-meter mosey." Something Holly'd always accused him of losing because he was such a sluggard. *Slower than a camel on holiday.* Whatever that implied. He'd still never been to Australia except to change planes for Antarctica. They had the world's largest herd of feral camels wandering through the Outback but he'd never seen one outside a zoo.

"Looks like." He saw the huffs of steam flurry out in front of her. Out of breath or out of patience? "We never finished—"

"I'm done, Holly."

"Try that again, mate. Think I got someone in my ear barking up the wrong tree."

"I'm done. That's my last *Send Mike to talk to the weeping witness* interview. Tad's at the beginning of this, I'm at the end." But was he done with her?

In answer, she punched his arm so hard and unexpectedly that even flailing his arms didn't keep him out of the powdery snow that exploded into the air when he fell.

She braced her fists on her hips and glared down at him. The sun made her hair shine the way it always did. His beautiful warrior. What had he called her? *A daily royal pain in the ass.* At least he'd gotten it mostly right.

"Well," he sat up and rubbed his injured arm, though the parka had absorbed the worst of the impact. "I guess that answers that."

"Answers what?"

"Never mind, Holly. It doesn't matter." At least he'd had the good sense to buy a long parka. Holly had teased him about it, but right now it protected his butt from the snow nicely, thank you very much.

There was a long enough silence for the sun to slip an edge out past Holly's hip and shine in his face.

"I don't get what's happening," Holly dropped...no, collapsed to her knees before him despite wearing only jeans. Collapsing wasn't any familiar part of her repertoire. "Something changed, Mike. Help me understand."

"And there it is."

"What?"

Mike rubbed at his face, smearing cold snow from his heavy gloves. He yanked one off to clear the icy crystals from his eyes. "The thing I hate the most."

"Me? What did I ever do to you?"

He raised his arm in demonstration, then winced at the pain.

"Okay, I might have done that." Holly reached out to pat his arm in a surprisingly gentle gesture—but withdrew her hand before she made contact.

"Not what I meant anyway."

"Well, you're the magic man with words. If you can't do it, I don't stand a chance."

"My action girl."

"Woman!"

He nodded but she was wrong. Holly would always have the youthful spring in her step like Supergirl. At ninety, she'd still have a bounce and a chaotic energy barely contained.

"Please, Mike."

There was something he'd never heard from her before. He waved a hand at...he didn't know what. "Sure, I can talk to the ladies."

"Like—" but she bit it off before she threw Klara in his face one more time. Small favors.

"Not like it's important most of the time. My job is more about keeping Miranda sane and you out of trouble. But when the turds hit the fan—"

"It's called shit for a reason, Mike."

He ignored her. "—you're the one who jumps out of planes to save Miranda. You're the one who—without even asking for my opinion—threw Andi off the team."

"I had to!"

"No, you *chose* to. I'm not saying you were wrong," he held up his hands defensively, "but I'm not saying you were right either. Have you looked at Miranda lately, really looked at her?"

"Well, she's been a bit more *Miranda* than usual and—"

He scooped up a fistful of snow and heaved it point blank at her face.

She fell back onto her butt with a squawk more of surprise than pain—the snow here was light and powdery.

"The woman's hanging on by the thinnest thread. When was the last time someone else's emotions bothered her? *Oh look, the pilot is crying. But what information does she have?* That's her being normal, unaware of others' emotions. Instead, she has to leave the building with her dog and the noise-canceling headphones on full isolation to survive a minute of it. She's disabled only if we treat her that way. Every inch of regression over these last months is because of us. *We're* the ones who are making her disabled, Holly. Not her. You and me!"

"You and me?"

"Yes! The moment you decided that Andi had to be off the team."

"But she—"

"I know what she did, Holly. I was there! And me? Me because I didn't try to stop or question or discuss what you decided. You know the only tool I have to keep track of Miranda's emotions now?"

Holly shook her head slowly, wiping her face but missing the powder caught in her hair and sparkling in the sun.

"I watch Meg. She's my only indication. Miranda's folded so far in on herself that it takes a trained dog to sniff it out. I sure can't anymore."

"Are you saying we should try to get Andi back? After what she *did*?" Holly's anger flashed red across her features without any thought or hesitation. At least there existed no question what she felt—ever.

"I'm saying we should discuss it. Like we didn't discuss it before you threw her *off* the team. You *and* I. Or better yet, we should ask Miranda. It's *her* team, Holly, not yours. It's her life, not yours. But that's not what I'm talking about anyway."

"Then *what*?"

Figuring he had nothing else to lose, "You're a Team of One, Holly. Did you even think of talking it over with me before you kicked Andi out? Don't bother answering, we both already know the answer to that one. Ever since you blew up the damn bridge that finished your team, you've been a Team of One. Maybe since you lost your brother in that flood and your parents threw you out. Maybe even before that when you led townies into the Outback for a week at a time to live on bush tucker simply because *you* could. I'm sick to death of being stuck out here on my own. I'm through. With this team, with you. I'm heading back to Denver. At least *that* I understand."

Holly's face did something he'd never seen before, it went wholly blank. In this moment, when he desperately needed to know what she was thinking, when he wished he could take back everything he'd just said, she was more blank faced than Miranda at her most desperate.

A high whine of a jet engine sounded behind him, growing louder and louder until he had to cover his ears again. He turned to see Miranda's Citation M2 rolling up the taxiway toward them.

"No! This. Is. Not. Happening!" His shout was drowned out, then the engines cycled down as the plane pulled up nearby.

The door swung down and Jeremy leaned out.

"Come on. There's another one." And he waved them urgently aboard.

He turned to look at Holly.

This couldn't be real. It really couldn't. One lousy conversation had been spread across two days now—and never completed.

Her blue eyes remained still.

Expressionless.

Watching him.

Waiting to see what *he'd* do.

What he should do was walk away.

What he *wanted* to do was walk away.

But Holly deserved the right to respond. To answer, if she wanted to try—for once!

He couldn't leave until she'd at least had the chance.

"Bloody fucking hell." He rose to his feet.

Then he held out a hand to help her up from the snow.

She stared at it for a long moment, then took it. But only long enough to pull herself up.

The distance between them as they walked toward the plane seemed to grow with every step.

36

"I'm happy we found you," Miranda said over the cockpit intercom once they were aloft.

Mike grunted.

"There are so many people."

He leaned into the gap between their seats and looked aft.

Miranda pictured them all too easily. Holly in the sideways seat behind Mike guaranteed her some buffer from the others. In the four main seats sat Jeremy, Kurt Anderson, the head of the SHK accident investigation authority, and a General Larsson, the chief of the Swedish Air Force. He'd been in the meeting with Liisa Salo. The last seat was taken by a two-star general with a NATO patch on his sleeve. He hadn't bothered to introduce himself. Was she supposed to know who he was? She hoped not because she didn't.

Tad had taken the rearmost seat, the cushioned toilet at the very rear.

"Yes, Miranda, that *is* a lot of people."

Mike always understood. And that small truth, validating her own observation. Or was it a feeling? Whichever it was, Mike made it that much more tolerable.

"Did they say why they were traveling with us?" he asked.

"General Larsson said he didn't want to risk being a single step away from our team."

"That's nice of him."

"Why?" Miranda had wondered if, like gravity or magnetism, risk fell off by the square of the distance. Perhaps this was a Counter-inverse Square Law she was unfamiliar with, where three steps away were nine times riskier than one step, rather than one-ninth as risky as a standard Inverse Square Law would dictate.

"It's a compliment, Miranda. It means that he's very impressed by the team and wants to make sure he's first to learn what we find out."

"But if you think it up, he wouldn't be first. And if you then tell me, he'd be third at the very closest."

"*Among* the first. Along with everyone else who is close by."

"Oh." That made sense. It should have been obvious without Mike explaining it. But it hadn't been. She'd never thought to chart her ease of comprehension over time, but it qualitatively felt as if it was becoming more of an issue with each passing day rather than less. She shied away from asking herself why. The memory of the two autistic meltdowns she'd suffered since Andi had left struck terror into her heart. Was she in a deep regression? A lifelong regression?

No, she wouldn't think about that.

"So, what happened?"

"Someone shot down a JAS 39E Gripen in Storuman, five hundred and sixty-three kilometers to the north." Then she glanced down at the console. "Four hundred and ninety-seven now. They used a FIM-92E Stinger."

Mike twisted to look at her.

"That's all they said, other than asking me to go. I'm not sure why, a military attack isn't a crash." She didn't look back, instead keeping her attention on the proximity radar. Mike hadn't taken over the radio work with air traffic control when he'd joined her in the cockpit. That in itself was unusual. Not that the communication in the fifty-minute flight through central Sweden required much attention, but he normally handled that. Nor did he offer to act as pilot-in-command. He usually liked the practice.

It was one of the reasons she'd decided to make the flight from their latest meeting in Washington, DC, to the Reykjavik ISASI conference in her own plane. It was near the Citation's limits, even with stops in St. Johns, Newfoundland, and Narsarsuaq, Greenland, for fuel. Within the US and Canada, Mike had never had reason to log time on long-distance over-water flights. Though she hadn't planned on continuing to Sweden.

A complete circumnavigation?

She'd never given it serious thought. In a different political time, they might have continued right around, but with Russian airspace closed, there were no achievable connections over the Pacific. Even Amelia Earhart's old route would require two flights beyond the M2's maximum range. Perhaps if she had a bigger jet. The M2 didn't have sufficient excess payload to place a large enough auxiliary fuel tank in the cabin to span the Hawaii-to-Oakland leg.

Only her and Mike?

But Mike would want to bring Holly.

And she would want to bring—

Miranda shied away from the painful thought.

She would want to bring *Meg*. The Glen of Imaal Terrier was her only true companion now. But even if the payload was restricted to Meg and herself, the M2 still lacked the range.

Perhaps she should look into trading up to the CJ4. But she didn't need a ten-passenger jet. She could barely justify the M2, though it was proving useful. Besides, that would be a different plane. She didn't like change and her autism *hated* it. Miranda knew this one now. In the year since her father's Mooney had burned, she'd only piloted the M2 and her Sabrejet. No, she'd stay with the familiar and forego any thoughts of a circumnavigation.

Mike unharnessed and rose to his feet though they weren't up to cruise altitude yet.

Before she had a chance to point out the violation of safety protocols, he headed aft. He didn't go far.

He knelt in the area between Holly's seat and the exit door. That was good. Unable to determine quite why, she'd been worried about them. Seeing them playing in the snow together as she'd taxied up to them had been very encouraging. This too.

37

HOLLY SAT TRAPPED BETWEEN TWO DIFFERENT WORLDS. UP forward, Mike and Miranda were isolated on the intercom over their headsets. Aft, the jet's sound insulation was good enough to allow conversation among the four facing seats without headsets, yet enough engine and wind noise penetrated the hull to keep her from overhearing a word without straining.

Only Meg had joined her in this nowhere land, coming to sit in her lap from the moment she'd sat down. Barred from her mistress' lap by her need to access the flight controls, Holly supposed she should feel complimented at being the dog's second choice.

Her position left her far too much time to contemplate Mike's declaration.

He was done with the NTSB and...done with her.

It was as if the words made no sense. Perhaps containing a hidden meaning beyond her capacity to uncover. Without Mike, would there even be a team? A Miranda? A Holly Harper? He was the glue that tied together everyone else's raging oddities. He—

—squatted in front of her as if conjured by her thoughts.

"Someone shot down a Gripen."

It took her a moment to translate Mike's words from noise to meaning. "Other than the attack on Ingrid Eklund's jet?"

"Shot," he reminded her. "With a Stinger."

"Where?"

"An hour north of here. Still in Sweden."

"One domino too many." She heard the pieces rattling against each other. Like they were being mixed together, not in some orderly line ready to fall.

"That's what I was thinking." He held up three fingers. "Dead Defence Minister on the LuftSvenska flight crashed by a sleeper-agent copilot. Sabotage with some tech rig on Ingrid's ejection handle. And now a direct shootdown."

She nodded. "So who would want to beat up on Sweden?"

Mike didn't answer and she didn't need to ask. He waited, asking her to confirm his thinking.

Why would someone want to harass Sweden? Who would have a real hate-on for them? Not war, but demoralizing, painful attacks.

"Demoralizing..." she tried the word aloud. "Who would want to...*punish* Sweden?" As soon as she asked, the answer was obvious.

Mike must have seen it in her face because he finally whispered, "NATO."

NATO wouldn't want to attack their newest member. But Russia was pissed as hell at Finland and now Sweden being granted membership. What better way to take out their anger than a whole series of hidden attacks.

"No. Wait. Article 5."

"Sure," Mike nodded. "An attack on one NATO member nation is an attack on all. But the language isn't that simple. It requires an *armed* attack, which the first two weren't. Does being shot down by a US-built Stinger missile count? I don't know. And NATO is only required to do whatever is necessary to *restore and maintain* regional security."

"Which means that as long as there is no direct threat to regional security..."

"It all becomes a gray area of whether or not to act."

Holly glanced aft at the generals who'd boarded—the two officers she'd busted in on while looking for Mike in the men's bathroom. The one-star with a Swedish arm patch and flyer wings had a place. But the two-star with a NATO patch on his sleeve? He finally made sense.

"Do you think he's here to..." she didn't want to finish the question, it made her shoulders hunch.

"...to decide if NATO needs to go to war? Yes, I'm afraid I do." Mike finished it for her.

"Against...Russia? But that's World War III."

Mike nodded carefully.

"Well, shit. That stinks worse than a bag of dingo breath."

"Never tried that myself," his half smile told her that he wasn't quite as done and gone as he thought he was. Except that wasn't the key topic of the moment.

"How do we find out what's going on?"

"Well, I thought that you'd take care of that."

"Me? Sure, mate, I'll just gather up my sexual wiles and bat my eyelashes—in ways you're so fond of pointing out—at that NATO two-star. I'll make him give me the nuclear launch codes while I'm at it."

Mike rolled his eyes. "*He* doesn't have the connections you do."

"He doesn't?" But then she remembered.

Maybe he didn't.

She pulled out her phone.

Mike patted her on the knee, then kissed her on the forehead before returning to the cockpit. Not half as done with her as he thought—at least she hoped that's what it meant.

38

Pizza? Frozen Stouffer's Meat Lovers Lasagna? A bag of Doritos with some plasticized fake guacamole dip?

Harry faced the refrigerator that Heidi had overstocked before she left.

His willpower always turned to crap the minute Heidi was gone farther than the office. With the best of intentions, he kept looking at Heidi's standard crackers, cheese, and carrot sticks with hummus lunch, and had no idea how she lived on that. Lunch was about salami sandwiches, which had become turkey ones. A foot-long loaded chili dog, which had become a bowl of chili. At least when he had a hack on, she let him hit the pizza hard—though even he could no longer face the meat-a-saur specials he used to live on. Just so damn heavy on the gut.

Of course, it wasn't lunchtime. It was barely seven a.m. So, he'd go for the cold pizza and some of last night's leftover spaghetti. Except he didn't see that anywhere. Oh, right, he'd finished both of those after Heidi's two a.m. opiate reminder call.

Wait? What was all the crap food doing here?

Oh, damn. He sniffled. Heidi knew he had no willpower

and was coddling him while he was laid up. Damn but that woman was awesome.

Still, the pang for junk lay there in his gut. Or was it just panic eating? His reputation felt like it was sliding down the drain. He hadn't uncovered trace one of Jeremy's copilot sleeper agent. Clean prints. No facial recognition anywhere before already being in place in Italy. Like he'd materialized out of thin air, which maybe he had.

If you didn't have a Star Trek transporter, what did you need to happen to make that your superpower? Not kryptonite or a radioactive spider. Not Doctor Strange's magic or being struck by Flash's lightning. Maybe— Maybe he needed more sleep.

His phone rang and he slammed the refrigerator closed, barely making good his escape, and crutched his way back to the bed, grabbing the phone before the last ring.

"Yo!"

"Yo, yourself, mate. I need to place a call."

"This isn't AT&T." Then he caught up with who was on the phone. "Holly?" She never called him. But she was also the only woman who CIA Director Clarissa Reese feared. That placed her just one thin notch below Heidi on his list of seriously cool people.

"That's who you're talking to."

"And you need to place a call?"

"Might've said something like that."

"Must be one hell of a call if you're pinging me."

"I'll be on the ground in thirty minutes. By that time I need an untraceable pipe, untraceable in either direction. No one can ever be allowed to know it existed—ever. I don't want even you to be able to see it. That tight."

He laughed.

Holly didn't.

Harry sobered. "What the hell?"

"This goes one bit sideways, it costs a very nice lady her life. And I'm not talking about me."

"You're never nice."

He meant it as a joke but the silence that crashed down left him plenty of time to pick out the sound of a jet engine on her end, the way it sounded inside a plane.

"Okay, what are the endpoints?"

"Me," Holly's voice sounded painfully businesslike, "on my encrypted phone in nowhere Sweden, and a number I'll give you at the time in Moscow. Is there any way to make sure the person is alone before you ring the phone?"

Harry could already picture about half the masking he'd need—thirty minutes was going to be tight for that level of obfuscation—when the question registered. "Uh, sure. Kinda. I can listen and, depending on her on-system fortification, maybe take a peek out both the front and back cameras. Of course, if it's in a purse or pocket, all you'll see is a bunch of fabric. Seen that enough times to gag a hamster. Better if I ring once and hang up. That way they draw it out, then I turn everything on."

"Okay, plan on doing that. I'll call you the second I'm down."

"Holly, about what I just said..." Harry stopped. He was talking to himself.

39

Inessa's phone rang a second time, five minutes after the first. No one there by the time she answered. It was a ten-digit number, just like all Moscow numbers, but not in any form she'd ever seen: 07734-07734.

This time, as she'd dragged her phone out of her purse, it had come into her hand upside down. Inverted, did the digits spell out...*hELLO-hELLO?* In English?

Yet no one was there when she answered.

Her husband worked at the FSB and she'd learned much from him how to look beyond the obvious. She, in turn, had helped him become one of the most powerful men in Russia's Federal Security Service—the KGB's replacement.

The obvious? Some prankster was ringing her phone. The non-obvious? Someone was ringing her phone but somehow knew she wasn't alone.

It was as good an excuse as any. This tearoom meeting had started late and continued to drag on tediously with nothing productive to show for two hours listening.

Every wife, mistress, and more than a few men wanted the ear of General Turgenev's wife now that it was clear he'd been chosen as General Murov's right hand. Murov ran the FSB and was in turn the president's right hand. That alone made her one of the most powerful women in the country. If they only knew the reality—well, she'd be dead.

Inessa was glad of the interruption. Information flowed to her in volumes that she'd never anticipated. Often from the sycophantic climbers hoping she'd pass to her husband some key revelation or cocked-sideways plan. But far more came from discontent or simply gossipy wives and mistresses of the oligarchy. She'd become a clearing house for so much information that she had to be selective about what she dared send to the West.

Her present rule: without at least two corroborations she ignored everything.

And her tea companion this afternoon, General Garin's mistress, had fallen so far since his sudden death—never say *execution* in modern Russia—that she had nothing to offer except her anguish.

"It's been lovely seeing you, dear. Please remember: the snail is coming, who knows when it arrives."

The girl took comfort from the old proverb, missing the truth that another snail coming for her was age. She was no longer twenty, and thirty loomed close. The chances of another such man as General Garin scooping her up was unlikely, especially not with the unstated stigma under which Garin had died. It now attached itself to the pretty brunette by association. What had made his death *most* unusual was that General Garin had been father to the president's mistress, but that very sinecure had made him careless.

Inessa bowed low to the old Chinese grandmother who no longer ran this tearoom but still came every day to watch over her daughter's efforts. She received a polite nod, more honor than most were given.

Inessa took a last look around as she wouldn't be able to

come here for a time. Not until Garin's lost mistress had found a lesser station to fall to and would be unable to afford to return regularly on the chance of Inessa visiting again. The low tables, tall vases, and the white-washed brick walls adorned with rolls of calligraphy and exquisite drawings offered a brief escape to another world that Inessa would miss.

When she bowed a second time, Old Grandmother watched her carefully. Had the wizened woman guessed that Inessa might not return for a long while?

Perhaps. But Inessa was out of time for such considerations. The first two calls had been precisely five minutes apart. She hoped there'd be a third, she doubted there'd be a fourth.

With thirty seconds to spare, she stepped outside to the sidewalk. A bitter wind sliced along the Moscow streets, rushing straight down from the Arctic. But she couldn't take a cab; most of them had listening devices, in addition to nosy drivers only too glad to make extra money reporting suspicious behaviors to the FSB's numerous minions. Even her husband's position wouldn't protect her from those.

She put her back to the wind and began to walk slowly south. Her apartment lay a few blocks to the west, but her husband's office lay five blocks to the south. Curiously, the closer she came to the Lubyanka Building, the safer she became. The FSB's monitors always made the mistake of thinking that sedition lay either inside the building or far away, creating a security gap around their headquarters in the heart of Moscow.

Her phone, now clutched in her hand, rang again—only once.

On the off chance that she was right, she held it facing outward and performed a slow turn. Other than passing cars and trucks, and a few men rushing by hunched as deeply as possible against the hard wind, she walked alone.

The phone rang again.

"Hello. Hello," she answered to prove that she'd received the message.

"Who shot your husband?" A woman asked.

For an instant Inessa froze in terror, then realized it was an identity test. A very specific one—something only two people in the world knew, three if she counted her husband. "You did. With a Taser."

"I did."

"How is my almost-sister?" Inessa asked in turn. It too might be construed as a test, but she truly wanted to know. She'd shared Miranda Chase's parents as the mentors who had taught her how to live life.

"She's been better. Not as bad as you last saw her, but..." Even the worried tone didn't scare her. As long as she never again had occasion to hear that poor woman's soul-scraping scream. Its memory still woke her on occasion from soundest sleep.

"Now tell me why you took such a risk for both of us by calling me directly. It must be very important." In fact, knowing who and what Holly Harper was, the biting Arctic wind was the warmest thing she felt.

"Would you know if the GRU were launching a clandestine attack on Sweden? Perhaps as punishment for joining NATO."

Inessa blinked in surprise. That was exactly the kind of information that *should* have come to her. The Armed Forces' Intelligence Directorate would be involved. Such an attack would take months of planning and should have easily filtered down in a society where the only true economy remaining lay in the trade of secrets.

"We have a maximum of two more minutes that we're safe to speak," Holly said when Inessa didn't immediately respond.

Rather than questioning who had hacked her phone and set up such a secure connection, Inessa sifted through everything she knew. She even considered the pitiful leavings that Garin's ex-mistress had offered like stray leaves left at the bottom of a tea cup's fine white porcelain.

"One minute," Holly counted down. She didn't push, but there was an urgency to her tone.

"Nothing. And I *should* have heard. I know many of the women in places to be overhearing of such a thing in both the Directorate and the elite military units they command directly."

"Then any guesses as to who?"

An old proverb came to mind. "Don't dig a hole for someone else or you will fall into it yourself."

"Someone setting up Russia to be the villain?"

"Perhaps. As if we were not already the world's antagonist. Does that help?"

"It might at that. Thank you."

"Do let Mir—" better not to use any names no matter how secure the call. "Please tell my almost-sister that I think of her each day."

"I will." And Holly was gone.

The bitter wind no longer caught and swirled about her heart. Finally there was a crime that her beloved country had not committed. She hoped that her Western friend made sure that Russia didn't pay the price for it.

40

"What if it wasn't Russia?" Mike repeated Holly's words in wonder. "But everything points to—"

"What if it wasn't?" she insisted. "Who stands to gain from that?"

"How did you..." But he didn't finish the question. She'd told him of the woman she'd met when she parachuted into Kaliningrad to rescue Miranda—a Russian patriot fighting to save her country from its own worst self.

They stood in the snow along the E12 road. There was no evidence to be had from the two vehicles that remained. A tow truck even now hauled the shattered VW Passat off into the failing daylight. The blue van, bullet-shot and spatter-painted with frozen brain matter, crouched beneath spotlights. Two p.m. and the three-hour day had already ended here in Storuman; the long winter twilight being hurried along by fast-gathering clouds.

It was cold enough that it hurt to breathe, though Mike figured that was better than smelling the dead guy's brains.

A trio of military police stood nearby with their submachine guns tucked in the crook of their arms, scanning the horizon for fresh attackers. Two police, locals by their gear, conducted a thin stream of traffic along the far shoulder.

By the van lay a pair of five-foot-long tubes, one still attached to what Holly had told him were targeting hardware for MANPADS. Man-Portable Air-Defense Systems, she'd had to explain. *Stinger. Nasty against aircraft. SAM—Surface-to-Air Missile.*

SAM he understood.

The Swedes had already traced the serial numbers to Pápa Air Base in Hungary. NATO's database also showed both Stinger missiles and a targeting system were still logged as being in weapons storage at the military base there.

The two-star NATO general they'd brought with them said that a combined SAS and Delta Force QRF—quick reaction force—had taken control of the storage site and all of its staff while they themselves had been flying from Uppsala to Storuman.

They are flying in a quartermaster team from Brussels to conduct a manual inventory against records.

Which would take forever. Pápa was a primary US-stocked supply point for all of NATO—they stored everything from rifle rounds to massive C-17 cargo jets capable of spanning the globe for whoever in NATO needed them.

Jeremy, Miranda, and Meg had been taken away on snowmobiles to inspect what remained of the cockpit of the downed Gripen. It would take a diver to inspect the rest of the plane, though there was little doubt about the sequence of events with so many witnesses.

A pair of Gripens raced by close overhead before circling down to land at the main runway beyond the trees. They'd come to reinforce the other two jets stationed here. Löjtnant Hugo Bodin, who had shot the blue van from his own Gripen, was presently in debrief with the Swedish general who had accompanied them. Neither general had wanted Mike and

Holly in the room, so they'd come out to see the wreckage. Thirty seconds had been enough. As it wasn't a crash scenario, Mike decided against arguing.

"Who else stands to gain?" Mike headed up the road to get clear of the roaring chain saw as they began clearing the shot-down tree that had landed atop the blue van, caving in the passenger compartment and pinning it in place. Nothing except the two Stingers' crates and a standard winter emergency kit had been in the rear.

"By attacking Sweden," Holly added from close beside him.

Every time Mike tried to think of someone shooting someone else on purpose, he automatically thought of the final gun battles that had ended his career as a Denver advertising mogul. Okay, not a mogul—he'd never climbed that high—but at least he'd been a player.

The Giovanni brothers had taken out their own sister for playing hardball in using Mike's ad agency to discredit their firms. But they hadn't counted on Mike feeding information to the FBI. The FBI heavyweights, the National Security Branch, had swooped in and cleared out the Giovannis—along with the military, congressional, and diplomatic corps contacts who'd greased the wheels in a massive military secret sales scam.

"If I hit you, you hit some other guy, then who in heck knows what loops back to bite us all in the ass," he summed it up for Holly. All he'd wanted back then was some fun with a hot lady and a good, lucrative con.

Back then?

Wasn't that what he wanted now?

Yes, he assured himself, *that's absolutely what I want.*

A passing truck swirled the falling snow, forcing them to close their eyes in its wake. Storm coming. The dark blue of the evening sky was disappearing much faster than the daylight. Heavy clouds sent thin, sharp flakes whirling down on a rising wind to sting his exposed face, clear portents of more to come.

"Who do you think, Holly?"

"Like I'd have a clue if you don't."

Well, he didn't. "We need someone smarter than us."

"Ooo, there's a toughie, mate. Should I start a list, or would Australia's latest census rolls be enough?"

Mike wanted to laugh. He really did. A laugh would help right now. Nope, not gonna happen.

"Heidi or Harry?" Holly suggested a little more realistically. "Or," she swallowed hard, "Clarissa?"

"Not my first choice." None of them were a fan of the CIA Director. Clarissa Reese was smart, effective, and as ruthless as one of Holly's saltie crocodiles with the scruples to match. "Who knows what her agenda is? I half think she'd welcome a war with the Russians as long as she could find a way to be running it."

Holly gazed off into the distance...a distance no longer showing beyond the snowstorm approaching over the wide flat land that had looked to stretch all the way to the North Pole.

"We'd better think of something soon. If we get snowed in here, we may not get out until the Spring thaw."

"I met someone." Holly said it so softly he'd have missed it, except the latest car whipping the snow at them was an electric Tesla.

Perfect. Of course she had. That explained...absolutely nothing. Unless it was Tad Jobson? But she'd said it wasn't, unless that had changed over the last hour.

She yanked out her phone, dialed, and waited. "Hello, Valentina. This is Holly Harper. We met last spring at Dulles International."

And Mike felt about two inches tall, short enough to get lost in the snow building up on the road's shoulder. When they'd been bringing Miranda back from the UK, after Andi left the team, Holly hadn't boarded the connecting flight to Seattle with the two of them. Instead, she'd slipped in twenty minutes later, the last second before they closed the cabin door.

Had an interesting meeting, was all the queen of Holly's Team of One had said. A week later, the law firm run by Andi Wu's family had ceased to exist as they were all arrested.

So who the hell was Valentina?

41

Eight a.m.

Val Mills glared at the clock as she answered her phone.

Russia didn't really wake up for business until nine a.m. Washington, DC, time. By five p.m. in Moscow, enough Russians had left work early and filtered into the bars and restaurants for her people to go to work.

As head of CIA's Russia desk, experience had taught her that those were her best intelligence gathering points. Which meant she slept in and worked late because the Russians appeared to think three or four in the morning their time was finally the hour to get drunk enough to turn stupid.

The in-between times left her plenty of opportunity to look at all the reports generated by DC, NATO, and EU people who wouldn't know Russia if it bit them. And foolishly trusted them until it did.

In her world, eight a.m. was early, but it rarely felt this harsh. Then she looked at the pillow beside her and decided that harsh might be a massive understatement.

Davey Willows, that new analyst on the Africa desk, lay beside her. Fifteen years her junior, or twenty, he'd brought an energy she'd long since assumed to be in her past despite her daily routine at the gym. Dance, drinks, and some serious sex had sustained them to nearly Moscow-late hours. As a woman of fifty who worked fourteen-hour days, she needed her beauty sleep. Or at least enough to function. Two hours didn't begin to cut it.

"Uh, who is this?" She tried again to focus on the voice jabbering on the phone.

The woman stopped, then slowly repeated herself as if speaking to a numbskull. She was. Or Val wished she was as a headache began throbbing.

Holly Harper?

Normally her brain cataloged names easily, but this wasn't one of her field operatives. One of her staffers or analysts? No.

Dulles International? Then she remembered the warrior she'd met at the airport's Dunkin' Donuts—now just Dunkin' of all ridiculous corporate name changes—last April. They'd met for mere minutes, and the woman had been thoroughly intimidating. Not nasty, simply so competent that it radiated off her in waves.

"Uh, hold on." She slid out of bed, away from the oblivious Davey Willows, and headed to her home office, only noting as she shut the door that she was naked. When was the last time she'd slept naked? More relevant, when was the last time she'd taken a significantly younger man into her bed so that she'd wanted to *be* naked?

There wasn't a scrap of clothing here in her office. Not so much as a paisley bandana. The tall glass windows of her condo looked out at that new skyscraper going up in the block across the road—thankfully to the side of her view of the Potomac.

The tiers of steel and concrete were filled with construction guys.

Easily able to see where the morning sunlight poured into her curtainless office.

She retreated to the most shadowed corner.

"Holly Harper." She said it to anchor her brain and battle the rising hangover that was the payback for the reason that so many things had happened the prior evening.

Haven't had that much to drink in years. Was she still drunk? Didn't matter. *Haven't consumed that much since He had decided to move on to a seventeen-year-old—one-third his age. If only he'd chosen a fifteen-year-old, I could have thrown him in jail.*

Christ, was that how I ended up in bed with Davey Willows? Trying to match he-who-must-not-be-named-ever-again? Pretty much dead on the money. Does following in his footsteps make me too sad to live? Oh yeah!

"Get it together, woman." Holly's laugh did more to sober her up than anything else.

Val froze, wondering how much of the interior dialog she'd mumbled aloud.

"I'm trying. Trust me, I'm trying." And quite why she was confessing that to a total stranger—

"Let's focus on Russia...for now," Holly's voice teased her hard enough for it to bounce off any still alcohol-soaked neurons and plunge directly into her hungover ones.

"Russia. Right. I'm good at Russia." Though her brain clearly remained offline.

"Have you seen the news on Sweden?"

"I thought we were talking about Russia?"

Holly sighed, then updated her on recent events. By the end of her explanation, Valentina felt painfully sober, and still very naked.

"Two questions. First, have you heard anything about this on the Russian grapevine?"

Valentina should have if it was there to find. It was the purpose of her job, to know what Russia would do next in advance of their actually doing it. "Uh...nope." Still sounding as dumb as a toadstool.

That reminded her how last night had started. Davey was a brilliant analyst. Discussion had led to drinks. Many drinks. Which had led to stupid, and not very skilled on his part, sex. She wasn't *so* out of practice that she couldn't judge that. His fearsomely youthful energy only compensated for so much, which last night had been more than enough for her. A rematch? Not without another serious round of alcohol she had no interest in repeating.

While still at the social, chatting-after-work drinks stage, he'd told her about the amazing communication systems they were discovering between plants—particularly fungal mycelium. The level of communication carried out underground included reproduction timing, water resource reporting, and even warnings of direct attack. He'd recently read an article that showed they basically screamed when cut down and other plants in the network responded by altering nutrient flows and caching energy—their sole defenses against the depredations of humankind.

Which meant that in taking Davey home, she'd been literally dumber than a *toadstool*.

"Okay, second question. Who wants to convince Sweden that Russia had attacked them?"

"Why would they... Oh. Punishment for joining NATO." Her brain finally came back online. She began pacing her office, as she often did during phone calls. The plush carpet felt good against her bare feet.

Bare feet.

Bare person.

She retreated to the shadows again and turned her back to avoid seeing if she'd attracted a leering lineup of construction workers.

"So, who might *frame* Russia? They'd do that because..." she often started questions to see how easily her subconscious filled them in.

"Article 5," she and Holly said in unison.

Val continued alone, "An attack on one is an attack on all. Do you seriously think someone is trying to provoke a war between NATO and Russia? Never mind." The question answered itself. Holly wouldn't have called her if she'd thought otherwise.

And someone trying to frame Russia almost made sense. But could she prove it?

"I'll need some time on this."

"Okay, I'll hold."

"Not so much with the time, I guess."

"Not so much," Holly agreed.

"Okay, let's start with the unlikely. I've seen no indications that the US particularly cares about Russia at the moment. We're too worried about China and Taiwan. And we'd much rather that Russia, NATO, and the EU take care of themselves wrangling over Ukraine for a while, which is why we're tossing enough arms their way to keep it out of our hair for now."

"And of all people, as a CIA director, you should have heard if it was the US sabotaging Sweden in Russia's name. China then?"

Val considered, caught herself starting to pace, then went and sat on the carpet in the back corner of her office. She held up one finger for the US simply to distract her body's unthinking tendencies from pacing. "They'd benefit from a war either way, but Russia would ask for aid if it became major. China's knows this and knows that we'd land hard on their asses if they did that."

"Scratch China," Holly noted.

Val held up a second finger. Then ticked off three more, "Southeast Asia is too far away. India has too many of its own problems with Pakistan and China to care. The Middle East is a narcissistic trainwreck at the moment. Anyone makes a wrong move and the Saudis will cut off their oil or the Israelis will circumcise them with a launch of Shrike missiles."

"Turkey."

Out of fingers because her other hand held the phone, Val raised the big toe on her right foot. "They're still benefitting from walking that thin line of appeasing both the US and Russia. In the last month or so they're finally realizing that Russia is falling apart after seeing how they're utterly failing at taking over Ukraine. After years of going the other way, Turkey is suddenly shifting to align more with the US. Though not a chance are they ready to cut ties with the East yet."

"That probably leaves the little people. I can't see the UK, France, or Germany doing something like this."

Val counted three more toes, leaving her staring at the pinky toe on her right foot.

The one on her bare right foot attached to her bare right leg.

She checked, she was still sitting down. Still no sight lines from the construction site to here behind the big philodendron. That was okay then. She stuck one of her five extended fingers into the soil. She made a mental note to water it today, then looked around for something to wipe away the dirt on, finally using the spine of Dostoevsky's *Crime and Punishment* in the original Russian. Rodion Raskolnikov was no smarter in Russian than he'd been in English.

Her foot was cramping from the effort to keep her toes spread.

Her little toe, low and to the right of all the bigger toes that — "No way."

"No way, what?"

"Picture a map of Europe, now picture the little toe of a right foot." And, once again, she'd proved that your average mushroom would blow her away on an IQ test.

"Uh..."

Of course Holly wouldn't have a chance of figuring out something as ridiculous as—

"Georgia?"

"Remember 2008," Val liked how that supported her argument. And that Holly *had* understood. Did that only move Holly up the intelligence quotient, or did they both get to outsmart a toadstool?

"That's weird as..." Holly tapered off.

"Yes, but it kind of fits." Plus it saved her from having to shift to her left foot to track more toe-country equivalencies. "They aren't a NATO member nation yet but they want to be. If I was them, I'd be scared as hell of Russia trying to pull a Ukraine on them before they can be accepted. That creates a major need to have someone else deal with Russia ASAP. They sent their Spec Ops teams into Donetsk and Crimea back in 2014, on the Ukrainian side, to help keep it out of their own back yard."

"It does fit." Holly paused for the span of thirty seconds while Val studied her left toes and wondered who hid under each of them. "Can you get me someone to talk to there?"

Val almost bungled that question in surprise. Holly had reached some warrior decision that fast. But Val wasn't drunk and mental activity had purged a significant portion of the hangover. Not someone *to call;* someone to talk to. This was the woman who had parachuted alone into Russia to rescue her friends.

Holly Harper would be headed to Georgia—in person.

"Yes, I have contacts there."

"Good. We'll be airborne soon. Five or six hours transit time."

"I'll be ready."

Holly paused before speaking, "You got it together, Val?"

It was nice of Holly to ask. An offer to listen, by someone

outside the CIA but with heavy-duty security clearance so that she could relax a bit. Val might take her up on that over drinks someday—over a *single* drink someday—but that's not what Holly needed right now.

"Yeah, I'm good to go."

"Goodonya!" And Holly hung up.

Val inspected her right toes and the five spread fingers of her right hand. Was Georgia logical, or was she sending Holly on a wild goose chase? She supposed that they'd know soon enough.

She slipped along the wall of her home office and ducked across the hall to her bedroom without crossing the construction project's sightlines.

Davey Wilson still slept the sleep of the sated.

Did she have it together? Not even close.

But if a seriously cute thirty-something-year-old—please let him be at least thirty—wanted to ravage her fifty-year-old body, who was she to complain. She had to leave for work soon; there wasn't any time to waste.

So she didn't waste any.

She was already naked after all, saving time right there.

Val, and her toes and fingers, pounced.

42

"How many more?" Chief Kancheli asked. *How many more attacks on Sweden would it take to tip NATO into war with Russia?*

Eight months as a direct-report to the Chief of the Georgian Intelligence Service, Pavle still shook with nerves each time he climbed the stairs to this office. Chief K—as he was known behind his back, and just as stone-faced as Agent K, Tommy Lee Jones, in *Men in Black*—loomed behind his desk.

Pavle did his best not to cower.

Chief K didn't need any artifice, like guest chairs with shortened legs, to loom.

The blocky triangular three-story building that was GIS headquarters squatted behind its towering protective wall. Only this one office and a deluxe conference room jutting above them all saw over the wall. The chief's office had floor-to-ceiling glass that looked out over the Tbilisi Sea as the nine-kilometer-long reservoir was known—he sat with his back to the only view, a backlit shadow of doom.

No taller than Pavle himself, he still loomed. Chief K went *all* the way back. Since the time of the breakaway from the collapsing Soviet Union over thirty years ago, Kancheli had adapted to the changing intelligence service until he had risen to the top fifteen years ago. Through it all—poverty, political chaos, the Rose Revolution, and Georgia's long hard climb into the top third of the world's Human Development Index—the wily bastard had been the lone survivor within the intelligence community.

Not that anyone would dare bring their tongue against him. Rumor said speaking ill of Chief K, even softly atop a distant mountaintop, was an assured death sentence. Perhaps even God himself might strike you down; someone definitely watched over the chief.

Kancheli had even managed to survive the brutal Russian war of 2008 in South Ossetia. The Russians had infiltrated massive troops through the Roki Tunnel, one of the few passages under the Caucasus Mountains to the north, then instigated the locals to draw the Georgian military into battle with random attacks leveling whole villages. When Georgia attempted to rout the rebels, the Russians had dropped the hammer.

Word was, if Chief Kancheli hadn't spotted the ploy when he did, the whole of Georgia might now be Russian. He'd escaped the Russians' ethnic cleansing of Georgians from South Ossetia with a withering scar all down the right side of his face and a limp that didn't stop him slipping unnoticed into your office and scaring the shit out of you with a snapped question.

Pavle met Kancheli's gaze as well as he could. "It's difficult to estimate. We know that they're still chasing cause and effect, though they're doing it awfully fast. Some sort of a civilian team —we think. We only had the two agents there in position to give us any form of a report. One is still returning from his putative holiday to Estonia and the other was the driver of this car."

Pavle held up a tablet computer and played the online

video he'd spotted. Some Swede had posted it minutes ago on social media. It showed a phalanx of security around a shattered blue van, and a badly mangled red VW Passat. A lovely blonde and an equally handsome guy huddled nearby.

"The man in the van was a fanatic. We convinced him that this was Allah's work and he is no great loss. The driver of the VW was our deep-cover man. Also, rumor has it that they dropped a Quick Reaction Force on the Hungarian Air Base where our fanatic liberated the Stingers."

"Exposure?"

"Our inside man in Hungary knows nothing beyond the money in his account. We're safe there. Still, I'd give NATO only hours before they start tracing the other missing armament."

"Then we should act quickly. There are other assets. Proceed."

Dismissed, Pavle felt the noose tighten about his neck with each step down to his office.

43

"I KNOW WHERE WE NEED TO GO. GEORGIA. THAT ONE," HOLLY held up her snow-caked right boot and pointed at it. "The one under the little toe."

His face must have reflected his inner *Huh?*

"Picture my foot on a map of Europe. Come on."

And she'd raced away. Mike hustled after her for the two kilometers from the destroyed van to Storuman Air Base through the growing storm.

The little toe? Really? Mike tried to picture it. Should it bother him that he could?

If a map of Europe with the width of a person's foot were laid out, Scandinavia would be the nail of the big toe. Twisting the foot at a slight outward angle placed France and Spain under the ball of the foot with the UK running close alongside. The Mediterranean as the arch. The big countries running down the toes: Germany, Poland, Ukraine. Then well to the right side of the foot, a small country beneath the little toe, Georgia.

He wished it didn't fit...but it did.

"Get NATO...and Russia's attention...to Sweden and Finland," Holly huffed out between blasts of ice-laden wind. "Georgia...keeps ticking away. Safe off...to the side."

Mike kept his breath for himself and stayed tight on her heels.

Once again, he was following along in Holly's wake. No consultation. No pause for calm consideration. Or for a deep breath.

Here's the answer. Go! Like she'd been fired out of a gun at birth and still showed no signs of slowing down.

Georgia? He wasn't even that clear on where the country Georgia was. Under the little toe, that much he understood. South of Turkey on the Mediterranean? No, that was Syria, Lebanon, and Israel all backed by Jordan. On the Black Sea? Ukraine and Russia across the top, Turkey across the bottom, oh, and Georgia to the east side of the sea.

Where were they going?

Again, obvious answer. Holly always jumped into the middle of the fray. Georgia.

"Hey! Whoa!"

Holly kept hustling ahead along the narrow road that served as a taxiway connecting the E12 highway to the military airfield back in the trees. With the wind mostly blocked—back here the approaching storm made pretty flurries—she had to have heard him.

And chosen to ignore him!

He grabbed the hood flopping off the back of her parka and gave it a hard yank. He caught her off-stride and she went tumbling into the snowbank.

She slapped for her knife as she rolled, but all her mitten grabbed was a handful of snowpants. His lucky day, again triggering her SASR attack mode, but *not* being stabbed by his lover.

Before she switched tactics and launched herself at him in some lethal form of hand-to-hand combat, he held up a gloved palm.

"Stop, Harper. Just stop!"

She remained hunkered in a crouch but didn't attack. Why had he ever thought this relationship was in any way charming? His near-death experience in Denver was one time too many. So why had he signed up to have it be a daily possibility by the woman sharing his bed?

"You're talking about flying to Georgia?"

Holly's glare answered that.

"Taking on whoever one-on-one?" Why did he bother asking? "Well, you can't take Miranda."

Holly rocked back on her heels and tipped her head sideways. At least now she was listening.

Then, so fast he never saw it happen, she grabbed his parka and dragged him into the snowbank with her.

He came up out of the snow sputtering—to see a Gripen jet zipping along the road, emerging from the swirling snow to overrun where he'd been standing moments before. The pilot looked down at him in surprise, probably wondering what the hell he was doing on a clearly posted No Access road. Then the heat of the exhaust washed over them in a thick stink of burned Jet A fuel.

He pushed to his feet—

And Holly yanked him down again—moments before the wingtip of the second jet passed through where his head had been.

He definitely should *not* have been thinking about near-death experiences. He'd forgotten fighter jets tended to travel in pairs. The rising wind and his parka's hood had masked the sounds.

Holly stood up, but Mike decided to remain in the snow.

"You can't take Miranda," he repeated from his place of safe repose.

"Why not?"

"Holly, when did you turn stupid? It doesn't become you."

Holly stared off into the distance. Her eyes finally refocused and she looked down at him, "Is she really that close to the edge?"

Mike wanted to point out she wasn't the only one. He let his silence be his answer.

Holly dropped down to sit in the snow opposite him. "They've downed three aircraft in twenty-four hours. We've got to stop this or the horror show is only just beginning."

"A horror show that's only going to push Miranda that much harder," Mike pointed out.

"And the World War that happens if NATO and Russia go head-to-head?"

She was right. Mike knew the answer as well. He hated it, of course, but something so obvious couldn't be brushed aside as easily as having his head pithed by the missile hanging from a fighter jet's wingtip.

He was done—except he wasn't.

He'd checked out. Ready to head home; a word that had only the dodgiest of meanings to him.

But if he walked away? War!

"Why the hell couldn't this have landed in someone else's lap?"

Holly flapped her hands helplessly. "We could call Drake or the President, but this whole scenario is only a guess. They'd probably laugh their asses off at us. Well, maybe not, but then we're all up in bureaucratic snarls and questions sent to the Georgian government who, if we're right, is the one trying to start the war in the first place. We're the action team on the ground, Mike. That means something. We have the best information and the lowest profile. No one can match that. Not before NATO General Sandor Kurbanov tells his people to pull the trigger on Article 5."

After looking both ways for passing jets, he rose carefully. "Let's go talk to Miranda."

"But—"

"We're on *her* team, Holly. Try to remember that."

44

Miranda forced herself to listen. Even with diagrams that Mike drew on the white board in the small room at Storuman Air Base that served as dining hall and conference room, she didn't understand how the pieces connected. Or perhaps she could understand them if she wanted to. But then why wouldn't she want to? They made it sound terribly important. She made a note that there had to be a difference, but she didn't understand that either.

The NATO general listened very carefully as if hanging on every word. How did one *hang* on a word? It didn't strike her as either a metaphor or a simile. She made a note to ask about that later as well.

Jeremy was actively nodding his head, asking only occasional questions.

When Mike was done and the silence stretched long enough that it was clear no one else had anything to ask, she sought the only clarification she could think of.

"Is there a plane crash in Georgia I need to know about? If so, I shouldn't go unless the GAA specifically requests my help.

The NTSB rarely travels outside the US except by explicit invitation of the country's investigating Aviation Authority."

"No, Miranda, there's no plane crash there."

"Then I don't understand what you're asking."

Mike didn't look to Holly as he so often did when he was thinking.

"There's nothing else we can learn from the Gripen," Miranda pointed out, "until they retrieve the rest of the airframe in the spring. And the SHK is far more qualified than I am to complete a review of that hardware."

Tad came in, tucking away his phone. "I was just calling home. What did I miss?"

Miranda did *not* want to look at him. Each time she did, she expected to see Andi; he was bigger than two Andis put into one body. He embodied the rotorcraft specialist role, except by doing so, he only served to remind her that much more frequently that Andi was gone.

Miranda turned away. "If there's nothing else, we can return to the ISASI conference by this evening. There's another day of lectures tomorrow. And I can return in time to present my own talk regarding the remote analysis methodology I applied during the Osprey crash last spring."

"And mine is two before that," Jeremy spoke up. "I'm speaking on advanced Black Box data recovery techniques. I forgot all about that."

The only other person in the room was the NATO two-star general. Other than giving his name, Sandor Kurbanov, and a side mention of Prague, he hadn't offered a word. But he hadn't missed any of the exchange.

Miranda didn't know what to say to Tad. Why would she tell people where to go? Her only criteria were whose specialties she needed for an investigation. To the conference? Surely Mike and Holly could judge whether the ISASI conference versus the confusing line of reasoning that advocated their journeying to Georgia was the correct choice.

"Jeremy and I will return to the conference."

"I think that's a good idea, Miranda, but Holly and I think we need to go make sure what is happening. Tad?" Mike asked.

"Hey, I'm along for the ride. Where we goin'?"

Mike turned back to face her. "One more request. Do you mind taking a commercial flight? It would help if we could take your jet to speed this along. Time is short."

"How is time ever short? Or long? The theory of General Relativity states that when moving at a sufficient percentage of the speed of light, time's passage changes duration in the relative time frame. But time has no dimension of length. Could you please explain that?"

Mike smiled for the first time since... She'd never tracked that, but it seemed like it had been a very long time. That was unusual for him. The ends of his mouth typically curved upward, but even that disappeared quickly into Neutral Face— she hoped that meant he was Okay. "Some other time, Miranda. Right now, we need to get moving. Is it okay to take the jet?"

She wished he'd be more specific, as they'd both be taking jets. He and Holly on the Citation M2, she herself on a LuftSvenska Airbus returning to Iceland. But, having phrased the question in her head, she now understood what he meant and nodded.

45

It wasn't until they'd dropped Miranda and Jeremy at Stockholm's Arlanda Airport and he'd asked for tower clearance to depart that it struck him.

Mike had never flown alone in the M2. And now he was planning on doing it across the entire width of Europe. At night. They'd left the snowstorm before reaching Stockholm, but they'd also left behind the sun and he wouldn't be catching up with it again on this flight.

"Tad," he called back into the cabin. "Come give me a hand?"

He should have asked Holly, she had basic piloting skills, but he simply wasn't in the mood to hash out his life at forty thousand feet. Forty-*one* thousand. They were eastbound traffic after all. Christ! He was becoming as anal in his thoughts as Miranda.

He'd take Tad any day. Let Holly rot in the rear along with the NATO two-star. Major General Sandor Kurbanov had placed a few calls of his own, then insisted on accompanying them by the simple expedient of climbing aboard and settling in one of the seats.

He still wasn't used to seeing a two-star without his entourage. The few times he'd been in the Pentagon, he'd witnessed the two-stars moving down the hall. It quickly became clear that colonels and one-stars served only one purpose, to flutter along in the wake of two-star generals. Of course, they in turn hustled along behind the threes and would faint if they were permitted in the presence of the fours. Mike wondered what the pecking orders were that defined the size of a general's entourage—it was *always* bigger than Kurbanov's none.

Oddly, the sole four-star he knew, the Chairman of the Joint Chiefs of Staff, shunned having any entourage whenever possible. Was that a sign of Kurbanov's importance?

Tad slid into Miranda's empty seat as if it wasn't completely wrong. Mike hadn't been able to shift across the aisle. It didn't actually matter as the M2 only required one pilot and the two control suites were identical on either side of the cockpit. But he still couldn't do it.

Tad took over the radio work with the ease of long practice, far more than Mike ever had.

Mike made a few nudges to the autopilot as it took them up to cruise altitude...at forty-one thousand. Next stop? Two hours down line. The Swedish general they had given a lift from Storuman back to Stockholm had arranged for them to refuel at Pápa Air Base in Hungary.

The M2 could have made the Stockholm to Tbilisi, Georgia, jaunt in a single passage, barely, if the direct route lay open. But Belarus, Ukraine, and Russia all lay between the two far corners of Europe. They all had exclusive no-fly airspaces—and a shooting war he wanted nothing to do with. It added nearly a full hour of flying time and another including the descent, refuel, and climb out, to jog clear of them. For the first time since the end of the Cold War, direct flights from Europe to China had become fantastically expensive to avoid Russian airspace. Direct from India to North America had ceased entirely, having to route through Europe or Singapore.

"Pogo stick," Tad rumbled over the intercom. "Go up and down a lot in this little jet."

"Well, the team," he didn't quite manage to say *we,* "is West Coast based out of Seattle. Fairbanks to Phoenix, this baby covers everything except Hawaii very neatly on a single tank."

"I bet. Sweet little machine, no offence, babe," he patted the top of the cockpit console. "Haven't been to Seattle. How's the pickin's there?"

Didn't the guy think about anything other than women? It was...exactly how past-Mike had been. Well, crap! Was that what future-Mike counted on with his planned return to Denver? Meandering through the fields of single women for a night here and a weekend there?

He hoped not.

Yet it sounded a little too close to reality.

"Have to set your sights higher than that." Mike wished he knew which one of them he meant that for.

"Says the man with the golden ticket."

Mike glanced over at him.

Tad didn't look over before he scoffed, "My mama didn't raise no blind boy. What is it with you two? Easy to see how bad she wanted to do it—"

Mike reached to cut off the intercom so that he didn't have to hear this.

"—but this boy had to near enough boot that pretty ass of hers to make her go talk to you."

Mike returned his hand to his lap, turning his attention forward. Through the darkened windscreen, he saw the lights of the Polish coast through the broken cloud cover. He glanced east, past Tad. Fifty miles over that way lay Kaliningrad. Holly had done the bravest thing he'd ever seen, jumping out of a plane little bigger than this one to rescue Miranda.

Never talked about it, of course.

Today she'd wanted—and not wanted—to come talk to him. And when she had, all they'd done was argue. He resisted the urge to glance aft.

Nope, he had no idea what was *with you two* either.

46

Holly wished she knew why Mike had asked for Tad's help in the cockpit instead of hers. Probably some crazy third-level motive she'd never guess: team indoctrination, feeling out his fit on the team, something to do with deciding if he was good enough for Miranda, or...

Or deluding herself. She'd pissed him off but good. But he'd get over it. Here he was, after all, following the mission through.

"No way is he leaving the team," she confirmed aloud.

"What makes you say that?" General Kurbanov's English was clear but stilted in the way only Slavs and other Eastern Europeans managed. It was the first comment he'd made that didn't sound like an order. Weirdly for a flag officer, he was less voluble than a house mouse.

"Our pilot thinks he's quitting the team. Not a chance."

"Don't be too certain. I have seen many good soldiers reach their limit and make drastic choices."

Like her quitting SASR by attempting to brain the Australian Governor General with her bare fists before walking out the door?

Shit, no question on that one. She'd loved Special Operations, had really come into her own as part of the Australian Defence Force. Yet she'd walked.

The only true indication she had of how they thought of her was that they hadn't dragged her back for going AWOL. Being away without leave ranked right down there with disobeying a direct order in a combat situation.

The out-processing officer—who'd finally tracked her down for the paperwork—had clearly been tempted to throw the desertion book at her. Instead, with a lot of brow-beating relish, he'd given her the heavy-handed reminder about what specifically and everything in general that fell under the umbrella of Australia's eight hundred-odd secrecy acts and related laws and regulations ad nauseum mandated by her security clearance.

However, the Governor General, after deciding she wasn't going to kill him, had granted her an honorable exit from the ADF for services rendered to the nation. She signed on the bottom line under: *Class C, partial invalidity, unfit for ADF employment but capable of performing own job outside the Australian Defence Force.*

Her invalidity was a bloody tearing rage.

They compartmentalized all the information she'd had valid *need-to-know* in the field because they were all territorial power-addled idiots. And it had gotten her entire team killed *and* buggered the mission so that they'd died for no purpose.

"Mike wouldn't do that," she told the general to reassure herself. Neither of them would win a game of Two-up with that play. "You're really not being a ray of light here, General."

"I have other concerns," he nodded toward the window.

"Like World War III."

He didn't deny it though she wished he had.

47

Holly wanted, *needed* to get off the plane at Pápa Air Base. Just five minutes. The small plane had begun to squeeze in on her as they covered the two hours from Sweden to Hungary.

No one on or off, the ground team had informed them when they landed.

She'd forgotten this was where the Stinger missiles used in Sweden had been stolen from.

Out the window, the guy overseeing the refueling had no relation to maintenance or even regular security forces. Special Operations—like recognized like. Besides, not a lot of teams carried HK416 rifles or were outfitted with fifty-thousand-dollar L3Harris night-vision goggles. Even fewer managed to look scruffy while doing it. The US Army's Delta Force often wore long hair and grew beards to blend in during undercover operations. And also because no one dared stop them if they were in the mood to grow one.

She'd like to go out and chat with the guy just for the hell of it.

She'd also like to dig for what else they'd unearthed on

base. It must have been bad to stop her from even climbing down to stretch her legs.

Asking Kurbanov didn't gain her anything except an uncertain shrug. He kept his window shade down and his attention on the files he'd been reading since wheels up in Sweden.

With nothing to read, she watched out the window. Fuelies, ground controller...all normal-normal except for Mr. Delta watching silently from ten yards back.

And then it struck her, the reason that Special Operations Forces were so successful at what they did. They didn't talk to outsiders, but they thrived on internal communication. Whatever reason he was there, it wouldn't be some poor uninformed sentry bloke. A Delta would know exactly why he was posted there and what he was guarding against.

It was cold out there. Spindrift blowing over the tarmac beneath a clear night sky that guaranteed at least five degrees below freezing to keep the snow loose like that and a brisk windchill. At least this time she pulled on her parka before clambering down the steps against the order not to disembark.

She ignored Mike's "Hey," at her back.

The Delta didn't unlimber his HK rifle as she approached. He didn't have to; he held it at the ready. Didn't say a word, even when she stopped three meters out—far enough to not be a threat, close enough that no one else would hear them over the roar of the fuel truck and the wind.

"Watch from hell." She's stood guard duty plenty of times in her past and it was boring as counting sand grains—except for the need to remain vigilant for every second.

He didn't answer, but scanned the air base and the plane to make sure she wasn't being a distraction.

"Former SASR." The Australian Special Air Service Regiment was their own version of the US's Delta Force.

He grunted an acknowledgment. He'd have already seen her training by how she walked.

"We're the team saddled with chasing the missing Stingers. Outside the fence."

That got his attention. It was unusual for Delta to be worrying about a security matter inside any base's perimeter fence. Like SASR, their usual role lay out in the field—way out in the field. Anti-terrorism force projection behind enemy lines was their specialty, especially if the enemy was classified as an ally and the intrusion had to remain very low profile—like invisible.

He scanned the area again through his night-vision gear, then eased the position of the rifle against his chest. The gesture told her to move a step closer.

Talking to someone wearing NVGs when you weren't threw most people, but no problem for her. The lower half of his face was covered by beard and the upper part with the four-scope L3Harris goggles—full-on cyborg. And lethal as shit.

Despite their tentative rapport, she was careful to keep her hands visible and still. She'd also turned enough that he'd be able to keep an eye on the knife sheathed along her thigh.

"What am I watching for out there?"

He stared at her in silence as the fuelie cycled down his truck's pumps, rolled up the hose and grounding wire, pulled the wheel chocks, and drove off.

Now it was just the two of them standing out in the bitter night.

One more scan of the airport.

Holly felt his gaze lock on the plane's door behind her. She turned, keeping her knife hip facing the Delta and shoved back her hood to see Tad half out of the doorway.

She made a brushing motion to herd him inside, to which he didn't react.

In the pilot's side window, Mike watched her. He shook his head.

At her or Tad?

He called out something that didn't reach her but Tad must have heard. He ducked inside, had some conversation with Mike, finally withdrawing like a bear into his cavern. Tad hunkered in that middle seat facing the door where she'd been earlier. It allowed him to remain inside, but practically shout *I'm watching you, buddy.*

A direct threat to a Delta operator. Holly resisted the urge to step over and close the passenger door in his face. Had as much sense as a dog barking at a croc. There was a reason dogs weren't allowed in Australian parks anywhere near water—crocs had learned fast that barking dog equaled easy meal.

Mike shook his head to himself, but continued to watch her through the window. Mike had never liked Tad Jobson. He was the one so damn good with people, maybe she needed to listen to that. Actually, it didn't take much to see why. Never being a combat grunt, he had all the field instincts of a flyboy who was always back at base or on his ship at night—none.

Holly turned her back on both of them.

"He's new," she offered the silent Delta.

He twisted his rifle slightly, no more than a wrist flex, as if asking whether she wanted him to shoot Tad. The height of Delta humor.

"Nah, I'd be the one who'd have to clean it up. And the boss wouldn't be happy with a hole in her pretty jet."

"The boss?" His NVGs aimed over her shoulder toward the cockpit for a half second as he spoke for the first time.

"She's not along. He's her copilot."

The two central tubes of his rig recentered on her face. The outer two, angled to either side like horns, would give him enough peripheral vision to watch the whole plane waiting behind her.

"Thought her copilot was a woman."

Holly resisted stumbling back. Andi Wu. Of course, the Delta would have been fed all the information about their team. Apparently it was a little dated, or was it a test? "Not for a while now, and never in the jet. Whirly-girl pilot."

"She rocked."

Holly closed her eyes. She'd never escape Andi Wu, neither her deeds nor her misdeeds. Special Operations Forces—especially Delta Force and Seal Team Six—were the 160th SOAR's primary customers. And Andi had been one of the Night Stalkers' very best. That this guy knew her sucked in so many spectacular ways. It sure didn't let her say aloud that the little bitch had betrayed the team eight months back. Didn't let her forget about Mike's insistence that she'd been preemptive in kicking Andi down the road.

"Low tech stuff." He said in a different voice.

She looked at him again, or tried to but a blast of wind began beating her face with her own parka's hood. He might actually be smiling by the time she wrestled it into submission.

"We started our inventory review at the top. Drones, drone controllers, heavy EM gear—all in place."

No electro-magnetic weapons or systems missing from inventory here at Pápa Air Base.

"A bunch of little shit still unaccounted for, but the big stuff tallies up fine. Other than that pair of Stingers, watch out for a pair of MK 22 ASRs in 7.62 config. Just inventoried those. Walked real recently. Still a long way to go on handhelds." Meaning rifles, handguns, grenade launchers, grenades... Not good. Very not good.

Which told her how much the US had stockpiled here in case of a surprise attack on NATO; they'd have had a large team at it for hours already. "So, no jets missing. That's something."

The Delta froze for a moment, then glanced toward the

distant flight line. "Uh, not my squad. I'll make sure someone checks."

Delta Force at its core was an Army unit. Meaning it suffered from Army-first thinking.

"Any Navy gear here as well?"

He nodded tentatively.

And she'd thought the winter was already cold.

Holly decided against wasting time worrying about missing jets or boats or whatever was supposed to be here. The fact that two ASRs had gone walkabout *real recently* was more than enough concern—the newest US Special Operations Command issue 7.62 mm Advanced Sniper Rifle. Under a mile, not much beat it, and definitely not at that light a caliber. She still preferred the extra half kilometer and big punch of a TAC-50 rifle heaving five times the mass downrange.

Were the ASRs long gone to some African war zone? In Sweden? Or waiting for her in Georgia?

No way to tell. And a weapon that could reach out and touch her from twelve hundred meters away wasn't something worth worrying about, much, because she'd never see it coming. She shrugged it off as well as possible and dug out an NTSB card.

"You hear about anything else gone astray, I'd like a head's up." No need to explain she was headed into the fray and needed to know what she faced.

He didn't take the card. Probably already had it. If not, someone back at their dedicated intelligence agency in Fort Belvoir, Virginia, would. Or there was no way he'd tell her. *No longer in the service, girl.* Nastier taste than a pint of two-buck Hammer 'N' Tongs draught.

"Right. Get my ass back on the plane. Get gone."

He twisted his rifle a few millimeters somewhere between a nod of acknowledgement and a perhaps teasing offer to shoot her if she stayed, then went back to scanning the area.

She offered him a single *Ha* that earned her a flicker of a smile. Okay, three-quarters teasing. She turned toward the plane.

On a night like this, there was no real worry about those ASRs. They weren't going to see anything out past a few hundred meters and the Delta's night vision could see that far.

She crawled back onto the plane and hoped that Mike could get them the hell out of here before the weather closed the place completely.

48

"HAVEN'T BEEN HERE IN A GOOD WHILE." TAD LEANED FORWARD to peer out the windscreen.

Mike almost bobbled the landing at Tbilisi International. "You what?"

The wheels banged down, but at least he didn't bounce the jet back into the air. He felt Holly glaring at his back for not being as good as Miranda.

"Sorry, buddy, shoulda waited till you were down." Tad kept looking about, not that there was anything to see at eleven at night except for the airport lights.

Mike decided against chewing out a Marine Corps aviator about sterile cockpit rules—no conversation not related to the flying moment was forbidden. He'd know that far better than Mike would.

"You've been here."

"Sure. Back when I was a baby Marine. We did a co-op training. In fact, this is where I got booted from mechanic to front seat. Got caught out showing my Georgian mechanic brothers what an American bird could do. Some damn two-bar," he stroked his shirt collar with two fingers denoting a captain's rank, "spotted me doing my dance and shoved me into the cockpit full-time. The GAF—Georgian Air Force—were trying to upgrade their fleet, mostly rusted-out Russian crap and their equally rusty tactics. Turn here," Tad pointed at a taxiway to the right.

Mike swung the plane to the right as he cleaned up the flaps and thrust attenuators.

Somehow Tad could both talk and keep up with the radio. Even after all of his years of flying, Mike still had to concentrate to understand aviation radio calls.

"Do you still know people to talk to here?"

"Sure, about what?"

Mike almost missed the next turn as he stared at Tad. "About what? Where the hell have you been?"

"Sittin' my ass right here in this seat. Doesn't mean I have a damn clue about what's goin' on, Mike. You guys have got me as confused as shit."

Mike tried to think back, but the decision to come to Georgia had happened out on the snowy highway when only he and Holly were there. And Tad hadn't been in the meeting with Miranda and General Kurbanov. "Uh, sorry, Tad. Didn't realize we were dragging you along without any details."

"It's cool, man. Figured I'm the new square on the block. Hazing like I'm a Ricky Recruit again. Kinda weird after fifteen years in the Corps to be on the outside. Seriously weird as I'm thinking about it."

"*Not* intentional," Mike followed where Tad was pointing toward a hangar on the northeast corner of the airport. "Just a lot happening really fast. Next time just ask."

"If you say so, boss." Tad clearly thought it was another level of hazing and, after the long flight, Mike didn't have the energy to argue.

A baton-wielding aircraft marshaler waved them into place. Clouds of his breath showed in the plane's lights. At least there was no snow on the runway but Mike felt a shiver though the plane's interior remained warm. The cold had never bothered him in Denver. Had his years with Miranda in the temperate clime of Puget Sound, Washington, thinned his blood that much?

The marshaler signaled the overhead X with crossed batons and Mike stopped, set the brake, and killed the engines. He tossed aside his seat harness, taking a deep breath for the first time in six hours. He loved to fly, but this passage had really taken it out of him. Yet he felt rather jazzed at having made such a flight on his own.

He twisted and flexed his muscles as he looked around.

They were parked way out in the back forty by the looks of it. The main terminal lay over a mile away at the far end of the runway. In between, a line of three 737s and two smaller jets were parked together—all painted white with red tails, winglets, and *Air Georgia* painted down the sides in a flowing script. They all had the reflective foil inside the cockpit windows and covers over the engines like they hadn't moved in a while.

Dead ahead sat a small cluster of Hind and Huey helicopters and a pair of Antonov An-28 twin-turboprop cargo planes, more appropriate for a museum than being painted Air Force gray.

Out here, they might have a long walk to find a rental car.

He turned to Tad, partly to delay starting the long cold walk. "Our theory is—"

"Holy shit!" Tad jammed himself back in his seat and stared out the front windscreen. His hand clenched hard enough that Mike wondered if he'd leave permanent marks on the leather of Miranda's seat.

Mike looked up, then figured he'd do a good job of finding out the answer for himself.

A pair of evil-looking trucks were racing toward them from

the military end of the field. They had gray-orange camouflage and weren't slowing.

If they rammed the jet's nose, he and Tad were going to be dead. The trucks were big enough that from the small jet he was looking dead-level at the driver. But that wasn't the focus of his attention.

Atop the big-wheeled truck, there was one of those turrets to protect a machine gunner. And poking out through the curved armor shield was the muzzle of a six-barreled M134 Dillon Minigun. He'd seen one cut a Honda Accord in two during a demo. But that wasn't the main memory. It made an unholy buzzsaw sound when fired—like God's table saw slicing the tablets for the Ten Commandments out of solid rock.

No time to run.

No time to—

Both trucks slammed on their brakes and slid sideways along the runway, coming to a stop mere meters from the jet in a clearly practiced move. The machine gun on the nearer truck aimed directly at his face.

It hurt to blink because his eyes had been so wide.

Then he noticed that the gun wasn't quite aimed at his face —it centered on Tad's.

The gunner waved. Not like a command, but more like spotting a buddy across a bar who he'd been saving a seat for.

Tad's laugh snapped Mike out of his frozen posture as hard and painfully as the sight of the attack had jammed him into it.

"That's my boys!" Tad launched himself from the seat and was out the door in seconds. The cold air swirled into the cockpit. More soldiers in camo gear jumped out of the trucks.

Mike watched in awe through the windscreen as they mobbed Tad, trading hugs, laughter, and back slaps that might kill a mortal man, and even an immortal one. He heard their shouts of, "Heard you on the air, brother." "Rousted the guys outta their racks." "Had to meet you proper."

"That's not something you see every day," Holly stood in the aisle and was leaning forward between the cockpit seats.

"What are they?" Mike managed to speak, though the dismounting soldier had slightly shifted the Minigun as he'd dismounted.

"Didgori. Homegrown and built on a heavy-duty Ford truck chassis. Hella tough machines."

"Uh, no, you don't see those every day." The unmanned gun now pointed directly at him. Ducking toward the side window didn't get him clear. Ducking the other way, he banged his head hard against Holly's.

"Hey! Ow!" She smacked him on the back of the head, as if colliding with her wasn't enough.

49

HOLLY FELT THE PLANE SHIFT SLIGHTLY BENEATH HER FEET. A boot scuff on carpet, almost masked by the noise from Tad's mates outside the plane.

She half turned to see Major General Sandor Kurbanov of NATO moving out of his seat. He shrugged on a parka, having never once taken off or even unbuttoned his uniform jacket, picked up his thin portfolio, and headed off the plane.

She heard the rear cargo hatch open as he grabbed his oversized hardshell briefcase.

Leaning sideways, she saw him talking on his phone as he circled around the group of soldiers from the trucks. A black Mercedes SUV had arrived unnoticed behind the pair of Didgori armored trucks. He climbed in and it sped off.

"Where do you think he's going?"

Mike still stared at the Minigun aimed his way as if it could shoot him with no one at the trigger. But in a single glance, his head shifted to track the departing SUV. "He say anything?"

Only that Kurbanov wouldn't be surprised if Mike left the team, but not a chance she'd be sharing that. She shook her head.

"Heard anything yet?"

Holly shook her head. She'd clutched her phone for the entire flight. No text. No voicemail. Not a peep from Val at the CIA's Russia desk.

She'd rather hear from Inessa. She'd even checked in with Harry back at the CIA with no luck. Holly didn't dare reach out again; it would put Innessa at risk—at greater risk than she already had. The FSB was evil, but they weren't stupid. And it would be for nothing, as Inessa would have sent something along if she'd thought of anything since their conversation.

Mike finished the shutdown checklist as they rehashed the idea that they'd been on a wild goose chase coming to Georgia, which was pretty pointless since they were already here. It proved even more pointless as they had no new information to work from. But she couldn't help herself. Kurbanov's words about the chances of Mike leaving kept echoing in her head. Maybe by talking to him, about anything, would keep him close.

And that realization shut her up as assuredly as a muzzle. She *wanted* to keep him close? Nope. Everyone close to her ended up dead. That Mike was still alive counted as one of the most surprising events in her life. Except she didn't care, right? Did that neutralize the hex and maybe her ill fortune wouldn't kill him?

Done with the checklist, Mike turned back to the gun. "It's like one of those paintings. No matter where you move, it stays aimed at your face." He leaned forward, shifted his head side-to-side, then leaned back.

Holly jerked back to avoid him banging her in the head again, then smacked him forward once again.

A double snap that she knew all too well triggered her reflexes.

Holly grabbed Mike by the shoulders of his NTSB jacket. She yanked him up from the copilot's seat as high as the jet's low ceiling would allow, then, twisting him as she fell backward into the aisle, dragged Mike down on top of her.

His full weight hammered down on her. She was going to be sore for a couple days, but a practiced set of flexions proved she hadn't broken anything.

She still held his shoulders and used them to shift him left and right, but he looked fine.

"Yeah, glad to see you too," Mike looked down at her as he lay fully atop her in the narrow aisle. "What brought that on? And what the hell is all that noise?"

Together they twisted to look out the passenger door, placing them cheek-to-cheek. Half the squad of soldiers who'd greeted Tad stared at them in surprise—she and Mike lay in the jet's aisle with their upper bodies visible through the door and their legs tangled up in the cockpit. The other half had heard the same thing she had and were scrambling for weapons.

There was a sharp thwap on the outside of the plane close above their heads. Before she turned, she saw one of the Georgian troopers beyond the door grab at his face as he tumbled backward.

There was a cry for a medic, but the downed man wouldn't be moving again. One of his eyes was now a bloody hole and the other one fixed and open.

One of the Didgori roared to life. The quiet scuffle of trained men loading up fast, followed by the heavy engine roar of the vehicle racing around the plane and away in the direction of the shooter. Others setting up a perimeter around their downed comrade and the medic.

Holly twisted and looked up to see where the round had punched through the plane's thin skin. There was a hole through the center of the padded sideways seat where she'd sat during all the Swedish hopping about. Then it had traveled out the open door to kill one of the Georgians.

A chance shot that, having no view, had missed its intended

target. Though if she and Mike hadn't turned cheek-to-cheek it would have passed through the back of his head. Lucky for him, not for the Georgian soldier.

Over Mike's shoulder, Holly looked into the cockpit and the two holes in opposite sides of the plane's windows. The shot that had triggered her reflexes to yank Mike from his seat had traveled at exactly the same angle. She'd wager that a line between them would pass through where her head had been before she pulled back—where Mike's head had been the instant before she'd smacked him forward.

The line traveled by a 7.62 mm round based on the size of the holes.

Two rounds several seconds apart. A bolt-action rifle. Time to manually throw the bolt and reset the shot, the amount of time it took her to haul Mike's ass out of his seat.

That close to losing Mike, twice. The chill that ran up her body had nothing to do with the cold December night.

50

Pavle had rolled out of bed to take the phone call without waking Elene. The vibration buzz on the nightstand and sudden illumination had been more than enough to roust him. Not as if he'd been sleeping anyway.

He'd convinced himself to allow a night for things to brew; he was the lead agent on the operation after all. If his idea worked, far more people would die in Sweden from the ensuing war than had already died from his plan, but counterintuitively that would be less awful. In that case, it would be a NATO-Russian war killing them. Russia was slaughtering Ukrainians—and getting slaughtered by them. That was war.

But if he himself launched the next phase of the plan he'd conceived, Chief Kancheli had drafted, and the two of them then refined, then the deaths would be his doing. That sat far less comfortably.

He chose one door and wished he'd chosen the other. From the living room he could have retreated to the kitchen or the second bedroom that they used as an office and overflow closet. Here in the bathroom he could sit on the toilet or the tub. With the heat turned down for the night, his feet were already cold against the tile. His thin pajama bottoms weren't going to help much.

The phone number was hidden, of course. He tried to think of the last time he'd received a call from an open number other than Elene—and couldn't.

"Pavle here."

"Sorry to wake you." Pavle knew that Chief Kancheli wouldn't regret it for a millisecond. Which meant something was escalating that even Chief K wasn't comfortable with. That proved damned hard to imagine.

"No problem, Chief." He wasn't about to admit that he was closer to a nervous breakdown than sleep. Elene had almost smothered him with care last night. Knowing something was wrong, and that he couldn't say what, had kicked her into some sort of overdrive excelling even his own mother when he'd been a boy.

"What's the status of Phase Four?"

"I, uh," he was already between two fires, "decided it was best to wait twenty-four hours. It would allow...us to observe possible developments before acting further."

There was a muffled mumbling in the background that continued long enough for Pavle to wonder if he'd fallen down a snake hole and the security branch would come blasting through his apartment door any minute.

"That," Chief K's voice sounded clear again, "is acceptable."

Pavle blew out a hard breath; Kancheli's version of highest praise. It didn't stop the shivers from the cold tile.

"What's your next step?"

Pavle glanced at his wrist; his watch lay on the nightstand beside Elene. He pulled the phone far enough away to see that it was already past two in the morning. "I...was planning to head to the office in a few hours. But I expect little information until our operative from the Gulf of Finland downing returns to work later in the morning, midday our time."

"I may have information for you by the time you arrive. Oh-eight-hundred. My office." And Chief K hung up.

Pavle set an alarm for six. Not a chance he'd be asleep, but better safe than sorry.

He slipped into the bedroom; the carpet exchanged the smooth tile's freeze for the chill of tiny spikes driving into his soles. Knowing that the carpet was soft didn't alter the sensation.

"Pavle?" Elene's voice a whisper into the darkness.

He followed it to enjoy a few hours curled up against her warmth.

With perfect understanding, she cradled him. With his nose planted against her breastbone through her flannel nightgown, either cheek cushioned by her lovely breasts and her hands stroking his hair, he felt safe for the first time in far too long.

She asked why he was crying; he hadn't realized he was.

When she asked again, he told her.

51

HOLLY'S PHONE BLASTED OUT A LOUD RING. SHE ALMOST LOST the round she'd been holding.

Her hands were so cold that it was hard to answer the phone.

"Yo."

"Yo?"

"Hi, Val. About to call you."

Actually Holly had been too busy over the last half hour to think about the director of the CIA's Russia desk.

After the gunshots, Tad's pals from the Georgian 43rd Mechanized Infantry had built a fast perimeter. The loan of bulletproof vests and helmets was appreciated. They wouldn't stop a direct hit by a 7.62 mm round, but they'd deflect a grazing shot.

The Georgians had charged head-on toward the shooter, finding no one and nothing. She'd looked it over with a trained eye, not even any stray brass. Someone had been careful.

The rounds must have been fired from close by the perimeter fence, but she found no fresh boot scuffs. There was an access road both inside and outside the line. The shooter had been in a vehicle but could have been on either side of the fence.

By pure chance, they'd found the single round, now clutched in her freezing hand.

After flying through the two acrylic windows, the first round had been stopped against the side of one of the Didgori armored trucks. Mostly spent, it had barely scuffed the truck's camo paint. A soldier found it when it rolled under his foot; good awareness that even a pebble a third of an inch across shouldn't be on the same pavement as jets. The other round was still buried in the dead soldier's face.

"M993," she'd guessed.

Tad had nodded his agreement. "Armor piercing to eighteen millimeters of RHA rolled steel." He had tapped a finger against one of the Didgori trucks. No thunk of thin metal, rather the soft thump like heavy steel. "Can still kinda see the black tip marking the round before it got all mushed up." M993s were marked with a black tip on the bullet.

The 43rd's commander had everyone there show their kit. The few who carried that round still had every one accounted for.

The bullet certainly would have had no trouble passing through her or Mike's head along with the two windows as the second round had proven. Miranda's Citation M2 was meant for commercial flight, not stopping NATO rounds. And the side windows were far thinner than the windshield because they wouldn't have to survive bird strikes at speed. The metal hull wasn't much thicker.

Mike had stepped up beside Tad. "No one this side of France has replacement windows in stock. They'll be sending out a team tomorrow to fix them, the seat, and the outside panel."

He'd been shot at, and still took care of business. Holly had seen plenty of soldiers come apart under similar circumstances.

She hadn't given him a thought in the last thirty minutes. She'd gotten him stashed inside an armored Didgori—rated to stop the size of armor-piercing round still resting so heavily in her palm—and focused on the battlefield.

And Mike had arranged to have Miranda's plane repaired as cool as a fresh draught.

It might be one of the most impressive acts of bravery she'd ever seen in a civilian—except Miranda. That wasn't really a fair comparison because Miranda's hyper-focused attention often didn't see the danger she was walking into during a crash investigation. But Holly had certainly seen trained soldiers crumble at their first time in such a near-death experience.

Now she could think about the *who* behind the *what*. Except she didn't have a clue.

"What have you got for me, Val?" Holly paced back and forth to try to build some body warmth. Also to avoid looking at this new side of Mike. Guys that she'd been sleeping with for three years weren't supposed to change, they were supposed to be comfortable as old shoes. She rolled the mangled 7.62 mm round back and forth across her palm.

"Place closes at three a.m. your time. Show up between three-fifteen and three-thirty. Ask for Max. I've texted you the address." Her phone chimed in her ear. "He's expecting you. I didn't tell him why, that's on you. And Holly?"

"Yeah."

"It probably won't lead anywhere, but he hears things. Don't fuck this up. He's a solid asset for us."

"Roger that, Val. And thanks."

"Yeah, right."

What had she done to earn the hard edge of Val's tongue? Though the CIA Russia Desk Director had sounded plenty rough all on her own this morning. What if it was Val's shit and not hers?

"After this is done, you, me, a pitcher of beer."

Val groaned. "Look, Holly, you owe me for connecting you to a CIA asset, so do me a favor."

"Sure."

"Never, ever again, under any circumstances mention alcohol in my presence."

"Sure thing," Holly agreed easily. "I'll just show up some afternoon with a slab of Coopers. I won't say a word."

"A slab?"

"Aussie for a case of beer. Makes an even dozen coldies for each of us, oughta loosen you up a wee bit."

"I need more aspirin," Val groaned and hung up.

Holly tucked away her phone after checking the time. She turned to the commander. "You have a ride I can borrow pronto?"

He slapped the hood of the Didgori truck next to him.

"I like the armor, but I was hoping for something a little more subtle."

52

"CAN WE PLEASE NOT CHARGE INTO THE UNKNOWN WITHOUT A plan? Just this once?" Mike didn't even know why he tried.

They'd been parked under the trees along the east side of Liberty Square in downtown Tbilisi for twenty minutes. The sleek black Mercedes was apparently the Georgian Defence Force's idea of low profile. They must have raided the VIP Motor Pool because nothing was too good for their buddy Tad Jobson.

Mike had stopped arguing about this not matching his idea of low profile when he felt the weight of the door as he swung it open. Up-armored enough to stop a .50 cal round, half again the diameter of the one that almost punched his permanent timecard at the airport.

While Holly, backed up by a dozen massively armed Georgian troopers, had led a scouting mission for the shooter, his ass had been stuck in a Didgori armored truck like a little girl. The only way to avoid the shakes was action. Except there were two patrolling troopers circling his vehicle, putatively guarding outward but equally effectively trapping him inside.

Unable to stop looking at the holes in Miranda's cockpit windows, he'd finally tracked down Cessna Citation service as a distraction. He'd finished the arrangements about the same time she'd finished her uninformative patrol.

Now, as they watched the entrance to the Bunker Bar, a slow trickle of patrons emerged into the bitter darkness. He recognized a last-call crowd when he saw one.

The entrance stood at the corner of Mikheil Somebody and Shalva Somebody Else Streets. He'd looked at each name a dozen times and still couldn't remember them. Noted mathematicians, local merchant princes, Georgian gods? Who knew.

Liberty Square turned out to be a parking lot. Maybe Mikheil and Shalva had been freedom fighters. Or poets. Weren't poets always writing about liberty? Or perhaps they'd invented pay-for-parking in Georgia.

The streets were narrow and tree-lined. The buildings all were two or three stories of yellow stone that had seen much better days. For all that, it looked to be a pleasant neighborhood—for three in the morning on a cold winter's night.

The final few patrons climbed the last of the stairs up to the sidewalk from a below street-level entrance. One braced a hand on the glass window of a convenience market and barfed up an impressive amount.

Mike had just been fantasizing that the store would open. He'd get a donut and some decent coffee... Now, not so much.

Holly hadn't answered Mike's request for a plan, instead clutched the steering wheel and stared at the last of the departing patrons, perhaps drawing imaginary targets on each one's forehead.

From the back, Tad finally spoke up. "Man's expecting us, don't particularly need a plan, do we?"

Mike would like if that was true for once, but he wouldn't be placing any high-dollar bets on it. Anything much over a buck would be too risky a proposition.

By three-fifteen, the trickle of patrons tapered off. One deciding to sleep off what remained of the morning in the market's doorway, his feet barely clear of the puddle of another man's vomit. The sicker had miraculously climbed into a car and driven away down the single one-way lane without hitting the cars parked to either side.

"On the move," Holly climbed out, leaving him and Tad no other option than to follow.

At the corner, she stopped to scan the streets and nearby windows. Tad, probably because he was a helicopter pilot, looked aloft. Mike kept his eye on the drunk in the doorway, but if he was shamming, he did a superb job of it.

Above the descending stairway, lit by a lone streetlight—the one beside it flickered too weakly to count—a brown awning stretched out to keep the rain off. A single word was printed on the dark fabric in blocky flame-color letters: Bunker. Like the world above had already been bombed and was afire.

As they descended beneath the streets of Tbilisi, Mike took one last breath of the chill air and hoped he had a chance to breathe it again.

The heavy steel door at the bottom of the flight had been propped open with a thin wedge that fell aside when Holly dragged it open.

Inside, another staircase led them several flights deeper beneath the street. At the bottom, another steel door, and they stepped into a darkened cavern—the only light shone in their faces.

There was a very distinct click that seemed to echo in the silence, one he'd learned to recognize from Holly's training out on the shooting range.

The sound of a safety being switched off on a rifle or shotgun.

Mike whispered, "I told you we should have a plan."

53

"I'M SO GLAD YOU RETURNED SAFELY, MIRANDA. MICHAEL DOES not come with you?" Klara Dahlberg looked about. She'd been sitting in the lobby bar with several other safety investigators though it was eleven at night here in Reykjavik. "Is he here for tomorrow's sessions?"

Miranda shook her head. "He and the others had something else to research. They are interested in the cause of the multiple incidents Sweden has recently experienced."

Klara turned to look down at her. Miranda kept her attention on the uneven ends of Klara's Nordic-blonde hair. Was the choppiness of the ends lapping a hand's length over each shoulder intentional? She kept her own hair trimmed as straight as possible, cut precisely to the lowest point of her jawline so that it tucked behind her ears without any stray ends tickling her neck. Andi had suggested she grow it out several times but now that she had gone, Miranda didn't see the purpose of such an experiment.

"And you do not go with them?"

"Jeremy and I were only concerned with the cause of the crashes themselves. Those have been resolved."

"So quickly?" Klara's voice sounded…

Miranda turned to Jeremy, "…aghast?"

He nodded.

She repeated the word a few times to herself. It was a nice word, but the sound didn't particularly fit the emotion. *Anger* had an edge. *Joy* sounded short and fun. *Aghast* sounded as if it should be a boat design: a dory, a sloop, a ghast.

"Sabotage twice and unfriendly fire a third time," Jeremy told her. "Not hard once we found the right thing to look at."

Klara gasped again. Yes, unlike *ghast,* gasp did fit the sound of surprise, yet it wasn't an emotion but rather a word representing a physical sound. She pulled out her notebook to compare the other emotion sounds with their correlative feelings on her emojis page, but was interrupted by others who'd stayed late in the bar. People. Gathering close.

Other attendees stood and joined them in ones and twos until eleven additional people had gathered around Klara. As the crowd grew about her, Miranda edged back. She scooped up Meg so that the terrier wouldn't get trampled by the unthinking herd.

A herd of people? All led by the ringing cowbell of Klara Dahlberg. That was her first double use of a metaphor. Miranda would have patted her own back as Andi had taught her, if her arms weren't full of terrier. And if it didn't make her so sad to think about Andi. And if she wasn't so very tired.

Or perhaps the gathering was Jeremy's doing. The various air-safety investigators were all listening to him discuss the three separate investigations they'd performed in the last thirty hours including transit time. They appeared more interested by the procedures than the events themselves.

A tall clean-shaven man with a chin as sharp as his Germanic accent—An analogy? How was she supposed to tell? —approached her. "Ms. Chase, if I might have a moment of your time?"

She looked at Jeremy still talking happily in the midst of the crowd / herd.

She looked at Meg, or tried to, but the dog had laid her head on Miranda's shoulder much the way Andi used to. Meg's back blocked Miranda's chin from traveling sufficiently to look down at the dog, though her soft fur and warmth were a comfort.

Holding Meg close, she allowed herself to be escorted to a deep chair by a low table well away from anyone else. He offered wine, she requested tea with milk from the waitress.

"You have been freshly returned from Sweden."

"Yes."

"Where you've been investigating crashes."

It wasn't a question, but she felt another yes was appropriate.

"What are your conclusions?"

Miranda lost interest. Jeremy had already stated their conclusions. She would leave, but then the waitress delivered her tea. She didn't wish to be rude and leave without drinking it. But it was still too hot, and the waitress was gone. Her mother used to put a small ice cube in her hot tea to cool it for her. She'd forgotten about that and how much she'd enjoyed hearing the sharp pops and studying the fracture patterns as they formed within the core of the ice.

But the waitress had moved on. Perhaps it didn't matter. By the thinness of the porcelain, the cup would have released sufficient thermal energy to become drinkable by the time the waitress was summoned and an ice cube brought.

"Allow me to rephrase," the man said.

She watched the formation of gentle thermal currents in the milk as the tea's surface cooled and subsided along the edges, exposing warmer liquid to the surface to, in turn, cool and subside.

"What are your *general* conclusions?"

"I'm..." She looked for his name tag. But in this environment, most of the conference attendees had removed their name badges for the night. They'd also had the advantage of thirty additional hours of knowing each other while she'd been traveling to Sweden and back. "...not skilled at general conclusions. You want to speak to Mike. But he isn't here."

"Indulge me," he sipped his wine but she felt that his eyes remained focused on her.

"In what?" The heat-driven currents in her teacup had subsided. A careful sip proved it needed another few minutes to cool sufficiently. "Oh, guessing. Mike is the best at it. Holly tends to jump to conclusions but is easily dissuaded from those. Or Andi. She was very good at that too." She'd been good at so many things. Miranda closed her eyes, but that did nothing to assuage the pain of her abrupt departure eight months ago. It still cut at her every day.

"Ms. Chase?" The man's deep voice dragged at her.

"Yes?" Opening her eyes proved difficult. Meg sleeping warmly against her chest wasn't helping.

"Oh dear," Klara Dahlberg hurried over. "You look utterly exhausted, Miranda. We must let you get to bed."

"My tea..."

"I'm sure they'd be happy to make you a fresh cup tomorrow. Come," Klara held out a hand.

Miranda handed Meg up to her. Klara took the terrier as if the dog might explode. Or perhaps she worried about Meg's light gray fur shedding on her burgundy blouse. But Meg woke up only long enough to snuggle into Klara's arms.

Miranda didn't remember the nameless man's question until she was in the elevator.

54

Holly barely resisted targeting the potential shooter. She could estimate the distance of the person wielding the gun, sight unseen. But the echoes of the underground room, especially not knowing its general shape, blurred his exact location.

Instead, she jerked the door closed behind her to protect Mike and Tad, then dove aside as she heaved her knife out of its sheath and upward, handle first, in a single clean yank.

With a sharp crack and a tinkle of glass, she smashed the light out.

She rolled into the room beyond, crashing into a set of chairs perched upside down on a table. Two of them landed on her as her knife clattered onto the stone floor behind her.

She pulled out her belt knife and the HK 9mm she'd favored in her SASR days. She didn't carry it often, but the shooter with the Stinger missile back in Sweden had set a definite tone to how the day might unfold.

The bar beyond wasn't dark, except by comparison to the bright light that had been shining into the entryway. She peeked through the fallen chairs.

In the sudden silence, she flicked off the safety. The bright click echoed off the arched brick ceiling. A long bar ran along the far wall.

Well to the left of where she'd expected, a big man with a thick beard and a bald head aimed a shotgun at her. He had it aimed directly at her squat under the table.

"What did you bring to a shotgun fight?" He called out.

"HK USP Tactical. Nine millimeter."

"That Aussie you speaking there, girl?"

"Might be," Holly admitted.

He swung the shotgun up to rest the barrel on his shoulder, offering her a clear view of it. If he clicked the safety on again, she didn't hear it.

"Benelli M4. Never actually shot one of those." She rose slowly, clicked on her own safety but did not holster it. "Why choose that over the Mossberg?"

"It's what they issued me first day in the GDF." Meaning he'd now shot it so often that it felt like a part of his arm.

"Roger that. Val says hi, by the way."

"Nice lady for a spook."

Unlike Val's boss, who was a stone-cold bitch. Holly kept that thought to herself.

There was a pounding on the door.

"Better let your friends in."

"Mind putting that away first?" Holly nodded toward the shotgun.

He held it up sideways, then together she holstered her sidearm and he safetied and slid the Benelli under the bar. "First two rounds are non-lethals."

She kept an eye on him as she moved to the door. Not wanting a surprise non-lethal in her back—depending on the round and where it hit, it might kill her anyway and would be guaranteed to hurt like hell if it didn't—she stomped on her knife where it lay on the floor hard enough to make it bounce upward a few inches. Hooking the toe of her boot under it, she lofted it up to hand height, grabbed it out of the air, and slid it into her sheath. As she'd told the Delta operator at the air base in Hungary, she'd had her fair share of boring watches. Always a chance to practice some pony trick.

Three steps back, she ran her butt into the door's crash bar.

Tad yanked it open and came in fast and low on her right with a Glock raised in both hands. Bad move. He stopped close enough that a single blast would have taken out the both of them—he'd have known that if he'd had some real ground combat training.

"You okay, Hol?" Mike voice was soft behind her.

She nodded. A couple of bruises from a dive and falling chairs were nothing new. Did he hear the concern in his own voice as he asked? Though she could hear General Kurbanov scoff at her attempt to read anything into that.

"You owe me a new entry light," the bartender announced over crossed arms with full-cuff tattoos running past his elbows. Arms almost as big as Tad's. Roaring flames.

"Shine it in someone else's face next time." Holly strode up to the bar.

She held out a hand, "Holly."

"Max." He didn't go for a finger-crusher, well, no more than she did. "Val didn't mention you were ADF."

Holly merely tilted her head in a, *Well, duh.* This wasn't the sort of guy she needed to tell she'd been in the SASR part of the Australian Defence Forces, any more than he had to say he was former GSOF. To prove the point, where a soldier's patch would land, his sleeveless black t-shirt exposed that the tattooed flames parted to embrace an arm-patch-shaped green-and-white art piece. Sword, wings, crossed arrows, and a trident over a Georgian Cross. That had to be Special Operations Forces; no other type of unit covered all those skills.

It was pretty but she preferred the simplicity of SASR's sword with wings she wore in a place only Mike had seen.

Val could sure pick them; she couldn't ask for a better contact—GSOF and a bartender would know and hear plenty.

"We've got a problem," she sat on a barstool. As Mike and Tad went to sit beside her, she spoke up, "Tad, check it out."

"Check what?"

Holly looked at Max and they both shared a slight smile. Good help was so hard to find. Tad had never been on a patrol. Mike shoved off his stool to go inspect the rest of the place to make sure they were alone. Holly knew that Mike hadn't known either, yet he understood effortlessly.

"Don't worry," Max waved him back to his seat, "already did the sweep. We're alone. Watched you out there for fifteen minutes." He turned over a tablet computer that had been lying on the bar and showed the image of the car they'd come in. Then the empty stairway they'd descended to get in.

"Guy in the doorway, too," Holly reminded him.

He nodded, then pulled out a cell phone and hit a speed dial. "You can head home. Thanks." And hung up. Moments later the guy who'd been lying in the door crossed into view as he circled the car once before departing. No sign of a stagger.

"Aw, crap!" Mike didn't look happy. "He fooled me. I was sure he was a drunk."

Holly smiled at Mike as she looked at him in the mirror over the bar. "Did you notice him lying down?"

Mike thought for a moment before shaking his head.

"A drunk you would have noticed. This guy settled down so smooth you wouldn't see him unless you were watching for that play."

Max grunted. "So, you've got a problem. Why are you talking to me?"

Holly had kept her other hand as near her sidearm as she dared without giving away what she was doing. She certainly wouldn't be depending on Tad for cover and, as far as she knew, Mike carried nothing bigger than the mini-Swiss Army knife on his keychain.

With Taz busy being a mom in Washington, DC, and Andi being thrown off the team, Holly hadn't realized until this moment quite how alone and isolated she'd become. If she lost Mike, then she'd be *way* out in the wind. Which meant it was time to wing it and see if she faced friend or foe.

"We're talking to you because we think the problem is here, in Georgia." Then she prepped herself to move fast without offering any outward sign. "Possible earmarks of Georgian Special Operations Forces."

55

"How can you tell me all this?" Elene hadn't shoved him out of bed in disgust, which counted as the only good thing to happen since this mission began.

"I can't. Shouldn't have. I'm so sorry." They lay facing each other in the dark, whispering from less than half a meter apart. And though their knees overlapped and she lightly clasped his hand in hers between them, he didn't think it would be welcome if he hid his face against her breasts again.

"Which means?"

He closed his eyes against the pain.

"I'm a dead woman if anyone finds out that I know."

Unable to look her in the face, he nodded, then shrugged. "No. Probably only interrogation for you." For himself? That one-and-done bullet to the brain.

"And my family?"

He looked at her face in the bit of streetlight reflected off the ceiling. Pavle couldn't tell if she'd wish them in trouble or not.

"Okay, you're right. It's a stupid question and I *don't* care."

Elene had a vision that focused solely on the future. It had become his favorite part of her. He spent hours dwelling on the past. How many times had he wished he'd been too drunk to write that memo to Chief Kancheli? Or that he *had* become a rock and roll drummer getting stoned with cute groupies rather than his role as Chief K's right-hand man. Trapped, now by his own words, into perpetrating a heinous attack on a friendly country?

After her brief week out of his life, Elene never mentioned her family again until this moment. Each time he asked, she shrugged him off and looked sad. He'd stopped asking.

"Pavle."

He nodded to show that he was listening.

"You're smart. You're too smart to get caught up in this when it comes apart. And you *know* it's going to come apart."

That gave him pause. This wasn't America with all of its leaks made by stupid people who wanted to show off to the media or their online gaming group.

Georgia operated differently. Chaotic restructurings, including the destruction and refounding of entire intelligence agencies, had shaken the country repeatedly since her 1991 independence from the Soviet Union.

If someone caught the Georgian Intelligence Service attacking Sweden, it would destroy the country's chances at membership in the EU and NATO. Then they'd be on their own when Russia tired of Ukraine's hard soil and turned their attention south again as they had in 2008.

Or perhaps the country's leaders would keep their hands clean, placing all blame on the GIS as a rogue agency. They'd gut the entire Georgian Intelligence Service—perhaps literally in his and Kancheli's case.

No, Kancheli would have thought of that; he'd survived every purge since independence over thirty years ago.

He would...

What would he do? Pavle tried to focus, tried to pretend he

was the one sitting in the lofty perch atop the GIS building with his back to the prettiest view in Tbilisi as a display of his power.

He would...

Pavle swore. "I woke up on a left leg."

"What? What is it, Pavle?" Elene's voice had tightened into a croak of worry at his idiom about having a truly bad day. Kancheli was Seven Fridays in a week's worth of bad.

"If you're right about it coming apart, Kancheli will have foreseen that. One guess who would take the fall."

"At least we'd be buried together," her soft laugh didn't sound resigned...or angry.

It was—

"So how do you save us, Pavle?"

—hopeful?

Save them? He had no idea.

56

"WE'VE BEEN ATTACKING SWEDEN?"

"It's a theory," Mike explained how it fit, without mentioning Holly's little-toe geography theory. Max didn't seem like the sort of guy that would impress.

"Hell of a distraction aiming the Russian president's attention at the far corner of Europe. Guy's a psycho, real hard to predict." Max had poured them each a stout or a lager from Georgian NaturAle.

Mike was more of a Pinot Noir man, but Holly gave the stout a solid four out of five. Tad had knocked back his lager like a Marine in a bar, not a man needing to stay sober on a dangerous mission. Only after he finished it, and saw Mike and Holly had taken little more than a taste, did he appear to realize what he'd done. Max refilled it without comment, but Tad worked on the second more slowly.

Max had a shot glass of Jack Daniel's Twice Barreled Whiskey neat that he hadn't touched yet. At upward of three hundred a bottle retail in the US, it had been a long time since Mike had tasted that. Max noticed his attention and slid the glass across. He tried to refuse, but Max poured himself another. They toasted each other and sipped. It didn't punch, it bloomed in his mouth. Each of the flavors—malt, cocoa, vanilla, sherry from the finishing barrels, and a soft cherry finish—came out and took a separate bow. A raised eyebrow of appreciation between them before they turned back to the matters at hand.

"You're talking to me, why?" Max had returned to crossed-arms mode.

Holly crossed hers in response, probably not understanding that for a guy, it wasn't only a distrust gesture, it was also simply comfortable.

Mike leaned in before she released her umbrage on their only contact's head. "We don't know your country, you do. If someone was doing this, who would it be? How do we find out and stop it before it turns into a war?"

"A war in Scandinavia sounds fine to me. That's fifteen hundred kilometers from here."

"Actually, twenty-one hundred and sixty-two if you want to avoid Russian and Belarusian airspace." And Mike remembered every forsaken minute of his first long solo flight without Miranda. In truth, his second. He didn't remember last April's flight nearly as well; he'd been too worried about flying an unfamiliar and bigger plane into Russian airspace to have time to contemplate the flight itself. The flight to Georgia had been practically mundane, even with the bad weather, which left him far too much time to think.

Max nodded, "Just my point."

"Are you a pilot?"

Max shook his head.

"I'll ask one other question then. You follow the jet stream much?"

Max squinted at him.

"Russia nukes Stockholm. It won't be Chernobyl with the meltdown fallout caught up in local winds spreading to Central and Northern Europe. They won't be putting down herds of Finnish reindeer and fighting new cancers across the region. It'll punch straight up into the jet stream, and you'll never guess where it gets dumped." Mike thumped his finger on the bar, then picked up his shot of whiskey so that his hand wouldn't shake. Even the thought of it hung like a black cloud seeping into the bar.

In reality, the jet stream would dump fallout from a Scandinavian strike on Moscow itself. And a retaliatory Moscow strike would mostly poison a lot of Siberians, but Max wouldn't know that. It would take a bomb on London or Paris for the heaviest fallout to be over Georgia because of the shape of the jet stream's meandering path over Europe.

Max looked up at the arched brick of his former bomb shelter lost in the shadows. The lights were off except for directly over where they sat.

Mike pushed, "And if all NATO pitches in and something goes astray, this place wouldn't stop a normal modern bomb. A nuke..." he shrugged as if he didn't care. It was a role, he was merely playing a role, that's all. But the lovely whiskey didn't warm his insides when he sipped it, instead it lit a furnace burning his gut into full churn.

He felt Holly staring at him, but he didn't dare look away. She would understand the technique and he'd wager that she wouldn't approve. For all her games, she was as straight-laced about the truth as they came, well, in any crowd without Miranda. Andi would have approved though.

Max's gaze met his the moment he looked down from the bar's ceiling. "Okay, made your point."

Mike waited.

Max looked away first. Not down in defeat, but up to the left, the *I'm thinking* quadrant for someone who communicated the way he did—quiet hands, steady eyes, all attention on the words.

"Yeah, I may know somebody. Can't reach out right now. I've got a place you can crash for a couple hours." He glanced at the UNIQ diver's watch on his wrist. "Make that four hours." The red-and-white Georgian flag on the dial had three words written below it in the curly script of Georgian.

"What's it say?" Mike asked. He'd never seen a UNIQ before, though he knew they were very high-end and built right here in Georgia. Mike himself wore a Lilienthal Berlin Meteorite for its clean lines. He liked the thin slice of actual meteorite used in the dial face.

Max glanced down at his watch in surprise, then smiled. "Georgian Special Forces. It's custom for the unit only. So you'd best not be fuckin' with me."

"Not for a single tick of the second hand."

Holly wore twenty-dollar Timex watches that she killed with alarming regularity. For Christmas he'd have to find her whatever the Australian equivalent was to Max's watch.

Then he jolted.

"What?" Max's eyes narrowed.

"Nothing," Mike swallowed against a dry throat. Then he knocked back the last of his whiskey, which burned all the way down.

Christmas lay two weeks off. He planned to be long gone by then. Way far away from Holly Harper.

57

PAVLE WAITED AT THE BASE OF THE HIGHEST STAIRCASE IN GIS headquarters. Neither he nor Elene had slept. Instead they'd talked through plots within plots, double crosses, and every other trick he had learned in the GIS—to no avail.

Everything he thought of, so could Chief Kancheli. And once thought of, the counter-move to it was easy enough to see.

Tell the president that Chief K had gone rogue—the president's family had been murdered by the Russian takeover of the Abkhazia region to the northwest and he would probably be thrilled at arranging a NATO attack on Russia.

Contact the Prime Minister—she and Kancheli had a history longer than the existence of the GIS.

The major general in command of the Georgian Defense Forces—no one would know better how ill-equipped the GDF was to repel a renewed attack. Ukraine had ten times the population and ten times the land area. From occupied Abkhazia and South Ossetia, the Russians could practically hit the three largest Georgian cities with artillery shells. No need for jets, drones, or warships.

Abort the operation—Pavle would be quietly executed and

any of a hundred overeager lower ranked staff would step in to finish the job.

Warn NATO—

That one was interesting. Though what hammer could they bring down? Georgia wasn't a NATO member and they had no direct power. It still seemed the best option. The question then? He couldn't exactly call the front desk in Brussels and ask for help to stop a war.

Besides, Chief K would have thought of that. Pavle's phone was bound to be monitored. Worse, for all he knew, Kancheli might have had all of NATO's phone numbers blocked by the three cell companies and the ten ISPs in the country. It wouldn't take even that much. The Georgian National Communications Commission only had five members and they controlled everything.

NATO. It was the only viable option he and Elene had come up with. He'd have to find some way to work the NATO angle—after this dreaded meeting with Chief Kancheli.

The chief's secretary nodded for him to proceed up the stairs. Tamar was a deceptively attractive woman with a model's flow of brunette hair, a particularly fine face and figure, and a notorious reputation for being utterly vicious. Anyone who spent a lot of time with Chief K would live in a permanent foul mood. Rumors about her ran the gamut, from cold fish all the way to castrating her lovers after their one night with her so that they'd never find pleasure with another. He'd never heard her speak, didn't even know if she could despite working here for years.

Pavle did know, from the time that he'd dropped a folder to the floor out of pure nerves, that she had an MP5K short barrel submachine gun slotted under her desk close by those lovely long legs. He always treated her with the utmost respect.

He checked his watch, 0800 exactly. Kancheli demanded punctuality.

Two men were in his office when Pavle reached the head of the stairs. They each had coffee and the remains of a Khachapuri. The malty smell of the cheese-and-egg bread boat made him wish he'd been able to eat. He'd skipped breakfast because he didn't want to barf from pure fear during this meeting.

"Ah, Pavle," Chief K waved him over. "There is someone I want you to meet. He's a great admirer of your work."

He crossed to shake the man's hand. They traded *gamarjobas,* good mornings.

"Pavle Rapava, my top analyst. Major General Sandor Kurbanov," Kancheli offered one of his chilly smiles, "of NATO."

Pavle felt his own hand go cold in the general's grasp. There would be no help from NATO, they *wanted* this war. Their chance to finally confront Russia once and for all.

He wasn't screwed; he was totally fucked.

58

"NOT LONG NOW."

They sat in the Bunker Bar, once more in the same positions they'd occupied four hours ago. He on the stools with Holly and Tad to either side and Max standing across from them.

Now, a large cast-iron skillet rested on a hot pad in the middle of the bar. In it were eggs poached atop a mixture of fried onion, tomato, walnut, and herbs. Max had provided them with forks and torn sections of sourdough bread as they ate communal style. Mike had never eaten Chirbuli before, but paired with the strong Turkish-style coffee, he almost felt as if he'd slept more than the few hours on the couch Max had pointed him to.

Holly looked like she hadn't slept a single second. Not his problem.

Tad looked as if he'd slept the straight eight of the pure of heart. Mike would really dislike the man if he wasn't so affable.

Or was he too affable?

He'd kept bantering back and forth with Max about military experience. The Georgian had actually opened up enough to tell some utterly bone chilling stories. He'd been deeply involved against Russia during the 2008 Russo-Georgian War. The only thing that ran deeper than his experience was his anger. It was pretty clear that he was more than half serious about delivering a suitcase nuke to the Russian president in person and pulling the trigger in person just to make sure he got his man.

How had Tad managed to not be in the room each time they discussed the Georgian trip? Because he was behind the scenes pulling strings? Did he really know so little about fixed-wing aircraft? His security clearance and ID had checked out, but that didn't stop a person from betraying those.

There was something off in all that bonhomie, but Mike couldn't lay his finger on it.

Warn Holly? Or keep an eye out himself?

In her current mood, if he mentioned his suspicions to her, she might go for answers with that damn knife of hers. So, it was all on him.

Tad's gift of the gab had coaxed Max into talking openly, which was more than Mike had achieved.

"A lot of Georgian Intelligence Service types come in here. Most are exactly what you'd expect."

"Oh great," Holly groaned.

Mike thought back to his FBI stooge days. Most Feebies were awful, some would have slept fine after putting a round through his head. But his handler had been a good guy, saving his life at a risk to his career when it really hit the fan.

"You've got one that's different?" Tad asked him.

Max shrugged. "I know who to ask."

Whatever he'd been waiting for happened. Max set down his fork and moved away from the bar. There was no sign of his tablet, so he wasn't watching the cameras. Mike caught him glancing up to the left again.

"Need to put on another egg. Answer the door."

As Max moved into the kitchen, Mike turned around, looking up to the left. There was a yellow light high up on the wall above the door. Not bright, just a single LED. As he watched, it went out. Close beside it, another one turned red. Followed seconds later by a knock on the door so tentative that he wouldn't have heard it if he hadn't been alerted. So much for his great psychoanalysis of Max's preferred mode of communication; his constant glances up and to the left had been watching his security lights.

As Mike reached the door, he glanced behind. Tad still sat on his stool; Holly was nowhere to be seen. Only past experience let him catch the sound of her knife coming out of its sheath somewhere back in the shadows.

He opened the door.

"Max..." The woman's voice died a few words later when she spotted Mike, which was just as well, he hadn't understood any of what she'd been saying.

She asked something with another *Max* sound in it.

Mike held out a hand. "Hello. I'm Mike Munroe. Max is cooking you some Chirbuli."

The woman didn't cross the threshold, she looked as ready to run as an altar boy caught drawing a Snidely Whiplash mustache and horn-rimmed glasses on a crucified Jesus—a feeling he remembered well. She stood tall, dusky brown hair to her shoulders with a pleasant face and a figure to match. Casual jeans and green blouse completed the picture.

Max called out from the kitchen, "In or out, girl. You're letting in a draft."

Not a breath of air crossed the threshold.

She scanned once more, her eyes hesitating on Tad still at the bar, then she stepped in, sidling around Mike.

He eased the door shut and still she jumped when the latch clicked home. *This* was the one they needed to help them?

Suddenly Mike felt far less confident than he had after talking to Max last night.

She twisted toward the door, perhaps ready to knock him aside in her escape. Then balked hard as Holly slid out of the shadows to stand beside him, blocking the door. Even five-ten with gold-blonde hair and a pale complexion, she found ways to be utterly invisible when in the mood.

He followed the woman's next glance and spotted the emergency exit but she didn't run for it.

Max returned from the kitchen. "Here. No runny middle, just the way you like it." He slid it into the pan still resting on the bar along with a fresh cup of coffee. Apparently she understood English. The woman hurried away from them, over to the bar.

"Spooky little thing, isn't she?" Holly whispered from close beside him.

"Roast in hell." The girl looked straight at them though her voice seemed to come from above. Nothing wrong with her hearing either.

Max pointed upward. "Arch acoustics. One point, Georgians. Zero for the Americans."

"Americans?" she asked, not taking the stool.

"What, you thought we were Russians?" Holly answered.

"No, Max would have already shot you if you were. GIS thugs?"

"I get that sometimes," Tad spoke up. "Being a thuggish sort of guy. But that girl is all sweetness and light." He shot a smile at Holly that said he wasn't done making a play for her. Mike wondered how one man found so many ways to be wrong. Not his concern. When Holly was ready, she'd put Tad down hard enough that he'd never forget it. By her looks, she was ready to perform a vivisection on him atop the bar this very moment.

"Could you two go squabble somewhere that isn't on the brink of war?" Mike moved toward the bar. "We're—"

"War?" The brief life that had come into the woman dissipated in a single breath.

"We're trying to stop one."

"War?" The woman sank onto the stool, would have gone to the floor if it hadn't stood close behind her. "Between Sweden and Russia?"

Now it was his turn to wish a stool stood close behind him.

59

"The problem is one you could not have foreseen," General Kurbanov stated.

Kancheli's grimace agreed.

Pavle stared out the vast window of the GIS building at the Tbilisi Sea. He should go out and drown himself there. That would solve...absolutely nothing.

"They called in an American investigator who is most unusual. I had the opportunity to observe her closely. Any further actions against their aircraft would be ill-advised at this time. She accurately identified in hours what should have taken them weeks for the first events. There was little time for public sentiment to swing negatively toward government reports as were predicted and necessary in your planning document."

Ongoing confusion and the public frustration with government's inability to find answers *had* been an essential element. Without that, it became simply a series of events somehow connected together and became more suspicious in their relationships than the events themselves.

"They weren't supposed to happen so close together," Pavle attempted to show his loyalty to the topic. "The Defence

Minister's trip was moved forward by a week. That the copilot saboteur was scheduled to fly both trips was a fortunate coincidence. He took matters into his own hands. Still, they should never have been connected."

"They were," Kurbanov waved a negligent hand to the northwest.

Then Pavle caught the fleeting expression on Chief Kancheli's face as the man reacted to Kurbanov's statement. Pavle wouldn't have noticed it if he hadn't been working so closely with the chief these last months. No, it wasn't the copilot who had jumped the gun. It was Kancheli. He was the one who had piled the three attacks so close together, ignoring the timeline Pavle had originally laid out.

Three separate investigation teams should have been called out, straining the general population's credulity.

Instead, they were already solved. The third because the clumsy oaf hadn't made good his escape despite equipping him with two Stinger missiles and a getaway driver.

Pavle bit his tongue to avoid reacting. If Kancheli wanted the copilot to take the blame for botching the timing, let him. Pavle could only pray that Chief K hadn't caught on that he now knew who had screwed up the plan.

Kurbanov missed everything. "I would recommend not implementing Phase Four as planned. You did well."

Pavle was glad that someone thought so.

Then he thought about his and Elene's plan to inform NATO and that here was the NATO general in charge of determining whether or not Russia had breached Article 5 to launch an attack. After that, he felt less glad.

"I would recommend escalating directly to Phase Five."

60

HOLLY'S PHONE CHIRPED. WITHOUT THE NORMAL PRESS OF BODIES to dampen the echoes, it filled the Bunker, making everyone jump. Except Max and Holly of course; that had been trained out of their systems. Or perhaps Max's sideways glance at Holly was a Spec Ops soldier's version of being startled.

All Mike knew was his heart skipped a beat, Tad splashed coffee on his pants, and the Georgian woman cried out.

Holly read the message. "Well, that's as much fun as tangling with a box jelly."

"A box jelly?"

"Sure, Max. Come hang out on our northern beaches of Oz in the summer, when the heat starts really cooking the beaches. The box jellyfish come in close to shore. A good sting and they send you back here in a box—the kind that are nailed shut from the outside." Holly's Strine was in full force.

But then she looked at the message again and he saw the humor collapse out of her.

"Hol?" Mike asked.

"From my new best buddy in Hungary. The one who offered to shoot Tad for me."

"He did *what?*"

They both ignored Tad. Mike hadn't thought about that. Had Tad been trying to stop Holly from learning what had gone missing for the NATO warehouses?

Mike, at least, had recognized the Delta Force operator for what he was. Why was he suddenly up to his knees in Spec Ops: Holly, Delta, and now Max? The woman who hadn't introduced herself didn't fit the bill, but he was ready to believe anything right about now.

Holly held up her phone. "I hate when I'm right."

Mike waited her out. He hated when she was right too and it took them both a moment to prepare themselves for whatever news she'd just received.

"Army's missing an AH-6 ULB."

Mike blinked hard, twice. No magic happened; he had no idea what that might be.

"The unmanned Little Bird helo?" Tad saved him. The Little Bird he knew. It was a small helo that could carry two pilots plus four special operators sitting outside on benches, or two pilots and a hell of a lot of weapons. In that latter version it was dubbed the Killer Egg. But he didn't know it could operate unmanned.

"Worse," Holly answered. "It's a stealth-enhanced version. They didn't note it was missing on the first pass because it's kept locked up and out of sight—at least it's supposed to be. And that's the good bit."

"What's the bad?" Max's arms bulged with muscle where he clenched them across his chest.

"Navy depot turned up missing a pair of Mark 46 torpedoes to go with it. They're little, designed for air drop. Three meters long and two-fifty kilos with fifty of that being explosive warhead. They'd do a real nice job of downing a submarine. Plenty nasty against a ship too."

"Holly, we're air investigators," Mike reminded her. "We

don't know crap about ships." Felt as if his barstool sloshed about under his butt. Torpedoes?

They looked at each other for several seconds, then both turned to Max.

"No, do not be doing of that. I know nothing of ships and boats. In 2008 we had nineteen, total. The Russians, they sink seven and steal all the little ones. I was in South Ossetia, two hundred kilometers from nearest boat. You, from Australia. You are surrounded by water."

Holly shook her head. "Big place, Australia. I grew up in the deep Outback, mate, a *thousand* klicks from anything bigger than a puddle. Our one river ran dry over half the year—on the wet years. Did my dance blowing up things, mostly planes and infrastructure."

"Ha! Knew there was reason I like you." He pulled up his t-shirt, revealed a jagged scar that crossed from his left belly to his right shoulder. "We captured Russian artillery, which blows up the third time we fired it. Piece of shit."

"Max is my cousin," the woman spoke up. "He's why I want to be a nurse. I saw how hard his recovery was." Her English was much better, though still heavily inflected in the Eastern European style.

"So, what do we do?"

Mike stared up at the ceiling for a while. He didn't know quite what he'd been thinking, swept up in yet another of Holly's leap-first plans. Sure, they would simply fly to Georgia, ask around to find out who had attacked Sweden to foment a war, and ask them to stop. *Good thinking there, Mike.*

"Where the hell is NATO General Kurbanov when you need him?"

61

Holly froze. That was a *hell* of a good question.

In fact...

"When did Kurbanov leave the plane? He flew in with us. When did he go?" Then she recalled. "He was off that plane close on Tad's heels."

Mike nodded. "I saw him grab his luggage and climb into a Mercedes SUV."

"How big was that luggage?"

Mike shook his head, and she hadn't seen it.

"I helped him load it into the cargo bay back in Stockholm," Tad held up his hands to make a shape in the air two-feet square. "About like so. On the heavy side."

Holly closed her eyes. How had she been so stupid? "Big enough and heavy enough to fit in an MK 22 ASR rifle with scope and rounds?"

Tad considered for a moment. "Diagonally, with the stock folded and the barrel removed. I'd say yes."

"A pair of those were missing from inventory in Pápa Air Base in Hungary. I'll bet General Kurbanov had one of those."

"Why?"

She shifted her attention from Tad to Mike and waited. She saw him thinking it through, damn but it was amazing to watch him at work. No shooting. No breaching charges. He simply stood there in the middle of the Bunker Bar and thought.

"How long to assemble the rifle?"

"Secure the barrel, load, add some optics and a flash suppressor," Holly would assume the guy wasn't Special Operations trained but still... "Under a minute."

"Why the delay between the two shots?" He knew crap about firearms, yet kept asking the right questions. Mike was so sexy when he did this.

"It's a bolt-action rifle with a five-round magazine." Holly demonstrated, swinging up a bolt, pulling it back to eject the spent shell, then ram it home and down to shove the next round from the magazine into the chamber. Finally, time to return a hand to the trigger and aim the weapon. About as long as it had taken her to haul Mike out of the copilot's seat and drag him down into the aisle on top of her.

"But why would he try to kill us?"

"Because," the woman at the bar spoke, "you were right about coming to Georgia to stop a war in Sweden. Pavle said that his boss had *another asset* who Pavle knew nothing about."

"And who's Pavle?"

"He," she offered in a slightly haughty tone, "is the second most important man in the Georgian Intelligence Service. And he's my fiancé."

"And who are you?"

She stopped and her shoulders slumped. "Me? I'm Elene. I'm nobody."

Holly wanted to give her a hard shake and some lecture on being somebody—because Holly remembered that feeling all too well herself from the sixteen years of growing up in her parents' home. But before she put thought into action, Mike spoke up.

"Then who the hell is Kurbanov? Why would a NATO general conspire with a non-NATO country to kill some flight investigators?"

Nobody appeared ready to answer that one.

62

MIRANDA ALWAYS ADAPTED QUICKLY TO TIME ZONE CHANGES. SHE
liked that Meg did the same. However, neither of them could
do it in a single night. And because both of them were still on
Swedish time, they were up at five a.m. Iceland time and
headed outside the ISASI conference hotel for a morning walk
in the December darkness. At this time of year, the sun
wouldn't rise for another six hours.

She wore her heaviest parka and given Meg her knitted dog
sweater that fit under her Therapy Dog vest. No one on the
team had owned up to the kind gift, not that she'd asked. If the
giver wished to remain anonymous, that was okay too. Meg
appreciated it on these cold days. It was very nice, matching the
dark geometrics of the thick Pendleton blanket on Miranda's
bed.

The multi-story glass atrium of the lobby gave the
impression of being outdoors with the night beyond the clear
ceiling. She hoped that Meg didn't think she was out of doors
until they were actually outside.

"Ms. Chase, going for a walk?" a man sat in the shadows in
one of the lobby chairs.

It was the man from the bar last night; he still wore no nametag. Though neither did she as the conference didn't begin for another four hours and Meg already knew her name.

"I'm sorry about leaving you to pay for my tea. I will..." she reached into her pocket but all she unearthed was her room key and a small roll of compostable dog-waste bags "...have to pay you back later."

"It was my pleasure. I'm only sorry that you were too tired to enjoy it."

Meg looked from her to the door. "Excuse me. Meg is waiting."

"Might I join you?" He rose to his feet and lifted a black woolen trench coat from where it had been draped over the arm of his chair.

She had her noise-canceling headphones in case he became troublesome. She'd rather be alone but Tante Daniels, her childhood therapist and eventual governess, had taught Miranda enough to suspect that would be rude. Nodding her assent, Miranda headed for the door. The man hurried ahead to hold it open for Meg.

The chill...she reached for the weather meter in her vest, except the vest remained in her room. The chill of...several degrees below freezing, wrapped around them.

"Last night I asked—"

"There's no need to repeat yourself." Then she covered her mouth. "Sorry, I didn't mean to interrupt."

"That's quite all right. Have you given the matter any thought?"

"I have made no *general* conclusions regarding the three incidents in Sweden. I did make three *specific* conclusions, which were reported to the proper Swedish and NATO authorities."

"NATO?"

"Yes. There was no need to report to the NTSB or FAA as we

were in an assistance role, not the primary investigating authority. General Kurbanov said he was sent to assess any Article 5 violations of the North Atlantic Treaty."

Meg was squatting along the edge of the front walkway and Miranda was keeping a close eye to see if Meg urinated or if she needed to unroll the first of an average two-point-three waste bags per day.

The man put his hand lightly on her arm and all she could do was stare at it.

A light touch used to freeze her mentally as well, but now it only stopped her physically—from doing *anything*. He was touching her, but not touching her. Being aware that all of her attention now lay trapped at the focal point of that contact didn't allow her to break the deadlock that it created. There and not there. Feeling it. And not. Torn between brushing it aside or clamping the contact hard against her arm; neither proved possible. Only the contact that—

Meg growled sharply. Then barked at the man.

Miranda heard the bark, but couldn't process why.

There was only the touch that wasn't a touch until—

The man stumbled away and her world snapped back into place.

"What's bothering her?"

Meg continued growling at him.

"You touched me."

"I didn't mean anything by it."

Miranda shushed Meg, then rubbed at her arm. The touch, which wasn't, still hovered on her nerve endings. And people wondered why she always avoided contact with other people. She also touched her headphones to assure herself they remained at the ready, though she wouldn't put them on yet. Except for the man, the quiet of the morning remained quite complete.

"I'm autistic. I find light touch very...distracting. Meg knows this."

"Well, I didn't. Please accept my apologies."

She nodded her acquiescence before petting Meg and returning to her walk. Meg didn't move to pee again, instead she watched the man carefully between steps forward.

"Ms. Chase. Please. A moment."

"How long is a moment? I've always wondered about that. My initial assumption that a moment ranged between greater than a second but less than a minute have been invalidated. Those requesting a moment typically use that as a premise to embark upon a far longer interruption than seems warranted by the word. I always find this curious. Should I be asking how long a moment do you wish for?"

"I'm concerned it will be a longer sort of moment."

"Can't it wait until after we complete our walk?" This time Meg squatted and made another patch of snow yellow. The terrier stepped forward and kicked fresh snow over it with her hind legs. She'd always been a very tidy dog.

"If I understand what you just said, I shouldn't have delayed my *moment* from last night to this morning."

"Is this about my autism or my specific conclusions?"

Meg resumed walking and sniffing more naturally as the man made no other unusual moves.

"It is about the man who *claimed* to be a NATO general investigating treaty violations of Article 5."

This time it was Miranda who stopped. She turned to him and noted that the second to top button of his trench coat had not been pushed fully through the buttonhole. Instead, it was three-quarters exposed and one-quarter hidden. Did that make the button uncomfortable? It wouldn't be the coat or the button manufacturer's intended design.

He looked down at his chest, then quickly set the button to rights as it should be. The coat's fabric lay better as well.

"This general—" the man began.

"Oh, why did you say, who *claimed* to be?"

"Because, I'm *Général de division aérienne,* what you would call a two-star major general, Pierre Vachon of France. I was traveling to Sweden particularly to meet with you regarding your recent investigations when I heard you were returning to Reykjavik; my plane arrived an hour earlier than yours. I'm the NATO department head for Article 5 investigations. More importantly, we have no General Kurbanov on our staff."

63

KOMMENDÖR KERSTIN HOLMGREN STUDIED THE SWEEP OF HER
sweet boat's radar. She'd been issued an all-speed order last
night to race to the eastern limits of the Gulf of Finland. At
thirty-seven knots, the seventy-meter-long Visby class corvette
HSwMS *Karlstad* had covered the four hundred kilometers
from Stockholm in under six hours.

She wished she knew *why* she'd brought His Swedish
Majesty's Ship here but those details weren't forthcoming yet.
Typical military, a lot of hurry-up-and-wait without ever
knowing quite why.

Thought it wasn't hard to guess. Someone had downed a
Gripen jet here at the edge of Russian territorial waters.
Command was scrambling to get some serious assets into place
in case it was the warning shot of a Russian *putsch* against
Scandinavia.

So far, *Karlstad* was the lone naval asset along the edge of
Russian territorial waters. She'd left the nearest submarine,
moving at half her speed, far behind. Never had a forty-
kilometer wide stretch of water felt as narrow. Estonia to the

south, Finland north, and nothing but Russia dead ahead. Drift ice, some of it a half-meter thick, added to the clutter.

The pair of Saab Gripens patrolling overhead counted for some comfort—though less than she liked after yesterday's events. She hoped for their sakes they didn't know that her attack-rigged AgustaWestland AW109M helicopter had been switched out for the AW109LUH search-and-rescue bird even as they'd raced out of port. Though the pilots must know of Major Eklund's forcible seat ejection and death by now, they might find it disconcerting to know that the *Karlstad* was more prepared to rescue them than to fight.

Karlstad boasted a complement of forty-three aboard plus the helicopter's crew of three. She'd sent all she dared to the bunks as they roared across the northern Baltic. What little they'd slept, with all sixteen megawatts of the four gas turbines driving the twin waterjet drives at top speed, was all they were going to get for a while.

"Engineering, I want a full system check after that high-speed run."

They acknowledged the order.

Tactical were at their scopes. She ordered battle rations. They were slower to distribute to the entire crew and less appealing, but the two cooks would deliver food and coffee to where the crew were rather than releasing them from duty stations to hit the galley.

The coming dawn was fast chasing away the darkest blue. If the Russians made a move, would it be in the short six hours of daylight? She hoped so. The Visby class corvettes were angular with stealth, fast with their big engines, had plenty of teeth for a fight, and had all the gear to fight at night.

But they were still a small boat stationed directly opposite St. Petersburg. And dodging through floating ice in the dark if fast maneuvering was required wouldn't go well at all.

Worse, they were also two years from the scheduled refit

that would give her anti-aircraft weaponry. All of her current armament assumed she'd be hunting subs or other ships. The recent Ukraine War had finally woken up the leaders to what their commanders had been saying for years. The next war was going to come mostly from the air: jets, drones, artillery, and more drones. The *Karlstad* remained ill-equipped to fend off those, though Kerstin would use her ship's armaments to the limit.

Tactical showed that a Finnish missile boat should be arriving in two hours. They were half the size of her Visby-class boat, but they did carry two different surface-to-air missile systems and she'd be happier once they were alongside.

Where was an American destroyer when she needed one? Probably sitting outside the mouth of the Baltic, *not wishing to appear provocative.* Eighteen hundred kilometers by sea placed them thirty-plus hours away. Useless bloody Yanks. They'd only be helpful after she was dead.

64

"HELLO, HOLLY. IS GENERAL KURBANOV STILL WITH YOU?"

As if that wasn't the question of the year. "Hi, Miranda. No, he isn't. Where are you?"

"Approximately thirty-five meters from the front door of the conference hotel."

Mike waggled his hands with spread fingers and offered a smile to Holly.

Yeah, from Miranda *approximately* meant she was between thirty-four and thirty-six meters away from the door. Actually, there'd been enough of a pause she might have pulled out her range meter to measure the precise distance. No, then she'd have reported the tenths as well.

"Why are you asking about Kurbanov?"

"I didn't."

Holly stared at the phone where she'd placed it on the bar before answering. "You just did, Miranda."

"Well, yes. That's technically accurate. But the person who wanted to know the answer isn't me. Does that mean that it's still my question or is it his?"

"It depends. Who is he?"

A man spoke up, "I'm *Général de division aérienne* Pierre Vachon."

"Seem to be a lot of you two-star types floating about."

"Perhaps. However, I *am* with NATO and can guarantee you that Major General Kurbanov is not."

Holly sighed. "So, no big surprise he tried to shoot us. Don't worry, Miranda, he missed."

"I had surmised that from your use of the word *tried*. I'm glad you aren't dead."

Max barked out a laugh but kept other thoughts to himself.

"Where are you now?" Général Vachon asked over the speakerphone.

"Not so sure about answering that. I'm not a big fan of major generals at the moment. The last one punched several holes in Miranda's jet while trying to punch holes in us." And she felt that her shoulders were still up around her ears with the tension of how close she'd come to losing Mike.

"My jet? He shot my *jet*?"

Elene furrowed her brow and whispered to Mike, "She's more worried about someone shooting her jet than shooting you?"

Mike rested a calming hand on her shoulder and answered as softly, "Shooting *at* us would be very distinct to Miranda from *actually* shooting her plane. One is safely complete. The other has consequences." Holly noted that he didn't mention the dead GDF soldier.

Holly returned her attention to the phone side of the conversation. "We've called in a repair team. We'll send the bill to Kurbanov as soon as we find him. First, Pierre buddy, can you prove who you are?"

Five seconds later her phone beeped with two images. One of a man bundled up in a trench coat outside a hotel at night.

The other of an ID with a matching picture. She used the security app on her phone to process the bar code on the ID. His scan passed muster, saying he was both himself and a top-ranking NATO officer.

But what would have happened if she'd thought to scan Kurbanov's ID?

Mike turned his own phone to face her. He'd done a search on Général Pierre Vachon on the NATO site—the photo matched. Then Mike flipped to another screen. No hits on a Sandor Kurbanov.

That'll teach us, he mouthed. He'd been the one all worried about Tad Jobson being authentic on his arrival. It made her feel better, no, *less worse* that neither of them had checked Kurbanov's identity.

She nodded. Neither of them had thought to question a two-star. Not a mistake either of them would make again.

"Okay," Holly patted Mike's sleeve in sympathy as he looked as gut-shot as she felt, "so, Pierre, we're in Georgia."

"The country? Why?"

By the time she and Mike had explained the thinking that had led them here, and Elene had been coaxed into speaking loudly enough to be heard, Général Vachon sounded ready to stroke out.

"...and we don't know how high it goes. At least to the top of the Georgian Intelligence Service. Possibly to the president or prime minister, even the military. But we don't know which if any yet."

"Get out of there. You're a civilian team and in way over your heads."

Holly glanced around the bar. Everyone's expression said he could go to hell, especially Elene's. She appeared to have slipped over into some kind of protect-my-man mode that reminded Holly of Mike's comment about Taz becoming more formidable as a mom than as an Air Force colonel.

Protect her man? Certainly a thought that Holly herself had never conjured up, not even about Mike. Except what had been her first priority after those two shots at the jet? Tucking him inside a Didgori *while* wearing a bulletproof vest.

"Over our heads," she answered for them. "Guess we'd better swim harder. Unless you have an action team just hanging out ready to invade a non-NATO member country? If you do, that would be totally peachy with us." Nobody's expression except Tad's agreed with that statement.

It earned her a thoughtful silence many heartbeats long.

"So what's your plan?"

"Easy. Find Kurbanov. Beat the shit out of him for trying to shoot my boyfriend."

That earned her a sharp look from Mike. Okay...maybe she shouldn't have said boyfriend. That implied things she'd rather not think about.

"After that?" Holly plunged back into the topic at hand. "Try to extract from him how to stop a war. Then I know about this bar here in Tbilisi where I plan to get seriously drunk. Maybe do some dancing."

Max smiled at her.

"What are you going to be doing from way over there in Iceland, General? Other than bothering Miranda."

Again the long pause.

"You could hunt down the missing ULB and torpedoes," Holly suggested.

"The what?"

Holly could almost get to enjoy this. "*Général de division aérienne* Pierre Vachon of the French Republic. You need to pay more attention to the little birds twittering at you from atop the ghost gum tree. Pápa Air Base lost an unmanned helo and a pair of Mark 46s. Have Miranda explain that to you if you need help, I'm out of time."

She hung up on the general, which was very satisfying.

Then she looked at the others. "Okay, open season on Kurbanov. Any ideas on how we find him?"

Holly really hoped that some old connection of Max's knew something.

But she didn't expect Elene to be the one tentatively raising her hand like she was still in kindergarten.

65

"YOU HAVE A VERY INTERESTING TEAM, MS. CHASE."

"I do? Why do you say that?" She'd never have thought to use that particular word to describe them.

"How good are they?"

Meg looked at the general. Miranda wanted to pull up her doggie emotion chart. Meg had neither angry-face nor happy-face. Perhaps waiting-face? "How good are they at what?"

"At what they're doing." His tone of voice shifted.

Meg's waiting-face shifted toward angry-face. She rose onto all fours. Preparing for a fight or to walk away?

Miranda answered carefully. "As I don't know what they're doing, I see no practical method of assessing their skills at their current tasks."

"At stopping a war?" The general's tone turned...fiercer?

Meg's answering growl sounded as if it came from a much bigger dog. She liked Meg, but making that sound? It reminded her too much of the Chow Chow that had once attacked her. Miranda took a careful step back hoping that she didn't hurt Meg's feelings. Meg appeared to only be watching the general, so maybe it was okay.

"I don't know. Roy has thanked them for doing precisely that a few times but I never quite understood why."

"Roy?" the general asked in a less...fierce...tone.

"President Roy Cole."

"Of the United States?"

"Yes, that one. Are there any other President Roy Coles? I only know of the one."

"Me too."

"Then why did you ask?"

She felt the general studying her.

Meg remained vigilant while he considered her question. When he didn't answer, she walked to the end of her leash to sniff at a lamppost rising from the snow. She piddled on it.

"What is a ULB and a Mark 46?" The general asked softly.

"A ULB is an unmanned Little Bird. It is a stealth-rigged version of an MH-6 helicopter capable of autonomous flight. The Mark 46 is a two-hundred-and-thirty-kilogram torpedo. The former is fully capable of carrying and delivering two of the latter over four hundred kilometers. Perhaps twice that distance if it's the Mission Enhanced Little Bird with the AACUS unit, that's Autonomous Aerial/Cargo Utility System, installed."

The general scrabbled at the top buttons of his trench coat, then reached inside to extract his phone from a breast pocket. He hurried away as he dialed.

She and Meg looked at each other, then resumed their walk.

Miranda hoped that he rebuttoned his coat properly this time.

66

PAVLE FELT THE PHONE BUZZ AGAINST HIS THIGH.

Elene often texted him funny little messages to brighten up his day. She also often sent him photos of her favorite bird, the Eurasian blue tit, a brightly blue, yellow, and black relative of the American chickadee.

But after last night's strategizing how to avoid war, she'd looked beaten, no more than a wisp of her usual self.

He hadn't been negative, honestly trying to consider her ideas, but the well he'd fallen down ran deep and the sides were too slick to climb. Every idea she'd put forth, he'd found too many reasons it wouldn't work.

When it buzzed again only seconds later, he risked slipping it out. Her innate positivity must have somehow reemerged since this morning. He wanted to bask in that for even a few seconds.

Kurbanov and Kancheli were discussing next steps, though all three of them agreed none should be needed. The next stage of the plan would create such a catastrophic event that battle would be engaged within hours.

It made the events to date appear to be mere harassment in comparison.

Pavle glanced down. No picture. A message, piled on top of two others.

Pavle. Call me.

Now, Pavle.

Please answer me.

What could possibly be so urgent?

He glanced at Kurbanov and Kancheli. They stood side-by-side gazing southeast out the office's big window. The morning sun sparkling off the Tbilisi Sea. Kancheli stood at a distinct cant, as if the winds of time were preparing to finally blow the chief aside. Couldn't happen soon enough.

Can't. Busy. He sent back.

The phone buzzed in his hand before he managed to return it to his pocket. He almost dropped it in surprise.

Now, Pavle! Call or meet me at the Chronicle.

He stared at the message; for her there existed no higher tone of urgency. If there was ever one place in Tbilisi—in the world—that Elene would never go under any circumstances, it was the Chronicle of Georgia.

Her father's first job out of school had been the first day of work on that monumental piece of art. From 1985 to 1991, he'd risen from laborer to the site manager's job. He'd become very close to the artist Zurab Tsereteli. His career and his fortune were made.

Until the collapse of the Soviet Union in 1991. The monument had been underwritten by the USSR. When work here in Georgia had stopped, Tsereteli had moved on. But not Elene's father.

Out of work, his reputation smeared by his work for the despised Soviets, the man had never recovered. Russia had occupied, then subjugated Georgia for two hundred and eight years and no one would forgive him such a trespass.

The Chronicle towered less than a kilometer to the north, clearly visible from Kancheli's office. Its thirty-five-meter-tall pillars of stone, bronze, and copper offered an all-round view that included the sea, the city, and the southern Caucasus Mountains. The life of Christ on the lower section of the pillars. Kings, queens, poets and artists above. And celebrations of Georgian life, like the harvest and world's oldest winemaking tradition reaching back over eight thousand years adorned the pillar tops.

Pavle had visited there many times—before Elene.

The work on the monument had continued slowly, but her father had refused to return to the site. Elene, raised to want no part of her brooding father, wanted no part of the work that had destroyed him either.

Pavle tucked the phone away. Keeping a hand on it in his pocket to suppress any further incoming buzzes, he crossed to stand beside Chief Kancheli.

"There are some things I must see to. I'll be back in a few minutes."

Kancheli barely acknowledged him. Once this mission was over...

Pavle swallowed hard.

You're too smart to get caught up in this when it comes apart, Elene had insisted.

If he was so smart...

There were only three futures.

One: this worked and he would be trapped as Chief K's hatchet man. A role he'd never survive for long.

Two: this worked and Kancheli erased Pavle's existence to protect the operation's secrecy.

Or three: Elene's prediction came true. *It is going to come apart.* And then they would both be executed; him as the fall guy and her for the secrets he'd told her.

He hurled down the stairs, for once not caring what

Kancheli's receptionist Tamar thought of him as he raced by. There was already a target on his back.

67

"Pavle!" Elene cried out the moment she answered her phone.

He squatted in one of the secure booths used for communicating with overseas agents, two floors below Kancheli's office. He prayed that Chief K didn't have these rooms monitored as well.

"I've been so afraid for you!" Her voice had lost all control.

"I'm fine, Elene. I'm completely fine." Which was the biggest lie of his life.

"You need...need...to listen to..." Her speech, choked by sobs, finally broke down completely.

"Elene?"

There was a brief sound of someone taking her phone and her sobs fell into the background.

"G'day, mate. I think we need to have a wee bit of a chat." A woman with a thick Australian accent covered Elene's background sobs.

"Who the fuck are you?"

"Aw, mate. I'm your new best gal."

"If you hurt so much as a hair on—"

"Not on the agenda, mate. Here, got a friend wanting to chat with you."

"Tell him to go—"

"Hey, buddy. You somewhere secure?"

Pavle knew the voice, but he couldn't place it. Familiar enough that he knew it well, but too out of context to pin down. It was deep and rough, like it spent more time being used to shout than talk. Like...

Shouting over a busy crowd and a dance band in a busy bar. To take a drink order.

"Somewhere secure? Yes, I am."

"Good. Let's leave names out of this. Answer the lady's questions. Time is running short. Your lady is fine with me."

"Uh, thanks. It really helps to know that."

Max was one of those people he knew well but knew nothing about. The man had poured him hundreds of drinks over the years. Had shared a toast with him when he and Elene became engaged. Always had a pleasant nod. And nothing much else beyond the story of his tattoos. Tattoos. GSOF. And when someone like Max introduced you to someone else...

"Okay, I'm listening."

"Good man." And Max faded into the background.

The Aussie returned. "Looking for a chap doing a dance in a NATO outfit. About five-eight, dark hair—"

"I've spent the last few hours with him."

"Aw, give the man a kewpie doll. Well done, mate. Where is the bloke?"

"Upstairs, meeting with Chief Kancheli. At GIS headquarters."

"Not the sort of squat I can go strolling into, I'm guessing."

"That would be a clear no."

There was a brief round of whispers he couldn't quite catch.

"Glass, rooftop office?"

"Yes."

"What's their plan?"

"I don't know much beyond the scale of it. Torpedoes from a helicopter and a boat somewhere, but they don't say which one. I think they're on the verge of shutting me out completely. Why is NATO conspiring with Kancheli?"

"NATO is asking the same question, mate."

"They're...what?" Pavle was missing something.

"That's two hints," the Aussie seemed to be enjoying this madness. "Do ye need a third? Chappie's doing a dance. NATO asking..."

Pavle finally caught on. "He's not NATO!"

"Ding! Ding! Ding! Stuffed koala bear with the kewpie doll. Ready to go for the big money?"

"Sure." It was all Pavle could think to say. Not NATO. Then his back door might still be open to get them out of this. But wait, she'd said that NATO was asking the question. He didn't have to reach out to them, they were already reaching out to him. "Yes. What can I do?"

"Can you get them out of that building?"

He laughed. "Not a chance. Rumor is that Kancheli has a panic room somewhere here that he lives inside of, like a vampire in his coffin."

A long silence, followed by a few more whispers.

"Is there a patio out front of that glass office? Can you get them both out on the roof?"

"Maybe..."

"Make that a yes and you get the dinky-di prize, mate."

"And what's that?"

"I give you a better than fifty percent chance of surviving this fiasco."

He didn't need to think about it, "I like those odds." Best he'd had since the day Kancheli had called him up to the office.

68

"Ms. Chase. If you would come with us please." Two men in military uniforms met her as she and Meg stepped back into the hotel lobby.

"I was planning on a shower and breakfast."

"This way, ma'am." The two men moved in closer. She stumbled backward against the glass door. Meg sprang in front of her and barked viciously at both of them.

"Ma'am, we've been instructed not to touch you. Please, could you just come with us."

Everything was a jumble. No sign of Jeremy yet this morning. Perhaps he was talking to Taz. Or had he been kidnapped?

And Mike and Holly were gone.

And that Tad Jobson had shown up claiming he could replace Andi, which was impossible. No one could replace her.

And the NATO general with the news that she'd been reporting confidential Swedish military information to an *imposter* general before he'd rushed away.

And Meg wouldn't stop barking.

And—

She dragged on her headphones and turned the noise-canceling up to full. It wasn't enough, and she started the audio track. It was ambient sound generated by transforming the frequency range of solar wind particles striking the Earth's magnetic field. There was a gentle swooping randomness that always helped to soothe her.

Then she scooped Meg up into her arms and looked around for what to do.

Everyone was looking at her. Meg was still barking, though Miranda felt more than heard that fact. But Meg was no contest for such weapons.

When one of the armed men waved a hand toward the direction they wanted her to go, she bowed to the inevitable. Keeping her head down so that she didn't have to see anyone, she went where they told her.

Meg stopped barking but kept banging the top of her head against Miranda's chin as she swiveled about to watch everything. After the third time the impact made her bite her tongue, she firmly clamped her jaw closed and lowered her chin to her chest to avoid further collisions.

They held open a door for her.

It was the lecture room for the conference sessions. Enough tables for all the attendees to sit comfortably and view one of the two large screens.

She recognized the sole occupant by the black woolen trench coat draped over the chair beside him. In the half hour since she'd last seen him, he appeared to have lost some control. An open briefcase sat on the white tablecloth. A computer, his phone, and a battered notepad were spread before him. None of their edges lines up.

Meg pushed up in her arms and looked over Miranda's shoulder. She turned part way so that she could see without blocking Meg's view.

The doors had closed, with the two men now on the outside.

A careful scan of the room showed that it was only the three of them, Général Vachon, herself, and Meg.

She saw the general was speaking to her.

Miranda stopped the solar wind music. When that appeared safe, she risked turning off the headphones.

Still okay.

Before she could take them off, there was a chaotic noise that had her jumping away from the double entry door and turning the noise-canceling back on.

Meg began barking again.

Finally, a man burst into the room, with one of the soldiers grabbing at him.

"Jeremy!" she called out.

His mouth moved.

She turned off her headphones, but didn't push them aside.

"Are you okay?" he repeated.

"I don't know!"

Jeremy glared around while trying to yank his arm out of the soldier's grasp who kept a firm hold on him.

Général Vachon waved the soldier aside. "It's okay. Leave him be."

Jeremy almost fell onto his face between the man releasing him and his efforts to reach Miranda. Not quite falling into Meg, he stopped a step away.

"Why aren't you okay?"

"I didn't say I wasn't. I said I didn't know. You need to ask the general."

Jeremy turned, then planted himself firmly between them as if he was trying to be Andi, Holly, Mike, and Taz all at once. "Well?"

"She's fine. I simply need to talk to her."

"And who are you?"

"NATO Général Pierre Vachon."

Jeremy glanced over his shoulder at her. "Didn't we already have one of those?"

"Kurbanov was a fake general," she told him.

"Really?" Jeremy blinked once, twice. "You know, that makes sense in a strange way. He never used his ID, always following someone else through security checkpoints. You never invited him on the plane with us, did you? Yet he joined in with—"

He spun to look at the general, then back at her.

"Holly, Mike, and Tad!"

"They're okay. At least Holly and Mike are. I would assume that they'd have mentioned if Tad wasn't."

"Oh." Jeremy took a deep breath, shook himself like Meg after a bath, and scratched Meg on the head. He turned to the general. "Is that what you wanted to talk about?"

"No."

69

"Holy hell, mate. That's beautiful." Holly wanted to take it out of his hands and give it a hug.

"Russian Orsis T-5000. Chambered in .338 Lapua Magnum." Max had extracted the impossibly nasty-looking rifle from the case in the back of his SUV, which they'd parked a hundred meters from the crest of the Chronicle Monument.

"Where did you lay your hands on that?"

"Oh, got it from this guy who hated to let it go."

"I can only imagine." It was Russia's newest sniper rifle. First shown in 2011, it had risen to be the sniper rifle of choice at the very top levels of the Russian clandestine services. She'd never actually seen one in the flesh. Only two ways a Russian sniper would let go of such a weapon, a lot of money or...

"I *talked* him out of it with this," he tapped the other case. "In 2014."

Holly sighed happily when she cracked it open. Inside lay the TAC-50 that she knew best. Both rifles reached past a kilometer and a half with ease. In 2014. That meant Max must have been among the Georgian volunteers to fight the Russian takeover of Crimea and far eastern Ukraine. At least one sniper had returned to Moscow in a box, without his rifle.

Mike dragged her aside. "Do you trust Tad?"

Holly couldn't answer at first. "I thought you were the one who checked out his credentials."

Mike shook his head. "I did. They came back clean. But... I've got an itch."

"Shit! Shit! Shit!" Mike's *itches* had saved all their lives more than once.

She made a point of looking casual as she scanned their team.

They'd planned to have Mike and Elene in civilian clothes to act as lookouts. Elene remained stock still by the passenger door as if the December morning had frozen her into a statue.

Max had rounded up three Georgian Defence Forces uniforms for the rest of them. Tad had walked to the edge of the empty parking lot and appeared to be admiring the view.

According to Max, the place was a good bet to be deserted on a chill winter weekday morning. But he'd taught Tad how to say, *Training exercise. Come back after one hour,* in passable Georgian. He had a good ear and looked dangerous enough to not argue with. Though he was probably the only black man in uniform anywhere in the country.

Holly eased back to Max's side as he reached for a submachine gun for Tad. She flashed him a quick Freeze hand sign and hoped that the signals were universal. He stopped.

Holly pushed the submachine gun under a blanket that had been drawn over the cases.

"Hey, Tad." As he turned from the view and ambled over, she picked up a handgun, dumped the magazine, and slammed in an empty mag. Then she turned to him and made a show of cycling the slide, catching and hiding the ejected live round from the chamber into her cupped fingers.

"We ready?" he asked. "Stunner of a place you folks have here. Even in winter, it's got this good feel to it."

"Here you go." Holly jammed the sidearm into his holster in case he could feel it was underweight for having no rounds. "Don't go shooting anybody with that." Because it was empty and wouldn't work.

"Deal!"

She trusted him, so what the hell did Mike know about Tad that she didn't?

"A hundred steps," Max nodded upslope.

No way to ask Mike or answer Max's questioning look. Time to switch to action mode. She dropped the question, then nodded.

"Uphill all the way."

A pair of giant columns guarded the steps. One looking properly Greek, its mate looking as if it had survived a battle between Picasso and a chain saw artist. At the head of the long flight rose sixteen pillars of stone ten stories tall. They were like some neat freak had rearranged Stonehenge into symmetrical rows and squared up all the rocks until perfectly smooth.

She scanned the tactical situation. Low trees blocked their view in most directions except where Tad had been. But the trees were sparse up the hillside.

"Okay, let's hustle." She resisted the temptation to race. They both needed slow and steady heartbeats at the top. Max's half smile acknowledged the choice and a bit of regret that they wouldn't be doing that.

Still, they took them faster than most would, traveling smoothly side-by-side, leaving the other three in their wake.

70

"You seem...nervous." Mike stepped up beside Elene after the others had moved off.

"I suppose."

Actually, by his assessment, she teetered near the edge of a nervous breakdown.

He offered his arm. She looked steadier after she looped a gloved hand around his parka's elbow. They began climbing the stairs at a much slower pace.

Tad had set off on a circular patrol around the lower level path.

"So, did you meet your fiancé here?"

That actually earned him a laugh. "I never, ever come here. This is where my father's hope and heart died. I sometimes think my mother got herself killed to get away from his dark cloud. She traveled to South Ossetia during the Russian War as a volunteer nurse. No training, simply to help. The Russians trapped them and killed everyone in the town as a part of their ethnic cleansing campaign."

"No good memories here."

"No. Pavle is my first truly good memories since Mother died."

Mike had to stop and catch his breath though they were barely half up the stairs and hadn't been hurrying.

Had *he* ever measured his life in good memories?

In good times, sure. Snow bunnies and fine restaurants. A con well played. A game won.

But good memories? How many of those did he have before joining Miranda's team? Before pairing up with Holly? That should be easy to answer but it wasn't.

They resumed their climb.

Yes, he wanted to go back to the good times. Life on Miranda's team had none of the ease and flow that came with surviving on his own and in his own way. It had also included a wide variety of near-death experiences, right up to last night's shooting.

Yet...

The memories were good. As if he actually fulfilled some purpose. But what a cost. The chaos. The near-death experiences. The crushing weight of each successive crisis.

They crested the last riser. His eyes didn't track the fantastic sculptures. Nor the sweeping views.

Instead, he spotted Max and Holly setting up on the southern parapet.

71

HOLLY STOOD ALONG THE WIDE STONE PARAPET OF THE Chronicle. It was as if it had been made for snipers. Chest high, smooth stone, and a sweeping view.

The Tbilisi Sea stretched away to the left. The morning sun still lay to the left and behind them offering excellent visibility. Any morning breeze had died and the chill air meant a minimum of turbulence.

The GIS headquarters building lay approximately a kilometer off and fifty meters lower. They couldn't ask for a better vantage point.

Frankly, she'd been worried about being caught out alongside Max. She hadn't shot a proper sniper rifle in years and it was a skill that staled quickly. But this shot would be almost easy. At half the rated effective range and a quarter of the longest recorded kill, she wouldn't be pushing the weapon's limits at all, only her own.

"You're zeroed for five hundred meters," Max's voice dropped to a sniper's whisper even with no one about to overhear them.

Not to be outdone, she answered, "I make the wind at five knots off the water and distance just shy of a kilometer."

"Eight hundred and thirty meters," Max held up his phone. "Google Maps."

Holly sighed and dialed the corrections into the scope, double-checking that she was dialing in the right direction to compensate for the amount of gravity-induced bullet drop across the distance past five hundred.

Their voices overlapped as they both looked up compensations for the denser cold air and the Earth's spin. The Coriolis effect became a notable factor especially as they were shooting just west of due south. In the full second of the bullet's travel time across eight hundred meters, the target would be carried sideways by...three inches due to the Earth's spin. She clicked in that setting as well.

"Are you sure, Holly?" Mike's voice close by her right side jolted her badly enough to add three extra clicks on the scope setting.

She carefully dialed the three clicks back before looking at him. He was standing there with Elene clutching his arm like she was a drowning woman. *Mike was always good with the women.* Is that what had happened to her? Swept away by that Mike magnetism? Maybe she *would* be better off if he was gone. "Am I sure about what?"

He nodded in the direction of the GIS headquarters. "Long time since you shot someone."

She turned back to her weapon. "These guys? I'm fine with it."

"Okay," his answer barely registered.

Yet she was aware of Max's sudden scrutiny. "I'm fine with it," she offered him a sniper's whisper that wouldn't even carry to Mike.

He didn't turn away.

"Just mind your own damn dials."

With her settings dialed in and checked, Holly turned her full attention to the target for the first time.

Through the scope, the triangular building with its rooftop glass office resolved into a heavy glass door. An area paved with slate between the door and the knee-high parapet along the roof's edge that she could cover in an easy sweep.

She checked her watch. At least five minutes to wait before Pavle would even start his part of the plan.

Most of being an effective sniper came down to patience.

She glanced aside at Mike. He'd walked off to wander among the monument's pillars with Elene on his arm.

Yeah, patience wouldn't be coming easy today.

72

"How could I possibly predict where that helicopter and its torpedoes will target?" Miranda felt weary to the very bones of the fingers that she was rubbing across her forehead. She, Jeremy, and Général Vachon had looked at everything known about the missing armaments.

The Unmanned Little Bird had been packed in a forty-foot-long high-cube container; high-cube meant that it was one foot taller than a standard shipping container, intended for over-height items—like the ULB. All that would be required to make it operational was mounting the six rotor blades onto the hub and pouring in sixty-two gallons of fuel—an operation requiring under fifteen minutes and no specialized personnel. The Mark 46 torpedoes were designed to mount quickly onto the helo's hard points.

"They could be fired into any harbor," she pictured the Swedish shoreline. "And they have hundreds of harbors. The Mark 46 torpedo has a range of eleven kilometers. They don't even have to fly it into the harbor; they could start the attack from out at sea."

"Patterns," Jeremy spoke up. "When we do a crash investigation, we're looking for patterns."

"And what doesn't fit into those patterns," Miranda stopped rubbing her forehead. "What's broken or missing? Or perhaps—"

"Shouldn't be there in the first place."

They thought so alike, Miranda had never minded Jeremy's interruptions.

"The attacks have all been against Swedish assets," Jeremy tapped the table rapidly with a pointed index finger as if the tablecloth held some secret location. But she understood his idea.

"General, can you look up all the locations of Swedish deployment? Especially ships and submarines."

They all turned to watch the big screens at the front of the conference room used for lecture slides during the sessions. His team at NATO were listening in on an open phone connection, and feeding their results back to his computer to show on the screen.

First they visited MarineTraffic.com.

From the Gulf of Bothnia to the north, Denmark to the south, and all the way up the Baltic to St. Petersburg, his map was soon covered with hundreds of tiny boat icons. Traffic flow, thick with cargo and fishing vessels. Because it was midwinter, there were very few pleasure or passenger vessels.

He selected vessels flagged as Swedish.

The three of them leaned in to study the map as it shifted. Nothing struck her as being unusual. All the patterns appeared normal, heavy traffic along the shore, fishing and small cargo vessels out in deeper waters.

"Anyone?" Général Vachon asked.

She looked at Jeremy and he shook his head. She matched the gesture.

"NATO secure traffic," Vachon spoke into his phone.

A far simpler map appeared onscreen.

"Sweden only," he called out.

Someone selected the Countries submenu and switched off everyone except Sweden.

Most of the icons showed ships in ports. Of their five submarines, only one was deep in the Baltic, halfway between Sweden and Helsinki, Finland.

"What's that one?" Jeremy pointed.

As soon as she saw it, she knew he was right.

Général Vachon hovered his mouse over the small icon.

A Visby-class corvette. Mid-channel in the Gulf of Finland close by Russian territorial waters where the Gripen pilot had been ejected and died on Daughter's Island.

The HSwMS *Karlstad* stood alone with four jets overhead.

The tip of the spear.

73

"ON THE MOVE," MAX WHISPERED.

Holly shifted the TAC-50 rifle into position and settled her gaze on the scope. Three men stepped out onto the patio of the GIS building eight hundred meters away.

And stayed clustered together.

Pavle was supposed to separate himself from the others, but they were moving together in a line. Were the two on the ends about to throw the one in the middle off the rooftop to kill him? Or was the man in the middle a target but keeping Pavle in place with a hand on his shoulder?

Then Holly spotted it.

She left the rifle, raced to the other side of the parapet's walkway and spotted Elene, still walking arm-in-arm with Mike through the monument.

"Elene! What color coat did Pavle wear this morning?"

"White with big red stripe! Georgia football team colors. I give to him as engagement present."

Holly turned back as Max's rifle cracked loudly.

He worked the bolt on his Orsis rifle before she even had

the TAC-50 fully in her hands. She'd realigned the scope to her eye as the Orsis barked a second time.

A man in the dark blue of a NATO uniform was already down.

As she watched, a man in a black coat, halfway back to the door, jerked sideways, a hat tumbling from his gray hair as he fell.

The man in the white jacket with the red stripe, probably now sprayed with blood, turned very slowly to look up at them. There was no way to read his expression at this distance.

74

"Patch it here." She stood at the rear of the bridge, watching the AW109LUH helo lifting off the *Karlstad's* rear helipad and circling wide to open the space.

Kerstin grabbed the handset by the deck commander's station when the phone buzzed.

"Kommendör Holmgren."

"Kommendör, this is NATO Général Pierre Vachon. We have reason to believe that you may be the target of an inbound Unmanned Little Bird helicopter armed with two American Mark 46 torpedoes."

"I have a ULB inbound right now with proper authorization. Urgent medical supplies. I've just cleared my helipad so it may land."

"Any authorization, it is forged. This is an *attaque* upon your ship. *Le tirer*. Shoot it! Shoot it now!"

Kerstin dropped the phone and snatched up a pair of binoculars.

"Distance to inbound?" She called out as she looked.

Even with the high-power binocs, it was little bigger than a ten-krona coin on the far side of her bridge.

"Seven kilometers and closing at one-seven-zero knots."

She grabbed the handset once again and punched for another frequency. "Gripen overwatch. This is *Karlstad*. We have reason to believe we're being targeted by approaching ULB Little Bird with twin torpedoes, heading nine-five degrees from our current position."

"Roger, *Karlstad*. Initiating pass."

She looked around for them, but couldn't spot them anywhere.

Then an unholy crack sounded overhead, like thunder and lightning had struck her ship. The lead Gripen had just unleashed a sonic boom as it passed over them.

"This is Four-Two," crackled over the radio. "Positive report of torpedoes on hardpoints."

"This is Four-Seven. Targeting. Fox three. Missile away."

As Kerstin watched through the binoculars, two tiny dots dropped away from the helo and plunged into the water—coming toward her ship.

One second too late, the Little Bird disappeared in a ball of fire.

75

Kurbanov's brains were splattered across the patio. He still had a face, but the side shot meant that he didn't really have a head anymore.

As Max and the Aussie had told him they would attempt, Chief Kancheli still lived, though not for long. His shoulder was mostly gone and blood was pumping out.

Pavle knelt clear of the fast-growing pool and grabbed Kancheli's chin, forcing his attention onto Pavle.

"The torpedo attack. Where and when?" He felt cruel interrupting the man's dying moments, he wanted to puke at the sight of his imminent death, but he felt a clarity of purpose that he'd been missing for a long time.

Kancheli groaned.

Pavle slapped him, hard, to force the man to focus.

"Too late," a bloody froth came to his lips. "You little mole-rat." He coughed. "Already gone. Done."

"Better a mole-rat than you," but he was talking to a dead man.

His phone rang. It would be the shooters asking what he'd witnessed.

At the same moment he heard a safety click off close behind him.

76

"FULL THROTTLE," KERSTIN ORDERED. "TURBINES AND DIESELS." Usually they were run as one or the other, but their power could be combined when the need was dire. "We've got torpedoes in the water." Definitely dire.

The bridge crew went impossibly silent as the *Karlstad* began accelerating.

"And you're heading straight toward them?" her first officer asked. Nice that he didn't add a *have-you-lost-your-mind* tone.

"It is faster to gather speed and then turn, rather than trying to spin the boat."

The waterjet drive could turn the boat exactly on its center if needed, but with the keel designing for moving ahead rather than sideways in water, it wasn't a fast maneuver. Instead, she'd get up speed and then carve a turn away from the two fish in the water.

"Ready depth charges, set for a spread of five, ten, and twenty meters depth. They're Mark 46 fish. They're designed to locate us, come in under the center of our keel, then explode to break our ship's back. We're not going to let that happen."

She'd trained for seventeen years for this moment. Ever

since her days as a cadet at the Naval Warfare Centre she'd dreamed of entering action. She was now older and wiser enough to hope that it *never* happened, but it didn't stop her desire to bring pain to the Russians. Too many years they'd been the bogeyman of all Europe and a chance beckoned to bring them down further than they'd already done to themselves in Ukraine.

Except the NATO general had said they were Mark 46 weapons. Those were US and NATO standard, not Russian.

Time to worry about that later.

When the ship hit twenty knots, she called out to the helmsman, "Start your turn. One-eighty about. Try not to hole us on any ice at this speed."

"Roger, Kommendör. Turning north and continuing for heading two-seven-zero." Due west.

The water jets were powerful enough that they would continue to accelerate through the turn. She leaned upslope as the ship heeled outward on the turn.

Kerstin resisted the urge to remind the helmsman not to heel so far over that one of the waterjet's intakes sucked air.

She needn't have worried. With the need to volley between ice floes, they were more jinking than carving their way around.

"Range?"

"Hard to estimate," tactical called out. "Sonar signature of a pea and we're making too much noise to listen. Two kilometers? They move at forty-plus knots. And," they all held on tightly as the ship rolled right, then left again, "they can run deep enough to avoid the ice."

"Roger that. Inform me at estimated one-kilometer closure."

"Aye, Kommendör."

Now it was a race. If the *Karlstad* could make a clean run, she hustled along at thirty-five knots, sixty-five kilometers per hour. The torpedoes had at least a five-knot advantage. But they had a limited range, running out of fuel after eleven kilometers. If she kept away from them for twelve kilometers, they might survive this. One way or another, this would all be over in nine minutes.

"Launch sonobuoys."

She didn't want a single meter per second less speed, so she didn't order the towed sonar array out as well.

"Buoys, one each kilometer."

They were covering that distance every fifty-six seconds running flat out—closer to every sixty-five seconds weaving through the ice. The problem was that the torpedo covered the same distance every forty-eight seconds with no turns. The fish needed under four minutes to make up a kilometer. They'd run out of fuel in nine minutes, or would if they hadn't caught up to her ship in eight.

The sonobuoy devices would listen for the sound of the torpedoes. The *Karlstad* was making far too much noise to listen effectively, especially astern. She didn't know how calculating the exact moment of impact would help. Morbid curiosity perhaps.

A waterjet was quiet enough to fool most acoustic homing capability, if they weren't running it flat out.

The *Karlstad* was running near her maximum speed when tactical called out one kilometer and closing. Four minutes to impact and she needed five and a half to outrun them. Time for a different solution.

"It won't be enough, Kommendör. We need to catch them with the depth charges."

Tactical's estimate matched her own.

Each time a torpedo lost its target lock, it would waste time and fuel circling to reacquire.

A depth charge, even if it didn't achieve the unlikely hit on a torpedo, would vaporize a large section of water.

That gave her an idea. The waterjets were very different

from propellors. An overrevved propellor would create some cavitation air bubbles, but for the most part they were massive chunks of bronze offering exceptional targets for a torpedo's homing electronics.

A waterjet, however, ejected a hard stream of water straight aft; the *Karlstad* was the supercharged version of a recreational jet ski. But, if they did turn hard enough to catch *air* in the waterjet, it would create a wall of bubbles behind the ship. In water, air bubbles acted as barriers to sound across all frequencies, including sonar. A torpedo's seeking ping would bounce and scatter off the air bubbles rather than her ship.

"Helm. Disable roll stabilizers. Slalom hard. Back and forth. Get the waterjet inlets to grab air on each turn."

"It will cost us speed, Kommendör."

"Roger that, proceed."

And everything that wasn't tied down or strapped in lurched toward the starboard side of the cabin as they turned to port.

Alarms screamed as the portside jet intake drew air.

Then silenced as helm sent them back the other direction, submerging one intake on his way to exposing the other.

77

PAVLE CAREFULLY MOVED HIS HANDS TO THE SIDE AND TURNED around very slowly.

Tamar stood in the open doorway.

The warm air escaping from the heated office to the winter air fluttered her hair like a photo shoot and pressed her skirt tightly against her thighs.

And the MP5K submachine gun she held was zeroed at his chest.

"Uh, Tamar, I don't know what happened..." If he could hear his own lie, she certainly could as well.

And he was so sick of lies he could scream.

"*T'rats'i!* No, I know exactly what happened. They were trying to start a war between NATO and Russia. They may have succeeded, I don't know if we stopped them in time."

She took another step out onto the rooftop patio.

Her eyes scanned from Kancheli to Kurbanov, then back to Kancheli.

Tamar opened her mouth to speak when the sharp crack of a bullet's supersonic passage resounded off the glass.

78

"Now that. That was sweet."

Holly worked the bolt to chamber another round before looking to see if she agreed with Max's assessment.

She did.

79

PAVLE HAD FLINCHED, BUT FELT NO PAIN. TAMAR HADN'T shot him.

Instead, she was cradling her hand and looking down at the MP5K.

In hindsight, he could see what happened.

One moment, the submachine gun centered rock steady on his chest as Tamar scanned the two corpses.

The next, the gun flew aside, skidding along the paving stones until it tumbled against the low parapet and stopped there.

As if by mutual consent, he and Tamar both moved close enough to look at it.

The small gun had been mostly folded in half by the round that had struck it side-on. He glanced back up at the Chronicle and wondered whether he had Max or the Aussie to thank for his reprieve.

The question remained as to how long a reprieve that might be.

Tamar looked at him and whispered the first words she'd ever spoken to him.

"Starting a war?"

Pavle nodded.

She sighed as she looked down at the remains of Chief Kancheli, "My father always was a bastard."

He almost laughed. His future father-in-law would be a delight compared to Kancheli.

80

SOMEONE ON THE BRIDGE MADE A HORRID RETCHING SOUND. Kerstin hoped that they didn't puke on some critical system.

Slaloming a seventy-meter corvette displacing over six hundred tonnes shared little with the feeling of a weaving ski boat. The ship didn't twist and dance, it *lurched* from one tack to the other.

Knowing that a couple hundred kilos of explosives was hunting them, with highly sophisticated electronics specializing in ignoring false signals, didn't help.

"Positive tracking," tactical called out. "Half a kilometer at eight-three degrees. Thirty seconds out."

She glanced at the clock. Three minutes before the torpedoes would be out of fuel.

"Launch a line of four depth charges."

The cans rolled out of the rear chute to tumble in the boat's wake. There they sank until the pressure gauge decided they'd reached their target depth. A hundred kilos of high explosive punched holes in the water and kicked fountains of foamed seawater skyward in clouds as tall as the *Karlstad* herself.

They repeated the exercise twice more.

One of the third group blasted a great double-thump of water aloft: the charge and one of the torpedoes.

All Kerstin could see was how close it lay off the stern. They survived that one by seconds.

"One down. Per the sonobuoy data, the other fish is circling to reacquire."

"Now! Helm," Kerstin called out. "Flank speed. Everything you've got."

She actually felt the big ship accelerate, pushing her back into her seat.

Now it was a pure race.

Each passing second brought more hope.

"Estimate zero fuel now," tactical called out.

Kerstin kept the *Karlstad* at flank for another five minutes before she dared ask.

"Anything from the sonobuoys?"

"Only us and the ice bumping about."

"Set speed for ten knots." She managed to keep her voice steady for the crew's sake and for her own.

Helm eased down the speed in a single knot at a time, looking ready to hammer back to flank speed at the least provocation.

Kerstin was in no mood to hurry him along.

The torpedo was designed to safely sink once it was out of fuel. But she certainly wasn't about to backtrack to make sure that it had.

She picked up the radio handset that had jammed in her seat cushion and punched back to the first radio frequency.

"Hello?"

"We're still here, Kommendör."

Kerstin considered. "So are we." Then she replaced the phone in its cradle.

81

"Not sure quite how to say this," Tad shifted from one foot to the other like a little boy who'd been caught with his hand in the cookie jar.

Mike had just finished checking over the work that the Gulfstream's team had done on Miranda's jet. Two new side windows, a new section of hull, and a new seat without a bullet hole in it. All clean.

The Georgian Prime Minister had insisted on his government paying for it, cheap for the price of never telling anyone what happened here.

In the last twenty-four hours, many other revelations had come to light.

Once they were face-to-face, or face-to-corpse, Max had recognized the fake General Kurbanov as a Turkish arms dealer who had stood to benefit more from a war than any country. His assets had been confiscated and converted into a large, anonymous reparation. Pavle had routed it through LuftSvenska to the families of those downed in the 737 crash.

Rolm Lindgren would be able to retire from the airline's presidency in relative peace.

Harry had finally penetrated the Italian flight school database sufficiently to unravel that Marco Marino had been Marko Marinin. The pilot who had crashed the 737 was indeed a Russian sleeper agent—but not working for Russia. He'd traded his attack to Kancheli for smuggling his family out of Russia through South Ossetia. To the media he became *a sole actor manic-depressive* who had falsified his psychological profile with the help of the now ruined Italian flight school scam.

Tamar had also revealed vast wealth gathered by her corrupt father, Chief Kancheli. He, post mortem, purchased two replacement Gripen jets for Sweden and made reparations to the pilots' families—and one prize bull.

"What's up, buddy?" Mike asked when Tad proved unable to continue.

The Prime Minister had put Pavle as probationary chief over the Georgian Intelligence Service. "Between you and Tamar Kancheli, you'll know better than anyone what needs to be cleaned out and what we should keep." Pavle had started with providing the short list of agents he'd used—Swedish and Delta Force action teams had already taken most of them down.

Pavle and Elene had promised them invitations to the wedding. Mike already knew what to get them for a present: he and Holly *not* showing up as reminders of this day.

Tad continued studying the ground as Holly strolled up with Max. The PM had wanted Max back in the GSOF, but he'd declined on the grounds that he had a bar to run. No mention was made of the highly restricted weapons that he'd liberated; the ones that he and Holly had used and that had once again disappeared from sight.

"Look," Tad finally found his voice. "You guys get into some heavy shit. I'm just a good ol' Southern-fried whirly-guy."

"It's not always like this," Mike assured him. Then thought

better of it, "In fact, it's almost never like this." *Almost.* And he couldn't ever thank Max enough for taking both of the kill shots so that Holly didn't have to. She was welcome to shatter as many submachine guns as she wanted, but he'd rather she never had to kill again. She might think she could brush it off, but he knew her too well and could see how each bit of her past ate at her.

He glanced over at Max, who was watching him.

Mike tipped his head ever so slightly toward Holly, then offered a small nod of thanks.

Max acknowledged it with little more than a twitch of his neck. Being Spec Ops, that was about right.

Tad was watching him too. "I'm not talking about what you guys had to do to stop this. That was A-1 squared-away. It's that you're in all...this." He waved a hand as if to encompass everything from the last three days. "International madness? Too heady for this boy. Give me a wrench and a bird to fly, and I'm good."

And Mike knew that's what had been raising the warning flags on Tad. Not that he was an unidentified agent for Kancheli and Kurbanov, but rather that he was visiting a world he'd never actually belong in.

How being a conman had prepared Mike himself to help avert a war better than Tad's years of military service was a question he'd never find the answer to. But for today—it was true.

"So what will you do?"

It was hard to tell with his dark complexion, but Tad appeared to be blushing. "My boys here with the 43rd Mechanized Battalion tell me they need someone to help the GDF shape up their helo program."

Holly laughed.

"I know, right? Way more my speed that what you folks are into. They've got some old Russian Mil birds and a double handful of Hueys. Feel like I can be useful here for a while. I'm retired military and I can't imagine the NTSB will miss me much."

"Going to help them take back South Ossetia?"

Tad shrugged that would be unlikely. The Russians had been occupying it since 2008.

"And nothing to do with the sultry Tamar?" Holly teased.

Tad had almost collapsed when he'd met the woman. This time he didn't blush, he grinned. "Might have asked Pavle to see if he could coax her to Max's bar. I've got me some smooth moves on the dance floor." He placed a hand on one hip and gyrated in a way Elvis might admire.

Mike saw the look on Max's face, just as he'd seen the look on Tamar's when they met. Killing her father was only the beginning of things that might go right between them.

Mike shook Tad's hand. "Gonna wish you luck on all fronts." Because he'd need a lot of it to slip in on Tamar with Max around.

"*Madloba.* Means *thanks* in this here place."

"Take back Ossetia," Holly said quietly after Tad had walked off to pull his luggage out of Miranda's plane.

"What's that?"

But Holly wasn't looking at him. She was staring off at the line of civilian jets parked halfway between their military corner of the airfield and the civilian terminal at the opposite end. A trio of Boeing 737s and two smaller jets painted in the colors of Air Georgia.

"What's up with those, Max?" she asked. "Haven't moved since we arrived."

"Bankrupt eighteen months ago, no buyers. The pandemic shutdown was harsh, but most of their routes were in and out of Russia. Ukraine War put and end to them."

Holly and Max exchanged some kind of look that Mike

couldn't interpret, but it left Max smiling almost as much as he had at meeting Tamar.

"Got me a bar to open." He shook both their hands and strolled off whistling.

"What was that about?"

"Just an idea. Can we get out of here?"

Mike hadn't heard such a good idea in a long time.

82

MIKE AND HOLLY SAT SIDE-BY-SIDE ON THE COUCH IN THE PACIFIC Northwest team house. The space between them close enough to reach across, yet neither of them did.

The flight back to Iceland had passed in silence. Dropping off Jeremy in DC, and the final long haul back across the country, not an unnecessary word had passed between them.

He expected to feel disappointment or affirmation or something other than a bone-deep weariness. He couldn't convince himself to buy in that the dozen time zones from Georgia to Gig Harbor, Washington, were the problem. He'd felt this way for four days now and it showed no signs of abating.

He also saw no signs of himself leaving and that was even more worrisome. Not as if he had all that much to pack, his life on the street had taught him to travel light through life. Even during the height of the Advanced Ads era—the day before it was erased from the face of Denver—he'd had an office with a studio apartment in the back, his car and plane, and a Premier season pass to the four Aspen ski mountains.

Yet each time he thought about packing, the prelude to walking out the door, he simply couldn't find the energy. If he stood up, he'd barf from the sheer weariness with it all. He was so sick of himself—but even that didn't get him to his feet.

It would help if Miranda came out of her room for more than meals and to walk Meg. But since their return from the conference, she didn't. And he couldn't bring himself to knock on her door to tell her he was leaving. He couldn't imagine which one of them would take it worse.

Instead, all he could recall was the line of body bags that would forever be on that Swedish ski slope. The look on Liisa Salo's face as she mourned a Swedish pilot she'd never met in the flesh. The pilot shot out of the sky on a quiet winter morning at Storuman. The final carnage on the rooftop in Georgia.

That was done, finished.

"Hey."

"Huh?"

Holly punched him on the arm and pointed at the TV screen.

A bright red *Breaking News* banner flashed upon the screen. Below it in the biggest font that would fit: *Plane crash in Georgia (country).*

He hit the volume. They'd both been such zombies since their return to the US that they hadn't even bothered to turn on the sound. Staring at the screen like monkeys watching a digital clock, that's how functional they were.

"We have limited information at this time," the voiceover snapped and crackled like it was only a marginal connection. The video had none of those issues.

It was a longshot view of a wide, two-lane road running straight into a towering cliff. Where you'd expect a tunnel, there was nothing but a wall of flames.

The words *Roki Tunnel, Georgia,* flashed up on the screen.

At the base of the cliffs to either side of the tunnel lay airplane wings, big ones—commercial-jet sized.

"Are those..." Mike couldn't believe what he was seeing. There was nothing particularly noteworthy about the wings, except how rapidly fire was taking hold of them. They were white.

"The winglets that curve up at the ends," Holly pointed. "Those are from a 737."

The winglets were red with white bands. "That's Fly Georgia's colors."

"But where's the plane fuselage?"

In answer, the film clip started over. Someone must have known ahead of time and set the camera in place.

The whole plane showed for just an instant. Then the wings slammed the cliffs and the fuselage of the plane shot into the tunnel.

The wings had time to become engulfed in flames.

Four seconds later, a blast of fire shot out of the tunnel and straight toward the camera, like it had been fired out of a cannon—or a tunnel.

The flame raced toward them so fast that they both shoved back into the couch to get away from it. But it roiled and dissipated before reaching the camera itself.

"Well, that'll take a while to clean up." Mike wondered how pissed the Russians would be over that. Someone had crashed a 737 *inside* the Roki Tunnel. In revenge, would Russia send a full invasion force through that tunnel—once it reopened—to rampage across South Ossetia and into Georgia?

"That's not a fire."

Mike waved a hand at the screen as if to ask what she was missing.

"No, Mike. Remember what I used to do—explosives

specialist. That's not a ruptured central wing tank and a blast of flame. Look at the initial delay, then how it flashed and faded in a single massive pulse," she pointed at the replay. Then she tipped her head, thinking hard.

He did his best not to admire the line of her neck. He was only here at the team house until he found the energy to pack everything. Then he'd leave. Sure. That sounded like a plan.

"The Georgian Air Force still flies the old Sukhoi Su-25KM Scorpion jets, right?"

As if he'd know. Talking to herself, she didn't wait for his answer.

"That means they have a stock of FAB-500s. Or at least the FAB-250s. Call it five hundred kilos, a half ton of high explosive..."

She leaned forward intently as they again reran the tongue of flame shooting out of the tunnel that still looked to him like a tongue of flame. Though he couldn't stop his own reaction, she didn't lean away when the burst of flame shot toward them.

"Nope. Not enough. A pair of the FAB-500s, a full tonne of bomb, or a quad of the 250s. Same-same. That matches. No, Mike," she turned back to him as if the conversation was no longer one-sided. "That's not fire. It's enough explosive to cave in a whole section of the tunnel. Maybe even— Oh, wait, that's only what came out *this* end. It's a tunnel, so call it two metric tonnes, as half shot toward Russia. Bet that surprised the living daylights out of them at the other end. The Roki Tunnel is almost four kilometers long, we need Jeremy or Miranda to run the calcs. The overpressure of the blast wave traveling as high as Mach 4 and compressing a four-kilometer-long tunnel of air would be nothing short of catastrophic."

"Going to be closed a while?"

Holly snorted. "Easier to dig a new tunnel than recover that mess. The last time it was damaged, it took them two and a half years to fix, and that was merely a bit of shelling at one end, not a deep blast like this one."

Flames continued to pour out the near end, but now rose like a fire instead of shooting out like an explosion.

It cut off abruptly when the tunnel end collapsed into a pile of rubble and the conflagration became trapped inside. The contained heat would melt or fracture whole sections of the interior, causing more cave-ins and leaving what remained unstable. It *would* be easier and safer to cut a fresh tunnel.

"I'll be buggered," Holly whispered in wonder. "He did it."

That's when Mike recalled the look between Max and Holly as they observed the abandoned Air Georgia planes. Combined with the technology used on the Unmanned Little Bird that had attacked the *Karlstad...*

Mike laughed aloud.

"What?"

"Général Pierre Vachon. Remember he was still there at the end, when we got back to the conference in Reykjavik."

"Sure, he debriefed us to make sure all the strings were tied into a knot no mere mortal soul could ever unravel. And I thought the Australian military's methods were convoluted. I bow to the NATO masters of changing reality to keep peace."

"Right," Mike nodded. "I also heard him in the bar asking Jeremy all about the AACUS unit. It's a hundred-pound plug-and-play box that turns a normal helicopter into an autonomous remote controlled one like the one that attacked the Swedish ship. Think maybe he helped Georgia slip one into an old 737 along with those bombs you mentioned?"

Holly looked from him to the screen, and began grinning like a fool.

"I'd guess that no one died crashing that plane. And I'd wager both NATO and Georgia are very glad to have that particular passage well plugged."

If they moved quickly, Georgia would be able to push through South Ossetia before Russia could reinforce the area using the much slower capabilities of an airlift. And it was winter, the tortuous Roki Pass that twisted over the Caucasus Mountains almost a full mile above the tunnel would still be snowbound for months to come. Plenty of time to fortify that as well.

Holly slung her arms about his neck and plastered a hard kiss of pure joy on him. "Madder than a passel of baby dingoes, but they bloody well did it."

They had.

And maybe they'd found what he'd been missing: hope.

If Georgia stood against the Russian bear, others might fight its expansion as well. This one act would ripple from Georgia to Sweden, leaving no one untouched. He and Holly held hands as they turned back to watch the broadcast.

Hope. Even a glimmer went *such* a long way.

He looked at Holly, still rapt at the replay. Not that anything in Georgia became news here in the States, but that bolt of flame or explosion or whatever Holly wanted to call it, racing toward the camera, made for damn good film. No one would be changing the channel soon and the broadcasters knew it.

Hope *did* go a long way. Was it strong enough that he might want to spend more of his life with...what had he called her, a daily royal pain in the ass of a woman? Perhaps that *was* something worth hoping for—even worth fighting for? He'd never fought for much in his life, always following the easy flow. Maybe the time to try had arrived.

He looked up at the ceiling, where Miranda remained ensconced in her room.

Hope.

He slipped out his phone and, without asking Holly, sent a text message.

Tomorrow. 0700. Same place.

Sometimes a Team of One was right and at other times desperately wrong. But what if something could be right for him, Holly, Miranda, *and* for the team?

He risked a small prayer that this time, acting as a Team of One himself, he would *not* be so very wrong.

EPILOGUE

"I'M HERE." ANDI DIDN'T OFFER ANYTHING MORE THAN THE simple statement in a dead tone. Not even to ask why Mike had contacted her. It was the same spot they'd found her watching the team house from the week after Holly threw her out, a block from the team's house in Gig Harbor, Washington.

It was a cool, crisp Pacific Northwest morning, a welcome relief after the deep chill of Sweden.

Mike had trouble believing the change that had come over Andi in these last months. A glance at Holly, the pain in her eyes, said that she hadn't missed the change either.

Andi came from serious money without flaunting it. She'd chosen the Army over law. Which had turned out to be a good choice when the family's San Francisco law firm had been caught selling military and Silicon Valley secrets to China and Russia *en masse*. She'd been one of the few members of her extended family not to be facing treason charges and decades in prison. Her mother and grandmother would never walk free again.

But the money and upbringing had always showed through. She'd had exceptional taste and always appeared as neat as a pin. Casual in high-end jeans, maybe a plain jewel-tone blouse of Indian cotton, and a fine-leather bomber jacket. Her black hair cut neat to her shoulders; her Army boots polished.

Now, the petite Chinese woman looked worn. Nothing major: a tattered cuff on her jeans, a small stain on her blouse, her hair hanging long and in need of a trim. And definitely worn down in one, far more important, way. Like Jeremy, she'd always been a positive force on the team. Unlike Jeremy, she'd done it from a steady, calm core that the Army had trained all the way into her bones. Or perhaps she'd been born that way.

Not now.

"What have you been doing, Andi?" Mike kept his voice soft.

"Flying," her voice as flat as her expression. None of the light that had so defined her remained in her face. "Robinson R-22s. Flight instructor."

Mike managed to suppress his gasp of horror. She'd been one of the best helicopter pilots—anywhere. Captain Andi Wu had been a lead for the 160th Night Stalkers Special Operations Aviation Regiment next-generation rotorcraft testing program. Making her perhaps *the* best small-helo combat pilot in any branch of the service. Coming to Miranda's team only after a horrid attack killed her copilot and the resultant PTSD ended her career prematurely.

For her to give lessons to beginners in the simplest of all helicopters was worse than any punishment he could have imagined.

Holly's action, and his own inaction, had damaged far more than breaking her away from Miranda.

"What are the rules?" Andi didn't look up, but she was facing Holly.

Holly's face was contorted in pain and indecision. She looked as if she wanted to embrace Andi herself and welcome her back with no other questions, as well as beat the shit out of her for what Andi had done. Holly turned to him with a desperate plea for help written clear in her eyes.

A team of two? Holly *had* listened to him—for once. Maybe it was a new beginning. There was that hope feeling again.

"Andi," he managed to suppress the tightness in his throat and speak normally around it. "There's only one rule: Miranda's."

Andi glanced up at him sideways through narrowed eyes.

"If she says you leave," Holly found her voice though he heard the tight pain in it, "all I wanna see is your soldier's ass hustling over the next ridge."

"And if she doesn't?"

Again Holly was struck dumb.

Mike shrugged. "It's her team, her life, and..." he took a steadying breath, "...her call." Whatever the consequences—which scared the crap out of him, though he remained vigilant not to show it.

He saw the motion he'd been watching for over Andi's head. He nodded upward.

"We didn't give her a heads up. It's all on you, Captain Andi Wu."

Andi turned so slowly it hurt to watch. As if she feared to see.

A block away, Miranda had come out the front door and headed down the front path to take Meg for her morning walk. Timed like clockwork; the way Miranda did everything these days.

At the sidewalk she turned away from them, following the exact same route every day, perhaps step-for-step. She moved at dog speed as Meg stopped to sniff at everything they passed. Meg's investigations created the only break in Miranda's metronomic rhythm.

They all watched her in silence.

Mike was about to reach out and give Andi a gentle push

when she jumped. She rubbed her butt where Holly had pinched her. But she didn't turn. It was almost like that too was familiar.

This time, after watching Miranda move away for another five or ten seconds, Andi started off at a slow walk. In moments she was running.

Mike leaned back against the hood of Andi's car and Holly leaned beside him. They both had their arms crossed; their elbows not quite touching.

No words.

Andi stopped twenty yards behind Miranda. Bent down and rested her hands against her knees though she couldn't be winded yet. After a desperately long pause, she must have found the nerve to straighten up and start walking again to bridge the final gap. The Night Stalker in her—with their motto of Night Stalkers Don't Quit—wasn't dead yet.

When she called out Miranda's name, Miranda kept going. She didn't have her headphones on, because that would be a safety issue on a street, though they were around her neck in case of some unexpected passerby.

"Oh no," Holly whispered and clutched his arm.

They saw Andi stumble to a halt and hesitate for a long moment before calling out again.

This time Miranda stopped and looked about, not quite turning around. Perhaps she couldn't believe what she was hearing. Finally, she turned to look fully behind her.

They stood too far away to read Miranda's expression, but Meg stopped sniffing about. Instead, she reached up to put both paws as high as she could on Miranda's leg. Her whine of concern carried all the way to them.

Miranda had dropped Meg's leash to grab her headphones with both hands.

"No, don't! Please please please..." Holly kept whispering.

Mike felt as frozen as the tableau before them: two women

stiffly five paces apart, Miranda's headphones half raised, and one very worried therapy dog.

He and Holly had talked over the best way to do this—another small piece of their new Team of Two. Having a sit-down talk with Miranda but without Andi? All four of them together so that he and Holly could mitigate any calamitous reactions? One or the other of them escorting Andi to Miranda? A phone call or video conference? They'd finally settled on leaving it up to the two women. They'd been the ones in love after all.

He only hoped that was enough. If it drove Miranda farther into her hole, she might never find her way out.

Though Miranda still clutched her half-raised headphones, they appeared to be talking.

"Look," Mike couldn't help from pointing, as if there was anything else he or Holly would be watching at this moment.

"What?"

"Look at Meg." The dog had dropped back onto all fours. She sniffed around Andi's ankles and received an absentminded pet for her troubles. Then, she sat and watched the two women closely but no more than that.

Holly's grip on his arm tightened enough to hurt but he didn't possess sufficient attention to ease her off.

It took five minutes—maybe ten, maybe two, afterward Mike had no way to tell—before Miranda, a woman who never ever initiated physical contact, released her headphones to rest on her shoulders and was the first to reach out. When they came together, laying their heads on each other's shoulders and remaining still in each other's arms, Mike glanced at Holly.

The woman who never cried—had tears streaming down her face. He wiped at them, but that only seemed to make more of them. He pulled out the handkerchief he'd rescued from his vest back in Sweden and handed it to her. She clutched it

tightly, but turned her face into his shoulder and truly wept—
as if all the past had been unleashed at once.

Mike held her hard against him and, in a call-the-Pope
miracle, she sagged against him and let herself be held.

He alone watched as the three of them, two women close
enough to rub shoulders and a dog trotting along happily
ahead of them, continued their walk. He watched them move
out of sight as he rubbed his palm up and down Holly's
shuddering back. This once, he didn't mind so much taking
care of a weeping woman.

NOTES

Once again, the real-world news has partially caught up with a Miranda story before it could be finished and published. Thankfully, as of publication, this is of technical rather than geopolitical interest.

On September 17th, 2023, while this story still remained in a rough draft, a Marine Corps F-35B Lightning II fighter jet crashed. An interesting detail is that the Marine Corps had to ask for the public's help to locate the crash. Why? After the pilot safely ejected, the plane's software did what it could to maintain stable flight for over sixty miles before coming down.

The fictional JAS 39E Gripen continuing to fly without Ingrid Eklund, after she was ejected, is no longer this author's conjecture. It is now a proven possibility.

AFTERWORD

If you enjoyed Gryphon
please consider leaving a review.
They really help.

Keep reading for an exciting excerpt from:
Miranda Chase #15, Wedgetail
(Coming summer 2024)

Be sure to visit:
https://mlbuchman.com/fan-club-freebies

- *Bonus Scene/Story*
- *Recipe from the book*
- *Character list, place maps, plane pictures, and more*

WEDGETAIL (EXCERPT)

IF YOU ENJOYED THAT, YOU'LL LOVE THIS TALE!

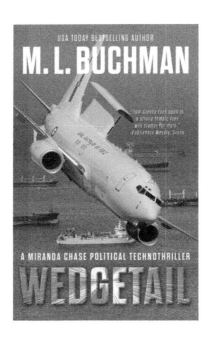

WEDGETAIL (EXCERPT)
CHANGI AIRPORT, SINGAPORE

"LOOK, I AGREED TO AUSTRALIA. I NEVER, *EVER* AGREED TO Tennant Creek." Holly hadn't won the argument in Seattle. Or on the flight across the Pacific to Singapore. In an hour, they'd be in the air to Darwin, and she'd probably lose the argument there again as well. Why was she doomed to revisit her childhood home deep in the Outback, a place she'd never intended to see again? And for some reason, the other three members of Miranda's NTSB air-crash investigation team were along for the ride.

"Not my doing, Hol."

"Mike, seriously. I keep making the same points and it keeps getting me the same result. The definition of dumb-ass stupid. Get me out of this!"

"Out of this? But it's lovely." He waved an expansive hand.

"You goofball." She poked her finger into his ribs, not sharply, but enough to let him know she was serious.

He was right, though, it *was* lovely. They stood in a giant butterfly garden built inside Singapore's Changi Airport. Fifty meters long, half that high and wide, and roofed with a great curved glass ceiling like a crystalline Quonset hut. Inside grew a flowering tropical forest, complete with an actual two-story waterfall, viewing platforms high and low, and a thousand or so butterflies in every color imaginable.

Mike had taken her to a much smaller butterfly garden in the Seattle Arboretum once. An actual date, which had been oddly sweet. Dating was a new aspect in their four years of sleeping together.

Strangest of all, she'd been charmed. Mike deserved another sharp poke for that, but she forced herself to behave.

The large tent, with a double-screened entrance, had been raised on the Arboretum's grass. Inside stood pots of flowers to entice the hundreds of butterflies released inside. In retrospect, she could see that most of the creatures had clung mournfully to the screening, dreaming of flapping about in the wider world beyond.

Not here. Amidst Singapore's jungle, they hid in trees, rested on flowers, fed on pineapple slices left out for them. Safe from predators and weather. Living out their lives in perfect security. More comfortable, but still a gilded cage?

She sure as hell didn't want to crawl back into the dog-kennel-sized cage of her past.

"Seriously, Holly?" Mike slid an arm around her waist. "I think you're fighting a lost cause. How many people do you know who can change Miranda's mind once she gets an idea?"

"You?"

"I honestly tried, Holly. I mean, I'm curious to see where you grew up, too, but I tried. It didn't work."

"Damn you for being decent. It makes it that much harder to complain." She stared at a white, yellow, orange, and black-trimmed butterfly that a nearby sign identified as a Painted Jezebel. Perfect. Just perfect.

A painted, immoral lady who always got what she wanted. *Stupid butterfly.*

Holly was doing her best to be a good and moral member of

the team. What had it earned her? A trip to Tennant Creek. And once Mike or Miranda saw where she came from, they'd never think decently of her again.

It had all begun over dinner a few months ago.

The four of them hadn't talked once about Andi's betrayal, her subsequent departure, or her return—not even tangentially. But the topic of a vacation came up. Their first attempt at a team vacation, hiking the Herriot Way around the Yorkshire Dales, had been the prelude to the unmitigated disaster of Captain Andi Wu leaving the team.

Go somewhere different? Andi had suggested.

The antipodes from the UK, Miranda had declared. That turned out to be in the Pacific Ocean south of New Zealand. Which had brought up the topic of Holly's homeland in Australia. Miranda had declared that as sufficiently *antipodal* and noted that she had an interest in the Australian Outback, based on Holly's stories of her survival adventures there. *You grew up there. You can be our guide.*

Somehow that had decided everything—leaving Holly to fight the line with all the effectiveness of a dying fish dragged onto the parched sands of her past. Her adventures? More like her *escape* from Tennant Creek into the tablelands to get *away* from her past.

"Andi? Should I ask Andi to try?"

Mike kissed her on the nose and almost earned a fist on his own. "Andi is still on tenterhooks around Miranda. She's not going to risk rocking the boat for a single second."

Holly sighed. It was too true. Andi had only been back a couple months after eight months gone. Everyone was much happier—even Holly herself, which she hadn't expected—but Andi was playing it very cool.

Even now, neither Miranda nor Andi wandered here with them inside the garden. Meg wasn't permitted in the garden despite her status as an autism therapy dog. *If my dog can't go, then I won't go.* To which Andi had added, *If you don't go, then I don't.*

Instead, they sat out by the blue tile pool in the middle of the concourse, with Meg perched on the wide ledge to watch koi as big as she was swimming lazily by.

"If I pray for a miracle and actually receive a dispensation from this abuse, does it mean that I need to believe in your Catholic God?"

"Hey! Not my God!" Mike held up his hands defensively. "He and I had a permanent falling out a couple decades ago. If I had to pick one, I'd probably go with worshipping Diana the Huntress. A scantily clad Holly Harper look-a-like, with a bow and arrow, running through the woods with her long hair streaming in the wind. Speaks Greek instead of Strine, but I can learn that. There's a definite image to improve my mood." He scooped his fingers through her gold-blonde hair and brushed it out behind her. He played with it more than ever since she'd started growing it out for him. Down to the middle of her shoulder blades and he was a goner. Guys were the strangest critters anywhere.

"Isn't she also the virgin goddess and the protector of childbirth?" Holly wondered where she'd picked up that tidbit as a bright orange something fluttered inches past her nose with wings as big as her palm. "So, are you saying you never want to have sex again or that you want to have a child with me? How do those two go together in one goddess, anyway?"

When Mike didn't answer, she looked over at him. He was studying a blue-and-black butterfly no bigger than the end of his thumb—too intently.

"No way, Mike Munroe. Tell me you did *not* just go there."

He grimaced. "Only for a second, and I assure you that it wasn't intentional."

"I should've stopped at the scantily clad image of me running through the woods."

"Don't forget the streaming hair." He wiped his forehead and didn't quite meet her gaze. "Uh, yeah. Let's stick with that."

Their relationship, since the mess in Sweden, had been better than ever. But there was this growing thing about taking The Next Step—or not. So far, they'd both remained careful not to go there, *until* she'd put her Army boot in it. *Real smooth, Harper.*

———

39,000' above Singapore

"I hate this place."

"Wouldn't be the Strait without you saying that," she replied as usual. Though Royal Australian Air Force Group Captain Rowena McCain couldn't argue. She'd flown more than two hundred patrols above the Strait. So often that she'd come to know it as well as her own hand. And now she could see the entire mess on her display.

It was a tactical nightmare, which had become like that itch that no amount of scratching eased. Constantly on the verge of collapse on every level: sea, air, and space. Even minor problems could have global ramifications.

"I *really* hate this place." Wing Commander Nick Neally completed the ritual that had existed since they'd both been lowly Flight Lieutenants on their first patrol here.

Nick, a great hulk of a man, sat at the console to her left; atypically dour for an Aussie, and brilliant at his job. She'd chosen him to sit at her left hand as the senior Surveillance Officer the moment they'd bumped her to the command seat—all of yesterday.

The Wedgetail—technically the Boeing 737 AEW&C, Airborne Early Warning and Control plane—was the hottest flying command in the RAAF. It was the only plane staffed by a

Group Captain, the equivalent of an American colonel. She had the responsibility *and* the power to order immediate action if needed.

"It's just a bit of clutter, mates," Squadron Leader Grant Felton laughed. "Place is bound to clear out someday." The diametric opposite of Nick, Grant would be chortling at some joke during his own funeral. Too bad he wasn't as funny as he thought he was—though he was definitely as handsome, but she'd long since refused to fall for that.

With her promotion last month to Group Captain—raising her to the highest ranked Black Australian in the RAAF—made her twice the target she'd ever been before. Especially in the eyes of a swagman like Grant. How could someone be so convinced of their own magnificence as a gift to the female gender? At least he tried to be funny about it, ever since she'd offered to recommend him for a lifetime of latrine duty in her next review. Which he referred to weekly, as if it was a bonding joke between them rather than an unvarnished threat.

They occupied the first three consoles in the main cabin of the E-7A Wedgetail patrol jet. Grant's title was Systems Officer, placing him at the forward end of the cabin closest to the main entry door and the cockpit. His job was to communicate with the two pilots forward and make sure that the plane stayed aloft and secure.

She sat next in the command seat, with Nick to her left managing the surveillance team.

Down the main cabin ranged seven more consoles, a total of ten. Six were along the left side of the plane and the remaining four to starboard. The count was split because of the large radio cabinets occupying the first two positions behind her and Grant's seats along the right side of the cabin.

Each station was mounted sideways against the hull and had a headset-wearing operator in a comfortable swivel seat facing outward. Every console was equipped with twin displays and radio controls that could talk to a nearby jet or anywhere on the globe via satellite with equal ease. Some flights only called for a few operators, but all ten stations were manned continuously when patrolling the Strait.

Nick oversaw six of the seven down-cabin stations. He had responsibility for surveillance of everything that happened outside the plane. He always managed to make sure that she was looking at the right thing at the right time. Nick had been doing that since their first day aboard; now she had the absolute faith of experience in him.

Grant managed his own console and the comm tech's at the first seat of the starboard row, close by the radio cabinets if there were any problems. Grant and the comm tech oversaw communications and the aircraft's operational integrity, including every type of radar and radio that could be packed into a single airframe.

Everything either Nick or Grant saw landed on her desk. At the moment, she was in command of security operations for the entire length of the Strait of Malacca.

Which left her in the middle...again. Story of her life.

She'd been a middle sister with two gung-ho brothers. One now a Footie star and the other a world-class sailor. But *she* was the commander set between the surveillance officer and the plane's systems officer. Not to mention being a single woman caught between a pair of RAAF bachelors. One with puppy-dog-sad eyes that saw the world all too clearly; the other convinced he knew far more about her than he did.

Nick tapped his screen, which highlighted a ship icon on hers.

Too fast for a fishing vessel, too small for a container ship.

"Satellite?" she asked.

"UK bird coming up over Sri Lanka. We'll have a visual five-minute window in three minutes."

"Roger that." Rowena went back to studying other shipping

activity while waiting to see if some pirate was desperate enough to commit his crime in the middle of the Strait itself.

In her two and a half decades of service, Rowena had seen plenty of ugly around these parts. Malacca wasn't going to be clearing out anytime soon, no matter Grant's prediction. The only thing that would stop this glut through the Strait was war. She'd gamed that all too often at headquarters; one of the ultimate no-win scenarios no matter how they looked at it.

The only way to bypass the Strait was a long haul south around Indonesia for the Strait of Lombok or on toward Australia and New Zealand. Their two countries were well out of the way, and they both liked that just fine.

At the three-klick-wide choke point where the Malacca opened out at Singapore, it wasn't unusual to have ships three hundred meters long that needed half an hour and six kilometers to stop, lined up a kilometer apart and sometimes two abreast. With the same passing in the opposite direction. And that was merely the big trade boys. Add in more little boats than bugs in a Outback termite mound, world sailors and local fisherman, and the occasional US Navy carrier groups complete with submarines. Then it started to get interesting.

The real trouble came because where there was congestion, there were pirates. The pressure of eight billion people on the planet made for a lot of poor—near enough half a billion of them within shooting distance of the Strait of Malacca—and a lot of those bearing no qualms about taking from the rich.

One poor ship had been robbed four times in a single passage. The first time for the crew's cash and valuables. Then someone pulled alongside and cross-pumped a hundred thousand gallons of diesel at gunpoint. Another pirate took twenty thousand more leaving her almost dry. The final pirates, finding the ship stripped, had ridden along for two days eating as much food as they could before disembarking. Thankfully, that hadn't been on Australia's watch.

As there were no flotillas of military ships passing through at the moment, the pirates were the focus of today's mission.

Of course, from up here in the Wedgetail, they could also keep an eye on the pissing match China led in much of the South China Sea. And not to forget Myanmar at the other end engaging anyone who'd listen to the latest military junta, which was no one with a pinch of common sense.

"Never two days the same," Grant teased.

"Each worse than the one before," Nick embraced his moroseness like an art form.

Unlike her prior commander, Rowena appreciated the banter. A standard patrol lasted twelve hours, unless something bad kicked in. Then they'd get a mid-air refueling and often hit twenty hours aloft. She could rotate some of the operators to the comfortable crew rest seats in the rear, but she never took advantage of that herself.

That created its own kind of trouble. Being labeled as an overachiever pleased the top levels of command but irritated those immediately above her. They assumed she was after their jobs, which she was. The fact that she was smarter than most of them put together, and everyone knew it, didn't help matters.

The man she replaced had aged out, rather than making the grade to Air Commodore. And she'd made her rank five years younger than he had. He'd managed only the barest civility when he turned over the Wedgetail to her command.

Neither Nick nor Grant aspired, both glad to be in straightforward service roles.

Rowena had her eye on those flag posts beginning a single rank above her with Air Commodore.

To make her next step? She had to hone her crew and her half-billion-dollar plane until they shone.

Under the Five Power Defence Arrangements with Singapore, the UK, New Zealand, and Malaysia, Australia helped to keep the trade moving as safely as possible throughout the region.

Australia's Wedgetails had proven to be major assets in achieving that and she planned for her plane to be the most effective one in the fleet.

But now that she was here, sea traffic wasn't her only mission.

"Talk to me about the air." She hit the top right button on the soft-touch pad beside her keyboard to flip her view, relegating the sea to her secondary screen and showing her the surrounding air space.

Nick flipped his screen to match. His three maritime staff specialists would alert him if anything went astray.

"About the same sorry state," Nick groused.

They flew at thirty-nine thousand feet over two of the busiest airports in the world: Singapore's Changi and Malaysia's Kuala Lumpur. The horizon lay four hundred kilometers away in all directions due to the Earth's curvature, and they could see out to nine hundred for aircraft at altitude. Everything from Ho Chi Minh City to Jakarta showed up on the screens—it almost made the clutter down in the Strait look rational. At least the shipping remained on the surface of the sea, other than the occasional submarine. The clutter of the air routes crisscrossed at every altitude imaginable.

But the Wedgetail wasn't called the most capable AEW&C plane aloft without reason. It specialized in sorting the noteworthy from the mundane at sea, in the air, and in near space out to a thousand kilometers. They might be watching the sea today, but if someone lofted a ballistic missile, the Wedgetail could find it before it left the atmosphere.

Rowena scaled her view to the closest hundred kilometers in all directions and began absorbing the patterns—something she did faster than anyone aboard. Always good to set a high bar for the staff.

The magic of her view was created in the back half of the plane.

Past the ten consoles and the small crew rest area, the aft half of the fuselage was closed off. From the wings back to the tail ranged some of the most sophisticated electronics anywhere. They controlled and fed the *Top Hat* radar antenna. The antenna—like a fat-handled dough scraper jammed into the spine of the plane by a giant trying to split the airplane in two—ran from the plane's mid-point to close before the tail and nearly as tall.

This was *not* the thirty-foot-wide spinning disk of the fifty-year-old E-3 Sentry AWACS planes. Those updated the radar view with one sweep every ten seconds. The E-7A Wedgetail's MESA—multi-role electronically scanned array—radar offered a continuous three-hundred-and-sixty-degree view: sea low, airspace mid, and space high.

"The boat's a service vessel. Registered. Called out to assist with a broken Number Two engine," Nick reported.

Rowena glanced over at his console and saw a low-angle satellite image, a static picture of the same boat, and basic registry information. It was one of many kept docked along the Strait like tow trucks pre-positioned on major highways during rush hour.

"Tell him to turn on his damn AIS." Ships were *supposed* to run with their Automatic Identification System transponder operating for just this reason.

After a quick radio call, the ship's ID blinked to life on the screen, reporting that the boat was who she said she was.

"Sounded hungover to me," Nick said in a voice that sounded that way. But then he always did, sober or not.

At her nod, he cleared the screen. One of the techs would keep an eye on it to make sure that it wasn't a false-flag operation or, if legitimate, that the ship they were assisting didn't break the traffic pattern in any dangerous fashion.

Back to studying the air traffic.

Commercial and cargo flights clustered in neat lines toward the major airports. Feeder flights appeared like flowers, their predictable patterns blooming outwards from major airports to smaller fields, then feeding back the other way. The only major field to the south was in Jakarta. Flights to Australia and New Zealand would rarely be routed through this airspace except for directly out of the major cities below.

Every pattern wove together on her monitor to make clear and predictable forms that—

"Who's this?"

She tapped her screen.

Nick glanced over at her console, squinted at it for a second, then turned back to his.

"Small plane," he reported. "Large bizjet class. Crossing at ninety degrees, heading zero-six-zero. Flight Level Four-Zero."

The Wedgetail flew northwest at thirty-nine thousand feet along the far-below Strait. The unknown flight flew northeast at forty thousand feet. Nowhere to the southwest to come from except the vast empty stretches of the Indian Ocean where the Malaysian airliner MH370 had disappeared a decade ago.

"Forty thousand should be a dead zone," she reminded Nick. "Verify."

"Verified."

Eastbound aircraft should be at Flight Level 37 or 41. With the westbound at 39 or 43, that provided a two thousand feet vertical buffer between planes going in opposite directions. Nobody should be at 40 unless they were in transition between flight levels.

"Identity?" Rowena asked.

"No transponder. Radar shows..." Nick kept working his keyboard.

In seconds he'd retuned the big Top Hot radar for Threat Sector emphasis in the direction of the unknown aircraft.

Focusing the entirety of the MESA radar on a single aircraft, vastly increased the detail.

"Bogey is a Dassault Falcon 2000 business jet. Typically, ten passenger and two crew. There's a belly extension I don't recognize. It isn't an antenna."

"Either its lost or—"

Grant slapped off his intercom headset. "What the bloody hell?" He was rubbing at his ears.

"Report?" Rowena asked when he didn't speak.

"Pray I'm hallucinating." He picked up the headset, held it near one ear, then dialed down the volume before pulling it back on. "Jackson? Boller?"

The Wedgetail's pilots' names.

Rowena tapped for the cockpit intercom channel. Nothing.

"What did you hear, Grant?"

"Screams. Like blood-curdling ones. Kind of sound you never want to hear—ever. Jackson? Boller?"

Grant undid his seat harness.

Rowena had been wearing only her lap belt, but out of the corner of her eye she saw Nick pulling on the two shoulder straps to make it a four-point harness. She did the same for herself.

Grant pounded on the door a few times. Then he keyed-in the unlock code on the external keypad beside the cockpit's safety door.

After waiting through the long pause that gave the pilots the option to override the unlock request, the three lights went green, indicating all three locks had opened.

He turned the handle and tugged.

Then harder.

He pulled his hand back and looked at it strangely for a moment, rubbing it. Then he ran his hand around the edge of the door.

Next, he shoved aside one earmuff of his headset, picked up

the intercom phone hung beside the door, and called out the pilot's names. He listened, then hung it up very slowly and turned to face her.

"I think we just lost the pilots."

———

Available at fine retailers everywhere:
Wedgetail
(Coming summer 20224)

And don't forget that review for Gryphon
They really help.

ABOUT THE AUTHOR

USA Today and Amazon #1 Bestseller M. L. "Matt" Buchman started writing on a flight south from Japan to ride his bicycle across the Australian Outback. Just part of a solo around-the-world trip that ultimately launched his writing career.

From the very beginning, his powerful female heroines insisted on putting character first, *then* a great adventure. He's since written over 75 action-adventure thrillers and military romantic suspense novels. And more than 200 short stories, and a fast-growing pile of read-by-author audiobooks.

PW declares of his Miranda Chase action-adventure thrillers: "Tom Clancy fans open to a strong female lead will clamor for more." About his military romantic thrillers: "Like Robert Ludlum and Nora Roberts had a book baby."

His fans say: "I want more now...of everything!" That his characters are even more insistent than his fans is a hoot. He is also the founder and editor of *Thrill Ride – the Magazine.*

As a 30-year project manager with a geophysics degree who has designed and built houses, flown and jumped out of planes, and solo-sailed a 50' ketch, he is awed by what is possible. He and his wife presently live on the North Shore of Massachusetts. More at: www.mlbuchman.com.

Other works by M. L. Buchman: *(* - also in audio)*

Action-Adventure Thrillers

Dead Chef
One Chef!
Two Chef!

Miranda Chase
Drone*
Thunderbolt*
Condor*
Ghostrider*
Raider*
Chinook*
Havoc*
White Top*
Start the Chase*
Lightning*
Skibird*
Nightwatch*
Osprey*
Gryphon*

Science Fiction / Fantasy

Deities Anonymous
Cookbook from Hell: Reheated
Saviors 101

Contemporary Romance

Eagle Cove
Return to Eagle Cove
Recipe for Eagle Cove
Longing for Eagle Cove
Keepsake for Eagle Cove

Love Abroad
Heart of the Cotswolds: England
Path of Love: Cinque Terre, Italy

Where Dreams
Where Dreams are Born
Where Dreams Reside
Where Dreams Are of Christmas*
Where Dreams Unfold
Where Dreams Are Written
Where Dreams Continue

Non-Fiction

Strategies for Success
Managing Your Inner Artist/Writer
Estate Planning for Authors*
Character Voice
Narrate and Record Your Own Audiobook*
Beyond Prince Charming: One Guy's Guide to Writing Men in Romance

Short Story Series by M. L. Buchman:

Action-Adventure Thrillers

Dead Chef

Miranda Chase Stories

Romantic Suspense

Antarctic Ice Fliers

US Coast Guard

Contemporary Romance

Eagle Cove

Other

Deities Anonymous (fantasy)

Single Titles

The Emily Beale Universe
(military romantic suspense)

The Night Stalkers
MAIN FLIGHT
The Night Is Mine
I Own the Dawn
Wait Until Dark
Take Over at Midnight
Light Up the Night
Bring On the Dusk
By Break of Day
Target of the Heart
Target Lock on Love
Target of Mine
Target of One's Own
NIGHT STALKERS HOLIDAYS
Daniel's Christmas*
Frank's Independence Day*
Peter's Christmas*
Christmas at Steel Beach
Zachary's Christmas*
Roy's Independence Day*
Damien's Christmas*
Christmas at Peleliu Cove

Henderson's Ranch
Nathan's Big Sky*
Big Sky, Loyal Heart*
Big Sky Dog Whisperer*
Tales of Henderson's Ranch*

Shadow Force: Psi
At the Slightest Sound*
At the Quietest Word*
At the Merest Glance*
At the Clearest Sensation*

White House Protection Force
Off the Leash*
On Your Mark*
In the Weeds*

Firehawks
Pure Heat
Full Blaze
Hot Point*
Flash of Fire*
Wild Fire
SMOKEJUMPERS
Wildfire at Dawn*
Wildfire at Larch Creek*
Wildfire on the Skagit*

Delta Force
Target Engaged*
Heart Strike*
Wild Justice*
Midnight Trust*

Emily Beale Universe Short Story Series
The Night Stalkers
The Night Stalkers Stories
The Night Stalkers CSAR
The Night Stalkers Wedding Stories
The Future Night Stalkers

Delta Force
Th Delta Force Shooters
The Delta Force Warriors

Firehawks
The Firehawks Lookouts
The Firehawks Hotshots
The Firebirds

White House Protection Force
Stories

Future Night Stalkers
Stories (Science Fiction)

SIGN UP FOR M. L. BUCHMAN'S NEWSLETTER TODAY

and receive:
Release News
Free Short Stories
a Free Book

Get your free book today. Do it now.
free-book.mlbuchman.com

Printed in Great Britain
by Amazon